SURRENDER

Book Four of
The Dragonfly Chronicles

USA Today Bestselling Author
Heather McCollum
Writing As

ELERI DRAKE

McCollum Creative Endeavors, LLC

McCollum Creative Endeavors
P.O. Box 1712
Apex, NC 27502

Cover design by Najla Qamber
Editing by Melinda DeJongh

E-Book ISBN: 978-1-962436-06-9

Print ISBN: 978-1-962436-07-6

Manufactured in the United States of America

*First Edition published by The Wild Rose Press under the name Heather McCollum, August 2013 *Second Edition, March 2026

For more information about Eleri Drake and Heather McCollum books, please check out her web site.

Eleri Drake Website

CONTENTS

DEDICATION

This book is dedicated to
Skye, Braden, and Irena, who have been fortunate enough to walk in the
steps of pharaohs.
Camel treks to the Sphinx, hot air balloon rides over the
Valley of the Kings, crawling through crypts— ahh, the adventure!
Thank you for taking me along in spirit!

FOREIGN WORDS USED IN SURRENDER

Aish Baladi (Arabic) – "bread of life," a flatbread eaten since ancient times

arrrr (Arabic) – word used to prod a camel forward

atsila (Cherokee, pronounced ah-chee-lah) – fire

babi (Arabic) - daddy

bayokav (Arabic) – stand up, common command to get a camel to rise

cac (Irish Gaelic) – dung, feces, excrement, used as mild curse

cingene (Arabic) – gypsy

dahabiah (Arabic) – a traditional, shallow-bottomed, two-masted sailing vessel used for passenger travel on the Nile River in Egypt

ghūl (Arabic) – ghoul or demon

fasieekh (Arabic) – gray mullet fish that's dried in the sun and then preserved in salt

keffiyeh (Arabic) - a traditional Middle Eastern cotton headdress or scarf, commonly worn by men

nar (Arabic) – fire

sahirat jayida (Arabic) – good witch

tenebris (Latin) – darkness, name of the wolf

thobe – a traditional, ankle-length, loose-fitting robe with long sleeves worn by men in northern Africa and the middle east

tuto (Ancient Greek) – owl, also the name of Kailin's owl

yalla (Arabic) – let's go, hurry up

TRIGGER WARNINGS

In SURRENDER there are episodes of claustrophobia. There is a young character with a disease that affects their ability to walk and breathe. And there are threats of assault, death, and demonic possession.

PROLOGUE

Luxor, Egypt
West Bank of the Nile
11 September 1848 AD

Anthony Fitzgerald Whitaker was born in 1815 and now he was going to die, in the dark, without a clue left behind of his whereabouts. He'd be a rotting companion to the mummy in its gold sarcophagus.

"Bloody hell." The dim glow of his lantern splashed across the colorful mosaic walls that would become his own tomb. He set the light down and covered his mouth with a dingy handkerchief against the three-thousand-year-old dust swirling around from the mudslide behind him. The roar of the flood surging from the Nile drowned out the wild thump of his heart. The rains of the previous week had weakened the ceiling of the tunnel he'd been exploring as part of the Egypt Exploration Society's expedition.

Stupid, paranoid, rash fool. Anthony berated himself silently so as not to use up more of the stagnant oxygen. He'd come down the unearthed steps at night, alone, in order to be the first to break through the millennia-old rubble from other floods. Almost as bad as the part about dying was the fact that no one would know that he'd found the mummy in a gold sarcophagus studded with jewels and lapis. Hidden for millennia, and now the Nile would likely break through and wash him away. *Poor bastard.* Though Anthony wasn't sure which one of them he was lamenting.

He scanned the stone walls. *No way out!* The only way to escape the tomb now was to wait until the Nile pushed itself inside and drowned him. He laughed a short burst that sounded more like a cough.

Light made him blink. He grimaced, trying to ignore the throb in his leg that had been hit by a falling boulder. He shuffled over to the golden sarcophagus, his dirty fingers brushing away the dust. "Son of Pharaoh Ramses II and Queen Nefertari, Amun-her-khepeshef, lies here," he read. But what held him in awe was the faint line of light that seemed to come from the seal around the sarcophagus, as if something glowed inside.

Anthony wiped his sleeve across his damp forehead. What was the source of the light? One that could maintain strength over thousands of years? He ran his hand over the etched glyphs across the shroud encapsulating King Ramses II's son and read aloud: "'I protect the Orb of Life by sealing it in here with me. A gift from an ancient magic, an ancient man. I gift it to the one who carries its mark. Beware its power and never let it fall into the hands of thirteen demons.'"

"Orb of Life?" Anthony murmured. A hint of a breeze flicked against the sweat of Anthony's nape, setting the hairs along his body in full alert. Light throbbed through the tomb for a split second, blinding him before disappearing so suddenly he wondered if he'd hit his head. On the other side of the king's son, large eyes in a small heart-shaped face stared back.

Anthony blinked several times, hard, squeezing his eyes shut, but the image of the girl remained. She was small, perhaps the same age as his friend's daughter, three or four years.

"Who...where?" he stuttered, the Orb forgotten. "From where did you come? How are you here?" Had she followed him down into the ground and hidden? *Good God!*

She gasped when she saw one of the king's servants lying beside the sarcophagus in a state of withered bones in bright cloth. "Come." He beckoned her closer. "He cannot hurt you. Come." She skirted around the skeleton toward his light.

Golden hair framed pale skin. *Definitely not a local.* Her clothes looked...old, historic, ancient really. Her breath fluttered in and out of her parted lips, and huge tears rolled down her cheeks. The child was in a mute panic. He had to calm her else she use up all their air before he could think of a way to get her out. So much for surrendering to the inevitable.

He touched her fragile shoulders and felt their rapid rise and fall. Her small hand held tightly to something that she clutched to her chest. "All will be—" He was going to say "well" but that was a blatant lie. "I'm going to try to get us out of here. I won't leave you." Her gaze leapt from wall to wall and then to the ceiling. Her breathing rushed through parted lips like the swollen current of the Nile beyond the walls.

Out of the darkness at the back of the crypt came a screech. The child leapt into his arms, and he scuffled them backward, his heels digging into the pebbly dirt. The sound of flapping preceded a bird hopping with large wings outstretched. *Bloody hell.* It was an owl, a great big owl. Now Anthony panted. "Did...did he come in with you?" Surely he would have noticed a giant bird flying with him into the hole he'd dug.

The child burrowed her face against Anthony's chest, her fragile frame shaking. Was she mute? Her heart pounded through her back as his hand lay across the rough weave of her dress.

The raptor landed at their feet, its obsidian, slightly slanted orbs set in a white feathered face. Wisdom and stoic strength emanated from the bird's gaze. Was it some unknown Egyptian god come to life?

Events had rapidly descended from tragic to impossible. He must be losing oxygen and hallucinating. Tears soaked his shirt, and he patted the girl's back. "I know," he whispered. "It looks dire."

She pointed with her unclasped hand at the rock ceiling and then jabbed her finger toward it several times.

"I'd like to go up too," he answered. "But there's a mountain of sand and stone on top of us and a raging river next to us." If he could suck the words back down his idiotic throat he'd do so. Terror pinched and pulled her sweet features into a mask of utter horror, and she cried out loud. Long, sucking sobs. Anthony tried to draw her back to him, but she pulled away to stand on the small, uncluttered circle of stone tiles radiating out like a sun. Standing with her hands out in front of her slight body, the girl stared up at the low ceiling where the owl swooped around the perimeter over the dusty artifacts left with the departed royal son. Was it looking for an exit?

"Out!" The tiny voice flooded the crypt with such power that Anthony swore the walls trembled. *Definitely not mute.* The girl panted and squeezed her eyes shut tight. Her hands lifted in fists at the ceiling.

"Out! Out! Out!" she screamed, the voice echoing so fiercely above the rush of water beyond that Anthony flattened palms over his ears. "Out!" The word blasted upward with wind and explosive force. "Out!"

Anthony hunkered down, his hands cradled over his head as the ceiling of the buried tomb shattered, exploding upward, blasting dirt, rocks, and three-thousand-year-old artifacts and tiles into the night sky. Several spears hidden in the walls released but were hurled upward with the rocks. He blinked and coughed as the dust tried to infiltrate his body.

"Out," the girl repeated, but the panic had ebbed as she stared at the empty sky above the huge hole. "Out," she whispered and glanced at Anthony.

He opened his mouth to speak but nothing came out except a startled curse as gravity deserted him. He floated upward with the girl, the owl leading the way into the open night air. When they landed on the edge of the flooded riverbank, Anthony stared down at the jagged stone lip marking the hole.

"Good bloody God," he swore and knelt before the child to look into the heart-shaped face. He swallowed, wiping his grimy hand against his dry mouth. What does one say in the face of such power? Was she a little goddess? A pale-faced pharaoh come to life? He opened his mouth and then closed it.

She shook. "Cold," she whispered.

A grin broke Anthony's dust-tight face, and he let out a loose laugh on an exhale. "That, my little queen, *I* can fix." He shrugged out of his coat and draped it around her shoulders. She snuggled deep into the folds and walked toward him. He opened his arms, and she stepped right into them. "Well now," he murmured, unused to the strange melting of his independent heart. Though she was obviously unrivaled in power, she was still a child in an adult world. If his instincts were working again, he'd bet that she didn't have parents here to protect her. "My little Cleopatra," he said. "Petite and beautiful and powerful enough to move armies."

"Kailin," she whispered and peered up at his face with the serious expression of one decades older. "I am Kailin." Although Anthony understood her words, her lips seemed to form others. She opened her fist to show a perfectly oval, polished piece of amber.

The owl screeched and landed nearby, apparently staying with its queen. Anthony shook his head and rested his palms gently on her slim shoulders. "Kailin. A pretty name for a pretty girl. But you'll always be the mighty Cleopatra to me."

CHAPTER ONE
NO ROMEO

Whitaker House Selby, England
05 September 1871

Kailin Whitaker perched on the crisp white edge of her perfectly made-up cot situated on the balcony overlooking the back gardens. Bruce always did such a lovely job with the sheets.

She inhaled the last of the summer jasmine wafting from the garden below and tilted the brittle paper, crisscrossed with her father's quick slashing script, toward the descending sun.

10 August 1871

Dearest Cleo,
The dry heat has made digging during the day nearly impossible. But once underground the coolness of the earth replenishes the body, not to mention the incredible mosaics

lining the latest tunnels. If I thought I could bribe or beg you to come see for yourself, I would.

Kailin laughed out loud but shivered just the same. She'd never set foot underground again. She pulled the knit jacket tighter around her shoulders as the evening breeze ruffled through the bushes below.

Cleo, I am treading along the footpaths of ancients! The very air smells of spice and history. And I am so close to finding the greatest treasure of all, the one we left behind. I would give anything to have you next to me when I finally obtain it. Again, impossible I know, but an old man can hope. Please know that when I hold the treasure, I will be thinking of you. I miss you.

Kailin smiled with a tug of heartache and blinked the ache from her eyes. *I miss you too, Papa.* She skimmed the rest of his details, her finger stopping on his last words.

The picture on the glyph describing the Orb was a dragonfly, and not just any dragonfly, mind you, but the same as the one on your arm. Would you perhaps know anything about it?

Kailin's fingers smoothed over her upper arm where the odd birthmark marked her as even more strange than she already was. Anthony had asked her many questions about her past through the years, his curiosity both annoying and endearing. But she couldn't remember her life before him. He'd dated her odd dress back almost nine hundred years. The strange words she'd spoken as a child, when she wasn't wearing the amber stone she'd been holding when he found her, had sounded like a dialect of the Celts of western Scotland.

Even now Kailin felt the familiar tug toward what they had deduced was her origin: a circle of ten monoliths soaring in a circle around a deep-rooted granite slab near the sea. Her gaze easily found the most direct route to it. The stone circles of England and Scotland had become her archeological passion over the years. And although Anthony grieved that he couldn't drag her below ground, he was pleased she'd chosen learning and science to flirting and frivolous hats.

As the sunset burned a thin line along the tops of the far trees, Kailin sipped the warm chocolate drink Bruce, her aging manservant, had pressed into her hands. The dark tang of barely sweetened chocolate swirled heat around her tongue and trailed down her throat into her middle, centering her, relaxing her.

"Dragonfly...hmm," she murmured to Tuto, her owl, perched motionless in the birch tree near the wall. The great barn owl turned his head in a fluid twist and chittered into the night. She smiled at her friend and stood, stretching. "Anthony is trying to lure me to Egypt again." She sighed. She hated to disappoint her father, but nothing would get her underground again, not even death. She'd had it written that her body was to be entombed above ground or burned on a pyre like a Celt or Viking. That would surely give the stuffy parlors and salons something to titter about.

Kailin exhaled and drew the pins from her long hair, letting it relax down around her shoulders. She stepped off the balcony through French doors and into her sanctuary, the only inside space in which she longed to be. Kailin glanced at the vast number of glass windows set into her round walls, all open to circulate the breezes and give the occupant the distinct feeling of being outside.

Kailin sat on the end of her large bed in the center of the room and glanced up at the painted mural of the sky. Several real birds roosted along the beams. Anthony had refused to install glass above her in case Kailin shattered it during a tantrum or nightmare, stabbing her underneath. So he'd had a mural commissioned for her to sleep under on rainy nights.

Kailin rolled her shoulders before willing the tiny buttons down her back to unhitch. The many ties and hooks opened with barely a thought, and she stepped out of her gown and petticoat. Yes, Anthony had quickly seen that in order to keep his house in one piece he needed to create a safe haven for his unusual ward. Luckily, he'd fallen in love with her as quickly as she had with him. Only his love for dusty mummies could draw him away from his beloved Cleo.

Kailin washed with the tepid water piped up to her own en suite water closet. She wiped the amber stone that rested against her breastbone and changed into a fresh white sleeping gown. She shook her head at the luxuries around her. After two months in the field, studying the monoliths on the coast of Scotland, her home felt like an overly plush palace.

Kailin brushed snarls from her hair and studied the night outside her balcony doors. Tuto soared by like a slice of moonlight with a mouse in his talons. Kailin left the walls of her room and stepped into the cooling, unhindered breath of darkness. The stars blinked above in the inky void. She picked out the constellations that she'd memorized growing up. Gemini, the twins; Cassiopeia, the queen; Pegasus, the winged horse; and Perseus, the hunter. She traced their forms into the legendary heroes and monsters. These were her friends, besides Tuto.

Her sadness scattered old rose petals and debris in the garden below before she could completely rein in the tug of self-pity. She curled up on her outdoor bed and unfolded Anthony's last letter. Hieroglyphs scrawled across the top border. A bird over another shape with a foot. The sign for life and then a serpent over a half circle and line.

"Life forever," she murmured and dropped her gaze to Anthony's smooth handwriting.

17 August 1871

Dearest Cleo,

I've been so blind. The Orb of Life is more powerful than we could imagine, and it seems the world around me is after it. I'm beginning to think that it should never be found. Unfortunately, I'm pretty close to unearthing it. And I think it's known. I'm being watched.

Cleo, you were so young when you found me. Do you remember it at all except for the parts that have plagued your nightmares? The mummy prince we found? I believe he was protecting the Orb. I think the dragonfly etched on it has some significance, something that ties it to our British Isles. If I can dig my way down to it again, I will be able to harness its power. But perhaps I should endeavor to turn in another direction all together.

I miss your keen decisions, my clever girl, your logical mind over what is right and wrong. I think perhaps I will come home to you soon. My bones are weary of all this intrigue.

My love always,
Anthony

Kailin read the letter three times in the fierce glow of the oil lamp before she realized the flames were blackening the glass globe. She tethered her magic, and the fire reduced to normal, but she couldn't tether her concern. Anthony was in trouble, more trouble than he wrote. For her father was exceedingly relaxed, a happy chap who was rarely ruffled. Giving up when he was so close to finding the biggest treasure of his life?

"What have you gotten yourself into, Papa?" she whispered and turned her head toward the rose trellis. Dousing the beacon that spotlighted her in the darkness, Kailin listened. A snap, a movement? Perhaps Bruce walked the grounds before bed. Or an animal stalked its dinner. She forced herself to breathe evenly, a necessary trick to control herself.

A face appeared over the balcony rail. *A man!* Without conscious thought, Kailin jumped up from the bed and hurled her magic at him. She gasped and forgot to exhale as she stared in terror. Not at the man, not at the possible consequences of acting on impulse, but at the inconceivable fact that the man continued to climb over the rail as if nothing had hit him. He jumped down onto her balcony and held out his hands, open palms forward.

"Whoa there. I'm not going to hurt you." His voice was deep, with an American drawl. "I'm merely a messenger." He wore brown trousers, a white linen shirt with the sleeves rolled up, and a wide-brimmed hat that had slipped to hang down his back. Moonlight glinted off his tawny hair. Broad shoulders tapered down along muscled arms to narrow hips.

He must be over six foot two. Kailin's blood pulsed energy through her, filling her with kinetic magic.

She drew in a breath and funneled her magic toward him. Leaves and small bits of debris blew past his form, but the man's wavy hair didn't even ruffle. *Good God!*

He took a step toward her, and she backed up, legs hitting the edge of the balcony bed.

"What are you?" she whispered and glanced around to find a manual weapon. Of course there weren't any. She'd never needed one before, not with her magic.

He stopped, eyes narrowing like he was trying to understand her question. Then his mouth turned up at the corners as his eyebrows rose. "What am I? Well, that's a new one." He shook his head. "I'm from the States but I'm a treasure hunter, mostly in Egypt." He extended his hand as if to shake hers. "I am Jackson, Jackson Black."

Kailin stared as his words sank in. Not a devil, not a proclaimed wizard of any type, but still able to block her powers. She tried once more to move him, but he stood there immune, a quizzical scrunching of his brows. Never before had she encountered someone or something that could stand against her magic.

Face relaxing, he withdrew his hand and pulled a piece of paper from his back pocket. "I don't usually sneak into ladies' bedrooms." He eyed her outdoor bed but didn't ask. "But your butler said you'd retired for the night and that I couldn't speak with you until morning."

"He was correct," Kailin snapped.

Jackson offered her the folded letter. "But this is something you'll want to see right away."

She didn't take it. Finally, he reached forward, and as quick as an asp striking, grabbed her wrist. Without thought, the control she kept tightly around her magic disappeared at his touch, but then so did her magic. She stared hard at their joined hands, watching him place the letter in her palm.

"You are Kailin Whitaker, daughter of the renowned Doctor Anthony Fitzgerald Whitaker?"

She nodded and inhaled, feeling her power return when he released her.

"Then you need to see that." He nodded toward the letter.

She opened the parchment while funneling her magic into the oil lamp behind her. It flared, casting a splash of light along the crinkled paper.

Kailin's eyes dashed across the typed words. Her chest gripped hard, holding her breath and her magic in a painful crush of panic. For a moment she forgot about the massive man invading her balcony and the loss of her magic when he touched her. Her entire being focused on the horror spelled out in boxy script. Anthony had been kidnapped.

She glanced at Jackson. "Who? Do you—"

He shook his head before she could get her words in the right order. "I don't know where they are keeping him. We're friends, your father and I."

"He's never mentioned you," she said and scanned the letter again. Orb? They, whoever they were, wanted the Orb of Life in exchange for her father.

"We dig together. Peers you could say. He talked about you a lot, Kailin. His intelligent, beautiful Kailin."

Jackson's mouth formed her name like a caress, but all she could do was stare back at him. "Do you have the Orb?" she asked.

He shook his head. "We were hot on the trail of it. Close, but then he gave up. Said he didn't want to find it. The next day he was gone and this letter was in his room, addressed to you. I owed it to him to deliver it."

"Why?" she asked. "Why do you owe it to him?"

Her question made his mouth tighten. "He's been good to me, let me help him."

Kailin turned toward her double doors and walked through. Jackson leaned against the door frame but didn't enter. "I will go," she said and yanked her canvas duffel bag out from under her indoor bed.

"At first light," Jackson suggested.

She turned to him, back straight, mouth tight as her shock wore off. "And where will you sleep?"

His eyes took in her bed and his mouth turned up into a lopsided grin that made Kailin's pulse jump. She frowned over her reaction. He seemed human enough, not a devil from her nightmares, but powerful enough to make her heart pound and steal her magic.

"I'm used to camping outside," he said, tipping his head toward the darkness beyond her oil lamp. "I'll make do in the gardens."

She stared for an exaggerated moment, as if his gaze held her captive. *Ridiculous.* She blinked hard and returned to her bag. "I will expect you at dawn, at the front door," she stressed. His chuckle faded as he jumped back over the rail.

For once Kailin locked her double doors. She'd sleep inside tonight, not trusting the man lurking in her gardens. *Jackson Black.* Her eyes narrowed as she ran over his words. A friend of Anthony's? Not likely. Could she trust him? Absolutely not. The man was immune to her powers. She frowned. But even worse, the man was a liar.

CHAPTER TWO
ON THE NILE

The breeze blew cool from the west off the Sahara as the sun sank below the banks of the Nile. Soon the scorching temperatures would plummet. Predictable, familiar, accepted. Jackson breathed in the unfettered air that reminded him of the unhindered wind off the prairie back home. Except at home, he could smell thunderstorms from far off, sliding with the cloud shadows across the flat land. Not something he usually noticed in Egypt.

Frogs chirped and long-legged birds rustled near the water's edge. A small herd of skittish gazelle picked at the shoreline, ever watchful of crocs.

He leaned against the outside wall of the main cabin of the small sailing dahabiah. The mid-sized vessel blew toward Luxor as fast as possible. The steamer from Alexandria would have been quicker without the wind, but there hadn't been a cabin available. And although *he* didn't mind sleeping on deck, a gentlewoman should. He chuckled darkly at the stars that twinkled above him. At least a normal, needlepointing, bustled-up gentlewoman should.

Jackson's gaze trailed after his thoughts toward Kailin Whitaker where she stood in a tan and white ensemble with wide-legged trousers that looked like a skirt when she stood with her legs together. She leaned against the low rail, her bare face in the breeze. Bathed in moonlight, the rosy glow on her cheeks paled into a smooth alabaster. She stared up at the stars, much like when he'd seen her that first night on her balcony. Straight and long, her back led up to her slender neck, where her golden hair twisted in a neat coil at her nape. She'd removed her veiled explorer's hat and leather gloves at dinner, performing her role with perfect aplomb, the rigid Ice Princess of England, every bit as solid and unyielding as the monoliths she studied in Scotland.

Jackson ran a hand along his stubbled cheek. He suspected that there was a flame burning within the ice, one that if stoked could shatter her practiced reserve. Though she'd only spoken to him when necessary, he'd seen fire in her blue eyes along the trip. How he loved a challenge.

The trek south had churned by rapidly. Jackson smiled at the memory of Kailin's flight from the house the morning after he'd leapt upon her balcony, the flustered butler trailing her with a scone. The man she called Bruce glared, making it perfectly clear that Jackson would have seen the end of a Brunswick rifle if Kailin hadn't insisted that she must leave to save Anthony. She'd also insisted on riding her mare instead of lounging in a carriage. Her one duffel and hearty pace made their departure from England nearly as fast as Jackson's arrival.

The flap of a wing caught Jackson's attention as the white-faced owl that had followed them along the road shot down through the air to land near Kailin at the rail. She ran one finger down the feathered head. It tipped and tilted sporadically as if listening to the night, its black, slanted eyes seemingly vacant.

She whispered something to it, and her musical lower-octave voice, like thick velvet, sent a sizzle down Jackson's body. The purr of her timbre was seductive, though he doubted she appreciated it. She laughed lightly, and the great raptor took off, becoming a spot of white in the growing darkness.

Jackson watched her turn and lean against the rail, and her eyes fell on him in the shadows. Not to be caught spying, he stepped out, his worn boots striding casually along the weathered planks. "Miss Whitaker." He inclined his head as he approached. She met his stare and then turned back to look out at the dark, churning water beneath them. A large snap along the shore stirred up a rustle of wings and a few frantic calls as several large herons took off for safer nesting.

Jackson leaned against the same rail, his elbow a small space away from Kailin's. "Aren't you worried"—he indicated the shadowed reeds where the croc had yanked a bird into a death roll underneath—"that your owl will make a meal for a croc?"

"Tuto can take care of himself." She paused and turned to him so that the wind pushed the stray curls back from her eyes. "He's as invincible as the pyramids." She laughed softly as if at some private joke.

The moonlight reflected in her eyes and revealed the silvery curve of her lips. Jackson hesitated. So the ice princess possessed a sense of humor.

"Tuto. Greek, for owl?"

She nodded and turned back to the coursing water. "My father named him when I was a child."

"When he found you?" he asked softly.

Kailin's face snapped toward him. Not many people knew that her origins were as mysterious as her seclusion, but he made it a point to find out everything he could when starting a project. And he'd just struck a chord.

"Yes, Tuto found me and my father," she purposely misinterpreted. Jackson let it go with a nod. "He's been with me ever since."

"He follows you," Jackson mentioned, his gaze flickering to the owl's silhouette against the half-moon.

"Everywhere." Kailin smiled, momentarily throwing Jackson's planned conversation off course. Damn, when the woman smiled it lit her whole face, a perfect porcelain reflection of the moon in the cool dark. She pulled her white, woven shawl closed.

"Anthony mentioned that you are in the same line of work as he, only in Scotland."

"Yes."

"So," he continued, "you know that digging and discovery can be hard, dirty, uncomfortable, even dangerous...for a woman especially."

Jackson would have felt triumph in the manipulation of the conversation, but the disappearance of Kailin's smile soured his victory.

"Yes, Mister Black, I am a woman and an archeologist. I understand discomfort and dirt. I think I can manage to get by without my tea and scones while gaining my father's freedom."

"Comfort aside, a rescue will be dangerous." Jackson studied her. The pert nose, the gently tipped eyes at the far edges, the soft curve of her lips upon one another. So delicate, yet so strong. "The men responsible for taking Anthony will be watching you."

Kailin smirked yet didn't meet his gaze for more than a brief second. "With any luck they will take me to him."

Jackson frowned. "And you will rescue him, like that." He snapped his fingers.

Kailin's eyes found his. She paused long as if contemplating how much she could trust him. "Yes." He waited, but she didn't continue. Apparently, she could only trust him enough for one-word answers.

Jackson grunted. "Perhaps we should retrieve the Orb first anyway. So they don't decide to shoot Anthony or you when we show up. These men aren't playing around. Anthony's room was ransacked when I found the letter."

The thought of rough, greedy men handling Kailin, touching her soft skin, stripping that mask of courage off her face, tightened his gut. He may be a bloody bastard treasure hunter, but he still had honor enough to protect a woman.

"Thank you for delivering the message. However, I won't need your services once we reach Luxor. I will pay you for your escort that far."

Jackson stared, his jaw dropping open. But his planned words did not fall out. She was trying to get rid of him. First of all, ladies didn't get rid of Jackson Black; he got rid of them. Secondly, it wasn't safe for an Englishwoman to travel alone in Egypt, camping outside or digging at a site, even if she wasn't in jeopardy of being kidnapped by those seeking the powerful Orb. Thirdly, her working without him wasn't part of the plan.

"The hell you won't need my services," he growled. "Even if you weren't a woman traveling alone in hostile territory, I know the last location your father was digging for the blasted Orb."

"I can figure that out from his letters and from knowing Anthony's mind."

"I can help you narrow it down to a specific vicinity. It will save time."

"I am certain, Mister Black, that I can find the coveted Orb as quickly as you can."

Jackson's eyes narrowed. "And I can crawl underground to retrieve it." Jackson watched fury and embarrassment pinch her features. Damn, he'd insulted her, but he needed to convince her that she needed him. It was common knowledge in archeology circles that Kailin Whitaker wouldn't go underground, and her balcony bed confirmed the fact that the brave lady before him was severely claustrophobic.

Kailin took a long inhale of the cool night air and exhaled. "Very well, then, Mister Black. Since you're so accomplished at slithering on your belly in the dirt, you may accompany me on my expedition."

With that, Kailin turned her straight back on him and walked toward the prow of the sailing vessel, her face into the wind.

He'd won, Jackson reminded himself as he watched her graceful shape saunter away. His plans were in motion. Kailin would be safe. Dr. Whitaker would be retrieved, and the Orb would be his. Jackson inhaled the wind and closed his eyes, slamming the dark images from his past back into their cell inside his chest.

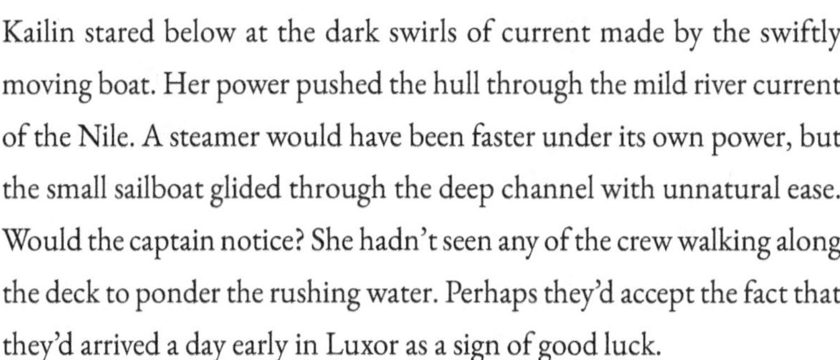

Kailin stared below at the dark swirls of current made by the swiftly moving boat. Her power pushed the hull through the mild river current of the Nile. A steamer would have been faster under its own power, but the small sailboat glided through the deep channel with unnatural ease. Would the captain notice? She hadn't seen any of the crew walking along the deck to ponder the rushing water. Perhaps they'd accept the fact that they'd arrived a day early in Luxor as a sign of good luck.

She watched Tuto dive below a low sand hill far out under the bright moon. It didn't matter what they thought, what anyone thought, as long as she got to Anthony before anything further happened to him.

Her forehead pinched, and she breathed slowly in through her nose to control the panic that could shatter her plan if she wasn't controlled. She wasn't fearful for herself. That would be hindering, and well, silly really. There wasn't much that could stop her—or hurt her, for that matter.

She frowned as her internal gaze formed around Jackson as he'd stood against her magic on the balcony, totally unaware of and unaffected by her power. *He* could stop her. The thought of his biceps straining against his sleeves hitched Kailin's breath. She'd witnessed his might as he'd broached her wall. She'd watched his tall grace as he rode before her along the road south. And now she'd seen the strength of his will behind his sharp, intelligent eyes as he played against her phobia to manipulate himself into a position of need on her expedition. *Jackson Black.* He was dangerous, not only physically but also emotionally. She exhaled through *O*-shaped lips to steady the slight rocking of the boat as they nearly flew down the center of the Nile.

I'll keep my distance. Her frown relaxed. They didn't call her Ice Princess for nothing.

The water swirled and Kailin breathed in the fresh air. Jackson had delivered her duffel to a cabin below. She'd have to go inside the ten-foot-square box at some point, but she'd never be able to sleep there. She scanned the deck. Several lounge chairs sat scattered for guests. Perfect. A blanket would keep her warm, and she'd pretend to doze off while watching the stars. Kailin strode with slow, measured steps toward the narrow stairs leading down into the depths. One more full breath and down. *In and out. Keep breathing.*

Releasing her magic slowly so the boat would glide under the natural power of the current, she trotted down the narrow steps. Reaching the bottom, Kailin kept her run under control as she strode to her quarters and turned the flimsy lock in the door with her mind. Click and slide. She was in.

"Good heavens," she murmured and concentrated on her thumping heart until it calmed slightly. Stars sparked in her periphery, and she fought to control the desperate need to suck in air. "It's like a bloody tomb."

She grabbed a blanket roll from the end of the netting-draped cot. "'Tis like a cramped sarcophagus." She'd brush her hair and rub the dust off her teeth outside. They'd disembark in the morning, and she would refresh herself at the hotel in Luxor where she planned to buy a second set of clothes for expedition, including suitable trousers.

Kailin turned and gasped, the air catching in her throat. The porcelain pitcher in the bowl near the small porthole rattled. Jackson Black's imposing, mountain of a body blocked the doorway. *Trapped!*

His head nearly brushed the ceiling. He stared with a lopsided grin at her full arms. "Vacating? It's customary to wait until the boat stops moving, preferably at a dock, before disembarking," he drawled.

Kailin cleared her throat and tipped her nose higher. "I dislike these accommodations. Until another room can be found, I will wait on deck."

"There are no other accommodations."

They stared at each other for a long moment. "You may have these," Kailin offered. "I prefer the outside anyway."

She stepped closer to him, which would force polite company to move aside. Apparently, Jackson Black wasn't polite company. He didn't even twitch as she walked up to him, invading his space. He grinned, a cocky tilt to his head.

Kailin frowned up at him. "Excuse me." Her shoulders tightened, and she breathed deeply. The room crowded her from behind and Jackson blocked her forward escape. In and out she breathed. "I...I need some air." The porcelain pitcher rattled in its basin behind her again, but Jackson didn't break the stare.

His grin faded to stone lines. "You're pale." Without further explanation, Jackson grabbed her valise and moved aside. His empty hand slid along the curve of Kailin's back to usher her out. She could feel the heat through her gown. Her heart leaped at the contact. Very few people had ever dared to touch her, dared to even meet the sharp stare she'd perfected.

Kailin's control slipped. She stopped mid-stride on the narrow line of the corridor. Jackson stopped with her, waiting, his hand still in place on her lower back. Kailin's gaze strayed to the paintings lining the short walls on either side of them. Her heart flew, her breathing hitched in and out, not smooth at all. Yet...the paintings hung, un-abused, un-rattled. As if only air wafted around them, not insanely unchecked magic.

"Shall I carry you?" Jackson's breath brushed against her ear where her hair cinched back into a tight bun.

"Out," she hissed and half expected the roof of the small boat to shatter upward into the night sky. But nothing happened. Only her own hyperventilating echoed in the silence around them. "I must get out." Kailin jerked forward, and Jackson's hand fell away as she sprinted toward the steep steps leading to freedom and the promise of fresh air.

"Damn," Jackson swore on an exhale behind her. The sound of paintings jumping from their nails and clattering against the hard floor punctuated the curse. But Kailin didn't care. She reached the top of the steps and flew to the railing. She gripped the wooden rail as hard as she tried to grip her power. Like a fish fighting against the line, Kailin fought to reel herself back in.

She breathed and imagined a bright blue sky, open and free, white puffy clouds high above. Her eyes closed as she imagined Tuto soaring up and through the azure with a gentle breeze. *In and out. Gentle, open, and free.* And little by little Kailin spooled in her magic, funneling it into the current surrounding the boat to speed it once more toward Luxor.

After several minutes she blinked open to reality, the deep blue-black shade of night across the desert. The splash of the water under her propulsion continued a constant lap and gurgle that melted into the background. In and out, she breathed, and eventually her fingers relaxed around the unpolished rail. Tuto flapped upward from a nearby tree as if he'd been checking on her.

"All's well," she whispered to the night, even though she felt weakness throughout her muscles like she'd physically climbed Druim Fada in western Scotland. How long had it been since she'd lost such control? Years.

Her forehead ached, and she rubbed cool fingertips along stretched skin there. The cabin, the corridor, they'd been too much. Even as she justified her weakness, blaming her reaction on the confining space, she knew it was not the complete reason she'd lost control. The skin tingled along her lower back where the man's hand had rested.

"He follows you. The owl." Jackson's voice shot through Kailin like cold lightning. He leaned forward against the rail she still clutched.

Kailin caught at the bolt of magic shooting up within her, forcing it into the controlled ribbon urging the boat onward. She turned to Jackson with an iced-over stare. "We look out for each other, keep each other company so that I do not have need for any other."

Jackson's glance slid away from her, ignoring her obvious request for solitude. Since the man wasn't ignorant, he blatantly chose to refuse her polite requests. He stared out over the Nile and the banks into the shadow-drenched desert.

"So, your one friend is an owl. Interesting." His tone mocked.

"I have other friends," Kailin defended and rifled through the small group of acquaintances and archeologists she knew. There was that man in Scotland who tried to talk to her several times on her last expedition, the one with the castle and sheep. Her brows furrowed. What was his name? There were the Macleans at Kilchurn Castle in the Highlands. They considered her a friend, didn't they?

Jackson stared down at her. "Ah yes, Miss Samantha McGivens. I'm sure she will be looking forward to reacquainting herself with you when we reach Luxor."

"Samantha McGivens?" Kailin hadn't seen the woman for years, not since finishing her degree. "She still resides in Luxor?" Kailin's eyes narrowed. "How do you know Miss McGivens? Know that we were...are friends?"

"Your father mentioned it," Jackson glanced back out at the swirling black water.

Kailin watched Jackson's ruggedly attractive profile. Strong jaw, perfectly sloped nose, good cheekbones. Striking, strong, and utterly dangerous. Not just physically dangerous to her since he was immune to her magic, but also dangerous because he loosened her control on it. Plus, she couldn't trust anything he said. He'd made that clear the first night on the balcony. Anthony only called her Cleo or Cleopatra, not Kailin, beloved or not.

Kailin paralleled his stare out over the water. *Samantha...hmm...* "I look forward to seeing her again. Does she know I journey to Luxor?"

"No. I know how to hold my tongue." Jackson's voice slid over the words with his drawl, which sounded almost scandalous there in the dark loneliness.

She blinked and glanced behind them at the local sailors securing lines. A few of them pointed toward the fast-moving water, and she turned back to watch out over the rail. "You, sir," she said, "have a way of saying things to make a woman frown."

A small chuckle cracked from his lips. "They either love me or despise me."

"Are those my choices?"

One of his eyebrows rose at her quip. "If they are, I fear you've already passed judgment."

Kailin grinned. "Firstly, I doubt you fear much, Mister Black. Secondly, judgment is something I do not have the authority nor the desire to pass on anyone." Her smile faded, dulled as past, childish pain tried to push upward. "I find those who judge to be...unworthy."

"Ah, but that is a judgment in itself, is it not?" Jackson's words didn't sound derisive, merely inquisitive.

Kailin looked sideways at him. "More of a method of self-preservation."

"Self-preservation? Why would a fortified castle worry over self-preservation?"

Kailin's lips tightened at the slight. Fortified castle indeed! She turned from the rail. "Good evening, Mister Black. I am finished with this exchange."

"Wait," he chuckled. "Miss Whitaker. Kailin." His voice reached out to her like a stroke of his warm fingers, taunting her with undoubtedly false sincerity. Was she gullible enough to turn back? No. Kailin took a step away. Jackson's hand shot out and grabbed hold of her upper arm. It was a gentle locking, but the results were anything but gentle.

The dahabiah stalled in the water with such a sudden impact that Kailin toppled sideways and right into Jackson's arms.

CHAPTER THREE
KAILIN BURN & NILE BUBBLE

The clean scent of leather and man coming from Jackson's warm chest engulfed Kailin, sending her heart thumping like African drums.

"Steady now," he said softly near her ear. Several deck hands ran past them up to the rail and peered overboard. "They won't see anything odd in the water, will they?" he whispered.

Jackson continued to hold her as she breathed, trying to tamp down her brimming fear. How did he mute her powers? First in the corridor, now on the deck. Both times he'd irritated her. The surge of magic would flare hot and ready but then disappeared upon his touch. She looked at him closely, and her breath stopped somewhere between her throat and her lungs. His eyes nearly twinkled with questioning mirth, yet his mouth was firm as if he too struggled.

"What are you?" she murmured above the loud gestures of the captain as he too peered over the side of the dahabiah.

The humor left his eyes. "Flesh and blood, miss. That's all. Like you, I suppose." Was he insinuating that he had magic of his own?

It was another reason Kailin must stay away from Jackson Black. "Release me." It was a command, but her tone waved a white flag. Kailin was tired. Tired of the physical exhaustion of controlling her magic and the rigors of the journey. Tired of the questions and worry about Anthony churning inside her. Tired of the emotional sparring with the utterly gorgeous, unfortunately perceptive treasure hunter who might be a wizard. "I must go."

"And where exactly are you going?" he asked.

The question added another problem. Kailin glanced around the small deck. She indicated the chaise lounges. "I will rest there. Get some air."

Kailin stepped away, and Jackson let his hand drop. She exhaled slowly as she walked, funneling her magic back into the water to propel the boat through the sluggish current. Her magic pulled upon the air around her to strengthen, but Kailin could control all the elements.

She sank onto the stretched mesh chair and pulled the folded blanket nearby across her lap. 'Twas more comfortable than sleeping on a stony ground beside a circle of stones.

She leaned her head back and searched the black sky for the friendly forms she knew. Kailin's face warmed at the blush. She pursed her lips tight. Yes, these friends might be untouchable, but they also couldn't hurt her. *And I can't hurt them.*

She followed the invisible lines connecting the pinprick lights until the outline of her friends appeared. She ignored Jackson where he stood talking to the captain. His easy drawl floated over the air toward her as if her ears were specifically attuned to it. *Annoying*!

Kailin forced her eyes to follow the lines of Orion, the great hunter. Scanning north, she traced the familiar guardian, Draco, the dragon. As a child she'd imagined the winged beast flying down to fight off hurtful whispers and the imagined demons haunting her nights. Anthony would shake his head at her fears, reassuring her that she was the most powerful force in existence. That she needn't fear anything or anyone.

A shiver rippled along Kailin's spine, and she pulled the wool blanket up over her chest to her neck. Because Kailin knew now that wasn't completely true. Her gaze moved from the slope of Draco's neck to Jackson standing against the rail. His gaze met hers without wavering. Yes, now Kailin knew that there were things out in the world that could hurt her, whether they be demons or magic or a single man.

⸺◦⸺

"The witch was so close I could smell the sweet fear in her blood!" Bechard, a blond, black-winged demon, roared into the inter-dimensional mist. A low grumbling like thunder amongst mountains followed in furious agreement from the other twelve demons dissolving in and out of their chosen forms.

Semiazaz, swathed in gray robes, his long white beard unrolled down his front, sat on his imagined throne, silent, brooding. He'd come so close to capturing both the dragonfly amulet and Gilla's third daughter, Katell, in the sixteenth century. Yet both had slipped through his sharp grasp.

"Drakkina!" hissed Bast, a sensuous catlike demon dressed in white Egyptian wrappings. "The priestess interferes again! When I catch her, I'll slice her skin, layer by layer, from her body."

"She doesn't have a body anymore," Semiazaz commented, a loose, far-away memory surfacing of a young beauty running barefoot through spring grass. He growled low and banished the picture along with the sickening sentiment it brought. "Drakkina's true body withered to dust long ago."

Bast flicked her tail which curved out of her robes. Her annoyance melted into a sly smile. "I'll give it back to her with the amulet. Then I'll skin her alive."

Semiazaz sighed, tired of dealing with the roiling emotions of twelve riotous, monstrous souls to which he was shackled. It had been three thousand years since Drakkina had bound them together to hinder their growth as the most powerful coven history had ever known. The thirteen demons must move together everywhere, agree in order to accomplish even simple tasks. It had taken nearly two thousand years for them to stop battling one another long enough to simply move. Quite the clever prison. Momentary pride whisked through Semiazaz as he thought of Drakkina's unique trap.

He glanced around at the figures in the temporal mist. Some of the demons manifested bodies, both beautiful and hideous. Others rested in the amorphic shifting of shadow. Three thousand years was long enough to learn that in order to escape they must act together. Semiazaz had mastered his emotions quickly and had become the leader of the group. Although dissension was a daily encumbrance, the group knew that a leader must be in place or they would battle impotently forever.

Semiazaz stroked his perfectly groomed beard. "The amulet is of great power. But to give Drakkina back her body and life we'd need the other half. There are always two parts to anything balanced, and balance creates power."

"Let us find the Orb of Life then." Deumis, a horned female demon, nodded from her corner.

Semiazaz rose from his gold throne to pace in the small circular space the demons left open in the middle, preferring to be as far from each other as possible. "The two together would certainly give her back her life."

"The amulet could do that alone," Bechard stated and flexed his wings.

Semiazaz shook his head and stared hard at the glinting maw of the tempest demon. "The amulet can give her corporeal form, but to give one back their life in full, full sensation, emotion, spirit, the two pieces must be linked."

Megaira, a lush female demon with serpents coiling her head like hair, hissed loudly from her perch. "Lest you forget, we couldn't even retrieve the amulet." The mask of beauty faded from her features leaving the horrific skeletal points of envious anger. "I want the Orb of Life! I want the amulet! I want Drakkina's body to twitch with agony!"

Semiazaz patted his hand down through the mist as if trying to calm her. "Yes, yes, we all want revenge."

"And life," Bast added.

"Apart from each other!" Bechard roared in his thundering voice that increased the tension in Semiazaz's imagined head.

Semiazaz could allow his body to dissolve, momentarily easing the pressure of keeping up his appearance, but to do so would show weakness. And amongst these monsters, weakness could easily overturn his rule. As much as the idea of resting seemed favorable, the thought of relinquishing his control over the group was frightful. It would take them another thousand years to decide on a new leader. And who knew where Bechard, the likely usurper, would take them.

"We *will* obtain the power to break apart," Semiazaz stated calmly, using his muted powers to enhance the volume of his voice to reach over Bechard's cursing and Bast's hissing. "And then you will have your revenge on the white witch. But…" His eyes met each of the burning orbs of his brethren.

"Before anyone else touches her, Drakkina is mine."

———◆○◆———

Drakkina's ethereal body flew under the moon and over the great pyramids. The land of the pharaohs, so full of ancient magic, resonated like a beacon, pulling her toward it. Her hand rubbed across the dragonfly amulet she imagined that she wore on a chain around her neck. When she'd worn the real amulet, it had pulled her south as it sought its mate, the Orb. Together they would create the circle of life, giving her power over life and death.

Drakkina huffed softly, her faint voice caught unnoticed in the breeze blowing along the Nile. As much as she'd like to be mortal again, she had a mission to finish first, a mission to save the world. She'd found three of Gilla's daughters already, hidden in time by her best student, Gilla, moments before the shackled demons killed her. But there was one daughter left, the other twin. After years of staying close to Kat and her broody mate in their new home in Scotland, Drakkina had meditated on finding pockets of magic where the last twin, Kailin, might exist. The amulet had sent her to Egypt where the Orb must be.

The silhouette of a white-faced barn owl dipped and rose across the large moon. The acrobatic movement and great height caught her attention. Did the animal hum with magic or was the power hidden between the grains of sand on the landscape below and in between the two-ton bricks of the pyramids? She cocked her head and pierced the night with her senses straight toward the feathered raptor.

The bird dove, a startled screech renting the air as if it had been shot. Had it felt her curiosity? Drakkina swooped toward the animal only to lose it close to the dark Egyptian hills. She hovered, listening, waiting, hunting. The resonance she had sensed was familiar. "Gilla?" she murmured. Finally, after years of searching for Katell's twin, could she have found her? Had the ancient magic shielded the child from her and from the demons?

A flutter heralded a screech. Drakkina dove downward, her dragonflies with their tissue-paper wings following. The rolling hills of cold sand spread below, and Drakkina's body lowered, her diaphanous sleeves billowing in the dry desert air. She floated downward and scowled at the wide wingspan and black, non-blinking eyes studying her as it followed her toward the sand.

"I'm a friend, fool bird," she said, her tone like arrowshots. The owl landed on a crate left littering the desert landscape and cocked its head. "Do you understand?" Drakkina settled on the sand without making an impression. "Are you Gilla's pet, a guardian for her last daughter?"

The bird stared, its obsidian eyes assessing. Drakkina sighed long and funneled a tendril of power to touch the silent owl. An echo of Gilla's great magic encompassed the creature, every feather, every miniscule part.

It hopped from foot to foot and ruffled its feathers as if ridding itself of her taint. "You feel that, don't you?" Drakkina glanced around at the night. The Nile snaked through nearly moonless landscape. "Where is your mistress then? You wouldn't fly far from her."

Drakkina pressed the imagined amulet she'd found with Katell, the other twin, against her imagined skin. She'd hidden the real necklace inside the sanctity of the ten standing stones in northwest Scotland.

The owl hissed low, and she felt a bit of its magic touch her diaphanous form.

"I am no demon, but it's certainly prudent of you to check." The tickle dissolved and the owl opened its wings. Drakkina indicated the distant river. "Lead on then." And the great protector leapt silently into the air.

——◦○◦——

Kailin breathed in deeply through her nose. The tangy smell of earth and water was a balm against her unpleasant dreams. She stretched her toes inside her laced boots and blinked upward at the gray-blue sky that lightened directly off the bow of the boat. East, they were moving east, not south. They must be traveling on the curve of the Nile that wound east, north of Thebes and Karnak. Kailin let the blanket fall down her arms and stretched them overhead, her eyes closed as she smiled. They'd made good time through the night, even without her interference. Her magic would have faded as she drifted off to sleep last night. Perhaps she'd made up enough time earlier in the evening. They should reach Luxor by the following morning.

Kailin's breath hitched as she turned and her gaze locked with Jackson's. He sat, two chaises down, feet crossed at the ankles, watching her. His cowboy hat sat on the small table next to him, allowing his casual, in-need-of-a-trim hair to blow in the breeze. She resisted the urge to check her hair with a quick pat.

"Good morning, Kailin… or Miss Whitaker," he drawled and raised his arms up in the air to interlock his fingers and stretch. Muscles bunched under his thin button-up traveling shirt. His hair sat tussled with waves around his head. He grinned and rubbed his strong, stubbled jaw, which added a roguish appeal to the casual charm of his brilliant gray eyes. Kailin fought to quell the giddy unease at having woken up near the man, as if they'd slept in the same room.

"What are you doing up here?" Her words came out a little breathless and she forced a smooth, calm exchange of air. "I did relinquish my cabin to you, Mister Black. If you are still trying to protect me in a misguided attempt to make yourself useful, you needn't, as I am more than capable of looking out for myself."

He shrugged and set his booted feet with a heavy clunk on the deck boards. "I too prefer to sleep under the stars. Does the constitution good. Growing up in wide open spaces"—he shook his head—"I spent many a night sleeping under God's canopy."

His answer irritated her. Why? Her lips pursed together. Certainly it wasn't because she'd hoped he'd admit to wanting to watch over her. Kailin rarely needed a protector. And when it was required for some social or cultural dictate, Anthony filled the role. Perhaps her irritation was merely that she sensed another lie.

She crossed her arms over her lap and turned back to the lightening sky. "Do you ever speak the truth, Mister Black, if that is indeed your name?" She turned her gaze to him when she heard a chuckle.

"Do you ever speak without a wasp flying free from your tongue, ready to strike, Miss Whitaker, or should I call you Doctor Whitaker?"

Kailin stared at the tanned American, his grin wry, and his eyes sparking with self-determined cleverness. He made her anxious, but she wasn't about to admit that to him. "You irritate me more than most, Mister Black." She tilted her head to examine him. "You invade my personal space, not physically like in the corridor but my"—she swirled her finger near her head—"emotional space." She nodded, satisfied with her description, happy to slap a label on it so it could be cataloged away like other common human responses.

"And Doctor Whitaker," she continued, "though accurate, causes more trouble than it's worth in this culture. Miss Whitaker is fine, although you have a tendency to hedge on the scandalous side of propriety by calling me by my given name seemingly whenever you please. Again, quite irritating."

He opened his mouth to say something, but she held up her hand. "And I am very aware that you answered my question with a question, thereby trying to change the subject."

Kailin crossed her arms over her chest and waited.

Jackson raised one eyebrow. "Yes." His gaze traced her features, and heat crept upward from Kailin's neckline.

"Yes, what?"

"Yes, I do speak the truth, when a lie is unnecessary. And yes, my name is Jackson Black."

"So you have deemed it unnecessary to lie about your name," Kailin parried and felt a tug at her lips as if a smile jockeyed for room to escape.

He laughed, a short chuckle that held the warmth of his gaze, and Kailin's heart took off like a spooked horse. Her fingers pressed against her breastbone as if to keep the wild steed inside her chest. Irritating. And *invigorating*, a small voice inside cried. *Ridiculous!*

She looked back out over the rail. "We are north of Thebes and Karnak, are we not?"

Jackson stood up and the glow of the rising sun broke over the edge of the far-off dunes, flooding him with an orange-yellow light. It was as if he reflected the unleashed solar power of the pharaoh's sun god himself. He walked to the rail and Kailin admired the way his rugged pants fit his hindquarters and muscular thighs like wavy sand over a landscape. He turned and for the briefest of heartbeats she stared at his groin before her gaze flew up his chest to his infuriating grin.

Kailin's face flamed with the sun. Long fingers caught in her wide trousers as she tried to force the blush to recede, but it continued along with Jackson's teasing look. She didn't notice anything except the heat in her cheeks until Jackson pivoted to lean out over the rail, giving her a view of his perfect arse. Heat climbed through her, turning her face scarlet.

"Kailin!" he yelled.

She swallowed hard over the sound of thrashing and splashing. Kailin leaped up from the chaise lounge and ran across the deck. Birds, reptiles, even some fish jumped from the water. Two crocodiles clawed their way up the steep bank on the opposite side of the small boat. Bubbles popped and boiled along the surface of the Nile. Heat steamed up from the surface. Jackson turned to her, a whispered order already on his lips. "Kailin, stop! The river...it's bloody boiling!"

CHAPTER FOUR
CLOSE ESCAPE

Air churned somewhere between Kailin's lungs and her lips, stuck. She forced a breath out. "Touch me, Mister Black."

Jackson's eyebrows lifted, but he didn't argue. He clasped her upper arms, yanking her into his chest. It was an embrace, and to anyone looking it would seem the rough grip of overcome lovers. Kailin's face flamed more.

"Don't let go of me," she whispered. He shook his head as he stared at her. As if he knew that her blush had caused the Nile to boil. His command to stop... *He knows.* Kailin swallowed and stared into his face.

After another minute the splashing died away, and Kailin felt her cheeks cool. She focused on the small scar under the indent of Jackson's chin, just visible beneath his unshaven shadow. He cleared his throat, but she didn't meet his eyes.

"So...Doctor Whitaker, for future reference. Do you embarrass easily?"

Refusing to heed her preference of title, the drawl sounded like a tease. His lips, full and inviting, turned upward. Kailin tilted her head backward, forcing herself to brave his gaze. "I'm merely asking," he continued without releasing her, "for when I take a bath. I'm prone to cleanliness so my chances of being caught in a boiling cauldron could be rather high."

He was teasing her, wasn't he? She didn't have any experience with teasing men, or women for that matter. Anthony and Bruce had sheltered her, even after she'd learned to control herself, for the most part.

"I...I don't know," she stuttered, totally at a loss as to what to say. His hands slid up to her shoulders and down her back across her rigid shoulder blades. "I avoid things to be embarrassed about. I...I don't usually lose control."

He chuckled low and Kailin watched the golden sun glint along the blond highlights shooting through his tawny hair. "Where is the fun in that?" His fingers stroked her back, and she stiffened as voices came around the corner.

Kailin drew back, latching onto her anger to rechill her composure. Eventually Jackson released his hold, and she leveraged some distance between them. "If I give way to my emotions, Mister Black, it can be unpleasant for those around me."

He stared hard at her as if examining a new species of animal.

She pursed her lips. "Perhaps," Kailin said, taking a full breath as she slid her cool persona back into place, "you may find it too worrisome to be in my company, Mister Black. Most do."

"I think I'll take my chances."

Kailin glanced at the points of her boots. "You seem to bring out the worst in me. It may not be healthy for you."

A little snort mixed with a chuckle. "I just won't bathe."

Her gaze shot back to his. "Oh, please do." She turned on her heel. "It would not be right to make all of Luxor suffer for your cowardice."

She grinned slightly as she walked away.

"And then there's the interesting fact that I'm immune to your...temper." His voice wafted across the deck to her, and her grin faded on an inhale. "Perhaps for the safety of Luxor I should touch you more, Doctor Whitaker."

The warmth tried to surface in Kailin's cheeks, but she was prepared this time. The taunts of others who whispered about her differences were something she'd learned to deal with early on. Like a steel cage descending around her, she cleaved through the words. At least enough to keep the fish of the Nile swimming. She grabbed her reticule and made her way to the cabin for a momentary refreshing.

Jackson watched Kailin descend the stairs with slow, steady steps, her head held high. "What are you?" he murmured. He'd heard all the rumors about the Ice Princess Whitaker but had categorized them as exaggerated excuses for no one being brave enough to talk to the highly intelligent, strawberry-blond beauty. Doctor Kailin Whitaker was indeed as stunning as described. Long wavy hair he'd glimpsed on her balcony that first night, had coiled against her slender neck where it had fallen from her bun during the night on the deck. Sharp blue eyes had met his gaze with infallible courage. They held intelligence and poise but also sadness, loneliness, and regret. Almost to match his own.

She had luscious lips, the perfect shade of natural pink to match the healthy color in her high cheekbones, and they turned upward into a smile when she watched her strange pet soar. Then there were the hills and valleys of her body. Without the unnatural cinching and bumping of a tight corset and large bum roll, Jackson could easily follow the slim line of her waist, a soft valley between her curved hips and her ample breasts. He preferred the shirt over a looser corset and parted tan skirt that she seemed to favor on expedition.

Kailin Whitaker was so much more than the doctor of archeology, so much more than the frigid, breathtaking beauty, so much more than a devious parlor illusionist.

Jackson had felt the tremor of magic before. After hunting for over a decade through curse-infested tunnels in the desert hills, he'd encountered his share of unexplained presence, the tingling pressure of power. Kailin Whitaker certainly possessed power of the magical kind. And she seemed barely able to control it. That had been a slip of control when she'd been blushing. She wasn't the type to purposely boil placid animals in their own river. He'd caught her perusal and she'd been embarrassed.

Jackson's frown smoothed into a cocky grin. She'd been watching him. Jackson chuckled, grabbed a long-poled net, and strode back to the rail. Perhaps he'd catch some poached tilapia or perch for breakfast.

⋅⋅⋅◆○◆⋅⋅⋅

Kailin concentrated on her balance as she stepped down the center of the thin plank of wood separating her from the murky harbor water. Parasol in one gloved hand, her small valise in the other, she blended into the milling crowd at the end of the pier. She stopped and breathed, trying not to wrinkle her nose at the tang of unwashed humanity and tainted water.

"Kailin, Doctor...Miss Whitaker, wait." She heard Jackson's command and ignored it. Her lips pursed tight as her heart skipped along in an annoying canter at the velvet twang of his voice. She'd had enough of Jackson Black and his bizarre influence on her control. He touched her and her magic disappeared. He gazed at her and her magic shot off like blind artillery trying to take out as many bystanders as possible. She'd find some other assistant to crawl through the tomb after the Orb.

Kailin wove through the throng in her simple blue walking dress that she'd donned that morning before they arrived, hoping she would pass unnoticed as a tourist. She'd made arrangements for her duffel bag to be delivered to Hotel Moudira, a reputable inn with open-air balconies overlooking a central garden. And it was Anthony's residence while on expedition in Luxor.

Kailin collapsed her parasol to hide easier within the mass of bustling humanity. No doubt Jackson would still find her. It was the way of irritatingly virile men, but she wouldn't be a bullseye. Kailin blended in with the flow of stately gentlemen and animated young socialites who rhapsodized over the temples they'd toured that morning. It was a mix of dark and easily burnt white skin and every shade in between, which was so much more interesting than the sea of pasty complexions she'd seen in London. Proper hushed tones and churlish whispers were replaced by children hawking wares, businessmen bartering, and open laughter unmuted by societal muzzles.

"Doctor Whitaker." Jackson's drawl flowed over the sea of heads and loud conversation.

Kailin made a rapid, risky decision, for anyone other than herself. She stepped into a narrow alley between the close-packed sand mortar buildings. It was cool there where the shadows hid. She worked her way between two low buildings, the steady murmur from the wharf and street muffled.

"There must be a back exit." But none were visible, only a sharp turn to run down another building with two more flanking her. She glanced up at the azure sky, a narrow ribbon between the buildings. "Good heavens." The heaviness of fear rushed through her as she realized how close the buildings stood. She glanced across the six-foot width to the other wall. Set into the hard packed earth and sand, the foundation could no more move than a mountain. Why then did it seem the two buildings were merging in on her?

Kailin inhaled the dry air. Even here in the shade of a dank alley, the arid breeze swept away any tidbit of mold, moss, or damp tang. Only sand and rock and a thin line of gold from the blazing noon sun above permeated the narrow path. Yet the air still felt sticky in Kailin's shallow breaths. She rested her hand along one wall and glanced at the way she had walked from the wharf. Perhaps Jackson had passed already, leaving it safe for her to exit back into the crowd. The smash of people was easier to deal with than the smash of hard walls. Even with the chasm of sky above, the buildings were entirely too close for comfort. With the way her control kept slipping, she'd hate to knock down the buildings in a panic. People could die.

Pebbles skittered as she pivoted back the way she'd come. Two quick steps. The glint of a knife flashed before her eyes before settling its cold line along her neck. The dank tang of an unwashed body engulfed her as a beefy arm yanked her against a solid chest.

"'Ello, miss."

—•—

"Bloody foolish woman," Jackson ground out as he shouldered through the press of workmen and tourists along the wharf. Kailin might have the academic intelligence to baffle most people on the planet, but she surely didn't have common sense if she thought striding without escort in a foreign port was safe for a lady. Apart from the everyday thieves, there were no doubt people watching for her arrival, people who were very capable of kidnapping. Although Jackson had to admit, kidnapping Kailin might be more difficult than anticipated. Perhaps he should watch for signs of fire.

A white lace parasol unfolded up ahead and Jackson surged forward toward the beacon. He grinned over the irony. Kailin was a woman ridiculously unafraid of villains but worried about the sun speckling the bridge of her nose. Jackson cut over through the thinning crowd.

A giggle escaped the lowered lace. "He actually asked me to crawl through the pyramid with him, Letia. Imagine that."

Damn. Obviously not Kailin.

Jackson's gaze moved upward, darting to every woman he could see. "Where are you?" he murmured and scanned the squatty sand-brick buildings. "You can't have just disappeared." Could she? Incredible strength and unnatural defense had been part of the rumors but not invisibility.

Jackson's gaze swept past the entrance to an alley. Would she duck down there to avoid him? The walls weren't terribly high. Maybe her phobia wouldn't affect her there. With one more glance in every direction without seeing the blue traveling dress and copper-blond hair tied in a bun under a parasol, Jackson jogged down the narrow corridor. Trash mixed with sand and pebbles along the sun-lightened path that looked empty. Damn, she must be lost in the throng. He turned to rush back out.

A sharp flutter zipped past his eye. He pivoted once more toward the back of the alley and watched the iridescent bug hover and dive. Another dragonfly followed, and then another. They darted back to him, encircling, and then took off farther down the corridor. "Hell," Jackson swore and jogged after the strange trio without thinking about the illogic of the direction. Too many times to count he'd successfully relied on gut feeling to guide him. He wasn't going to question it now.

He rounded the corner. In a flash of instinct tied directly to his gut, Jackson drew and cocked his Remington. The pistol was an extension of his hand and eye. The very spot he focused on would be shot through with one quiver of his finger. And right now he focused on the bent nose of the bastard holding a knife to Kailin's lovely throat.

"Mister Black, wait."

Jackson's eye didn't blink, didn't waver from his target. "Let her go. Now." The last word came out between the small crack of his clenched teeth. "Or there'll be a hole through your skull." The man's brittle lips pulled back in a leer that revealed yellow, broken teeth. His dark tan skin and clothing showed him to be a local. The knife and sneer showed him to be a criminal.

"No, Jackson." The sound of his given name across her tongue tugged him. Jackson's gaze barely flickered to Kailin, but he saw her swallow against the blade. Anger shot through all his muscles, and he fought to control his trigger finger. "Sir, take me to my father. I am surely a greater prize than the Orb. Once you surrender me to the one who hired you, I can be forced to take him to his trinket."

"Call off your man," the bastard said.

"Jackson, let—"

"He's not with the group holding your father" Jackson cut her off as he stared into the dark eyes of the enemy. "He's a local thief taking advantage of your stupidity for walking alone through a deserted alley."

The bastard shrugged. "Perhaps I am." The man lowered slightly to put Kailin directly before his face. He inhaled loudly. "Perhaps not. I will take Miss to her babi."

"The hell you will," Jackson growled and stepped to the side. Kailin inhaled sharply and Jackson froze, his gaze set on the dirty blade at her throat. Kailin's eyes widened as she looked over his head. Several dragonflies zipped past his shoulders to swarm around the thief turned lecherous kidnapper. The man cursed and removed his arm from Kailin to swat at the little storm of glittery wings diving toward his face.

Jackson jumped forward, taking advantage of the distraction. But the thief was already flat against the wall. His red eyes bulged out of his heavily bearded face. "I...I can't move," came from the slim opening between his lips. He blinked as the dragonflies seemed to aim for his eyes.

The piercing screech of an owl splintered the muffled sounds from the street behind. Tuto, her pet, soared down, flapping its great wingspan before the thief's face. The man cursed in Arabic.

Kailin still stared behind Jackson, and he whirled. Hovering several feet from the pebbly dirt was a ghost or spirit, a woman. Her robes flowed around her on invisible breezes. Dragonflies circled her ancient but smooth face, landing and taking off from her loose, long hair. Excitement lightened her eyes to a pale blue, and a smile curved her lips. *I've found you.*

The woman's lips hadn't moved, but Jackson had plainly heard her voice, a deeply feminine rumble, in his head. The woman's merry eyes moved to the thief jammed up against the wall.

My dragonflies learned to go for the eyes and mouth from your sister's butterflies. She waved an arm, and her little army shot back to join the others around her.

Kailin's eyes narrowed. "Who are you?"

"I am Drakkina, Gilla and Druce's teacher," the apparition said out loud. Jackson couldn't tell how old she was, because her image changed slightly every second. She smiled at the owl, who sat at the base of Kailin's feet. "Good to see you are taking care of your mistress."

"Gilla and Druce?" Kailin said, questions in her tone.

"Let me go," slurred the thief, his lips still frozen. Was Kailin holding him against the wall?

Gilla was your mother.

Jackson looked between the four: thief, owl, Kailin, ghost. He lowered his gun halfway to his side. None of his experience could help him with this bizarre situation. Only the sound of shallow breathing came from the thief. The dragonflies zipped noiselessly as if they were half-concocted hallucinations. Jackson blinked hard but the images continued to dive through the air around the ghost.

"This isn't the place for introductions or explanations," he said. He glanced down the empty alley. "I'm taking you to your hotel, Kailin."

The ghost's gaze turned to him, scrutinizing, appreciating. One of her eyebrows arched high. *Tall, virile, strong. A good mate for Gilla's daughter.*

Mate?

Kailin's gaze flickered toward Jackson and her cheeks pinkened. She'd heard the ghost's assessment in her head too.

The thief behind her groaned, his face turning red.

"Kailin." Jackson stepped forward and touched her hand before she baked the thief alive. The man slumped to the ground, his knife skittering across the packed sand. Jackson kicked the slightly melted weapon away, but the man didn't look like he had any intent of trying to follow it. "You're lucky you survived today, bloody bastard," Jackson said. "Think again before attacking anyone." Tuto pecked at the man's arm several times before taking off, his huge wings lifting him into a swoop toward the alley mouth.

Jackson propelled Kailin around and past the floating apparition. Did it follow? Did the thief get off the ground? Didn't matter. He needed to get Kailin out of the alley and to safety. This was also a rare moment when she seemed too stunned to argue with him.

"What the hell were you thinking?" he growled slightly above a whisper as they stepped back into the public stream. "Going off alone was foolish enough, but then walking down an alley off the wharf at Luxor? And then letting the bastard hold you." Jackson paused in his tirade and his step but then continued to propel Kailin through the street. He signaled a hackney and lifted her in. Without releasing her elbow, he followed, clipping a few directions to the driver in the local Arabic. The man hefted the small conveyance onto his shoulders and took off through the milling people. Jackson scanned the crowd. No doubt they were being watched.

"You can let go of me now," Kailin said in a firm voice. "I won't jump from a moving cart."

Her arm was slender, strong beneath his fingers. He didn't want to let go. "I wouldn't want to be responsible for the baking of any locals."

Kailin's eyes flashed at him, color high in her cheeks. Why did he bait her? It was apparently dangerous—for bystanders at least. "You would be responsible for that," she whispered quickly. "I've never before lost control like I do when you are near me."

He moved close to her and inhaled the sweet flower smell of her skin. "And yet when I touch you..." He let the sentence hang, enjoying the sound of the word *touch*.

Her blue eyes stared into his as if trying to decipher an ancient warning in a crypt. The slight golden hue encircling her iris made the color take on a greenish tint around the periphery.

"What *are* you?" she whispered, searching his eyes.

"What are *you*?" he answered back.

"I asked first." Her soft pink lips twisted into a petulant line. She had lips made for yielding if she'd ever let someone.

That someone is me. Mine, whispered through Jackson's head and he almost turned to look for the ghost. But the timbre was his, not hers. *You are mine.* The thought screamed through his head, hardening his gut.

"The ghost said I was your mate," he answered.

"Do you know who she is?" Kailin asked, not taking the bait.

He gave a brief shake, barely seen. "She seems to know you. Gilla's daughter?"

Kailin glanced down, her shoulders lowering back into the dingy cushion of the seat. Her gloved finger rubbed along her upper arm. "She knows of my parents."

"I thought Doctor Whitaker was your father. I didn't know you had a mother."

Kailin's gaze snapped back to him. "Everyone has a mother, whether they know of her or not. Anthony has been my father for as long as I can remember. He and Bruce played the part of mother too. I have no knowledge of my mother by blood, but be assured, Mister Black, I was birthed by someone."

Moisture in Kailin's blue eyes turned them greenish and Jackson wished once again that he had the forethought for polite dialogue. The pit of his stomach churned with guilt and regret. Tears were his downfall more than any firearm. By now he should be dead a hundred times over with as many tears as he'd seen. And Kailin's could surely cripple him. If she knew the power she had, she'd no doubt wield it over him like her magic.

Jackson glanced away from the proof of his brutish behavior. He breathed in the heat rolling off the nearby sands as they dodged foot traffic away from the wharf.

"I apologize for any offense," he said slowly, considering each word before uttering it this time. He filtered out pity from his voice. "And as for mothers, they are...important. I am sorry you did not know yours."

She did not snap back, didn't say anything, but Jackson felt her gaze. They rode in silence until they stopped before a three-story building with an ornate arched doorway flanked by potted palms.

The etched stone, cleverly stacked, blended with the sand-colored bricks of the town, but turquoise-and-red mosaics depicted Egyptian scenery along the walls. Gold painted steps led up to glass doors where a local boy in a red bellman costume stood ready to open and close the portal. Hotel Moudira stood like an oasis in the arid city. Ladies in fresh gowns brandishing parasols and gentlemen wearing trousers with matching vests climbed the steps to a deck with umbrella-shaded tables to saunter into the cool relief of the reception area.

Jackson helped Kailin down from the hackney and paid the driver. She added her own coin to the lucky lad's hand. He smiled and bobbed at her generosity.

"No need to pay double," Jackson said and grabbed her valise.

"In case it was his father whom I incapacitated in the alley." She took her valise from him and turned away.

Jackson watched the straight line of Kailin's back as she stepped before him up the steep staircase. It seemed that the ice princess hefted the chains of guilt as well as he did. Jackson caught up to her pace in two strides. He offered her his arm. Observing polite manners only, he was certain, she rested her fingers on his forearm. But she neither pressed nor faltered on her way up the steep climb. The woman was rugged and had a strong heart. Each layer he peeled back from Doctor Kailin Whitaker made Jackson want to uncover even more.

CHAPTER FIVE
HOTEL MOUDIRA

Kailin stepped into the ornate lobby and crossed it while walking next to Jackson. Curious stares and bending heads flanked her. She folded a veil of aloof respectability around herself, concentrating on constricting the bubbles of magic and anxiety popping around under the familiar façade. Familiar, yes, but also exhausting.

She sighed softly. How she missed the quiet majesty and resonating silence of the Highland mountains, the harsh land too difficult and cold for most tourists. She'd been able to excavate and study the historic mysteries of the landscape and carved rocks without the constant need for control. Even with all the modern amenities and expensive luxuries offered here, she'd be much less comfortable and much more tired.

"Another sigh?" Jackson spoke softly.

Kailin stared straight ahead at the reservation desk. "I find that I am homesick for my wide-open skies and mountains. God's creations are much more relaxing than this man-made opulence. I fear I am tired of it already."

"Hmm… That I understand," Jackson murmured and Kailin looked sharply at him.

"Do you? I thought you spent your time here, hunting for manmade opulence."

He tipped his head as if agreeing to part of her observation. "I didn't always crawl in the sand looking for trinkets." His cocky half-smile sobered. "I grew up under wide-open skies west of the Mississippi River in the States. I understand homesickness, Doctor Whitaker."

She glanced about for eavesdroppers. "Miss Whitaker, please."

"Oh, but to be merely walking amongst the wildflowers and prairie grass, where you would feel comfortable being everything that you are, Miss Whitaker."

Kailin blinked and her tight mouth softened. That was all she would permit. Perhaps he did know something then of the strain she felt. The weight of everything, not merely of walls and ceilings, but of judgment and societal cages. A man raised under constant reminder of God's grandeur must have something of a humble heart, although Jackson Black's heart seemed way too cocky to be humble.

"Your eyes give you away," he whispered near her ear as she turned back to the registration desk. The manager signaled that he would be right with her and she nodded.

"How so?" she asked though kept her eyes cast away.

"They soften, harden, flash, and reflect the emotions trying to pound their way out of that mask you wear. People say you are made of ice, but it is all a façade to hide yourself."

Kailin swallowed hard and forced her voice to remain smooth, aloof. "How annoying of you to notice."

He laughed with what sounded like appreciation for her wit. It made her mouth soften again, the corners rising on their own accord.

"May I help you?" The manager stepped before them. He eyed Jackson critically and turned more to her. Did the man know Jackson?

"My father was abducted from your establishment, Mister...?" She found it best to reveal the most important information first. None of this small talk on which people seemed to waste considerable breath.

"Willep," the man sputtered. He looked to be in his middle years, a bit paunchy, but a man who took great care in getting his mustache to curl on the ends to points.

Kailin nodded coolly. "His name is Doctor Anthony Whitaker." The manager's face continued to redden, and she felt Jackson's hand clasp her elbow. Even though the need for constant self-restraint disappeared, she frowned at Jackson. It wasn't her out-of-control magic that heated the paunchy man's face but his own embarrassment at allowing such an atrocity to occur in his hotel.

"The magistrate has taken all the information, madam. We are doing all we can to find him I assure you."

"I am *Miss* Whitaker, and I am sure you are investigating." She forced a cool smile to assure the man that she wasn't hostile, merely efficient. "I will require a room with an outside balcony and access to my father's room and possessions. My bag was brought from the wharf earlier."

The manager nodded and his gaze drifted to Jackson.

"Mister Black will need a separate room," she added.

Jackson tipped his hat slightly with an amused grin. "As the lady says."

The manager blinked several times. Perhaps he wasn't used to such directness from a woman, especially with a man at her side.

Kailin glanced at Jackson. A casual grin sat across his lips. He apparently had no problem with her leadership abilities even if it stretched the lines of social etiquette. It wasn't that she thought she could handle the conversation better—well, perhaps she could—but that she was used to taking charge. She was the leader on her small expeditions and digs. It suited her. In this way she could relax in her own skin even when playing the role of civilized lady.

The manager rang a bell and a lad, perhaps barely considered a man in British society, stepped promptly from around a potted fern with her canvas duffel in hand. The manager dangled two keys for the boy. "Room 302 for Miss Whitaker." He turned to her. "It was your father's room. I will have the box of his belongings brought up to you. The room has been used since…it was vacated last month."

Her lips tightened with disapproval. There would be no studying the room for evidence of the crime, not when the man had righted and cleaned it so he could continue to rent it out. Her gaze narrowed as she stared at him like a cobra ready to strike.

The manager's gaze snapped away as if he were a rabbit running from her bite. "Room 306 for Mister Black, Avil," he said.

"Thank you, Mister Willep," Kailin said and turned to follow the boy struggling with the keys while his two hands held her duffel. It was heavy, and the boy's arms were thin.

"Much obliged," Jackson said, tipped his hat and stepped forward. Without a word, he took the bag from the boy, placating him with a few words in Arabic. Jackson nodded for him to proceed, and the boy waved them to follow. Jackson's own duffel slung against his narrow hips as he walked ahead of Kailin. Occasionally he glanced back to ascertain she was still there.

"Don't fear, Mister Black," Kailin called. "I will scream if anyone tries to abduct me on the way to the room."

"I'm only making sure you're not ducking alone down any more alleys on the way." Several bystanders stared at their banter. Really, current mores were so ridiculous. Perhaps that's why she preferred studying long-dead societies to the annoyingly alive one she lived within.

With curious eyes taking in her every gesture and glance, Kailin kept her gaze level with Jackson's back where his hair lay in waves against his neck. The way the muscles played through his shirt as he hauled their luggage was stimulating enough.

She pursed her lips and fought to keep her gaze from sliding down to where she knew his pants lay perfectly against his bum. If she wasn't careful all the ferns in the hotel would shrivel with the irritating heat the man lit in her. She'd never before had such a reaction to an individual. Even embarrassed or irritated at the parade of eligible men Anthony and Bruce insisted she be exposed to, she didn't lose control of her magic. Jackson Black was different. He loosened the tight knots she purposely tangled around her talent to keep it under control.

Room 302 looked like any other simple suite. Kailin strode through the confines of the walls to the balcony doors, swinging them wide to the dry open air. She leaned against the rail and overlooked a tamed central garden. A trickling waterfall fed a rock pond with large goldfish. Wrought iron tables with chairs sat at random intervals amongst the manicured beds, which flanked an inlaid stone path. Quaint, pretty, but more importantly... Kailin glanced upwards at the empty sky. *Open.*

Kailin measured the breadth of the small balcony in her mind. It was big enough to accommodate some cushions from the lounge inside. Yes, she'd be comfortable enough here. She turned to investigate her father's old room.

Avil waited in the corridor while Jackson strode across the room to the rail and leaned over. "Three floors up. Safe enough."

"Apparently not for my father." Kailin began her inspection of the room. "They must have come through the door. Were there signs of forced entry?" she asked Avil and felt the amber stone she wore on a chain around her neck warm. It translated her words into Arabic for the lad, but her lips formed the words in English.

Avil shook his head, eyes still wide as moons.

"I did not see, *madam*, but I did not have to repair the door afterwards," the boy said, the stone translating his Arabic for her. He touched the door jamb as if looking for evidence and shook his head. "No broken wood."

Kailin nodded, her bun rubbing against her nape. She reached behind and cupped her neck to soothe the ache already building there and surveyed the rest of the orderly room.

Two potted ferns flanked the balcony doors, and a miniature palm stood in the corner next to a large wardrobe, which Jackson checked for criminals. Green curtains tied back around a regular-sized bed with matching coverlet and plump rust-colored pillows. A small chandelier in orange and burnt-umber cut glass hung from the ceiling in the center of the room, and a wooden chest sat on the floor against the bed's footboard. She lifted the lid. Extra blankets and a robe sat folded inside. Several paintings depicting Egyptian artifacts hung about the room and a water pitcher with basin perched on a wooden table near the balcony door. A rich rug in a matching palette covered the polished wood floor. No obvious signs of scuffle. Kailin bent to the rug and lifted it. Dust, crumbs, but nothing else.

A silent movement on the balcony accompanied Avil's gasp and Jackson's chuckle. "Your pet has found you."

Tuto perched on the rail, his head swiveling in a disjointed perusal of his new roost. She smiled. "He's never far from me."

She turned toward Jackson, the smile still in place. His grin relaxed, and their gazes locked for a full breath. Kailin blinked several times while the flutters in her stomach made it hard to inhale fully.

"I suppose you're safe enough for now," Jackson murmured. He gestured to the boy who clutched the side of the door jamb, his body half out in the hall. "On to room 306. I will come back to escort you below for dinner at seven."

"I will eat in," she said. It was definitely best to keep her distance from the man.

"Rather closed in here," Jackson said. "There's a cool breeze that comes from the wharf as the sun drops. It's more refreshing along the front promenade."

"Hmm..." Kailin hesitated, feeling the trail of perspiration gathering under the bodice of her blue traveling costume. His argument was good; she'd give him that.

"Seven-thirty," she said. She looked at Avil . "I would like to bathe before dinner if that can be arranged." The boy promised to send a bathing tub with water. She nodded a thank-you.

"Would you be in need of assistance?" Jackson drawled in English. Kailin could hardly swallow against the hard flutter of her heart. She paused, mesmerized by the fire reflected in his wolfish eyes. They were the eyes of a rogue, a gambler and treasure hunter. *And a liar.* Kailin clamped a cold fist on the heat pooling in her stomach. "I could hire a maid for you," he continued.

She blinked, her brow taut. Could she have possibly misunderstood his look? Heat rose in her cheeks, and Avil pulled at his high collar as if feeling the rise in temperature.

Kailin thought of her stones back in Scotland. Cold, hard, rough, and solid. They were the literal rocks she held onto to control her magic. She breathed evenly, rebuilding her control.

"No need, Mister Black." Clipped precision chilled her voice to ice. *'Tis as it must be.* "I can care for myself. I've done so my entire life."

"Ah, another thing we have in common, Doctor Whitaker." Jackson tipped his head and followed Avil out the door.

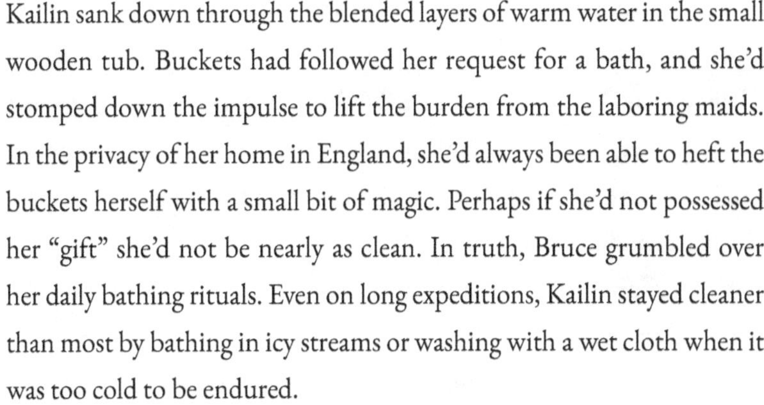

Kailin sank down through the blended layers of warm water in the small wooden tub. Buckets had followed her request for a bath, and she'd stomped down the impulse to lift the burden from the laboring maids. In the privacy of her home in England, she'd always been able to heft the buckets herself with a small bit of magic. Perhaps if she'd not possessed her "gift" she'd not be nearly as clean. In truth, Bruce grumbled over her daily bathing rituals. Even on long expeditions, Kailin stayed cleaner than most by bathing in icy streams or washing with a wet cloth when it was too cold to be endured.

But this bath was pure luxury. Kailin let her head fall back to rest on the high back. Her knees broke the water where she sat mostly submerged. Her breasts teased the surface. A slight rising of steam hovered, scented with the addition of her favorite rose-and-mint oil.

Kailin breathed and closed her eyes, allowing the knots in her back and shoulders to warm and untangle along with her nerves. In through the nose, out through the lips. She exchanged air and channeled her mind toward her favorite mental destination, the stone circle.

High in the rugged terrain of western Scotland, within earshot of crashing waves, sat a circle of ten soaring stone monoliths. An immense slab table sat in the center, rooted to the ground. Kailin breathed deeply of the rose and mint and let her mind float amongst the wildflowers growing there, unharassed by the confines of polite society, living their lives outdoors under God's immense sky.

The stone circle had been Kailin's first expedition. She'd barely been of an age to venture into the marketplace alone when Anthony had broken down and taken her. She smiled at the memory of poor Bruce blustering the whole way as they climbed crumbling boulders and rode along washed-out mountain roads. She hadn't known what she would find, but she'd known something was pulling her. Ever since she could remember she'd felt tugged north and west, toward the circle.

Bruce had stood trout-mouthed while Anthony said "and there it is" when they'd broken through the thick evergreens and first spied the magnificent circle. A giddy bubble of tickling warmth had flooded Kailin's senses with well-being, and the constant pulling had stopped. She had found her true home.

Kailin rubbed her wrinkling fingers along her skin, washing away the grime of travel. A quick glance showed Tuto perched on the balcony, keeping watch or falling asleep, she wasn't sure. She closed her eyes again. She was safe even if her eternal watch guard napped.

The handsome face of Jackson Black surfaced behind her lids, disrupting her calm visualization. Kailin dimmed his features as she tried to remember the exact structure of the granite slab in the stones. The pocked surface grew tiny microcosms of moss and lichen, giving it a green velvety surface. She'd actually slept in its comfort, lulled by the hum of magic weaving amongst the sentries, chasing the nightmares back into the tombs she refused to enter again.

The lightning in that aggravating man's storm-gray eyes sparked in her mind. "Damn," she murmured, squeezing her eyes. The memory of his touch, his warm hands through the fabric of her gown, sent a heavy heat down through her belly.

Kailin scratched gently along the dragonfly-shaped birthmark on her upper arm, and she opened her eyes. Had she been bitten by a mosquito?

Tuto ruffled his feathers in the background, and the filmy iridescent wings of several dragonflies zipped in from the evening-shrouded garden. Water splashed over the side of the tub as Kailin sat upright, her head snapping around. She wasn't alone.

CHAPTER SIX
PRIESTESS, SPIRIT, CRONE, OR WITCH?

"Gilla's daughter," the smiling spirit said and floated down toward the damp floor.

Kailin's heart pounded, her magic ready to strike, but she kept her voice level. "You are Drakkina," Kailin said and sank into the water so only her neck broke the surface. *Naked and in the tub.* She'd only be more vulnerable if she were trapped in a tomb hyperventilating.

"What are you?" she asked with an icy staccato.

"Good question." The spirit canted her head. "I feel great power radiating from you."

Kailin followed her inquisitive glance around the room. She swallowed, breathed, and gingerly lowered the table, pitcher, and trunk back to the floor. They could have smashed a would-be assassin, but Kailin knew they'd be no use against this apparition.

"Perhaps you are the wisest of your sisters too?" Drakkina asked.

Kailin nearly shot out of the water. "Sisters? You know more of my blood relations?"

Drakkina nodded, her eyes shifting briefly to Tuto who watched her but did not enter the room. Did her owl find the woman no threat or was she holding her friend at bay?

"Yes, I knew Gilla, your father, Druce, and your siblings. You look very much like your twin, Katell." She flicked her fingers toward Kailin's right cheek. "Without the scars, of course."

Kailin's breath stuttered somewhere around her collarbone. "My...my twin?" Where had she come by scars?

"Don't you remember her? Well, you were young, four I believe. She didn't remember you at first either."

"Where is she?" Kailin stood up out of the water. The bathing sheet flashed through the air into her hands. Sloshing water over the side, she stepped out and wrapped herself in the clinging linen. Tall and straight, she stared at the apparition.

The woman frowned slightly. "Not somewhere you can find her, without my help that is."

Kailin watched the spirit carefully. "Is my mother with her?" She was grateful for Anthony and Bruce for raising her outside the confining strictures that trussed up genteel young ladies, but she'd begrudgingly envied the ladies walking down the streets with their mothers, sharing delight in shop window displays.

Drakkina's face softened. "No." She blinked quickly, a very human gesture in a strangely changing face. One moment the ghost looked young and then faint lines cut grooves into her skin as she aged into a wise sage. "She died, not long after she sent you away to safety."

Kailin's legs wobbled, and she sat on the edge of her bed. Images that haunted her nightmares of rising above a cold swirl of chaos came back to her, making her blink. "Why?" She looked at the spirit. "How did she die?"

Drakkina floated lower, closer. "Listen carefully, Kailin." Her eyes pierced. "The world is in jeopardy. A coven of thirteen demons grew so powerful they were able to slip past my defenses."

"They killed my mother?"

Drakkina nodded. "They killed many." Her face tightened, and a shimmer of moisture shone in her eyes. "Stole good souls." She paused. Her striking blue eyes reflected the light, showing pain. "They seek power to steal the world, control the world by cutting the temporal lines that hold all times apart. If they are successful, all times will crush together until the world is overrun, unrecognizable. Billions will die or wish they'd died."

"And killing my mother?" Kailin whispered.

Drakkina's diaphanous feet touched the woven rug. "First they killed your father and stripped his powers. He was a great wizard, one of my best students. But Druce was cocky, a common fault of handsome warriors." She shook her head. "He met them alone and they shredded away his essence for their own until only the husk of his physical body remained.

With his added strength, they were strong enough to breach your mother's massive defenses. She fought to save you and your siblings. When she knew she couldn't hold them off much longer, she threaded each one of you into time, into a different time, hidden away from the demons."

"And from each other," Kailin murmured.

"It was safer to live separate, harder to trace."

"The demons sought us for our magic then?"

"Seek you," Drakkina corrected her eyes growing wide. "Gilla sent her magic with each of you. You received the—"

"Ability to move things," Kailin finished softly.

Drakkina snorted. "Aye, the ability to move things. Sounds so simple and benign, but I have a feeling that you've had a difficult time keeping it under control." She motioned to the colorful vase that hovered.

"I've had no instruction," Kailin said and concentrated on setting the West African vase down. Its bottom tapped on a small table as it came to rest.

Drakkina floated to stand before her, her hands by her sides as dragonflies flitted around her white, braided hair. "Gilla was right. You are very strong. I think she sensed it in you as a babe. The magic she sent with you was her strongest. Power to manipulate the elemental parts of physical objects."

"So"—Kailin hesitated, her brow tense— "when...Gilla sent me away with her last ability, she died."

"She was weak from fighting and had no magical defenses left. Only her mother's ability to love with ferocity remained." Drakkina mumbled and shook her head. "She died quickly, child, without torture. The demons thought she was still powerful and required their entire focus to crush. She dissolved instantaneously once they attacked." Drakkina shook her head as if regret weighted her form.

"Couldn't you do anything?" Kailin searched her lined face.

Drakkina closed her pale blue eyes. "I did. I saved the world. I made sure you all got away. I did what must be done." She opened her eyes. "And I continue to work to save this world even though I'm no longer in it."

"You're dead," Kailin stated the obvious, "but haven't moved on to God." She flapped her hand overhead.

"I've not seen your God. I hear the wisdom of the Earth Mother. Some say they are one and the same." Drakkina pursed her thin lips tighter. "And I'm mostly dead." She glanced at her chest, where an amulet hung with a dragonfly centered on it. "When I wear my physical necklace, its power gives my body true form."

Kailin clasped her bath sheet with both hands and stood, leaning toward the misty form. She glanced at her arm where her brown birthmark sat. "It has the same symbol."

Drakkina smiled. "'Tis my symbol. The dragonfly. Vulnerable in form but resilient and powerful in spirit." Several dragonflies zipped around the room as if they understood her praise.

"I'm marked with your symbol?"

"Each of Gilla and Druce's children have my symbol on their bodies. A gift from me." She smiled. "It draws you four sisters toward your origin and the safety of my protection."

"The circle of stones in Scotland."

"'Twas where your home once sat."

Kailin plopped back down on the edge of the chair. "My home."

"You are safe there, at least until the final battle when you and your mate, along with your sisters and their mates, fight the thirteen devils that will stop at nothing to steal the world and use it as their playground."

Kailin's lips parted, her mind taking in all the spirit's words. They swirled inside her like a desert cyclone.

"You are the last sister I needed to find," Drakkina continued. "Now I will help you find your soul mate, and we will be ready to defeat Semiazaz's coven."

"Semiazaz? My soul mate?" The details the crone threw at her were like pebbles shot about in the storm within her head.

Drakkina glanced down at her beringed hands and twirled one simple silver band around her finger. "Semiazaz is their leader. And yes, Jackson Black is your soul mate." She flipped her hand casually toward the door. "That handsome rogue ready to fight for you in the alley."

"No." Kailin jumped to her feet, nearly dropping the bath towel. "The man is absolutely not my soul mate, if there even is such a thing. Soul mates are labels used in fairytales and fancies wished for by foolish girls. Soul mates have nothing to do with real life."

"Does your magic work on him?" Drakkina's eyebrow rose.

"No, but—"

Drakkina held up her hand. "Has your talent ever failed you before?"

"No, but—"

"He's the one then. It's been the same for each of your sisters." Drakkina shrugged. "It matters little how you feel about him now. You're tied to one another on a level so fundamental to your being that you might as well give up fighting your attraction to him"—she eyed Kailin knowingly—"and marry him now. Anything else is a waste of your energy. Energy you could be using to mate." Drakkina's dragonflies danced around her even faster as if in some carnal bacchanalian revelry.

Kailin leapt off the chair, her damp hair snaking around her shoulders as she shook her head. "What?! No! There will absolutely be no mating."

Crash! The door splintered inward as Jackson's huge boot came thudding down. He held a revolver in each hand, his eyes wild as he searched the room. His guns aimed at the floating spirit, but his eyes focused entirely on Kailin.

Behind him, a young, dark-haired maid gasped and dropped a box. Tuto swooped through the room at the commotion. The maid screamed and ran back down the hall. Tuto circled and landed on a post of the bed, surveying the scene below for threats. A man in his thirties and an elderly woman stopped to stare through the wrecked door. "Good Lord," the man in the hall exclaimed. "What is this about?"

Jackson's gaze traveled Kailin's length in the clinging sheet, and her face began to heat. He crossed to her, one gun tucked away, the other still ready to meet the unseen threat.

"You screamed," he said and shook out of his blue jacket. He laid it about her shoulders, awkwardly closing it in front with one hand.

"I was startled," was all Kailin could say as her face flamed. Her gaze flitted from the ruined door and guests to Drakkina to Jackson. Kailin felt the light touch of Jackson's fingers on her arm through the jacket. Could he mute her powers without touching her skin? As he increased pressure, the molten magic inside her faded.

"A misunderstanding," Jackson said to the room and lowered his gun, although his glance hesitated on Drakkina who had retreated to a dark corner. "The bird startled her."

"Well, I certainly imagine so," the elderly woman said and held a monocular up to stare at Tuto from the doorway.

The well-tailored man continued to watch Kailin. "You're going to have to find another room." His proper English accent held notes of gentry. "And I'm sure the hotel will require payment."

"Thank you for the obvious," Jackson said. "Please be kind enough to send for the manager while Doctor Whitaker finds some clothes."

"Doctor?" the woman said, eyeing Kailin with a critical eye as if having a brain was worse than standing in a room with strangers wrapped only in a towel.

"Miss Whitaker," Kailin corrected.

"Come along, Henry." The elderly woman tugged on the man's arm.

"Go along, Aunt Gertrude. I must see that his lady is unharmed."

"She's unharmed."

"I'm unharmed."

Jackson and Kailin spoke at the same time, making the man's gaze shift from one to the other before he glanced downward. The matronly lade sniffed and continued on down the corridor.

"I believe the maid was bringing this for you." Henry picked the box up and carried it into the room, placing it on the bed. "I can stay until the maid sends someone if you are in need." Henry looked at Jackson, which was quite brave considering the gun Jackson held.

"She's in need of privacy, not an audience," Jackson growled. He indicated the hallway with his gun, but the man stood his ground.

"I would hear it from the lady," Henry said.

Kailin wet her very dry lips. "Thank you, sir, but Mister Black is my assistant. He is fully trustworthy." She choked a little as the lie curled like bitter coffee around her tongue. Jackson frowned. "He will merely prop the door up and guard it from the outside while I dress." She turned to meet Jackson's frown. His eyes searched the corner where Drakkina floated. He must be able to see her. "All is safe here," she assured both men.

Jackson replaced his second gun in a holster he wore around his narrow hips like an American cowboy. Kailin snapped her eyes up from his strong thighs and buttocks. She breathed and suppressed the warmth in her face.

"You heard her," Jackson said, shooing Henry out of the room. "All is safe here." He grumbled a curse as he hauled the door upright and fit it into the gaping hole.

"Just send for me, Henry Dallinton, if you have need, Miss Whitaker," came from the other side, followed by the sound of footsteps clipping away.

Kailin yanked underclothes out of the trunk, her glance going back and forth between the propped door and Drakkina. When she was certain no one but Drakkina could see her, she took Jackson's coat from her shoulders, setting it open on the bed. A second of thought was all that was needed to dry the damp garment, and she ignored the pleasant scent of the man, which emanated from it. Kailin turned away, dropping the towel, and threw her white, high neck smock over her head, pulled on a pair of drawers, and followed them both with her stays.

"He can sense you, but the others cannot," she whispered while using her magic to tighten and secure the ties behind her. She set the bustle pad around her waist, a much-needed yet ridiculous contraption to give her the silhouette that English culture dictated.

Jackson Black is apparently sensitive to magic. A good match for Gilla's daughter. The words came through Kailin's mind, and she paused. The witch might be dead, or mostly dead, but she was certainly powerful. A chill ratcheted up each of Kailin's vertebra. What else could Drakkina do? What could she teach her?

"I need to know more about everything." Kailin threw on a yellow petticoat, settling it to rest on her hips and cinching it to bustle slightly in the back over the pad into a short train. Then came the overgown in green silk embroidered with swirls of gold thread. It was her one dinner gown. She would find at least one more while here, as well as some more expedition clothing.

In time. Right now, your task is to fall in love.

The woman pointed a long finger toward the door. Kailin frowned with tight lips and glared at her. She shook her head. "I will not fall in love merely because you order it," she whispered through compressed teeth.

Neither did your sisters. The spirit met Kailin's frown with her own. *Waste of time but I won't interfere. I've learned.* Dragonflies zipped around the room. Tuto's head swiveled as he followed the insects. Kailin watched the glittery wings fade while in flight. When she looked back to the spirit, she was gone.

Kailin exhaled a huff and used her magic to flip the little buttons closed at her nape and at her wrists. Her mind spun crazily around the information she'd learned. Her mother, murdered by demons that now searched for her and her sisters and planned to kill them to take over the world. It read like some wild story, too bizarre even for *Lloyd's Weekly*. She would relegate the whole thing to temporary, stress-induced psychosis.

But Drakkina... Kailin's lips tightened into a tense line. She ran a finger over her birthmark, now encased modestly in green silk. The apparition was real.

"Uh..." Jackson hesitated, his voice only slightly muffled by the heavy door. "Do you need help dressing?"

Good God. Did the man think she'd actually invite him in to dress her? The thought of his strong hands sliding along her skin as he tightened her stays made Kailin's heart tip into a fast run, heating her cheeks. She really had to get ahold of her reactions to the man. Why did he affect her so easily?

Jackson Black is your soul mate. Drakkina's words wafted through her mind, and she slapped them away with a quick shake of her head.

"I will be out as soon as I can, Mister Black," Kailin said. "I've been dressing myself for quite a long time now. Buttons and long hair take time," she added to soften the response.

Silence answered her, and she momentarily closed her eyes at the sting of it. Did he think she was a shrew like the rest of the world? She'd never cared before and had fostered the impression to keep people away. But the thought of the rugged, strong man falling for the persona that she'd grown into made her stomach clench.

Kailin pressed cool fingertips into the gentle indents at her temples while her mind dried and wove her hair into a tight plait that then tucked under into a lovely, intricate bun. She opened her eyes and used her fingers to tease out a few curls around her face. It softened her look. She applied a beeswax balm with the essence of mint to her lips to defend against the dry air blowing in from the desert.

Kailin grabbed her silk reticule and straightened the layers of green and gold skirts. "Silly contraption," she whispered at her reflection in the polished glass over the African vase. On expedition she did away with such social strictures, which was part of why she preferred the field to the drawing room. Kailin exhaled long and eyed the propped door.

Tuto stretched his wings and dove from the bedpost through the open balcony doors. Kailin certainly hoped there was another room with a balcony available. Although given the opportunity she could fix the door herself.

"I am presentable," she called.

Strong fingers appeared on both edges of the door and Jackson slid the oak to the inside wall.

Jackson's gaze turned to her and she waited, actually held her breath as those piercing eyes took in her appearance. She fought the simpering urge to check her hair. *He is not my soul mate. There's no such thing.*

Jackson's brows rose with appreciation, and a curve nudged the slightly parted corner of his mouth. "Well now."

Those two simple words shot like a firework through her. Kailin cleared her throat and inhaled, walking to her bed to retrieve his dark blue frock coat. "Thank you," she said, handing the heavy garment to him.

Jackson worked it on over a cream-colored shirt and vest, which he wore with a minimal cravat in a dark blue to match the jacket and tailored brown trousers. Only his double gun holster, buckled to sit low on his hips, pulled him out of a gentleman's dinner party. His brown hair was slightly damp and drying in waves above his ears, and he'd shaved the stubble off his strong jawline. "Shall we?" His silky drawl held his smile.

Jackson offered his elbow for her to rest her bare fingertips. "From a water nymph to a lovely lady in a mere dozen minutes." Jackson grinned as they stepped through the doorway. The finger of his free hand rose to toy with a curl by her cheek. "Even your hair has dried." He tipped his head slightly and Kailin shot her gaze back in front of her so she wouldn't trip on the ornate runner down the corridor.

"How inappropriate of you to notice," she whispered, but the breathless way her words brushed across her lips made the rebuke sound more like a lover's purr. She blushed deeply, her fingers curling into his arm. If she let go now, the entire hotel could shoot up into flames, baking them alive.

"Success lies in the details," he answered as if they discussed racehorses instead of her appearance. "I hunt treasure, Miss Doctor Whitaker," he said, using both of her titles, and stepped lightly next to her down the carpeted staircase. "One must pay attention to every aspect of life in order to unearth the prize."

They walked casually across the lobby where large hats fought for space on women whispering on the arms of their stalwart gentlemen. "Do you view me as a prize to be unearthed?" Kailin asked softly and continued to stare ahead. She should stop the conversation, the quiet fencing. Perhaps he wouldn't answer. Then she could remain silent having had the last word.

She breathed in the cool dry air that wafted off the desert as the sand quickly surrendered the baking heat of the day. Kailin reached for the iron arm of the chair, but Jackson pulled it out from the table. As she bent to sit, adjusting the ridiculous bulbous bustle into the rounded cushion, Jackson's warm breath grazed her ear.

"Prize? Rather a treasure, a grand cache buried deep within a mountain of gloriously enticing *rock*." He slid her seat in to the table, completely without her help, as if she were a child.

Jackson kept her fingertips in his warm grasp as he rounded the small table and sat. Clever man. Infuriating man!

She kept her voice low. "I would pull my hand from yours, Mister Black, but I fear I would unleash mass destruction with my ire." Kailin met his gaze with her own steel. "Rock indeed," she muttered. It was the look that had sent men of great means scurrying out of her way. Yet Jackson Black merely stared back, a spark of battle in his storm-gray eyes.

Kailin wet her lips with the wine provided in a glass before her, her fingers still tight in his grip. Her tongue licked at the underside up her upper lip, over her teeth. Jackson's grin faded, his eyes narrowing as if he were a pointer catching the scent. Carefully, Kailin slid her fingers from his grasp and kept her hand palm down on the smooth tablecloth. At once the enclosed flame of the small candle between them leaped and danced. She breathed deeply. "Be warned, Mister Black. This rock has a tendency to crush."

His frown hedged once again into appreciation. "I think," he said and lifted his own wine glass, "the world has far more to fear from your lava, Doctor Whitaker." He raised one eyebrow and tilted his head slightly to one side. "Except when I touch you. Curious?" He took a drink of his wine.

The waiter cleared his throat, and Kailin's gaze snapped to him. How much had the man heard?

Kailin breathed slowly, imagining cool snow drifting over her. A gust of cold snapped at the overhanging awning. Several hats blew, followed by feminine screeches. Kailin closed her eyes in defeat. Jackson Black completely shattered her control. It was as if she were a child of four again just figuring out how to drop the garden pebbles before they hit poor Bruce when he wouldn't let her have a third dessert.

"Would you like to move inside?" the waiter asked as several groups stampeded into the hotel lobby. "There seems to be a storm rising."

Jackson looked expectantly at Kailin. "No," she managed to say. "The breeze suits me." The waiter bowed, took their orders and retreated. With a calming thought of gentle sun, the breeze died and the heat of the day could still be felt.

Jackson glanced around. "Nice way to gain privacy." He regarded her shrewdly as if trying to figure out exactly what she was or could do.

Kailin had always hidden her powers except from Anthony and Bruce, who were desperate to keep her safe from torturous scientific study. Unfortunately, she had a temper so there had been a few mishaps throughout the years. A picture of Samantha McGivens, drenched and screaming, flashed into her mind only to be covered quickly with a mental bandage. *Cover and lock it away. Breathe and imagine peace.* Anthony's words had meant to calm her into control, but they didn't always work.

Kailin swallowed some more wine. She tapped her nails on the table. What to say? She glanced around too. "The weather changes in Egypt so rapidly. I've found it is best to wait it out."

Jackson nodded, his perfectly formed lips puckering for a moment before pulling back into a casual grin. Kailin saw a hint of white, straight teeth. She took another sip of wine and her stomach growled. If their food didn't arrive soon, the wine would surely muddle her head.

Jackson leaned back in his chair and surveyed her while Kailin made a point to look out over the milling street below the hotel. Locals pulled carts alongside donkeys. Merchants closed up brightly colored shops, extinguishing oil lamps. Children ran barefoot races, laughter in their innocent, dirty faces.

Kailin smiled softly. "They are so free," she said and Jackson followed her gaze. "Free and happy."

He leaned forward and filled her empty wine glass. "Everyone has manacles." Her gaze turned to his. He tipped his chin toward the urchins. "Theirs happens to be poverty, cultural instability, heartlessness of the ruling class, and famine."

Kailin's smile faded with a nod. "You are right."

"How many chains do you endure, Kailin Whitaker?"

Warmth penetrated her tense muscles with the wine. She laughed a bitter snort and covered her mouth. "More than you can imagine, Mister Black. But at the same time, not enough."

He leaned forward across the table, his stormy eyes connecting with her own on a level that shackled her to him. "And what would happen, Kailin," he asked, stressing her given name, "if you were to let yourself break free? Unlock the fetters that hold you back?"

Her eyebrows rose. "I am quite frightening."

He leaned closer. "I don't scare easily. So tell me, Kailin..." His voice had mellowed even more like a warm, inviting river, drawing her to its source. "What would happen if you let go?"

She laughed, a twinkling titter that must have come from too much wine and no food. She blinked. "But don't you know, Mister Black?"

He smiled with her but shook his head, waiting.

Her words were a conspiratorial whisper. "The world would come to an end."

CHAPTER SEVEN
SINGED

Jackson's eyes narrowed, and his lips opened with a half-formed question.

The waiter came through the doors with a silver-laden cart. Kailin realized that she had practically laid across the round veranda table to meet Jackson over the candle in the middle.

The aroma of poached fish with dates filled Kailin's senses. She straightened the beige napkin in her lap and nodded to the waiter, who set the steaming dishes before them. She immediately picked up a fork and broke some of the fish away from its spiky little bones. The flavors filled her mouth. "Mmmm..." She relished the salt and sweet that mixed in each bite. "Delicious." The wine paired perfectly with it.

She indicated Jackson's untouched plate of fish with her fork. "Try it. It's heavenly." She stabbed the flaky white meat and smiled triumphantly as he too began to eat. Oh, how she loved getting the last word.

A flaw, Anthony had laughed appreciatively as he tried to tame her stubborn ways as an adolescent. A flaw perhaps, in this culture, but it gave Kailin a sense of staying in control. And control was essential. It was who she must be to keep her magic from destroying those around her. She could never slough off the chains that Jackson teased her about. She shivered slightly at the horror.

"Cold?" Jackson asked.

She shook her head and chewed. Two small groups of patrons once again braved the veranda. The descending cold was mollified by the heat curling around inside her. Part wine, part churned up power, part—she swallowed and glanced down at her hands. Part Jackson Black's velvet voice.

He glanced into the twilight. "The apparition... Does she haunt you?"

He said the words so matter-of-factly, Kailin coughed. She touched the napkin to her lips. "I've never seen her before today."

"What does she want?"

For us to mate and fall in love. The thought made her words squeak a bit when she answered. "She has some story about a demonic apocalypse that I must help stop." Kailin took another drink of wine. "And to tell me I have sisters."

"Apocalypse?"

"Something about thirteen demons trying to cut the temporal threads that hold reality together."

"What does all that mean?" he asked, his fork halfway to his mouth.

"I didn't have time to dig for details before you crashed through the door." Kailin took another sip of wine. She knew better than to trust the water, but all this wine was not ideal either.

"You yelled "no" twice, and your voice was raised."

She leaned forward, her fingers perched on the edge of the table. "You could have knocked."

She signaled the waiter in the doorway who hurried over. "Do you have any hot chocolate, perhaps with a dollop of cream?" The waiter nodded and headed inside.

Two more bites under Jackson's patient scrutiny, and the waiter was already back with a pot and a cup of loose tea leaves. He set them before her on the pristine tablecloth. "Pardon, Miss Whitaker, but we have only tea. Cook will send for chocolate, for tomorrow." Kailin sighed but smiled her thanks.

A trill of high-pitched laughter fluttered up the steps as a feather-bedecked hat bobbed into view. A woman, slender and perfectly dressed in fashionable white lace and silk, stepped onto the veranda on the arm of the Englishman from the hallway, Henry Dallinton. His gaze moved from the lady on his arm to Kailin. Surprise turned to a smile on his face.

"Devil," Jackson cursed under his breath.

Henry propelled the lady in a patient yet straight path toward their table. As they stopped, the woman looked down past a pale, perfectly formed nose and gasped. Kailin's hand clenched and dropped to the table, hitting the handle of the cup. It flipped, scattering loose tea leaves across the white tablecloth before rolling off the edge. Before it hit the floor, Kailin's magic latched onto it, setting it with a clink against the stone tiles near her ankle. Henry glanced down at it with a bewildered look.

"Kailin Whitaker." The woman glanced at the leaf-strewn tablecloth. "Never far from dirt." The words would be good-natured teasing if said with a genuine smile. The upturned lips on Samantha McGivens' face, though, were anything but genuine.

Jackson's chair scraped back as he stood. Kailin could only stare at the bedecked woman, her pinched face framed by white feathers. "And

Jackson Black," Jackson said, bowing ever so slightly. He totally ignored Henry. Samantha's lips relaxed into a soft smile at Jackson's handsome face.

Kailin's inside crawled with serpents. *Wretched! Wretched night!* As if sensing her unease, Tuto swooped down from an obelisk across the square to land on the rail of the veranda. His head swiveled around to identify the threat. Fathomless black eyes rested on the couple. Several women screeched and again a stampede ensued into the lobby. The frustrated waiter cursed softly in Egyptian Arabic and followed the group with his heavily laden cart.

Samantha jumped, clinging to Henry's arm. "And your bird," she said with wide eyes. "Half a dozen years, and it's still alive and following you." She whipped long, gloved fingers toward Tuto. "Shoo, you vulture."

"Tuto is a barn owl, Samantha. Not a vulture," Kailin said with stifled stubbornness. She picked up her thin china cup and placed it back on the table. There wasn't even a chip from the dainty flowers painted along its rim.

Henry's forehead wrinkled. "Goodness," he drawled in his British accent, but then smiled, his gaze going between Samantha and Kailin. "You two know one another."

Samantha turned her long lashes back to Jackson, purposely misinterpreting Henry's comment. "I'm certain that I would remember meeting Mister Black." She held out the gloved hand which Jackson took. He shook it as if she were a gentleman on the street.

Samantha's eyes widened and she drew back, clasping both of her hands before her chest before gesturing toward Kailin. "Henry, this is an old acquaintance, Doctor Kailin Whitaker." Kailin resisted the urge to roll her eyes at the obvious slight that the title was meant to give.

Henry bowed. "Henry Dallinton if you remember." He straightened. "I am here to escort my aunt, Lady Gertrude Vandemeer, while she visits friends in Cairo. I'm afraid I wasn't able to properly introduce myself earlier, Doctor Whitaker."

"Proper introductions aren't required when one is standing naked beneath a bath cloth," Jackson said, his eyes on Samantha. Kailin swung her foot under the table, but of course the infuriating man was out of reach. With him being immune to her magic, she couldn't even pinch him or tweak his nose.

"Naked?" Samantha said, her voice loud and full of scandal.

Kailin swore she saw Jackson's lips twitch.

"'Twas a misunderstanding," Kailin said with a flip of her hand. "I was startled and Jackson, Mister Black, kicked in the door to my room." Kailin spoke evenly as if she were explaining a mildly interesting commotion over the price of fresh fish. "I had just stepped from the tub. Mister Dallinton stopped in the hall to offer assistance."

Henry smiled at Kailin, and she took a large sip from her wine glass. No one said anything while she swirled the dry tang from one cheek to the other and swallowed. *Bloody wretched evening*, Kailin thought and took another swallow.

After a long moment of silence, Jackson sat down. "Are you two here for dinner or meeting friends?" he asked though it didn't seem like he truly cared. Perhaps he wasn't comfortable with silence like Kailin was. She often used silence as an effective weapon, along with a direct stare. Make things uncomfortable and people usually retreated. Since she despised retreating herself, she'd spent her whole life silently pushing others away.

"Henry and I are close friends," Samantha said and snaked her hand through Henry's arm. "We came to sample some of the hotel's fabulous menu." She tipped her head, making her bouquet of white and black feathers quiver and dance. "And what brings you here, dear? I never thought I'd see you back amongst the pyramids."

Kailin's stomach clenched, and she fought to breathe slowly. Certainly, everyone within the archeology circle must know about her missing father. And yet, this spoiled, ridiculously pampered socialite acted as if Anthony's kidnapping was not noteworthy.

"I've come to rescue my father, Samantha." Kailin felt the heat rise in her cheeks.

"Oh, yes, yes." She flapped her silky limp hands. "Father was quite beside himself when Anthony Whitaker disappeared." She blinked her cow eyes, glancing at the hotel. "And wasn't it from this very establishment?"

Henry's face pinched in concern. "Your father's been kidnapped?" And then with much more horror in his voice. "And *you've* come to retrieve him? From the villains who took him?" Henry's gaze moved with helpless appeal to Jackson who forked some fish into his mouth.

Jackson shrugged, swallowed, and nodded. "She's tougher than she looks."

"Ridiculous." Henry twitched with dismay.

"Father said Anthony was being foolish," Samantha continued. "That he knew of some relic or something, but he wouldn't unearth it. Anthony said it was better left buried."

All this Kailin already knew from her father's letters. They all looked at her for confirmation, but she neither denied nor acknowledged what Samantha had said.

Instead, she turned her gaze to the horrified man. "Do not fear for my safety, Mister Dallinton. I will be whole and hearty when this is over.

Though I have little doubt the kidnappers will wish they had never heard of Doctor Anthony Whitaker when I am finished."

Kailin sipped her wine to punctuate her boast. She heard Jackson chuckle under his breath. This made her smile. The feeling was rare enough to make her pause. When was the last time someone had made her smile? Someone other than Tuto, Bruce, or Anthony?

Henry sputtered and Samantha frowned at having her information ignored rather than craved by Kailin. "You will get yourself into trouble, as usual," Samantha said, her feathers nodding with agreement. "You are but a woman, and not very influential. You would do best to hire someone to retrieve what the kidnappers desire." Samantha smiled at Jackson like he might be her favorite flavor of cream. "Someone big and brave like"—Henry stood up straighter—"Mister Black, here."

Henry deflated, and his lips pinched with peevish annoyance.

Samantha had the audacity to wet her bottom lip with the tip of her tongue, resting her teeth upon it. Like she used to do around the young officials her father brought home for dinners.

Whether it was the wine or the memories of the mean-spirited girl forced on her as a childhood friend that ignited the fuse inside Kailin, she wasn't sure and didn't care. Fury exploded inside Kailin at the lustful spark in Samantha's eyes as she salivated over Jackson. Like the lava Jackson had mentioned in their earlier battle of words, red hot power seeped beyond the tight lid of control Kailin had clamped down on her magic.

Samantha moved closer to Jackson and rested her delicate hand on his shoulder. "Perhaps, Mister Black, you would like to attend a little soirée I am holding tomorrow evening at our grand mansion along the east bank. There is a lovely view of the Luxor Temple across the river." Her eyes never left Jackson. "And of course, you may come too, Kailin. All British subjects in the area have been invited. Father would likely talk with you."

The heat continued to grow inside Kailin, and she concentrated on breathing to keep the flame of the candle on the table from growing too high. *Wretched woman, wretched night!* She barely noticed Tuto gliding overhead, watching. Her pet hissed softly. A warning? Kailin sniffed the faint acrid tang of smoke.

"Good God!" Henry huffed and jumped forward. "Samantha! You're on fire!"

Both Henry and Jackson leapt into action while Tuto swooped down to investigate. Samantha screamed, her gloves flailing around her head. Black-tipped Kittiwake and pure white Snowy Egret feathers in her large hat were being eaten by a growing ring of fire, crowning the woman with a halo sent straight from Lucifer himself.

Instead of whipping off the hat first, Henry grabbed a large pitcher of water from a nearby table and sloshed it over the inferno of Samantha's hat. She screamed again, not from fear or pain but from the slap of cold water, which sluiced down her face and darkened a trail down her silk bodice.

Jackson grabbed the still-smoldering hat from her head, which brought some pinned faux ringlets with it. He stamped the flames out, leaving what looked like a small creature of feathers and curls smoldering, its now lifeless body laying limp on the stone terrace. He stepped immediately to Kailin's side and rested his hand on her shoulder.

Jackson's handsome face was open in something close to amused shock, but there was a pinch of worry on his forehead. Kailin turned away. What must he think of her? Her stomach sank down and it was all she could do not to run away from the spectacle, punctuated by Samantha's hysterical shrieking. People from the lobby and indoor restaurant had emerged to watch the theatrics.

Water still dotted Samantha's face, and Kailin handed her a napkin. Samantha snatched it from her fingers and dabbed at her cheeks while her other hand pressed against the top of her head where half her curls had disappeared.

Henry patted ineffectually at her dress. "Miss Samantha, I don't know what—"

"Leave it!" Samantha cut in. Henry removed his jacket and draped it around her shoulders.

She glared at Kailin, which made her dark eyes look like the slits of a venomous serpent. Kailin burned with embarrassment and hoped Jackson wouldn't remove his hand. "You did this," Samantha hissed low. "Again!"

"I dumped the water," Henry offered, trying to milk the venom from Samantha's words. "I am so sorry, Miss Samantha. Do not blame Miss Whitaker for my foolishness."

Kailin sighed. "It seems we are destined to be disagreeable together, Samantha. For that I am truly sorry."

Samantha shook her dripping head, her tone seething. "Escort me home, Henry." She turned on her heels. Her shoes squished as she walked to the steps leading down. The charred, drowned faux hair and feathered hat sat in a pile on the stone patio. The harried waiter picked it up with pinched fingers as if it were a dead bird and threw it off the far side of the balcony to land in an alley. The patrons filtered away, whispering, and Jackson found his seat.

He took a bite of fish while Kailin stared down at her hands on the table. "Well," he drawled after a moment, "that was interesting."

Kailin released a half-sigh, half-groan, and her shoulders sank. She let the chair hold her form, the only thing to prevent her from crumpling to the ground. The pressure of tears built behind her eyes, but she fought to keep them inside. She closed them just in case. "You asked me, Mister Black, what would happen if I released the chains holding me. If I...relaxed, surrendered to my emotions." She glanced up at him.

Jackson stared over his glass of wine as he sipped. There was no judgment in his eyes, no condemnation. But she didn't need his disapproval to revile herself.

She forged small trails with her fingertip through the scattered tea leaves still on the tabletop. "As you can see, I don't make many friends." She tried to keep the pity out of her voice, but the words themselves sounded pitiful. She shook her head and forced a smile to hitch up the corners of her lips.

He set the glass down and leaned in. "I'm guessing that Samantha McGivens is no friend to anyone unless there's something advantageous in it for her."

Kailin drew in a thin breath as the sharp ache in her chest dulled. She nodded.

A slow smile spread across Jackson's face. "Tell me, Miss Whitaker," he said, using the name she'd asked him to use. "Miss Samantha said, 'again. You did this, again.'" His rough voice made a poor imitation of Samantha's screech, but the words were the same. Laughter danced in his eyes as he lifted his brows with expectant patience.

Kailin shook her head. She looked into Jackson's curious gaze for a long moment, deciding. He'd seen her at her worst tonight and hadn't run away. Kailin took a slow breath and exhaled. "The last time I was here"—she glanced from side to side and lowered her voice—"well...I set her on fire. I threw several glasses of punch on her to put it out before it could do permanent damage. She was once more a victim of my lack of control."

Kailin met his gaze evenly, waiting. Jackson stared and then with a huge exhale he laughed. It wasn't brief or soft. He laughed loud long chuckles that caused a blip of a giggle to escape Kailin. *Terrible!* It must be the wine.

Kailin held fingers against her lips to prevent any more merriment to escape at Samantha's expense. "Now stop. No one deserves to be lit on fire."

Jackson laughed all the harder, his chair tipping back onto two legs. His face was open with rugged charm. He lifted his arms overhead to clasp his fingers, and his biceps bunched against his coat sleeves. Kailin swallowed another giggle and tore her eyes away from his masculine physique before her face heated again.

"I'd argue that statement," Jackson said, a grin remaining on his lips, lips that looked soft and inviting. Lord, how much wine had she drunk?

His gaze connected with hers. "You certainly don't have an easy time of it, do you, Atsila."

He had no idea. "A...chee...la?" she asked, touching the amber stone through her bodice. "Fire?"

One corner of Jackson's lips quirked up in a lopsided grin. "You know Cherokee?"

"Only a bit," she lied.

He shook his head, ruffling his waves of brown hair. "Not many know the words of the Indians in the States."

"But you do."

"Yeah." He rubbed his smooth jaw. "I lived Southwest of Missouri in the States, west of the mighty Mississippi River in Indian Territory."

She straightened in her seat, regaining her composure. She brushed the tea leaves back into the cup. "I don't need a nickname, Mister Black. And I certainly don't need your pity."

"Oh, are we back to that then?"

She opened her mouth to retort, but closed it, suddenly very weary from trying and failing to wrangle her powers into submission. She pushed upward slowly. "I think I should find my room for the night."

Jackson stood. "I will talk to the manager about getting you a new room."

Kailin waved her hand. If they hadn't fixed the door yet, she'd do it herself if she could have a moment of privacy in the hall. "My current room will do."

"The door—"

"Easily righted, and I will move the wardrobe against it to prevent intruders." They walked across the lobby where onlookers stared and speculated.

Leaving the lobby behind they climbed the sweeping staircase. "You really don't need anyone, do you?" Jackson said.

"Everyone needs someone," she murmured and glanced beside her where he climbed. "For instance, you can crawl underground."

He nodded. "A rare talent indeed."

Her lips turned up in a tired grin. "And as far as I can tell, you aren't flammable."

ALONE OR LONELY?

Jackson woke to predawn darkness, his muscles tense. What had woken him? Forcing even breaths, he waited, unmoving on the small bed draped in mosquito netting.

"Blasted cowherd," came a whisper from the shadows. "Wake!"

Jackson didn't even twitch at the spirit woman's command. What did she want? And how could he gain the upper hand when dealing with someone as uncatchable as this ghost?

A pebble bounced off the quilt that he lay atop. Still, he resisted the reflex to fight. A faint buzz tickled along his bare legs. He cracked his eyes the tiniest line to see the iridescent wings of dragonflies flittering around him.

The apparition floated closer, and he let his lids shut again, breathing evenly.

"Cac!" the spirit woman cursed. "Open your eyes!"

"Why?" his deep voice shot into the darkness as his eyes snapped open. He rolled off the bed in a smooth release of muscle and pent power.

The spirit gasped, dissolving into an iridescent shade of white smoke that faded like vapor. Within a heartbeat she was back. "You play games, warrior," she chastised. "While Kailin roams the dark streets alone."

"Bloody hell," Jackson swore and yanked his trousers from the back of a chair. He slammed his legs into them, pulling up his suspenders, and followed that with socks and boots. He should have slept outside her door. "Where the hell is she?" He grabbed his gun belt and his shirt from beside the bed. He was out the door only half dressed, jogging down the silent, dark corridor.

The crone floated along at his pace. "A street to the west. Her owl follows her."

"Where is she headed?"

"I'm not certain. Her mind is closed to me."

Jackson heard annoyance in the spirit's voice. A round of questions bombarded his mind only to dissolve as his thoughts came to focus on only one thing. Kailin. The woman looked for trouble and refused any type of help. She had power, more so than any he'd encountered in his decade of digging in cursed tombs. But so far, her power seemed more trouble to her than helpful.

"Her magic is great if it keeps you out," he said and wondered if the apparition could read his thoughts.

"Her magic is wild," the crone said. "I can teach her to harness it like I taught her mother."

Jackson hurried along the sleepy avenue away from the hotel. Only a handful of people braved the streets in the pre-light of day. Two drunkards dragged themselves home. A prostitute hurried by, only too aware that the shadows were dangerous. *She's smarter than Kailin.*

A shadow elongated into a man, half hidden on the stoop. Jackson pulled his gun, his hand wrapping around its familiar weight, the metal and smooth wood fitting into his palm. Smoke encircled the man's bearded face, a turban wrapped upon his head.

Would the US hire locals to follow Kailin? He kept his eyes on the man as he passed, but he didn't make a move. Could his own government be watching *him*? The idea cinched the twisting inside him even tighter, and he again glanced at the crone floating beside him. If she could read his mind...

Overhead, the silhouetted wingspan of an owl sliced noiselessly through the lightening sky. Kailin must be close. With the black turning to gray, Jackson could make out boot tracks in the thin layer of sand and dirt, boot tracks that looked too small to be made by a man. He turned a corner.

Kailin stood tall, her arms out to the side, straight and proud while a man held her wrists. Fury gushed inside Jackson. The cocking of his gun echoed in the stark silence. "Release her." His calm words ground out like the gravelly scrape of a sarcophagus lid.

The man dropped his arms and backed away from Kailin. "I...I do not hurt Miss. I am friend"—he bobbed his head like a frightened bird—"to Miss Whitaker."

Kailin turned, a pale shirt held before her. "Jackson?" Kailin's eyes moved to the crone who hovered with hands on her hips. Tuto landed on the top of the awning outside what looked like a small home that doubled as a shop. The man jumped, his eyes bulging out under the great owl's predatory stare. He babbled in Arabic. He didn't seem to see the apparition.

Jackson lowered his gun. "What are you doing?"

She exhaled with mild frustration. "I'm buying supplies." She shook the piece of clothing, and he could tell it was made of sturdy material for expedition. "I packed light, expecting to purchase supplies here." She produced a few coins from the tan, wide-legged trousers she wore and handed them to the nervous shop keep, who hurried away.

The crone huffed behind him, and Jackson's relief at finding Kailin unabused turned to anger. "So you came out in the dark, alone?"

Kailin picked up a gown in shades of gold from the top of a barrel and draped it over one arm, along with the shirt and a folded pair of trousers. "It is nearly dawn, and what do I have to fear?" She watched the nervous merchant, who hurried forward to set a pair of matching gold slippers on top of the pile in her arms. "Thank you," she said, and the merchant ran back to the door of his shop, shutting it firmly behind him.

Jackson stared at her. "You..." He shook his head. "You were hoping they'd take you. The kidnappers."

Kailin's eyebrows rose as she walked toward him. "It would save a lot of time and trouble."

Jackson re-holstered his Remington. "You don't have control." He touched her bare wrist. "What if there is someone else who mutes your power," he whispered.

Kailin pushed her shopping into his arms, her face stone. "There's only one of you."

Jackson frowned at his suddenly full arms. "How do you know that?"

Kailin's gaze flashed to the spirit woman still hovering nearby, but she didn't answer. Her gaze reconnected with his, her eyes narrowing. "So as long as you stay away from me, I'll be fine."

Jackson exhaled in a gust, which fluttered a couple yellow feathers stitched to the tops of her slippers. He was the one who should be angry. She was continuously putting herself in jeopardy despite the magic she possessed, a magic that could cause havoc.

"Doctor Kailin Whitaker," he said. "For a woman as smart as you supposedly are, I'm sadly surprised by your foolishness." That got her attention. She turned sharp eyes on him.

He set the load of fabric on top of the barrel and ignored one of the slippers falling to the dusty ground. "Let me guess. Your plan is to go into their nest, knock them around, and pull your father out."

She blinked, an obvious tell that he'd guessed right.

"So what happens next?" He stepped close to her so that the front of her skirts brushed his legs. "They will know you have powers greater than they could imagine, powers they will want to use. That is, unless you kill them all." He left the threat hanging.

Kailin cleared her throat. "Killing is not in my nature."

"Lucky for the world."

Her face began to redden, and he touched her wrist again. "If you follow this rash plan of yours, you will become the next target, the next prize, a weapon to be used. They will take your father again since it is obvious you love him, maybe even that manservant back in England. They will make you do things under threat of them coming to harm."

"I can keep them safe," she murmured but Jackson smelled victory.

"So you will force these two proud men to hide behind your skirts for the rest of their lives. Anthony won't be able to dig and discover any longer. The kidnappers will figure out a way to get to you, but Anthony won't let them take you, probably not that Bruce fellow either. They will protect you until they are killed." His teeth came nearly together as he spoke the last words. "You will lose them both, and you will be alone."

Kailin crossed her arms before her. "What do you suppose I do then?"

Yes! Finally, the proud, powerful, beautiful woman was ready to listen to him. His gut twisted with guilt, but he stamped it down. Things were unfolding as they should, and everything would work out in the end. Kailin would get her father back and she wouldn't become a target. Jackson would.

He caught her gaze. "We find the Orb and we exchange it for your father's safe return, like they asked."

"What if the Orb of Life is dangerous like my father thinks?"

"Chances are it is merely a valuable trinket that some big-time collector is demanding for a large price." He kept his face casual, his eyes relaxed. He wouldn't let the US government have it anyway, so it didn't matter what their plans were.

Kailin pursed her lips. The dawn light cast a soft glow over her smooth skin and long lashes. He could read the indecision in her face, her intelligence weighing his words against her perception of him. And what was that exactly? Did she think he was the assistant to her father, an amateur treasure hunter? Or did she see more?

"All right," Kailin said, "I won't go steal Anthony away from them, even though I certainly could." She walked over and scooped up the fallen slipper, brushing off some dirt.

"Certainly," Jackson said, mollified, "but not without raising interest about what you could do in their hands."

He caught a faint shiver running through Kailin's shoulders. He hated putting the thought in her head, but she must see the danger. There were all types of power in the world. Not the type that could throw things around and light ridiculous hat feathers on fire. The power of manipulation and ransom were as strong. And the men who held her father knew precisely how to wield their weapons.

Kailin set the slipper next to the first and lifted the bundle once more and looked back toward the opening of the alley. "The merchant says he can rent us animals, camels or burros, to take us to our dig."

"Camels get us there quicker. And since I'm your assistant, I will secure them."

She hesitated but finally nodded and strode toward the exit. On the waking street, she walked next to Jackson in silence. When one of the slippers fell off a third time, Jackson took the layers of fabric from her arms, handing her the slippers to carry.

They reached the hotel steps. "We will start out tomorrow at midmorning," Kailin said. "I will see you again then."

He shook his head. "First, I will escort you to the McGivens' party tonight. Second, we will leave at dawn while it's still cool."

Her brows rose with the edge of mockery. "You want to attend a soirée?"

Jackson nodded to the boy who held the door open for them. He lowered his voice as they strode across the tiled reception hall. "Every American and Brit was invited. It's the perfect audience."

"Exactly why I won't be go—"

"You should let it be known how worried you are about your father and how you're going to do what the kidnappers demand to free him."

"I may not be allowed across the threshold," Kailin said, staring straight ahead as they climbed the carpeted steps to the bedrooms above.

"Doctor McGivens will surely want to see his old friend's daughter." Mutiny tightened her classic features, so he persisted. "Even if the kidnappers aren't present, they will hear. It will keep Anthony safer if they know you're going along with their demands."

The stubborn glint faded from Kailin's eyes with two blinks. "Very well thought out."

He smiled. "Perhaps I have another use besides crawling on my belly in the dirt and saving the locals from infernos."

They stopped before the repaired door of her room. Without the help of a key, Jackson heard the lock turning, and Kailin pushed into her room. His gaze took in the empty space and closed balcony doors. He followed her inside, scanning for danger. He looked inside the wardrobe, but it only held the traveling gown she'd worn yesterday.

"It's good I purchased an evening ensemble if we must go," she said.

Jackson couldn't agree more. The gold of the fabric would match the strands in her hair.

Kailin scooped the gold dress and other items from his arms, turning her straight back on him to spread them across the bed. The golden gown she'd purchased had little round buttons down the back like a single-file line of soldiers ready to protect her naked form underneath, keeping all intruders out. What would it take to breach that line of resistance? Jackson was a treasure hunter after all.

After a short nap, that had unfortunately been filled with a blush-worthy dream, Kailin descended the hotel steps into the heat of afternoon Luxor. Could Drakkina broach her dreams? Why else would she have given into the lustful fantasy about the man she had absolutely no control over? A man she didn't trust?

Jackson stood, leaning against the balustrade, writing in a small book. He met her gaze and pushed off with his boot. "I visited your merchant friend and secured four camels, the camel caretaker, water, wine, fresh fruits, breads, cheeses, and additional blankets. I already have tents and outdoor survival gear."

Kailin glanced around meaningfully. "And you carry all this in your pocket?"

He grinned. "The caravan leaves at dawn tomorrow. They will come to the front of the hotel."

Kailin nodded to the busy thoroughfare that ran before Hotel Moudira. "It will give the gossip mongers plenty to talk about."

"The better to be seen."

Under the bright blue sky, fish mongers called and merchants held up pinch pots of spices to passersby. Carts rattled along the hard packed dirt roads with baskets and pails of milk. Burros and camels jingled with stately tourists in their ridiculous riding outfits perched on their backs. Kailin breathed in the heat that was so intense that her tongue felt cool inside her mouth.

Despite the high temperatures that continued through the end of summer, Kailin loved the atmosphere. The very air was infused with tantalizing mystery and unknown spices. But it didn't hold excitement as it had before. Not with Anthony missing.

Her mind drifted to the spirit and her ominous words. End of the world? Soul mate. The last two words tickled sensation down into her stomach. She shook her head. Jackson Black—her soul mate? He was rash, way too casual in his approach to life but then annoyingly stubborn about things. His gaze held truth, but he hid things, tweaked details. She frowned, reminding herself that he hadn't yet mentioned the pet name by which Anthony referred to her. Her father always called her Cleo after the great Egyptian queen, Cleopatra.

Kailin's lips tightened. Jackson's charm had lowered her defenses. She should tighten them. Refreeze the icy fortress that protected her.

"Relax," Jackson's voice soothed next to her and she startled. He cupped a warm hand over hers where it clutched like a talon to the rail. "Let's find some good food and even better wine."

A squeeze of panic twisted Kailin's stomach, momentarily numbing her need for food. "I want to inspect my gown and slippers and do something with my hair for tonight. I think I'll have some food sent up."

Jackson studied her mask of cool etiquette. He frowned slightly. "I'll escort you back up then."

"No need," she said and turned. "I really am fine on my own." She walked away quickly before he could argue. He didn't follow.

Disappointment swelled heavy in her stomach. She lifted her chin and climbed the steps. *Ridiculous.* She needed to put space between them. Her fear extended to people as well as tombs. She liked space. Why then did she feel the ache of loneliness as the distance grew between them?

CHAPTER NINE
SOIRÉE

Jackson tied a white silk cravat into a simple, sophisticated knot in the front of his neck. He shrugged into the black evening jacket. His broad shoulders strained against the fit. He hadn't time to have it properly tailored, but it would do. And even though he'd have been more comfortable in trousers and a duster, tonight required pomp. He set the low crown top hat on his head and grabbed his gloves.

He stopped before Kailin's door.

Rap. Rap.

"A moment, please," she called from within. Hearing her voice meant she was fine. Of course she was, but he exhaled anyway and leaned against the wall to survey the empty corridor. No one lurked, although they were certainly being watched. The men who had taken Anthony Whitaker were very powerful. They weren't likely to let Jackson's plan run its course without intervention. He'd have to stay close to Kailin at all times. The thought opened his chest, making it easier to breathe.

The door swung inward without the sound of a lock turning first. Jackson frowned. "The door should be locked at all..." His scold trailed off as Kailin stepped forward. *Bloody hell.* She was exquisite.

The low lamps cast a golden glow along her rosy cheeks and pink, full lips. Her red-golden hair was caught up in a soft weave, a blue comb crowning the glorious stack of curls. Long lashes framed her blue eyes. Jackson's gaze slid down the soft column of her throat, taking in the modestly high neckline that hugged her assets perfectly. The dress of gold silk molded to her slender waist to bell out in a full skirt that draped into a high bustle behind.

Tips of the matching slippers she'd balanced earlier peeked from the satin line of ribbon edging the hem. A waterfall of embroidered flowers and swirls cascaded from her waist to the floor. The light swish of silk punctuated the silence of the room as she walked into the hall. With a glance from her, the oil lamps extinguished within the room, leaving only the sconce in the hall to light her face.

Kailin smiled, her eyes assessing his attire. Her face transformed into an even more glorious gem with that simple expression.

"You are dressed quite handsomely," Kailin said and placed her gloved fingers lightly on his arm.

He instantly raised it level and cleared his throat. "And you are...beyond exquisite." She tilted her head, accepting his compliment, and he saw the darkness of a blush on her cheeks. Jackson led them down the corridor. "I will have to touch you all night if a compliment makes you burn."

"What?" she asked, breathless, her slipper catching on the stairs.

"You blush so easily. And you will receive compliments all night. I wouldn't want you to torch Miss Samantha's house as well as her hat. Since I seem to stop your—"

Kailin flapped her other hand. "Yes, yes, of course." She frowned with a sideways glance in his direction. He grinned back. "You have a way of saying things, Mister Black, that makes you sound...dirty."

"I thought you liked dirt, Doctor Whitaker," he drawled, merely to see another blush warm her cheeks. She huffed in indignation. "Never fear," he said before she could storm off. "I will contain myself when we are amongst the civilized."

She snorted. "I'd hardly include some of tonight's attendees in the realm of civilized."

"Agreed." He tipped his head. So she was aware of the underlying snake pit of rivalry, swindling, and greed. "I prefer to face a hundred decayed mummies in dark tombs to the false pleasantries at these gatherings."

She looked sideways at him, her smile still in place. "Ballrooms have the same effect on me as dark tombs, especially those ballrooms filled with vipers. Perhaps you best stay close to me tonight else I raze the roof."

Jackson signaled the carriage he'd arranged. As the open-air barouche approached, he glanced around. "Any sign of your ghost?"

"Not at present, though she seems to show up without much warning."

"Much?"

Kailin's hand grazed her upper arm. "I have a birthmark, a dragonfly. She says all my siblings are marked with one." He helped her into the four-wheeled carriage and passed the other half of the payment to the driver he'd arranged.

He sat down next to her so they'd both face forward. "What does this birthmark do?"

"It tingles, sort of itches when she's near."

Jackson's lips came close to her ear, and he inhaled her fresh floral scent. "Make sure to tell me when you start to tingle then."

Kailin inhaled quickly but nodded with a casual agreement. Her eyes flitted to the open night sky. She smiled softly. "How lovely. No roof."

Jackson ignored the tang of the docks that mixed with the breeze whirling in from the chilling desert. "Fresh air. It's good for the body and soul." He winked at her and she leaned back into the leather seat, her head tilted back to stare up at the stars. Her lovely neck was fully exposed, and a yearning to kiss it came over Jackson. Her skin would be fragrant and soft and warm. He'd make the pulse jump into a gallop as he kissed it. He felt his cock harden and was glad for the long evening coat that would hide it.

They rattled through the shadowed streets toward a wealthy area near the American embassy. His eyes glanced at the star-spangled flag snapping a sporadic tattoo in the night. Would he ever see the wide-open plains of home again? Home? That hadn't existed for years now. He hardened himself against the homesickness.

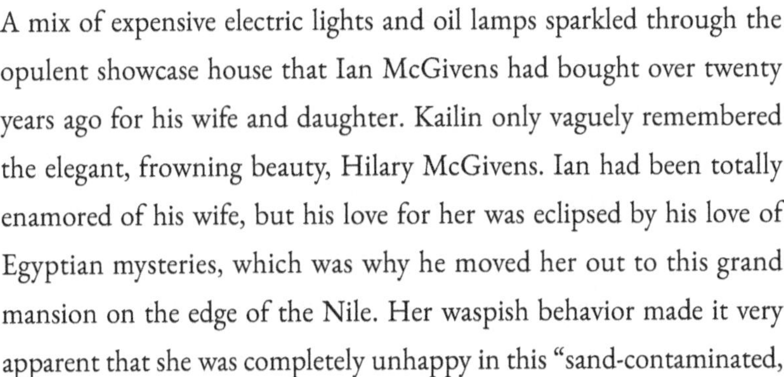

A mix of expensive electric lights and oil lamps sparkled through the opulent showcase house that Ian McGivens had bought over twenty years ago for his wife and daughter. Kailin only vaguely remembered the elegant, frowning beauty, Hilary McGivens. Ian had been totally enamored of his wife, but his love for her was eclipsed by his love of Egyptian mysteries, which was why he moved her out to this grand mansion on the edge of the Nile. Her waspish behavior made it very apparent that she was completely unhappy in this "sand-contaminated, dirty, backward country." Hilary died of a bacterial infection when Samantha was young.

Samantha was very much like her mother, except that she had never lived anywhere else so her longings for a different life were less severe. Although that was the only thing less severe in the replica.

Kailin allowed Jackson to help her from the carriage. He'd already paid the driver. *Where does he gain his money?* Kailin realized she had absolutely no idea regarding Jackson Black's financial health. Unless one made significant discoveries, archeologists were only rich in spirit and adventure, not in coin.

The suspicion shriveled into an inconsequential pondering as Jackson's warm breath grazed her ear. "Hold your head high, Doctor Whitaker. You are far more intelligent than these snobs, and you're absolutely stunning."

The compliment warmed her inside, somehow melting and strengthening her at the same time. What an odd combination. As they climbed the marble steps toward the white-gloved Egyptian footmen, Kailin concentrated on breathing evenly and presenting her chilled, sophisticated-casual smile that she'd perfected for such evenings when she was forced to mingle in polite crowds.

"Kailin!" Doctor Ian McGivens called when he saw them enter. His bearded mouth turned up into a sincere smile. He begged pardon of the man and woman at his side and strode across the black-and-white-tiled foyer, meeting them under a crystal chandelier that probably cost as much as one of the footmen would earn in his entire lifetime. Ian's eyes flicked to Jackson and back to Kailin, but he didn't stop his momentum. Ian's hand slid between Jackson and Kailin to clasp her shoulders. He squeezed gently, as close to a hug she would get in this arena, and Jackson stepped to the side to give him room.

"Ian," she said with a genuine smile. "It's good to see you."

His gaze slid down her form. "You look absolutely royal in gold." He indicated her gown, but then his smile faded. "I'm so sorry that it's because of these horrific goings-on that you've had to leave your lovely Scottish coastline." His hands slid down her arms to clasp her hands in his. "We will find Anthony."

"I plan to do just that," she said.

"You? By yourself?"

Kailin glanced at Jackson. "With my assistant, Mister Black."

Jackson tipped his hat. "Good evening, Doctor McGivens."

Ian nodded to him. "Yes, yes, I had heard someone had gone to inform her or I would have gone myself. You are back sooner than I imagined."

"Doctor Kailin Whitaker travels quickly," Jackson said.

Ian smiled and nodded. "All these years of expedition. Makes one quite flexible and fast to migrate." He turned back to Kailin. "I'm so glad to see you, my dear, but I do worry about your involvement. Anthony's kidnappers are powerful and professional. The local police have not been able to find any leads."

Kailin squeezed his hand. "Don't worry. I have a lead which Mister Black and I will be following very soon. There is no doubt that I will retrieve what the kidnappers want in return for my father." There, the message was delivered. May Ian spread it at will.

Ian lowered his voice. "The Orb? That's what they want, isn't it?"

Kailin glanced at Jackson's frown but nodded anyway. "What do you know about it?" she asked Ian.

He shook his head. "Not much. Your father was quite obsessed with it, but then suddenly gave it up. Said it wasn't worth the danger of retrieval." Ian said this as if he couldn't fathom the concern.

"Perhaps my father has finally grown up," Kailin said.

"You mean grown old," Ian grumbled. He pulled her gently along toward a long table laden with small bits of tasty fare and three large Champagne fountains. Jackson stalked behind her like a well-heeled guard dog.

"I begged him to give me his notes," Ian continued. "Said I would go after it myself, but he refused. If he doesn't get to discover it, he doesn't want anyone else to either."

Kailin patted Ian's arm. "Sounds like the two of you haven't changed much."

Ian smiled dismally at that. "Well, good luck finding the unfindable. Say..." He stopped. "I could help you."

Jackson stepped closer. "I've already taken that position."

"But I have notes, an idea of where Anthony was looking," Ian said.

"Mister Black worked alongside my father and has similar information. We will be successful."

Ian's eyes narrowed as he scanned Jackson from his polished black shoes to his hat. "Worked alongside Anthony Whitaker? I'd have known if he'd gotten himself a brawny boulder-pusher."

Jackson grinned casually at the description. "Doctor Whitaker didn't like to publicize the fact that he might need some extra muscle to help with his digs. He's a rather private sort."

Ian sniffed, one eyebrow rising. "That's certainly accurate," he murmured and handed a fluted glass of Champagne to Kailin.

"Damn the devil," Jackson murmured and took a sip of his sparkling wine.

Kailin turned to see Henry Dallinton break away from a small group of gentlemen to stride across the ballroom. "Miss Whitaker. How wonderful to see you here."

Ian leaned in to her. "If you won't take me along, I best get started on trying to find it myself." He walked away.

"I need the Orb for my father, not for myself," Kailin called as Henry stepped up like an expectant puppy.

Ian raised his hand and turned his head only to glance at her. He smiled. "Of course, I will give it to you after I am certain I'm given credit for its discovery. *I'm* not through yet finding the glory of the pharaohs." He laughed then and walked away.

"Good God, is he planning to set out tonight?" Kailin said and glanced at Jackson. Henry still stood there waiting to be acknowledged. She gave him a quick smile.

"We'll be ahead of him by at least a week," Jackson said, his gaze hardening as he stared at Henry. "Dallinton." He nodded.

Henry responded in kind but turned immediately to Kailin. "More talk of rescuing your father?"

"It is foremost in my mind," Kailin said.

"Of course, of course," Henry assured. "As it should be." He frowned. "I only hope you will exercise safety and restraint. I would hate to see anything unpleasant happen to you."

"That's my job," Jackson said.

Henry eyed Jackson up and down much like Ian had. "Of course, but digging through sand and rocks is not easy work. It is wrought with peril."

Kailin frowned. She should be used to the chauvinistic view of women in the archeology circle, but comments about her fragility still riled her. She'd love to show these men what kind of strength she had to move sand and rocks.

"Do remember, Mister Dallinton," she said stiffly, her ice façade easily slipping along the familiar ruts created over the years. "That I am a doctor of archaeology, well respected in Britain and beyond. I understand the discomforts and perils of expedition. *I* will not take foolish risks." She looked at Jackson and felt the corners of her lips edge upward. "That's Mister Black's job."

She took a sip of the Champagne and let the bubbles tickle her nose and warm her throat on its way down. Perhaps more Champagne was needed in order to maneuver through this night. Though she was fairly certain the wine had contributed to the feather inferno at the hotel.

Henry bobbed his head. "Please take no offense. I am not used to such a strong woman hidden within such a delicately beautiful form. I only worry about preserving such spirit."

A flattering apology. Better than more pompous spouting of female failings. Kailin nodded, accepting his words.

A high-pitched trill of laughter edged with disparaging condemnation filtered through the chamber music and low murmur of the crowd. Samantha McGivens. Kailin's stomach squeezed on reflex, hitching the Champagne up in her stomach. She set her glass down.

Henry made a soft noise that sounded like a curse before turning apologetic eyes to her. His expression alone made it obvious who Samantha must be pointing out.

"She really is a lovely woman most of the time," he apologized, frowning. "I believe she has a difficult time with your beauty overshadowing her own. It brings out the worst in her."

Kailin focused on his kind brown eyes, and her tight lips softened.

"Smooth, Dallinton," Jackson said as he took her elbow. "I think we'll find a more enjoyable room so as not to torment Miss McGivens any longer."

Kailin let Jackson guide her toward the adjoining room, but his words irritated her. "And why wouldn't I want to torment Samantha?" she asked with sarcasm.

Jackson leaned into her. "Because I don't feel like stomping fire out of the drapes just yet, Atsila."

"Let's leave then," she hissed as judgmental eyes fastened on her when they entered. She was caught between the piercing chuckles of Samantha and her friends behind her and the pointed stares before her. Inside she quivered. Outside she stood tall, an ice statue with a razor stare.

"We've only been here a quarter hour."

"I'm very efficient," she insisted.

"You need to spread word about our expedition."

She huffed through clenched teeth. "Impossible," she breathed. "I don't mingle. Ian and Henry are as far as I'm going to spread word. They'll do the rest."

Jackson's other hand reached over to cover hers where it sat on his arm. The warmth of his palm permeated her glove. She glanced at him, their eyes connecting instantly. He led her to a shallow alcove and blocked her view of the floor where several pairs rotated through a quadrille.

Jackson's gaze bored into hers. "Kailin," he murmured, and the name on his tongue said with such intensity caught her breath. "Dallinton may be a blue-blooded ass but he's right about Samantha." She tried to look down but he caught her chin with the crook of one finger. "You are easily the most beautiful woman here. If people are staring at you, it's because you are more beautiful than a golden idol buried with a king."

Kailin sniffed a laugh, a lightness filling her. "You don't give mainstream complements, do you." She looked down at her gold ensemble. "The silk and stitching are lovely."

"Not the gown, you, Kailin. You're beautiful. You could be in rags and still outshine the loveliest queen in Egypt." Jackson's face was intense without his usual mask of humor. "You really don't know that, do you?"

Kailin's breath caught somewhere in her chest as she clung to his words. He released her chin, but her eyes stayed locked to his, as if they were a raft in this pool of sharks. Jackson's finger brushed her cheek, and his brow furrowed. "So strong yet you let these people bother you."

She answered with a sigh. Yes, these people—this world—bothered her, to use Jackson's words. She was an outsider. Even with Anthony as a father, her strange reactions and introverted demeanor had fostered whispers and open criticism. So she'd taken on the ice-façade to protect herself. Unfortunately, Jackson Black seemed to melt it easily.

Jackson's intensity faded back into a casual grin. "If they only knew how you could turn this party inside out," he whispered and raised his eyebrows.

A full smile broke across Kailin's mouth. "I'm tempted, so you better not stray far." It felt good having someone other than her anxious father know of her secret so openly. Hiding one's true self from the world was taxing.

"I will stay by you *all* night if you let me, Atsila."

CHAPTER TEN
NEW ACQUAINTANCES

Had Jackson asked to sleep with her? The emphasis on the word "all" certainly bent the question toward carnal.

Kailin opened her mouth, unable to think of a retort before a tall, dark man walked up to stand before them.

He bowed stiffly. "Doctor Whitaker, I am Doctor Hasani Moghadam." The man completely ignored Jackson. "I have had the intellectual pleasure of studying your father's many great findings and adventures." One of his eyebrows rose over deep brown eyes. "I have little doubt that you are definitely as interesting."

Kailin tipped her head slightly and ignored the murmured curse from Jackson. "It is always nice to meet one of my father's contemporaries," she said simply. If she'd allow herself to admit it, the man was a bit intimidating.

He inclined his head to match her response. "If your guard permits, would you accompany me through the next dance?"

Guard? Very well, Jackson was a guard, protecting the world against her spontaneous wrath, but that's not what this elegant, glint-eyed Egyptian man meant. In this stuffy, male-centric, pompous world Jackson did serve as the figurehead of a guard, much like Anthony had done for her. So why did the man's question irritate her so much?

Kailin looked at Jackson with sharp eyes. "Do you permit?"

Jackson choked slightly but sobered. "You have my permission, Doctor Whitaker." He looked at Moghadam. "Make sure you return her to my side the moment the dance is concluded. Doctor Whitaker must not tire herself as we have a grand expedition planned."

It was the opening she'd need without sounding like she had an agenda. Jackson was clever. Kailin kept her grin to herself as the man escorted her to the center of the floor.

Doctor Moghadam stood as tall as Jackson, so he was nearly a head above the others. His strong hand found her waist quickly as a waltz started. He led her in the basic step easily, his eyes turned down to study her.

"You are leading an expedition here in Egypt?" he began.

"Yes, in order to save my father."

"Aye, an unfortunate incident. I am sorry," he said though his words seemed stilted like he was thinking about something else. "So...you are leading an expedition to find him?"

She smiled slightly. "Not exactly. The kidnappers want a certain treasure that my father was close to finding. I will discover it and exchange it for him."

Moghadam frowned, a darkness in his eyes that sent a chill down Kailin's back. "Why have *you* find it, why not find it themselves?"

Kailin swallowed and applied the arrogant mask. "I assume they have tried, but they cannot."

"And you can?"

"Certainly."

He continued the steps with smooth grace though his face paused before breaking into a toothy grin. "You are...as confident as people say."

She had to smile at that. "Is that what they say? Confident?"

He returned her sly smile. "The most slandered people are the most interesting ones." He tipped his head slightly, reminding her of a hawk zeroing in on a mouse. "Ice queen was mentioned. Much rivaled for her beauty. Arresting, starkly intelligent, disconcerting."

"Thank you, I think," she bantered back, stomping down the old discomfort of being studied and judged.

He bowed his head. "So much like the beautiful Queen Cleopatra." She glanced upward, his dark eyes meeting hers and her breath hitched. Cleopatra? Cleo? Did he know Anthony?

The music ended yet he continued to hold her in the circle of his arms. "Perhaps you could use a guide, a Marc Anthony, strong and sure with an army at his service to help you in your quest."

"The job's already taken," Jackson said beside her and Kailin inhaled, blinking. The spell was broken. She almost shook her head as if she'd been hypnotized by some carnival magician.

Moghadam dropped his arms and stepped back. Kailin felt Jackson's arm under hers. Moghadam laughed. "I see no army, Mister Black."

"Numbers do not equal strength, Mister Moghadam."

"Doctor Moghadam," he corrected stiffly.

Jackson turned to Kailin. "I think it's time to retire. I wouldn't have you exhausted before our big hunt."

"When do you leave?" Moghadam asked.

"In the morning," Kailin murmured. "Good evening, Doctor."

Jackson walked evenly beside her, not in front or behind, out of the dancing room toward the foyer.

"Jackson!" A high-pitched call came across the expanse of the packed room. They stopped together, heads turning in time with the rest of the room. What lady yelled across a ballroom filled with social snobs? Against the back wall a very young woman sat with a middle-aged chaperone waving her hand toward them.

The girl looked delicate sitting amongst ruffles of violet, still shy of full womanhood, sixteen or seventeen years old. Her face was sweet, innocent and wide-eyed, her smile pure with joy at seeing Jackson. Kailin's stomach, already wound tight, twisted painfully. *Ridiculous reaction.* Of course Jackson should have friends in Luxor. It added some credibility to his story of working here.

Jackson took a step toward the radiant girl-woman but didn't surrender Kailin's hand. When she didn't step with him, he stopped and turned. "Kailin, I need to greet Cassy. I didn't know she would be attending." He frowned. "She shouldn't be attending."

"I'll wait here," Kailin said and tried extricating her hand, but he wouldn't let go.

"Remember the curtains," he joked, meeting her frown with a grin. "Come. Meet Cassy."

Kailin took large steps so as not to look like he was pulling her along, which of course he was. Good God, the man was taking her to meet a lovely girl who was obviously on very close terms with him if she risked ridicule in order to flag him down. She was much too young for him, wasn't she?

The closer they walked the more brilliant the sweet smile beamed. The guardian whispered something in her ear and Cassy folded her flapping hands in her lap.

"Oh Jackson, I thought it was you, but Mrs. Pierce wouldn't leave my side to fetch you." The young woman's smile turned to Kailin, but she didn't stand.

"Hello."

Jackson finally released Kailin's hand and leaned in to kiss the girl's cheek. He kept bent forward talking in soft tones. When he stood, she was blushing. So, Kailin thought, she wasn't the only one he made blush. Ah, but could the girl torch the drapes? Doubtful.

Anger slid through her. The woman was a child, too young for a man of Jackson's age and worldliness.

Just when Kailin thought to tug him away, perhaps to save his mortal soul, Jackson grabbed her hand and pulled her closer. The girl still didn't rise but looked up expectantly.

"Cassandra, this is Doctor Kailin Whitaker, with whom I'm going on expedition. Doctor Whitaker, please meet Cassandra Black, my little sister."

Cassandra leaned forward and clasped Kailin's other hand. "So pleased to meet you. Jackson mentioned you on his last visit, and I've read several of your papers."

Sister? The title ricocheted around inside Kailin's head like a moth stirred up by a lamp. She paused for only a second before regaining her practiced smile. "So nice to meet you," Kailin said. "I'm glad you two were able to see one another again before we head out."

"Oh yes," Cassandra said and gave Jackson a little frown. "You don't come around enough. Poor Mrs. Pierce must entertain me all day."

The smiling lady with brown hair held up in a neat bun patted her shoulder affectionately. "Since you are with her, Mister Black," Mrs. Pierce said. "I will fetch us some punch and confections."

"Oh yes, thank you, Mrs. Pierce." Cassandra smiled enthusiastically. "I especially like anything iced in chocolate."

Mrs. Pierce chuckled. "How could I forget?" She strode off with brisk efficiency so that people parted to let her through.

A lively tune was struck in the adjoining room they had quit, and Cassandra glanced at it and sighed.

"Why don't you two have a dance," Kailin suggested. Surely she could sit in the corner eating chocolate for the girl who obviously wanted to take a turn.

The girl's face froze and then another blush took it over as she smoothed her dress over her knees. "I'm afraid my dancing days are over." It was then that Kailin noticed the wheelchair under the layers of gown. "Walking these days is difficult enough. I don't think even Jackson could carry me through a whole dance." She smiled, though her eyes looked sad. "But I heartily enjoy the music. That's why I forced Mrs. Pierce to bring me when we received the invitation."

Cassandra looked sternly at Jackson. "So don't reprimand her for taking me out. She bundled me in blankets to the point of smothering me and refuses to leave my side. In fact, make her use the privy before you leave else she'll be uncomfortable the whole night."

Cassandra hadn't paused once during the whole explanation. Kailin stared as Jackson kissed the top of his sister's head. It was clear that he loved her. Kailin's chest tightened and a sting scratched behind her eyes. This girl didn't look for pity or whine for attention. She simply wanted to hear the music and enjoy her fragile life.

"When we return," Kailin said softly, then cleared her throat. "We will bring music to your home and Jackson will dance with you until he can no longer stand."

The girl giggled. Kailin didn't look at Jackson, but she felt his stare. Cassandra leaned back in her chair, suddenly looking tired, yet the smile remained around her delicate lips. She really was beautiful and now that she looked, Kailin could spot the similarities between brother and sister. Thick hair framed fine features. And she had Jackson's intriguing gray-blue eyes. Although hers were completely open, without suspicion, caution, or speculation. But she also looked a bit too fragile, too lean, as if sickness indeed plagued her.

Mrs. Pierce returned with a plate of cookies and a footman carrying a tray of punch. They each took one and sipped. After two chocolate-dipped shortbreads, Cassandra looked more revived.

"Doctor Whitaker?"

"Kailin, please."

"Only if I am Cassy to you." Kailin smiled and nodded. "Good then, Kailin, tell me about the soaring stones you are studying, the great monoliths of the western Highlands. I have read your last three papers debating their purpose and origins. Do you still believe they were used for some type of ghastly ritual? Because I think there could be other possibilities."

Kailin blinked several times and heard Jackson chuckle beside her. "Cassy may be quite...fluffy on the outside, but her mind is quicker than most."

"Fluffy?" Cassy flounced the skirts around her still legs. "Well yes, I suppose I do like ruffles."

Kailin breathed long and took the seat beside the girl. "I had first thought the circle was used for rituals because I found several nicks in the stone slab at the center of the stones, as if it were used as a sacrificial table. However..." Kailin thought of Drakkina's words that the place had once been Kailin's home. "Now I'm not certain. Perhaps it was a table, used in a household."

Cassy's eyes grew rounder. "So domestic. But human history has been peppered by so much violence. Even the holy bible talks of sacrifice. Your new theory would be revolutionary."

"What if the stones were magical wards," Kailin conjectured. "Set to protect a small house in the center."

"Like a magical fence." Cassy nodded. "The diameter of the stones leaves adequate room for a dwelling."

Kailin smiled. The girl was quite clever and had a remarkable memory if she remembered the dimensions from the paper. Sweet and smart and enjoyable to be with. Kailin continued to debate the pros and cons of her recent theory with Cassy until Mrs. Pierce came back from the privy.

"Miss Cassandra," her chaperone said. "It is getting late. We should retire to the warmth of your home." She glanced at Jackson. "Perhaps your brother could help us find our conveyance."

"Certainly," Jackson said. "You and Kailin can continue your theories after our expedition."

"Perhaps one day you can journey to the stones to see them in person," Kailin offered. "They really are astounding when you stand silently in their mighty presence."

Cassy smiled politely and nodded, but Kailin spotted the hopelessness in her eyes. Determination had propelled Kailin through most of her life, and she wasn't giving up on Cassy without giving it a try. She squeezed the girl's hand. "We'll figure something out," she whispered by her ear and stood.

Jackson pushed the wheelchair through the throng, Mrs. Pierce and Kailin following behind. As they neared the foyer, the crowd thinned and Jackson paused to ask the butler to call for both conveyances.

"Leaving so soon?" Samantha McGivens crooned, a Champagne glass in her hand. She tilted it precariously. Several of the ladies near the glittering fountains tittered. Kailin wasn't sure if their snickers were for Samantha or her or Cassy.

"Oh well, you weren't much of a socialite," Samantha continued. She turned to the delicate waspish faces standing along the punch table. "Kailin always preferred to roll in the dirt with the men rather than keep clean like a *normal* lady." She shrugged her slender shoulders. "Perhaps it has to do with never having a mother." Samantha turned back to her, triumph in her overly open eyes. "Pity." Apparently, Samantha was punishing her for the hat incident. But bringing up her lack of mother for revenge's sake was beyond spiteful.

Kailin's blood boiled. While Mrs. McGivens lived, Samantha had flaunted her mother before Kailin. The shrewish girl had maliciously pouted in pity for her. Kailin had continually turned the other cheek, not wanting to cause more trouble. However, in front of everyone at the soirée, in front of Jackson and her new friend, she couldn't turn away in silence. What type of an example would that be for Cassy, who must suffer snide remarks at her infirmity?

Kailin stood tall. "Everyone has a mother, Samantha," she replied like a slight ripple on a glassy lake of calm. "You were fortunate to know yours." By now the room had hushed as people strained to hear Kailin's peaceful words. "Honor her memory, Samantha"—Kailin's gaze dropped to the slanted glass of Champagne in Samantha's gloved hand—"instead of washing it away with spirits."

Kailin turned, her gaze even but blind to her audience as Jackson chuckled. "She's about ready to burst," he whispered near Kailin's ear. The brush of his breath did strange things to her pulse. But Samantha's voice shattered the giddiness.

"What would you know about honor?" Samantha seethed. "Your only associates are dirty natives, tomb robbers, and cripples who take invitations far too literally."

Kailin rooted to the marble floor, shock making movement impossible. Mrs. Pierce *tsk*ed beneath her breath and patted Cassy's shoulder. Jackson cursed, his hand moving toward the gun Kailin had seen at his hip under his jacket. Exactly what he would do with a Remington to defend his sister at a soirée, she hadn't the slightest idea. There was no time to see because right then three unfortunate things happened at once. Samantha laughed evilly, Kailin saw Cassy wipe away an escaped tear, and Jackson let go of Kailin's hand.

CHAPTER ELEVEN
SPLASH

Geysers, three of them, shot up from the Champagne fountains, straight to the twenty-foot ostentatious gold-accented ceiling. Samantha screamed when even the Champagne in her glass shot up, spraying into her face with enough force to blast up her perfectly pinched nose. Her lady friends behind her suffered the same fate. They coughed, sneezed, and gagged, mopping at their faces. Glass shattered as they dropped their now-empty flutes.

"Bloody hell," Jackson swore and grabbed Kailin's hand. He glanced at the drapes behind the buffet table, but they hung straight and un-charred, although speckled and stained.

"You!" Samantha screamed and blew her nose into Henry Dallinton's offered handkerchief. She stomped her foot and pointed a soggy gloved finger directly at Kailin. Along the refreshment table men dabbed and women wailed and sniffled. Every guest near the tables was drenched with chilled Champagne.

"Damn," Kailin whispered.

Several servants inspected the three empty Champagne fountains cautiously, as if they might spontaneously refill and explode in their faces. Kailin blinked and stared only at Jackson, pleading in her eyes. "At least it wasn't fire," she murmured.

The frozen mask of shock on his face cracked into a warm smile. She was amazing.

"You did this!" Samantha screamed. The curls around her face hung like wet noodles and a dark swath of drink stained the front of her gown.

Henry and the other male attendees tried to comfort the women that had been caught in Kailin's explosion. It was a cacophony of dabbing handkerchiefs like a sea of dancing white flags. Shrill voices reprimanded as breasts were accidently or purposely pressed. At least one woman of weak countenance swooned.

"You!" Samantha yanked her wet glove off and flung it toward Kailin, but it dropped with soggy weight onto the floor between them. "You did this!"

"Again," Kailin sighed on a whisper.

Jackson couldn't hold back his merriment any longer. Laughter broke from him and he shook his head. "Doctor McGivens," he called to Ian. "You throw one hell of a party." He bowed slightly to the irate woman. "Good evening to you, Miss McGivens. If I were you, I'd be thankful that your gown wasn't fashioned of feathers."

Kailin wasn't moving, so Jackson tugged slightly to prod her. "Come along, Mrs. Pierce," Jackson said to Cassy's guardian. "I believe the party will be wrapping up soon." The footman held open the front door with a bewildered stare that followed them to Cassy's closed conveyance.

Jackson lifted his sister into the hired coach and wrapped blankets around her legs.

Cassy stared wide-eyed at Kailin. "Was that...did you do that?" Cassy asked.

"Now Cassy, that's how rumors start," Jackson said.

"How...?"

He kissed her cheek. "If she did, you've made a very powerful friend."

His sweet sister was devoid of friends except for the widowed Mrs. Pierce who was paid to watch after her. It wasn't the first time he wondered if it had been a mistake to bring her here to Egypt when her illness progressed. Egypt was the land of magic like nowhere else on the globe. If he was going to save her, she needed to be close. Yet she also needed a friend. One who wouldn't pity or demean her for her differences.

"Powerful indeed," Cassy said, glancing at Kailin. "Did you see the look on Samantha McGivens' face?"

"Goodnight, Cassy." He'd planted the seed of friendship. Perhaps even if Kailin hated him when this was all finished, she'd still be kind to his sister. He would add it to his list of ardent hopes.

Cassy leaned out the window and waved to Kailin. "Thank you, Kailin. That was the most fun I've had—ever."

Kailin smiled back cautiously. "We will visit when we return." She waved and the landau rattled off.

Jackson helped Kailin up into their waiting barouche even though she could have easily done so herself. But she let him. She must be in shock. She'd publicly displayed her abilities to a room full of powerful tongue-waggers. Would people believe Samantha that Kailin had been the one responsible? Kailin sat frozen beside him.

"That should give them something to talk about," he commented as the carriage jolted into movement.

Kailin sighed and a small chuckle escaped her, higher pitched than usual, as if hysteria picked at her resilience. She laughed again and fell backwards into the well-worn leather seat, her hand against her chest. He grinned as they trotted through the nearly empty streets toward the hotel.

Jackson helped Kailin down and paid the driver. Avil, who apparently also watched the doors at night, held the door open for the two of them. The boy bowed low like Jackson was a bloody pharaoh.

Kailin's face was a mask of blank beauty. She hadn't said a word after the brief fit of humor. She took his proffered arm, and he escorted her across the vacant lobby. No doubt the elite were all still at the McGivens', dabbing and conjecturing. Hopefully they had more Champagne or it would be a very dull evening.

Jackson led Kailin up the steps to the third floor. She still hadn't said anything. He stopped her before she could enter her room. Her gaze had fallen to the tips of her silk slippers.

"Kailin?" She didn't look up. Jackson crooked his finger under her chin and slowly lifted. His stomach clenched, his face tightening. Tears glistened in her deep blue eyes. They shone like small, dark pools of pain, embarrassment, and regret. He didn't ask, didn't really need to know anything more than that she hurt.

"Atsila," he whispered and pulled her forward. And she actually stepped into his offered comfort. Jackson encircled her slender frame in a hug, firm but gentle. She pressed her forehead into his chest, burying her face against him.

He felt the slight tremble of her shoulders as she sobbed silently. His hand stroked down her curls, down her back. Again and again he followed the path, gently trying to rub away the hurt. He felt as if he bled while he held her. He was helpless and completely unsure how to handle her sorrow.

"She deserved it, you know," he said.

Kailin's shoulders trembled harder, and he pinched his lips tight. *Bloody hell.* "It could have been worse. You could have burnt the whole place down around them."

A sob escaped her. *Damn.* He was failing. He sighed long and wrapped both arms around her, offering his warmth and strength instead of his idiotic, inadequate words. He couldn't seem to get anything right around her. "It was my fault anyway," he said. "I let go of you."

Her shoulders stilled, and she sniffed. Kailin nodded against him.

Anger was better than tears. He'd take the blame over her pain any day. "I'm the one who insisted we attend. I'd promised to stay attached to you and then I let go." He grazed her head with his chin as he nodded. "I was definitely to blame."

She sniffed and pulled back slightly. Wet lashes spiked out from watery eyes. "You did promise."

"I should be horse whipped."

A smile quirked along her soft lips. He stared at them, wondering once again what they would taste like, how they would feel against his.

"It's a good thing I can't do anything to you," she murmured.

"Hmm...agreed." He ran his thumb along her cheek, smudging out a tear trail. "With the way you blush, I'd have fared much worse than the feathers by now."

Kailin glanced down. The lighting in the corridor was dim, but he could tell that he'd brought on another blush. He leaned closer. "If I keep saying things to make you burn, Atsila, you won't be able to let go of me. Perhaps that's my strategy."

She glanced up. Her face tilted so close to his, only inches apart. Was he taking advantage of her vulnerability? Hell yes. He was not one to pass on golden opportunities.

Jackson lowered slowly, giving her time to return to her chilly senses. Instead her eyes fluttered shut and Jackson closed the gap. Soft, warm, yielding, her lips tasted as perfect as he'd imagined. He gently tilted her head to feel more of her, deepening the kiss. His pulse shot off into a race as his blood ignited. With a fire born of need and curiosity about this puzzling woman, he pulled Kailin into him, wrapping himself around her slender form.

A soft murmur rose from her, like a moan. The noise thrummed through him, fanning the fire. Her small hand came up between them. "We're...in the hall."

Jackson's gaze raked the empty corridor. She was right, of course. Some twit like Henry Dallinton or his condemning aunt was liable to walk through any moment. Kailin produced a key from her reticule. He grabbed it, thrusting and turning the lock. The door swung and he rushed her through. The darkness embraced them at once and he closed the door, pulling her back where she belonged, in his arms. She didn't fight him at all. His hands caught her face, warm, tipped toward him. He lowered to her lips gently, again waiting for her ice to break the moment. Her lips pressed against him and her fingers grabbed at the back of his hair.

Jackson let out a groan as the floodgates slammed open. *Must stop soon*! Too much longer and he'd ruin everything. Too much more and he wouldn't be able to pull away. And he must pull away. She'd hate him all the more later if he didn't.

A wild screech tore through the room. Jackson twisted, flattening Kailin to the wall, his body shielding her. The balcony doors stood open and Kailin's great owl swooped into the room, its black silhouette huge inside.

"Tuto!" Kailin yelled as the bird screeched again and hurtled toward her bed. Kailin shoved Jackson away and slid out from behind him to stand on her own. In a second the three lamps in the room sparked into flames.

Jackson's gaze flew around the compartment, hunting the shadows with his trusty Remington drawn. Even if he couldn't see it, there was a threat. The owl's talons shredded the ornate spread over the mattress, tearing back the bedding. Kailin gasped.

"Stand back!" Jackson yelled, but Kailin ran around to the foot of the bed where Tuto flapped wild wings and pounced onto a writhing serpent.

"No, Tuto! It'll strike you!" she screamed and with a flick of her hand, Tuto lurched backwards, hurled by Kailin's immense powers, but the serpent twisted in his talons, its head lunging for purchase. Kailin's fingers flicked together like a pair of scissors. The snake's head broke from its long body to thump on the floor.

Tuto dropped the still-squirming body and landed on the bed, blinking. If an owl could look rattled, her pet certainly did. "Good God, are you hurt?" Kailin ran to her friend, her hands gentle as she smoothed his feathers. The flames in the lamps grew in their glass containers around the room, obliterating the shadows.

Jackson approached the dark-colored serpent that still wriggled with recent death on the rug, a stain of bright blood streaking from its severed body. The scales reflected the dancing lamplight.

"An asp. In your bed."

"An Egyptian Cobra, scientific name *Naja haje*, one of the most venomous snakes of North Africa." She brushed loose hair from her forehead. "But it's also called an asp. Like the one that was rumored to have killed Cleopatra." She blew out an exhale and turned to kiss Tuto's feathered head. "You could have been killed."

"You, Kailin, could have been killed," Jackson said and strode to the open doors of the balcony, leaning over the rail. A trellis of climbing jasmine stood beside the balcony. Jackson's lips tightened. Hell, she'd slept out here last night where anyone could climb right up next to her. His gaze raked the interior garden, but no one moved in the shadows. The asp was possibly planted hours ago. By whom?

He turned to the room where Kailin continued to inspect Tuto. Jackson strode inside and yanked back the rest of the bedding, but no more assassins lay in wait. He shook his head as his heart raced. "One bite would have killed you."

"How did it get in here?" she asked as she straightened each of Tuto's broad wings, tenderly rotating them. The bird shook its feathered crown but allowed her inspection.

"Someone put it there."

Kailin's gaze pierced him. "Someone wants me dead?"

"The bed was made. I don't know of asps that climb trellises on their own to snuggle under sheets."

Tuto hopped to the end of the bed. Jackson stood to the side so the bird could spread its wings. It swooped low in the small room and shot out of the open balcony doors.

"Who wants me dead?" Kailin sat back on her heels in the middle of the rumpled sheets. "I thought the kidnappers needed me alive to get the Orb."

Jackson nodded. He pinched the bridge of his nose. "Another party?" He stared at her. "Maybe someone who doesn't want you to find the Orb."

"Doctor Moghadam called me Cleopatra. He wanted to go with me on expedition."

"Moghadam," Jackson mulled over. He'd check into the doctor through his contacts in the city.

"I thought he might know my father well," she continued.

Jackson raised one eyebrow and tried to focus on Kailin's serious features instead of the way her bare legs peeked from her gown when she shifted to her hip. "Why did you think that? Did he mention Anthony by name?"

Kailin shook her head, her eyes narrowing slightly. "Because of the Cleopatra reference he made to me."

Jackson knew he should be catching on but hadn't a clue how that bridged. He waited.

Kailin released a long breath. "My father calls me Cleo after Queen Cleopatra. Ever since he found me." Kailin pinned him with a sharp look. Her head tilted so that her loosened curls cascaded down one shoulder. "And it is very...disconcerting that you don't know that, Mister Black, since you are my father's assistant and he has spoken so often of me to you."

Jackson stood rooted beside the bed, his eyes relaxed even though his mind turned over this new information. He could lie, but it froze on his tongue. He watched Kailin's demeanor freeze in increments, as if ice slowly replaced her warm blood. Minutes ago, their shared laughter, then her tears, then the kiss had dissolved barriers. Then one ridiculous detail that he hadn't investigated made her wrap herself back in ice.

Her eyes sparked with crystalline glass as her chin solidified, pursing her soft lips into a thin line. Her back straightened so that she seemed to grow inches in her position amongst the pillows, pillows that right now could have had her hair spread across them instead. *Bloody hell!* What had he gotten himself into?

"Who exactly are you, Mister Black?" She said the words with such cold precision that they nearly puffed out white in the room as if she were outside on the western plains on a winter morning.

He opened his mouth, not knowing what would come out. The truth?

Kailin gasped, slapping a hand over her upper arm.

Instinct to protect, Jackson dove for her, his hands grabbing for the unseen threat. Another snake? A different poisonous creature? Had it already bitten? Was he too late?

CHAPTER TWELVE
TINGLING

Jackson's body was revved with desperate energy. If Kailin was bitten there was little hope he could help. The thought pounded hard in his temples, and he engulfed her in a hug, rolling her to the side in a billowing of gold silk and petticoats. He grabbed her arm. Perhaps he could suck the venom out.

"What are you doing?" Kailin sputtered, her head half buried by the pillows. Jackson swatted the velvety squares off the bed.

"Where is it?"

"Where is what?"

"Whatever bit you? It could bite you again." In one swift jerk, Jackson tore the length of sleeve from Kailin's arm.

"What? Wait! Stop!" she shouted and struggled upright.

Jackson held up her arm and rubbed his fingers along her doe-like skin, ignoring how enticingly it contrasted with his own. Only a brown shape lay along her pale limb. A bruise? He leaned into it. "It's a dragonfly," he murmured.

Kailin snatched her arm back. "My birthmark."

His eyes searched the tossed covers. He flipped over several remaining pillows. "No snake then."

"Already in bed together. Wonderful." The enthusiastic whisper came from the shadows behind him. Jackson rolled off the bed, his gun drawn before he stood to his full height. The apparition smiled.

Kailin tumbled off the other side, nearly falling on her face in her haste. "We're not in bed together." She scrambled upright, tugging on her bodice to set it correctly in place. The missing sleeve and falling hair gave her a look of being either ravished or attacked by a bear.

"Well, you should be." The ghost who called herself Drakkina frowned. "You're as stubborn as your sisters."

"And if we were," Kailin continued, "you shouldn't be checking in on us. That would be *bloody* rude."

Her feminine voice, spitting such anger, was like a kitten imitating a tiger. Although Kailin Whitaker certainly had claws. Claws, a clever mind, and barely controlled power. The combination could explode like a barrel of lit gunpowder.

Drakkina waved her hand and several dragonflies jumped off to zip around the room. "I would have left if you'd been indisposed." She pointed at Kailin's bare arm. "You will always know when I'm near."

"The tingling sensation."

Drakkina nodded. So that was the source of Kailin's gasp, not a venomous bite but a tingling birthmark Kailin had mentioned before. Jackson felt the need to sit but didn't budge. Drakkina frowned at his gun.

"All you warriors want to kill me. First of all, I'm on the side of good." Her lips tightened. "I'm on your side," she reiterated as if needing to make that clear. Could the witch read his mind? "Second, your bullets can't hurt me. I'm already dead, for now, anyway."

"Why are you haunting Kailin?" Jackson asked and lowered his weapon, though he didn't re-holster it. "You need to move on to wherever you need to go." He wouldn't give it a name, as he had wondered where a devil like himself would end up.

"I am not haunting anyone." She sniffed. "I'm completing a mission to save this world, which includes finding all of Gilla's daughters and their soul mates to fight the final battle against Semiazaz and his coven of demons."

"Wait. Soul mates?" Jackson asked.

Kailin grumbled something under her breath. Jackson looked at her. "Is this the apocalypse you mentioned earlier?"

Kailin's eyes grew round and her arms angled out from her body. "You think us being soul mates is the equivalent of an all-consuming end to the world?"

"Do you?"

Drakkina chuckled. "Aye, passion. Good, good. "'Tis merely a matter of time then. I won't have to interfere. 'Tis best I don't anyway. Love takes its own bloody time. I thought Merewin and Hauk would never get past their stubborn natures."

Jackson glanced between Kailin and the ghost. "You mean me, a soul mate for Kailin." His heart began to beat faster like when he'd seen the cobra in the bed.

Kailin let loose a sarcastic chuckle and paced back to the bed to sit on the edge. "Hardly!" Relief and annoyance prickled through him.

Drakkina frowned at Kailin and nodded to Jackson. "Her magic doesn't work on you, correct?"

Jackson stared, his mind ticking through the scenes of him calming Kailin's storm. Drakkina took that as an affirmative. "Therefore, you are her soul mate. And the link between each daughter and her mate is important in order to gather enough power to defeat the demons."

"Who are these..." He hesitated, feeling foolish talking about beings that only existed in hellfire sermons.

"Demons," Drakkina finished for him.

"Of which I've seen no evidence," Kailin said.

Drakkina ignored her. "A group of thirteen corrupted, powerful souls who are determined to collect enough magical power to break the web of time holding all eras in their proper place.

"If they succeed, time will no longer have meaning. All of humanity that has ever lived will be resurrected and placed back on this small planet, piled upon one another, starving, tormented, dying all over again hideous deaths. Everyone you care about, everyone you've ever cared about, every generation of every family will live again in agony, only to be toyed with and tortured for fun and game. Some may escape Semiazaz's far-reaching attention, but they will live in hiding until the meager resources of this planet give out."

"Why would they do that?" he asked.

Drakkina threw her hands wide. "Why do demons do anything? To cause havoc out of a sense of revenge and resentment, grow huge on dark power, feed on pain and suffering." Drakkina lowered her arms and pointed at him. "Don't underestimate them. They will stop at nothing to succeed. I bound them three millennia ago to stall their progress, but they've learned to work together." Her gaze dropped as if weighed down by guilt. "Now I fear they're even angrier."

"You could be making this all up," Jackson said. "To toy with us. Perhaps *you* are the demon."

Drakkina pierced him with a pale blue-eyed stare. "Treasure hunter. You understand the call of the hunt."

Jackson supposed he did. He'd been hunting for fossils on the plains as a boy and had first come to Egypt as a young man after seeing gold treasure and a sarcophagus in a traveling show back in the States. He'd been hunting his whole life and was now on the biggest hunt of all, one that meant life or death. Jackson nodded under the spirit's scrutiny.

"These monsters hunt power." Drakkina jabbed her finger in Kailin's direction. "And Kailin is the most powerful of Gilla's daughters."

Jackson's hand contracted into a fist. "They're hunting Kailin?"

"Yes, cowherd."

"I've never, in all my years, seen them, heard them, detected them in any way," Kailin said, crossing her arms before her. The bare one still looked odd, as if she'd been in a bar brawl.

"They haven't found you yet, but they found your twin."

Kailin dropped her arms. "Is she still alive?"

"Not in this year, but yes, she survived. They also nearly found Merewin. They are getting better at hunting you all. I think the final battle that my oracle predicted is nearing. It is only a matter of time before they sense you. The magic of the stones in Scotland and the vast power still ingrained in the pharaohs' monuments have masked you and your mother's power, the power that you can barely contain."

"Do you...? Could you..." Kailin began, her stare quite serious on the spirit. "Could you teach me to control this gift from my mother?"

Drakkina grinned slowly and nodded. "I taught her. I can teach you."

"When?"

"Now, except I seem to have interrupted something I probably shouldn't have." Drakkina's gaze flicked to the bed. Kailin blushed and the oil lamps flared hot, sparking bright light through the room.

"We were dealing with a snake in the bed," Kailin said.

Drakkina grinned, eyeing Jackson. "I bet 'twas a big snake." She laughed. "Like I said, I'll leave you to it."

The flames shot up out the tops of the lamps, cutting off Drakkina's cackles. Jackson immediately grabbed Kailin's hands and the flames retreated. "It was an Egyptian cobra," he said, "venomous and likely meant to kill Kailin."

Drakkina sobered. "A human hunts you too?"

"Apparently," Kailin said, and her blush began to recede.

"Well don't die," Drakkina ordered and looked at Jackson. "You either. The world needs you two, like the rest." Her gaze moved back to Kailin. "You'll want to meet your sisters. You can't do that dead unless, of course, the demons win and they bring you back to devour you."

"Maybe they only want to devour you," Kailin murmured.

"Why are you trying to save a world you no longer live in?" Jackson asked. Some motives seemed pure on the surface, but underneath they reeked of corruption.

Drakkina's lips tightened. She looked for a moment like she wouldn't answer, but then her lips relaxed and opened. "I'm tied to this world, tied to Gilla's daughters through ancient spells." She met Kailin's questioning gaze. "I gave my oath to your mother to protect all of you and your world."

She swallowed, and the dragonflies zipping about came to hover close to her, some of them flickering like a caress against her cheek. "I lived in this world too once, long ago. I remember it. And I remember the feeling of loss, loss at the hands of ultimate evil." She looked up. "As long as I can, I will fight it. If I stop, I truly will be dead. They will have won. Not to mention that if they bring me back in corporeal form, they will seek me and take great pleasure in torturing me for shackling them all these years."

Silence sat between them like a thick triangle of questions and muffled thoughts. Jackson was the first to move, slowly releasing Kailin's hand. "Perhaps the lessons can begin tomorrow on our expedition. It is late tonight. Kailin needs sleep."

"So do you," Kailin said indignantly.

"So do I," Jackson parroted.

Drakkina flipped her hand around. "I will keep watch with your pet." She indicated the balcony where Tuto perched on the rail, surveying the garden below, perhaps for more snakes or human assassins. The spirit began to fade. "Tomorrow then." And she was gone.

Jackson watched Kailin's shoulders slump. "No more tingling?" he asked and she shook her head without looking at him. "I suppose we should get some sleep. The camels will be here at dawn."

She nodded, still mute.

"Where do you plan to sleep?" he asked.

"On the balcony."

Tuto and Drakkina would no doubt guard the balcony and gardens below. He would guard the door. "I'll take the bed then."

Kailin's face snapped toward him. "The bed in your own room."

He unbuckled his holster, and his belt and gun slid off over his narrow hips. They clunked heavily on the nightstand next to the bed. "I'm not leaving your side, not now that I know someone is trying to kill you."

He walked to the balcony while she sputtered behind him like a kitten who'd been thrown in a bowl of water. She had moved the divan out on the narrow balcony. He riffled through the linens, checking for more surprises. The only thing that assaulted him was the light floral scent that permeated the sheets from Kailin's time sleeping there last night. He exhaled the enticing aroma and turned. "All clear out here. Tuto and the ghost are keeping watch in the garden. No one will get by me inside."

"I will be fine. You need to go to your own rooms. What will people think?"

Jackson came up close to her inside the room. "People will not know and if they somehow find out"— his lips quirked up a bit at the corner—"I'll merely explain to them that we are soul mates." He winked then just to watch anger light the blue in her eyes. The ghost was right; there was passion between them. Which was good because he much preferred fury to apathetic avoidance.

The oil lamps flared, and he grabbed for her hands, but she tucked them behind her back like an errant child. "No bonfire tonight." He slid his palm along the side of her neck, touching the soft skin. She tried to step away, but his fingers curled at her nape, stopping her. "I plan to sleep in that bed, and if there are any flames in it, it will be when we're in it together."

"Oooo!" Kailin stomped her feet but grabbed his hands, pulling them from her neck. "When Drakkina teaches me how to control my magic, I'll have no need for you at all anymore. You can crawl back into whatever hole liars stew in."

Jackson's grin faded. "Maybe when you learn to trust me with the whole truth, I'll learn to trust you." He released her hands and strode to the bed, leaving her gaping in the middle of the room. He stretched out on top of her bed and doused the flame nearest him.

"Goodnight, Doctor Whitaker."

CHAPTER THIRTEEN
JOURNEY INTO THE DESERT

Four one-humped dromedary camels stood before the Hotel Moudira. Three were saddled with colorful woven mats in the traditional fashion, tassels dangling evenly around. The fourth beast served to carry the supplies Jackson had arranged the day before. A young Egyptian man stood silently beside them.

Kailin had sent word to Musa, Anthony's lifelong manservant and guide when he visited Egypt, only to hear the shocking news that he had been taken along with her father. Hopefully he hadn't been murdered for the simple reason of not being of value. The thought twisted inside her, making it harder for her to keep her cool, controlled demeanor.

Kailin studied the new guide, Qeb, as she sipped from a tall mug of warm dark chocolate with cream. He was between twenty and thirty years of age, she guessed, and wore a traditional white thobe or basic dress to his ankles with a keffiyeh head wrap. Several curved knives with colorfully swathed handles hung from a mustard-brown belt tied loosely around the thobe. Worn leather sandals were the locally preferred hiking boots.

Qeb smiled cautiously at Kailin and nodded, his eyes flicking down to his hem in a nervous bow. There was too little time to fully inspect the man's background. There had been enough delay having to travel from England to Egypt.

Jackson inspected the leather bags and bedrolls tied to the fourth camel. He wore trousers with boots and a long-enduring leather expedition jacket that lay comfortably across his broad shoulders like a second skin. A wide-brimmed hat sat on his head in more of an American West style than the popular rounder brimmed hats the Brits wore. It fit him, as if it belonged there even when his mount had a hump instead of a sleek neck and flowing mane.

He ran his hand down the nose of one camel and let it lip away some fresh stalks from his palm. Qeb had brought the animals watered and fed that morning. Kailin had settled her hotel bill and only waited for Jackson's signal to head out. It came in the form of a nod.

She stifled a yawn from not having slept well knowing he lay only yards away in her bedchamber, probably without a shred of clothing. Every time her mind wandered to the minute details of his kiss, she'd remind herself tersely about his lie. Why had he said that he was close friends with Anthony? To convince her to come with him quickly? Why was he even involved in trying to liberate her father if he didn't know him? What was in it for Jackson Black?

Kailin pushed the bombardment of questions aside as she stepped onto the courtesy step and propped her foot in the stirrup.

"A lift?" Jackson's gentle rumble sent her heart galloping, and she concentrated on holding in her powers along with her breath. What would happen if she were incapacitated? Would her powers run amok or would they wilt along with her body if she fainted? She never had before, but it seemed the only way to restrain her magic was to restrain her breath, which could lead to the inadvertent triggering of the experiment.

She inhaled and lifted herself into the saddle attached behind the single hump, her balloon-like tan trousers straddling the beast. The material tapered in below the knee where tall leather boots protected her lower legs. They were a natural brown, not black, which would absorb the heat.

"As you see, Mister Black, I need no help. I am schooled in camel riding. I did spend much of my childhood here." Sometimes she wore the more respectable wide-leg trousers until reaching the vacant desert, but there might be no time to change before they camped that night, and she wasn't about to slow the pace of the caravan by not being secure in the saddle.

Jackson's hat tilted back as he looked up at her, a wisp of his hair peeking out along his forehead. "Would you care to lead the way then?"

She nodded crisply and glanced at the road toward the Valley of the Kings. It would take two days of riding to reach the spot where she'd been entombed with Anthony long ago. The hole she'd blown apart was in fact on the edge of a slope leading down to the sometimes-surging Nile. The original entrance to the tomb had collapsed and Anthony had managed to guide her in filling the hole that night after she'd calmed. Due to the churning water so close to the hole, no expedition had advanced in that particular area.

Anthony had explained how he'd fished Kailin from the flood waters. Her parents presumed dead and anonymous, he'd had little trouble adopting her when no family could be found.

Kailin breathed deeply as she tapped the camel with the leather-tipped rod. The animal started its slow sway out into the street like a heavy barge breaking free of the dock. Perching behind the camel's hump provided a secure seat even if they picked up speed. They walked in a line along the narrow streets leading down toward the water where they'd moored the other day. Merchants, still wrapped in layers to guard against the morning chill, set out wares for the day.

Kailin glanced at the ascending sun. It wouldn't take long before the chill burned away, leaving a baking heat. That was the way of the desert, extremes. Baking heat with the sun and bone-chilling cold with its lack.

She watched Jackson from the corner of her eye. He coaxed out the scorching heat in her. She preferred the chill of aloofness, had grown accustomed to its numbing protection. Yet Jackson Black, with a deep stare, a caress of voice, the minute upturn of a wicked grin, could melt her ice, evaporating it into steam so that she became hot baked sand within his gaze.

Kailin touched the long scarf that held her wide-brimmed explorer's hat on top of her head. She'd wrapped it with white gauzy material that would help keep out sun, sand, and any peripheral glances at the man who had become a torment to her calm civility. Instead, she would continue to introspectively consider the serpentine questions about his motives as her eyes roamed the smooth landscape beyond the green vegetation flanking the Nile. The hotel sat on the West Bank so there was no need to cross the wide waterway. They would head west and then south along the flood line of the Nile. The reburied tomb lay along a hill two day's journey south.

Kailin glanced behind as they left the main street to head toward open countryside beyond the bustle of the town center. Would they be followed? Watched? Would those responsible for the deadly snake seek to assassinate her as she rode toward the Orb? Or would they wait for a more private moment? She could stop any weapon if she saw it coming. It was the unexpected that could kill her.

Kailin held her breath and waited until her heart calmed. Her back stiffened as she turned forward. She wouldn't let fear delay her. Perhaps it was good that Jackson came with her. Another set of watchful eyes could sway the line from death to life. And she must stay alive to save Anthony—and perhaps the whole world, if the Wiccan priestess was to be believed.

Jackson kicked his mount and moved closer, his eyes scanning the hills in the distance before them. "A covered conveyance may have been a better idea."

"I've yet to see a coach on expedition," she said with a forced smile in her voice.

"I don't like this," he murmured. "It's difficult to hide on a desert. I'd rather we stay along the Nile where trees and vegetation offer cover."

"Any ideas about who might not want me to proceed?"

Jackson was silent for a long moment. "There are radical groups who feel British discovery is akin to desecration of the dead."

"Technically I suppose that is what we do," she said, her eyes squinting back at the sun cresting the edge of the Nile beyond a series of low shacks.

"They attack any archeological expedition in order to stall and, as they see it, protect their long-buried kings," he added.

"Have these radicals tried to kill the explorers before the expedition even started?"

"Not that I have heard. Someone seems desperate to stop you."

Kailin huffed with indignation to mask the chill that snapped along her shoulders. "Well, I'm not dead, and I'm not scared off."

Jackson pulled his hat forward to shade his eyes. "No, you are most definitely alive." She held her breath to hold her blush. "And the bravest woman I've yet met."

She had to laugh at that. If he could see the goose bumps along her arms he might think differently. "Braver than your sister, risking ridicule and illness to attend a nest of vipers last night? I think not."

His lips quirked into a gentle grin. "Cassy is more desperate for entertainment apart from dear Mrs. Pierce than she is brave. But yes, you two would do well together, I think. Both brave and ready to face the world no matter your perceived disadvantages."

Kailin blinked. She certainly perceived her lack of control as a disadvantage but fought to hide that. Did Jackson realize the length of her struggle, her exhaustion at times?

"If you don't mind me asking," Kailin said slowly. "What is the illness that plagues your sister?"

"Poliomyelitis, an illness that attacks the spinal system, causing paralysis. She contracted it last spring after our parents died back in the States from influenza. She seemed to recover but I think the shock of being on her own there weakened her greatly." Jackson said the words evenly, his gaze outward once more.

"You weren't home, in the States, when your parents died and Cassy was sick?" she asked.

His lips tightened in the hard set of his face. "No."

"How did you hear?"

"By wire that they had died, but I didn't know Cassy was sick until Mrs. Pierce sent word that her heart had become so weak and she could no longer walk. It was the first I'd heard of her illness."

"Yet you blame yourself," Kailin said beneath her breath.

"I should have returned immediately. She was barely older than a child."

"But you did go to her."

He nodded and touched the rim of his hat. "She was so weak by that time I feared she would die immediately. I stayed months, nursing her with Mrs. Pierce."

"She grew strong enough to make the voyage to Egypt." Kailin studied Jackson's profile as he stared straight ahead. "Why? Why bring her halfway across the world?"

Kailin brushed at her arm a half second before an iridescent blue dragonfly alighted on the knobby head of the camel. If the creature noticed, he didn't show any sign, not even a twitch of his ear.

"The ghost," Jackson said, his gaze shifting in a slow scan of the air around them.

"Why did you bring Cassy here?" Kailin insisted.

Qeb rattled through a short burst of exclamations in Arabic as a swarm of dragonflies whirled around them like a small locust storm. Jackson spoke calmly back to the wide-eyed Qeb. "They don't bite," Jackson replied in the same dialect, which Kailin understood because of the amber stone.

Drakkina didn't show herself, but as the warming breeze teased a curl out of Kailin's bun, she heard the spirit-woman's voice. *I'm keeping watch. No demons. No assassins. Yet. Stay close to your mate.*

Kailin let out a frustrated huff and glanced at Jackson. He gave her only the slight tip of a nod, but it was enough to show he'd heard Drakkina's words. Mate? Kailin felt her blush begin to grow. Good God, what would she set on fire out here? Her eyes scanned the low scraggly bushes that marked the border of the floodplain.

Lesson one, Drakkina's voice floated into Kailin's mind. *Imagine your magic as a bubble held inside.*

Kailin already thought of her power as a bubble inside. She reinforced the image and softly exhaled. The bubble image remained; her magic remained trapped inside. She inhaled a calm ribbon of dry air. The bubble continued.

Lesson two, shrink your bubble until it's small enough to feel like a hard pebble inside. Then tuck it deep behind your rib, in the center of your heart, to be released upon your command.

Kailin packed around the bubble like a translucent snowball, forcing it to contract. The walls thickened until they became opaque marble. She'd closed her eyes, her fingers wrapped tightly into the woven layers of saddle and guide rope. Her muscles flexed in her arms as if she wrestled the magic. She bullied it into a tight star that sparked and glinted, enlarging and contracting until she compacted it into a pea-sized pebble.

Opening her eyes, she saw Jackson watching her from beneath his brim. "Well done." His face was serious. "Maybe you won't need me much longer." His lips quirked upward in a wry grin. "I'm sure Qeb could crawl on his belly down in the dirt for you."

Kailin patted a handkerchief against her forehead to dab away the light sheen of sweat from her efforts. The dry breeze sent a shiver along her skin. "Somehow I don't think getting rid of you will be that easy."

His grin widened until she could see his white, even teeth behind his lips she'd been pressed against last night. Kailin yanked the mental image of the glittering pebble into her mind.

Jackson chuckled. "We archeologists are a tenacious lot."

"You mean treasure hunter." She indicated him with a bent of her head. "There is a vast difference."

"We both decipher clues, follow our instincts, hunt down every known bit of information and dig for lost treasure."

Kailin nodded. "But it is what we do afterwards that makes the distinction." She looked closely at Jackson. "Exactly what do you plan to do after we find the Orb, Mister Black?"

"Get your father back, Doctor Whitaker," he answered without hesitation.

Kailin weighed his words. They came smoothly, with the undisturbed glassy surface of truth or...the chiseled rut of rehearsed lines. What was she missing? There was more to Jackson Black than what he presented. The bits of information he gave were puzzle pieces that didn't quite fit together.

"What I mean, Mister Black, is"—and she leaned a bit toward him—"what is in this for you? Treasure hunters don't merely come along for the ride. And don't try to spill the same lies about being Anthony's assistant. If you didn't know my father's name for me, you don't know him." She straightened in the shifting saddle but kept her body flexible to absorb the camel's gait. Her eyes narrowed. "You don't know *me*."

"I know you prefer chocolate to tea or wine, with a dollop of frothy cream. I know that you will throw yourself in harm's way to save your pet and that the mask of ice you wear is only that, a mask." He leaned closer but his voice didn't diminish. "That your heart is as kind and warm as your mind is clever and your wit is a razor's edge." Jackson's eyes connected to her gaze like a chain. "I know, Kailin Whitaker, what makes your blood fly, your heart pound. I know the intoxicating warmth of your body pressed to mine and I know the enticing way you taste."

Kailin managed to pull in a wisp of breath. "You overstep propriety," she whispered.

"On a continual basis."

Kailin glanced at Qeb. "Does he understand English?"

A wicked glance sparked Jackson's eye. "Shall we see?" He straightened and looked at the guide. Qeb smiled, showing a line of chipped, tarnished teeth. "The lady is beautiful." Jackson didn't look at Kailin and neither did Qeb. But he nodded as if agreeing.

"Jackson, don't." A blush started and Jackson held his finger and thumb apart as if he held a small marble. She huffed at his reminder to keep her magic contracted.

"I have kissed her," he continued. "She tastes like honey and smells like summer flowers. I plan to kiss her again."

Kiss her again! Kailin opened her mouth, eyes wide. She'd called him a liar and questioned his motives, yet he spoke of kissing her again. She narrowed her eyes and stretched her Ice Queen mask tight across her skin.

Qeb nodded, but his eyes didn't stray to her. Jackson glanced her way, ignoring her scathing look. "I'd say we are fairly safe."

As long as I don't speak. Kailin clasped the amber stone through her shirt where it rode above the line of her loose corset.

He turned back to Qeb and spoke quickly in Arabic about the camels being solid beasts. Qeb nodded and rattled off a reply. He smiled fondly and slid his hand over the camel's neck that he led across the shifting sand.

Kailin swayed in her saddle and let her gaze wash over the hills in the distance, yet she barely saw them. She breathed in, breathed out. Several exchanges later she realized that he'd never answered her questions. Instead he'd rattled her with his preposterous flattery and outrageous words.

"You think, Mister Black, that you are smooth enough, audacious enough, to knock me from my senses. You think you are clever enough to evade my suspicions." She looked at him, an icy stare meant to leach the triumph and humor from his eyes. "You. Are. Not. What do you want?"

Jackson's gaze met hers in an unwavering battle. "You've named me a treasure hunter, Doctor Whitaker. If you are accurate, you've answered your own question. I want treasure."

Kailin's heart beat hard. "You will take the Orb then," she accused.

"I hardly think that the Orb is the only treasure to be found in the tomb that holds it. You can use whatever you need to free your father." He held her stare, fusing with it, holding it hostage. "The rest is mine."

Kailin stared back across the few feet separating them as they swayed in a tandem rhythm on their mounts. "Anthony gets credit for the discovery," she bargained.

Jackson nodded once. "What does a treasure hunter care for fame? I am here for the money." He shrugged, his smile gone.

The planes of his face had hardened, giving him the look of an outlaw. Rugged, beguiling, dangerous. She traced the lines of his cheeks with her gaze, bringing her to his mouth that was so expressive and the only thing soft about the man. Jackson Black was untamed, full of passion and fire. What would it be like to lose herself in the flames of his embrace? Heat fanned down through her body, licking along her veins like little flames.

"Nar!" Qeb shouted and pointed wildly behind her. "Fire!"

CHAPTER FOURTEEN
WAVES OF SAND

"Bloody hell!" Jackson yanked his camel in the direction Qeb jabbed his finger. Birds shot up from a line of low bushes marking the edge of the flood plain. Several snakes slithered in *S*-curves across the warming sand. "Control, Atsila!" he shouted as he jumped down and grabbed a thick blanket from the pack.

Kailin bristled at his command, but the splashing of two crocodiles sliding into the Nile made her groan. "Good God." Kailin breathed and found her magic. It had expanded inside her chest with her carnal thoughts, nearly overflowing the bounds of her body. She imagined it small, clasping the wildly growing beast and pressing it inward. Reluctantly, fighting like a child used to little restriction, it struggled back into the hard shell of a pebble. Kailin opened her eyes. Qeb and Jackson beat at the flames that licked across the brittle scrub.

Kailin stared up at the clear, arid sky. Moisture? Was there any? She searched the waves of heat that had begun to roll off the sand like an oven. Affecting the weather was much easier on the British Isles where humidity hung pregnant in the air. Here, the sun sucked at and the sand relinquished any moisture in the earth. Only a thin line of clouds formed above them as they worked. Nothing that could squelch flames.

The scrub connected to a long line of bushes running back toward an irrigated field. If she didn't stop the fire, the farmer would lose his crops, livelihood, and food. Kailin urged her camel closer to the escaping line of flame even though it stubbornly resisted. She finally gave up on pushing the animal onward, knowing that one couldn't make a camel do anything he didn't want to do.

"Cover," she said and flipped her hand in the air, releasing the pebble, letting it expand toward the target. Sand surged up in a wave along the fire line. The wave crested and fell, dropping on top of the flames, smothering them. "Cover," she repeated and flipped another wave of hot crystalline earth. The dried skeletal bushes disappeared under the blanket of sand, and so did the flames. Kailin's gaze scanned the line, looking for smoldering twigs, but nothing except a long, raised bed of sand remained.

Jackson stood at one end, holding the woolen blanket he'd been thumping the flames with. Sweat glistened off his face as he stared at her. She watched his chest expand and contract with a long breath. Qeb stood with his blanket at his feet, arms dropped to the side, eyes wide as gold pans as he stared at her.

"Ghūl," Qeb said and backed up, his palms outward as if fending off an animal about ready to attack.

"No," Jackson answered. "No demon." He shook his head at the guide and switched to Arabic. "Sahirat jayida." He looked back at Kailin. "One who can't control her magic."

"That was not my fault," Kailin said as Jackson tossed the singed blanket over the back of his camel.

"Because my motives angered you?" Jackson countered, one eyebrow raised. Qeb remounted but kept his cautious gaze on Kailin. "I gave you what you asked for. The truth. Your temper is your own fault, not mine."

Kailin fought the blush she knew crept up her neck.

She kept her magic locked behind her rib cage. Her anger was indeed misplaced. Most people didn't usually start by blaming themselves, not if there were other appropriate outlets for the emotion. Yet this was being pointed out by the very man who hurled her far beyond mere irritation right into abject fury and some other emotion that sent her blood racing to spots she'd rather ignore.

Jackson had finally been honest. He wasn't there for her, wasn't intrigued by her. Maybe he was curious about her magic, or the spirit woman, or even the crone's prophecy about the end of the world. But it wasn't Kailin Whitaker that tethered him to this expedition. He was a treasure hunter and had seized an opportunity for gain. He was finally being honest, and she was angry about it.

"Your motives are what they are. The fact that you've been lying to me angered me," she said, her words as dry and flat as stale toast. "I will not work with someone I cannot trust."

"I rather doubt that Qeb will stay to help you after that show."

Kailin let her eyes roam over the dunes ahead. To turn around would be wasteful. Time was important. She didn't know what conditions Anthony was enduring. Kailin literally ground her teeth, her eyes half-mast, as she followed the sloped contours of the desert beyond. Blast her ridiculous claustrophobia. Without it, she could do this alone.

That would reveal my abilities, her conscience whispered and she clenched her teeth at the truth. If a woman, cinched in by societal ropes, not to mention the tight corsets and the restriction of bustles, was able to find and excavate an undiscovered tomb without aid, people would question.

Her eyes caught the dark outline of a lone rider at the crest of one sultry hill, watching their progress. Was he one of the kidnappers? Or an assassin with an unknown motive for stopping her? Or only a farmer curious about the smoke? The dark figure disappeared.

"Very well, Mister Black. Feel free to continue your treasure hunt." She swung around to pierce him with razor scrutiny. "You can have all the other riches, but the Orb is mine and even though I may not be able to light you on fire"—not that she could ever light anyone on fire purposely, but the threat felt good sliding off her tongue—"I can certainly move mountains if someone gets in my way."

Kailin didn't wait for a response but tapped her camel into movement, like a rocking vessel upon the waves of sand. Jackson Black could turn around and go back to Luxor if he wished. She could certainly take care of herself, society be damned.

⸺◆⸺

The rocking of the camel beneath Jackson marked the time as well as the sun moving above. He watched Kailin untie the gauzy ribbon from under her chin. In a swift tug, she un-hatted herself, revealing her silky blond hair. The sun plucked the red highlights from the mass of glorious waves swept high to reveal the gentle slope of her nape. She leaned over the camel's neck and attached her hat to the saddle. In another quick flourish, she draped her long white scarf over her head and wrapped it in front of her face.

Even in the headdress usually reserved for Arab men, Kailin couldn't hide her assets. The wind off the barren hills of sand yanked and twisted at her body, molding her modest traveling costume to her woman's figure. The scarf fought to contain her hair, but a few golden tresses broke free to dance in the breezes like silky ribbons.

He kept behind her, giving her time, giving him time to adjust to her condemnation. Jackson wiped his arm across his gritty brow and scanned the horizon of sand. It was better for her to know some of the truth, enough to keep her from lowering her guard around him. Because she shouldn't lower her guard.

His lips pressed into a line of acceptance, acceptance of who he was. He was a treasure hunter and in some circles a scoundrel. He played dangerous games well. He risked much since he had little to lose and slid along the razor edge between honor and self-gratification with ease. She shouldn't tangle her young, pure heart with his.

Besides, he had more significant matters to consider, more important than the lovely slope of Kailin's neck that the wind flattened the scarf against, more critical than the strength and grace she exhibited with each sway of the camel's stride, and much more vital than those damn curls flapping about.

Jackson caught sight of a rider off to the right along a dune. A single rider on a camel.

"Cingene?" Qeb asked.

"Could be a Bedouin," Jackson answered in Arabic. "But keep alert." Qeb nodded and continued to scan the terrain. They were in the open, but soon night and the approaching hills would obscure threats.

They made camp in a small valley between dunes when the sun dropped below the hills and the temperature plummeted with it. The winds at times could whip across the desert at night with a cold fury that seemed like a personal vendetta against humankind. Kailin didn't complain. The camels were set loose to rest, with one of them tethered.

The animals would stay together. If one remained, the others would as well.

Jackson made a small fire in the circle created by the resting beasts. Their bulk and the dunes blocked the little light, and the wind scattered the smoke into the inky black sky. Hard cheese, fresh brown bread, wine, and smoked fasieekh were rationed amongst the three. Not knowing precisely how long it would take to excavate the area Anthony Whitaker had been exploring made it difficult to plan the division of food. Jackson would try to catch some of the scarce wildlife along the way. Snake meat could be roasted easily over a campfire.

Jackson lowered to the cold sand near the fire and washed down his meal with watered wine. His gaze settled on Kailin without conscious thought. She picked at her fish with delicate fingers, catching her thumb and forefinger between her lips. Jackson's breath hitched in his throat as she licked the digits and slowly pulled them from her mouth. She bit off a chunk of bread and chewed, the gentle curve of her jaw working the rough texture. Bloody hell, the woman was a torment.

Jackson shifted uncomfortably on the ground and drank some more wine. He stood to find the jug of washing water and scrubbed a damp rag over his face and neck. He took time to scrub his teeth too. When he glanced at the fire, Kailin was gone. He was back to it in three strides. "Where?"

Qeb pointed past the camels to a low rise. In the blue-black night, Jackson spotted Kailin's outline against the white sand. She stretched out flat on her back along the gentle incline.

Jackson strode from the warmth of the fire, grabbing the wool blanket from the back of her camel. As the brightness of the fire faded from his eyes, the night surrendered its shield, and he could see the vast dark landscape. Kailin lay staring up at the enormous sky. Her face looked like a narrow pale moon on the night landscape. She'd opened her scarf so that it pillowed her head and her hair framed loosely around her, devoid of hairpins.

Jackson stood several feet away, staring at her silent repose.

"What do you want?" she asked after a minute.

"If you intend to sleep out here, unprotected, at least wrap up in a blanket." Jackson unfolded the woolen rectangle and draped it over the subtle hills and valleys of her body.

"Thank you," she said with a chill that mimicked the wind.

He stood for another minute and looked up at the sky. Stars shot the night with diamond-like beauty. He inhaled the clear air and for a moment he stood once again on the prairie back home, the huge night sky enveloping him in awe.

"Do you require something else?" Kailin asked.

"No, I'm admiring the stars."

"Hmm..." She trailed off. "Exquisite display once you step beyond the comfort of the fire. I prefer it."

Jackson lowered to the sand next to her but kept several feet of buffer between them. "That's the way of it. Viewing the most beautiful things on this earth requires surrender of comfort and security. Anything amazing requires risk."

Silence. Jackson reclined until he too was flat on the incline, staring up at the stars. The cold from the sand crept through his linen shirt. The moon was only a sliver, giving the stars their chance to shine bright. He traced the familiar outlines. Gemini, the twins, linked like one with outstretched feet. His hero, Orion, the great hunter, held his bow ready.

"I used to believe Orion would protect me at night when I slept under him," Jackson murmured as he traced the bow with his gaze.

"Hardly. He was slain by Scorpius," Kailin said and her finger lifted to the outline of the scorpion. "It is Sagittarius's arrow that is poised to pierce the villain's heart. Although his outline looks more like a teapot to me. There's even a cloud of steam coming from the spout." She pointed.

Jackson traced the archer with his gaze. She was right. Some of the stars of Sagittarius did look like the outline of a teapot.

"So, if any of the great heroes or beasts of the sky are able to protect us, it would be Sagittarius," Kailin said and shrugged her slender shoulders in the sand. "Certainly not the foolish Cassiopeia. She spends half the night upside down on her throne. Mayhap Perseus and his won head of Medusa will turn the villains to stone."

"Perseus," Jackson said, the word caught in the night breeze that blew between them. "Of course he would protect you, a beautiful maiden like his Andromeda."

Kailin's head moved slightly, as if her gaze shifted to his profile, but he continued to stare up at the stars, so bright he could easily pick out the outlines.

"You are versed in the constellations?" Kailin asked.

A smooth chuckle came out of Jackson on a breath. "I spent a lot of time under the stars, guiding cattle when I was young. The stars were our guide, the figures were my friends, the legends my favorite stories."

"It seems we have the same friends," Kailin whispered and looked back to the sky.

"You spend a lot of time with them, sleeping outdoors."

He saw her nod in his periphery. "Steadfast, ready to listen on every clear night, not very opinionated," she joked. She paused and her voice wavered. "They are unbreakable and loyal. I am myself with them."

They stared upwards together in silence. Questions curled on Jackson's tongue. Had she no human friends? No one to talk and laugh with, no one to confide in? Were Anthony and her manservant in England the only people who didn't judge her as odd, a beautiful Ice Queen better left untouched? She was so intelligent, creative, spirited. She would make a wonderful friend for his sister.

Jackson kept silent. Kailin wouldn't want his words, would probably dislike him even more for what she would perceive as pity. Pity would ice her over when she'd finally relaxed enough to talk to him.

"Where did you watch the stars?" she asked. "On the plains of Indian Territory? Is that where Cassy was when she got sick?"

"Yeah. To both questions."

"And your parents."

"They're buried under the wide-open sky." His voice flattened. "I'll be damned if I bury Cassy with them."

"You never answered my question before," Kailin said. "About why you brought Cassy to Egypt."

Jackson paused, weighing his words. "I couldn't take care of her half a world away."

"I would have thought you'd stay with her there. You spoke of homesickness. Why wouldn't you tend her in the States?"

"Treasure hunter, remember. The only treasures on the plains are rich earth and golden harvests. I'm not a farmer."

"You do like to dig in the dirt," she countered, the smallest hint of a smile in her voice.

He laughed softly. "Not when there is nothing to find but worms, rocks, and manure."

"Look," she said, pointing to the sharp tail of a star. It glowed in a diffusing arc across the sky. "A dying star."

"I believe it is referred to less morbidly as a shooting star," he said as the trail faded. "Make a wish on it."

"I don't make wishes on the death of friends," she whispered. "No matter how glorious they are as they burst and fade to be forgotten."

"Only forgotten from billions of miles away. The death of something so incredible would surely affect those close by. They would never forget her brilliance."

Kailin's chin turned again and she adjusted slightly toward him. "You wish, then."

"Hmm, I wish...that Cassy will walk again and live a happy, long life." He felt Kailin's stare. He rolled his head slowly to meet her gaze.

"That doesn't sound like a treasure hunter." Kailin blinked at him in the dark.

Was she closer to him? It seemed only a few inches separated them now. The edge of her blanket warmed his arm. "Treasure is different for different people," he said.

"Defining the treasure defines the hunter," Kailin said. Jackson's gaze moved to her shadowed lips, their perfect shape as she formed the gentle remarks. "In that way we are all treasure hunters, Mister Black."

"What is your treasure, Doctor Whitaker?" he asked, his voice rough compared to the smooth ribbon of her words. The sand in between them marking the space seemed to disintegrate, dissolving like sugar in hot water.

What would she do if he kissed her? Slap him? Melt into him like the night before? The risk was very much worth the treasure. Jackson pushed slowly up onto his elbow and leaned over her. Kailin's eyes watched him, waiting. He gave her time to frown, bite out a cutting remark, jab him in the chest. All she did was readjust slightly to keep the connection between their gazes.

"Control," she whispered.

He stilled, tension gripping between his shoulder blades. Was that her word for stop?

"My treasure," she said, "is control and the knowledge of my origin. That is what I want, for what I hunt. A normal life, also, I think."

The grim tension in his mouth relaxed. "Normal is boring, and you, Kailin Whitaker, are anything but boring."

Jackson lowered his head and felt a sharp breeze skim the top of his head at the same time the sand on either side of him popped in small plumes. *Arrows!*

"Hell!" he growled low and rolled on top of Kailin. She gasped but didn't question his intentions. A sudden thought ripped through him.

"Kailin, are you hit?" he breathed along her ear.

"No," she exhaled. "Where are they coming from?" She gasped softly as another arrow sliced through the sand several feet to her right. They were exposed, easy targets.

Jackson wrapped his body around Kailin's, the wool blanket sandwiched in between them, and rolled with her. She yelped but tucked inside the cage of his chest and arms as they slid and flipped like a log down the slope of sand. Jackson heard the thumps of arrows hitting behind them and whizzing across them.

"Let go of me," Kailin demanded when they reached the bottom. "I can't stop them when you're touching me." Her words came out in a rush.

Jackson released her but hated the feeling of exposing her. "Hurry then."

Kailin half sat, half leaned on her elbows in the sand. She placed her palms outward as an owl screeched overhead. "Back," she whispered. The sounds of jostled horses over the rise preceded Arabic cursing. Several men from the sound of it. Anger, white and blinding, shot through Jackson. Who the hell was shooting at them? They could have killed Kailin.

Jackson leapt up and cocked his Remington. Bullets trumped arrows any day.

"Jackson!" Kailin called after him as he climbed up the slope, his head ducked, feet churning in the slipping sand.

"Back!" she called again and horses neighed and sand blew in a wave in front of him toward the men he could now see in the shadows.

He ducked along the ridge and counted. Six, eight, ten men fought with their horses as they danced wildly in the unnatural sandstorm while Kailin's owl dove upon them. Who the hell were they? What game were they playing? Were they part of the organization that had hired him?

The horses pranced and reared so that his shot in the dark would be just that; he didn't want to hit an innocent animal or be blamed for the death of a compatriot. He fired over them, exploding through the jumble of curses and neighs.

The shadows ducked, yanking their horses. He fired again, scanning the dark group for any man breaking the line of confusion to come closer. One large shadow emerged, the glint of a blade in his hand. Finally, someone he could shoot. Not fatally, but in a place that would prevent his escape. The man would talk once Jackson explained the consequences for keeping his silence. He watched the giant stride out of the fray. Jackson concentrated on the way his shadow moved, picking out what he thought was the man's knee.

"Back," came the whisper behind him and the advancing shadow flew backwards, disappearing into the night landscape with a hard thump and a rain of sand.

He turned. "I was planning to shoot that one."

"I think he'd rather be thrown than killed."

"I wasn't going to kill him, only stop him so we could get some answers," he said through his teeth. "Like why they are trying to kill us, or rather you."

Qeb had dropped to the sand, yelling questions in Arabic. The villainous group mounted their spooked horses and took off into the desert night, Tuto flapping and diving against their backs.

"Back," Kailin murmured once more, but only sand shifted ahead of them. All had fled and had taken the answers with them. Jackson heard her drop to the dune.

"We'll take turns keeping watch through the night," Jackson told Qeb. The guide nodded, but his round eyes, reflecting the small amount of moonlight, were focused on Kailin.

A breeze whistled across the sand and Kailin shivered.

"You go with Qeb back to the camels and sleep," Jackson said. "I'll take the first watch around the perimeter."

She looked like she would argue but didn't. "Wake me if anyone returns. I would rather not have blood spilt."

"It's your blood that they seem intent on spilling," he clipped. Anger tensed through him. If she hadn't pushed the large bandit away, he could be questioning him now, discovering the group's mission. If arrows hadn't suddenly peppered the sand around them, he could be kissing Kailin right now, reveling in her warmth, tasting her.

He watched Kailin's straight back melt into the night and reemerge in the glow of the fire. She stepped gracefully around a camel's head and sat before the embers as if at ease in the hostile environment. She stretched her arms and rewrapped the scarf around her hair and shoulders. She poked at the coals of the wood they'd fed into it with an iron stick she'd brought. The outdoors suited her. She was too much to contain within walls, almost too much to contain within her perfectly formed body.

Mine, rippled through Jackson's thoughts. *My woman.* He half growled, half groaned. Not likely. Not now and certainly not later, after he stole the Orb from her.

CHAPTER FIFTEEN
MISTAKES WERE MADE

"Cac," Drakkina cursed on a breath as her unfocused eyes picked out the details of human misery swirling in the shadows of her scrying bowl. The future was still unstable, too easily swayed toward the darkest of outcomes.

She imagined herself sitting cross-legged on the stone table in the center of the ten soaring monoliths that had stood since being erected under the direction of druids nearly two millennia ago. Clouds of vapor hovered about her as if they held their own consciousnesses, charged with potential. Every movement of every living thing influenced the currents forming in the future wash of gray. Sometimes the vapor would swirl in upon itself and sometimes it would billow out as the past blew against the future, influencing it.

She sat between moments in an amorphous soup of non-existence. The thin planes of time formed an intricate web around her as she rested in the empty space reserved for the future. It was here that she could scry the most clearly, see into the possible events to come.

Dragonflies rested on her silk robes. The energy to create their lithe forms was so minute that she conjured them as easily as she pretended to breathe. She closed her eyes.

"Dearest Earth Mother, forgive me," she prayed. "Help me help your world, your children. Free them from their hideous fates." *Free me from mine.* She opened her eyes to stare into her bowl and gasped at the man's face hovering there.

His jawline was firm and covered with a short beard. Eyes of blue stared back at her, eyes tinged with gold and laughter. She reached forward as if to sift her fingers through his soft waves of hair but stopped above the water. Drakkina couldn't breathe. The weight of the image was too heavy. The man smiled at her gently and whispered something through the mist, his lips forming declarations, making oaths he could not keep.

Drakkina blinked against the pain. Why did the Earth Mother show him? What torture was this?

"Eógan," she whispered and blinked to clear the moisture from her sight. She should close her eyes, not let him inside where he'd weaken her. She had to be strong to win this war for humankind, to exact her revenge on the monster who'd taken her love. Yet she couldn't close her eyes, not when she could stare into his face, memorizing the curve of his cheek, the slope of his nose, the length of his lashes, the small lines at the corners of his eyes.

"Why?" she asked with a hitch. "Why show him to me?" As Drakkina stared into the eyes of the man she'd lost, his eyes narrowed slightly. The twinkle of humor glinted sharper, the blue darkening and spreading until only a pinpoint of black sat in the middle. Eógan's hair lengthened and his beard grew, snaking down toward his chest, icing to crisp white.

Drakkina leaped back, nearly falling from her imagined perch as she viewed the malicious face of cruel, demonic power.

"Semiazaz," she hissed. "Deceiver, thief of souls, devil!" The demon's face reflected brutal triumph. He smiled softly, his lips moving in direct imitation of Eógan's words.

Drakkina shook her head and spit into his face. "No more! Show me no more!" With a flip of her hand, Drakkina upended the wide scrying bowl, sending it flying off the table to fall amongst the buttercups and cornflowers, waving in their illusion around the base of the stone table.

She purged a long, open-lipped sob into her palms, releasing a flood of loss and soul-twisting grief to engulf her, drown her. For long minutes she surrendered to the anguish she had ignored for so long that she'd thought it had disappeared. It hadn't.

Stomped down pain didn't dissolve with avoidance. It waited, a bomb, ticking patiently, waiting for the chance to detonate. Pain must be extracted like millions of fragments of piercing shrapnel from all parts of one's existence. It was impossible to extract them all.

Drakkina sobbed, her hands wet, her heart sore. "Eógan," she whispered, his face renewed in her memory. "I'm sorry. I wanted too much." She wiped a worn cloth over her face and inhaled the fragrance of soft pine and summery warmth. She traced a finger along the faded lines of color in the binding cloth they'd used at their wedding as her dragonflies danced around her, caressing her hair and face with feathery wings. Drakkina tipped her chin up, her eyes to the gray swirls of space between the lines creating the woven landscape of time.

"Earth Mother," she whispered and felt her heart grow strong as she inhaled a cleansing breath. Despite her sins, the goddess of creation had indeed answered Drakkina's prayer. Drakkina's tears had forged her soul, beaten it with memories into something stronger. Eógan's face sat clear once more in her mind, the reason she would defeat this coven. To save the world, yes, to save herself from a torturous rebirth and death, of course, but also to deliver vengeance against the beast who'd taken her love.

———◦◦◦———

Kailin stood in the predawn light pushing her shirttails farther into her trousers, which had come askew. She rolled her shoulders and twisted side to side, stretching sore muscles from riding and sleeping on the sand. One camel blinked in her direction but didn't move otherwise. "Too early for you," she whispered as she walked over to him. Kailin ran a finger along its curved snout to between the beast's ears. They flicked as she scratched absently.

Where was Jackson? Her stomach tightened at the niggling thought that he might have left her during the night. Which was ridiculous since she barely wanted him on this expedition. Kailin turned in a tight circle and stopped, her exhale full of unacknowledged relief.

The outline of a large man stood along the ridge, wide-brimmed hat, broad shoulders, long nose of a gun held along a straight leg. Kailin stepped from the shelter of the camels and retrieved the long jacket she always wore on expedition. It was tailored, cut like a woman's riding coat, but it was formed from butter-soft leather. She caught at her hair, blowing around her face, and stared in his direction.

As if Jackson felt her gaze, he turned. The sun slid like a thin rail along the sand at his feet, burning upwards, breaking into dawn in the east. Their gazes connected for a long moment before Jackson turned once more for a quick scan of the surrounding dunes and step-slid down the hill back toward their camp. Kailin scooted behind a dense set of bushes that they'd assigned as their privy and managed to relieve herself and wash before Jackson finished his round of the perimeter and returned.

"No villains?" Kailin asked as he stepped up. She worked fingers through her hair, weaving it into a loose braid to fall down her back.

A smile curved his lips. "None beyond myself."

She snorted softly and tied a scrap of fabric to the end of her braid. "We better get started." She glanced at Qeb, who was still snoring.

"Aye, aye captain," Jackson said, his gaze traveling down her instead of jumping right into preparations. There was appreciation in his face.

She picked up her scarf and snapped it to scatter away the sand. "What?"

"I will have to get you a Stetson when we return," he said and touched the brim of his tan hat. "Nothing keeps the sun and rain off the face better." He nodded toward her outfit. "And it would match your gear." Perfect white teeth flashed from his smile.

Kailin tipped her head to the side, studying the rugged man. "But then I'll look like a cowboy." Her tight mouth relaxed as she watched him tie a brightly colored bandana around his collar. His smile was contagious.

He nodded to her rounded expedition hat. "Camel herder or cowboy," he said and shrugged with a full smile. "Not too far off."

Kailin pointed to him. "Treasure hunter." Then she touched the tip of her finger to her own chest. "Archeologist. Very different creatures."

Jackson stepped closer. Would he kiss her again? Out here in the open, the dawn light revealing them to... Well, there wasn't anyone there except the sleeping guide. He leaned his face closer to hers, and her lips parted slightly in the shadow of his wide-brimmed hat.

He shook his head slowly. "Actually, Kailin, I don't think we are very different at all." His hand came up and he rubbed a thumb over her cheek before moving past her toward the blackened circle of their spent fire.

Kailin inhaled a shaky breath that she hid by looking down to check her pocket for her expedition notebook. It was there, tucked inside with two five-inch sharpened pencils. She concentrated on the thought of cool water keeping her pebble of power from expanding.

"Yalla," Jackson said and kicked Qeb's foot as he walked by toward the camel he'd been riding. The guide snorted and jerked upward, his blurry eyes scanning the camp like he'd forgotten where he'd bedded down for the night. He scratched his head and stretched.

After a quick bite of bread and figs, Kailin stepped up to her kneeling camel. She stretched down to touch her toes, enjoying the pull of the muscles down the backs of her legs. Rolling up through the length of her back she twisted, and her gaze fell on Jackson.

He stood near his camel, arms crossed, legs braced, watching. Qeb was nowhere to be seen. Before she could turn back Jackson was already striding across the distance.

"I can help you get settled," he offered.

"I'll be fine." She grabbed hold of the leather and fabric saddle and pulled upon the pebble from behind her breastbone that would help her rise. But it dissolved away instantly and completely as Jackson's hands fell on either side of her hips. He lifted her swiftly across the colorfully tasseled saddle. She huffed as she straightened, placing her spread legs in the familiar places. "I could have done that."

"And let Qeb and anyone else who may be watching see you levitate over a camel." He gave one shake of his head, and his gaze darted down to where he pulled on the saddle's straps, adjusting and tightening, brushing against her calf.

He moved to the camel's head. "Bayokav."

Kailin clenched her thighs together as the camel's back legs straightened, throwing her forward. An unsuspecting rider might be dislodged but not Kailin, who had been raised on camels. The beast's front legs then straightened, pushing her back as it stood, her perch now nearly ten feet high.

Jackson patted the camel's jaw and looked up at Kailin, the grin on his unshaven face giving him the look of a scoundrel. "Somehow you're even graceful on the back of a rising camel. And those britches suit you. Layers of skirts and fluff must feel like manacles on a woman. Holds you down." He tilted his head. "Is that why you like expeditions?"

Kailin felt warm inside at the praise, but she kept her words icy. "I never said I like expeditions."

"You didn't have to. You explore all over Scotland and seem unusually content sleeping on the ground before a fire on a desert."

She looked down from her perch to meet his gaze. "I like expeditions because there are far fewer people out in the wild. And I don't like people."

Her ice-sharpened words did not seem to shock him. He smiled and tipped his hat. "We have that in common too." Turning, he strode to his own camel.

Qeb was already seated on his camel with the fourth one tethered behind. He waved the back of his fingers as if he shooed them forward. *Good Lord!* Had he been watching all along?

Kailin shielded her eyes against the piercing sun where it glared over the dunes now. She would keep the sun to her left this morning, in the east as they traveled south toward the outcropping of rock at the end of the hills that snaked back in toward the Nile's banks. To a sunken spot where the Nile had probably flooded hundreds of times since the tomb that she and Anthony had been trapped in had originally been dug.

The flood waters might still be too high to attempt the original entrance. Each year the Nile flooded to its highest in September. It was near the end of September, and the floodplains would still be full. She would have to enter near where she'd exited twenty years ago. A shiver tickled through her at the memory. Arms numbing to the tips of her fingers, her heart jumped into a panicked race. *Not me*, she corrected and breathed deeply. It was Jackson's job to crawl underground.

Kailin tapped her camel with the small crop, and it rolled forward, blinking its long lashes. She made clicking noises and patted its neck. She liked camels. Their lumbering gait was often mistaken for stubbornness, yet their feet and bodies combined into vessels that could maneuver through the extremes of the Sahara with relative ease. The camel's body swayed as his wide toes padded across the shifting sand of the landscape.

They climbed out of the gully and into the brightness of another crisp autumn morning on the Egyptian desert. As Kailin buttoned her leather jacket against the chill, she knew that she'd be shrugging out of it before too long, once the sun baked the crystals beneath them.

Jackson's camel strode briskly toward her, wide steps that caught up with her slow sway. "So where was your ghost last night?" he asked. "We could have used her."

Kailin kept her gaze forward. "She seems to show up when it suits her agenda."

"Do you believe her? That she's saving the world from demons?"

Did she? "She's passionate about it. Those who have passion for something are either captivated by that something or insane," she said, glancing at him.

He chuckled and adjusted his hat. "Is that your definition of passion then? Something that captivates you or makes you insane?"

Kailin shrugged. "Perhaps. Both make you lose control."

Jackson rode for several rocking steps before speaking. "You can't abide the loss of control, can you?" he said softly, his voice like brushed velvet.

"You've seen the havoc my loss of control can wreak." Her gaze slid toward him but then back out across the desert.

"So you avoid all passion."

"Unfettered emotion is passion and insanity." She shook her head. "I practice control for the sake of those around me." She lifted an eyebrow and looked sideways toward him. "For the sake of the world." She smiled grimly. Let him think on that for a while. He didn't know how much power she had inside. She barely knew herself. How could she safely explore it? No, it was best to practice constant restraint. Maybe Drakkina knew the extent of the damage she could render.

They rode through the day, even eating in the sway of the gentle beasts that seemed like they could meander forever. Sometimes Kailin swore her camel seemed asleep as his knobby legs propelled him forward across the baking sands.

She'd removed her jacket but was glad for the long linen sleeves to keep the sun from burning her skin. The scarf shielded her face and neck with its gauzy white length.

Occasionally Kailin would glance over at Jackson, who swayed casually in the saddle like a man accustomed to the boredom of a long ride across sameness. His hat sat low over his brow, shielding the sun from his eyes. A white bandana wrapped around his neck with the same protective effect as her long scarf

Kailin turned her attention back to the blue sky, the rays of sun shooting down, the smooth hills of windblown sand, the outcropping of rocks and occasional discarded remains of past expeditions. Her mind lost interest after four hours of the same sight, the same rolling gait, the same sultry sun. Even the constant watch for the villains from the night before dulled as time rocked onward with the steps of the camel. It was as if they sailed across a sea of sand, watching for land ahead.

A length of blond hair that had tugged free touched her cheek and tickled across her lip. Kailin caught it, returning it to the confines of her scarf. She ran her tongue over her lip to banish the itch that the tickle had started. The memory of Jackson's taste stirred in her mind. His tongue had touched her there, explored her lips and the line in between. Strong yet gentle, he'd teased a response from her easily, melting her ice as quickly as the desert sun could melt an icicle.

Kailin turned in her seat to find Jackson staring at her. She caught her breath and reached to hold tightly to the pebble of her magic that pulsed inside her. Jackson nodded, touching the front brim of his hat.

She jerked her gaze back out to the rolling hills of sand. *Good Lord!* It was as if the blasted man could read her thoughts. He couldn't have seen her lick her lip or the blush that had risen in her cheeks. She let her breath out in a long, silent sigh, determined not to think about the cut of Jackson's shirt across his wide shoulders, the thickness of his wheat-colored hair, the strength of his jaw and hands. She exhaled once more and purposely focused on the terrain.

Ugh. How did Anthony stand it? Hours and hours of watching nothing but sand? Her gloriously green Scotland was far superior in transitions. Mountains, forests, weather, all of it full of challenges and changes. Here the challenge was sameness, cut edges of tan sand, chasing winds, slow ups and downs of stinging crystal that moved under the invisible hand molding the hills and valleys. Slow endurance saved the soul on the Sahara, which was why the camel flourished here.

Kailin reached into the leather bag tied to the colorful saddle and retrieved her favorite novel, *Pride and Prejudice*. She flipped through the worn pages until she found the description of Elizabeth Bennet's loud and hectic family: four sisters, an abysmally inappropriate mother, and a patient father. Large and mostly accepting of one another, Kailin read the familiar words half with envy and half with curiosity. What a different life hers would have been if she'd indeed been surrounded by her sisters, sisters that did exist out there somewhere in time, a place to which Drakkina could travel and possibly take her.

Drakkina, she called in her mind. *Are you about? Where are you?* She waited, but her birthmark did nothing. Kailin concentrated on the small dragonfly shape and imagined her pebble moving toward it, to lie upon it, opening and growing slightly.

The tingle that shot up her arm surprised her and she inhaled sharply.

"What is it?" Jackson said, his gun already out of its holster as he pushed his camel closer behind her.

"My birthmark."

In front of them, waves of heat lifted from the uniform crystal landscape. The image undulated and shifted into the folds and creases of a face. Large eyes sank into the hill with shaped ridges for eyebrows. A nose pushed out like a mountain range down the length of the hill to molded lips out of sand. The sand had been sculpted into a familiar face.

Kailin rubbed at her arm where the birthmark blazed softly like someone scratching at a sunburn. Jackson pushed the brim of his hat back and leaned forward along the camel's saddle. "Bloody hell."

CHAPTER SIXTEEN
NO PASSION

"Daughter of Gilla, I am here." Several dragonflies launched out of clear air to encircle Kailin. She watched, mesmerized, by the disembodied face molded from sand, the lips moving with her words. The entire face must be twenty feet tall across the rise of a sand hill. The camels flicked their ears and blinked as their riders halted them. Qeb bowed low over his camel's neck, whispering what sounded like a prayer,

"Where were you last night?" Jackson asked quietly next to her. "We had a nighttime visit you could have warned us about."

Drakkina frowned. "I have things to do." She waved a hand toward them. "I see you survived. You are aware of the threat now. Between your guns and Kailin's power, I doubt any mortal creature could kill you if you pay attention. Watching for the immortal threat is my purpose." She looked closely between them. "Have you two realized your attachment yet?"

Kailin's stomach clenched. "Mister Black is helping me find a relic that I will trade for my father's life. There is no...attachment happening."

"It will happen eventually," she said. The sand shifted so that she appeared to shake her head. "You are beautiful. He is rugged, strong, and handsome. You should give in to the attraction between you two, the passion," she instructed. How could eyes made from sand look piercing? The camels walked sideways up the dune and Drakkina's face sank back into the slope.

"Kailin does not like passion," Jackson commented. Kailin cut him a sharp look.

"Doesn't like passion? Ha!" echoed in the wind. Drakkina reappeared as a floating form up ahead. "You have your parents' blood in you, daughter of Gilla and Druce. Passion forged their power." The spirit's hand flapped toward her. "It forged you and your sisters. Passion is what fuels hope, love, the core of humanity. Not like it? Then you should say that you don't like life."

"Of course I like life," Kailin said, her eyes and lips tight. "And hope and all those wonderful elements of happiness. I merely said passion for me is dangerous, akin to waving a lit taper near explosives."

"Perhaps you need to explode first and then judge the results," Drakkina said, a twinkle in her eye.

Jackson coughed, and Kailin gripped her pebble of magic hard as her blush rolled up her neck like a rising tide of lava. "The world may not withstand it," Kailin grumbled.

"Nonsense," Drakkina rebuffed. "Your magic does no harm when that man touches you." She pointed at Jackson. "I would say that if you want to ever delve into the carnal world of the flesh, he would be the one to do so with."

Kailin's eyes closed as she fought the fire prickling her skin. After a moment she blinked them open but stared straight ahead. She wouldn't, couldn't look behind at Jackson. Certainly, he'd heard

Drakkina's pronouncement. The tactless crone hadn't shut him out of any conversation thus far.

"To where are you journeying?" Drakkina's gaze scanned the surrounding dunes.

"To find the artifact I mentioned," Kailin said, with a good dose of condescension.

"I see you've been practicing control."

Kailin gave the slightest nod, her lips still pinched.

"Only one brush fire," Jackson said, bringing Kailin's glare. It only made the grin on his face spread. "She seems to have an affinity for flames."

"I don't just set things on fire. I can produce water also," Kailin defended. "If there is any to be found in the air. I also move things."

Jackson shrugged. "When you lose control, you tend to set things on fire."

Drakkina pinched her lips and frowned. "If the power gets away from you during a battle with the coven, you could do more harm than good." Her pale gaze shot toward Jackson. "She will be a target above her sisters. She holds the most power; once the demons realize that, they will attack her first. If they kill her and strip it away, we haven't a chance of winning."

A tremor slid along Kailin's back at the spirit's words. Not only could she fail herself if she lost control, but she would also fail Anthony and the entire human race if she didn't learn how to properly control her mother's gift. Or rather, her mother's curse.

"When is this battle supposed to happen?" Jackson asked, his casual tone replaced by a sharp dryness that reminded Kailin of a cobra ready to strike.

"It is coming," Drakkina answered. "Sooner than I originally thought. The demons are better attuned to what to search for among the lines of time. They know you will all return to the stone circle where the slab awaits."

"The stone table," Kailin said, watching Drakkina closely.

Drakkina nodded. "It has served as many things. The table in your family home for one, but it was created before the stone circle was formed, a sacred place dedicated to the Earth Mother. Some have said it was the Earth Mother's laboring place as she gave birth to the world. The ring was erected by her priests in the generations that followed. The priests wove great magic between them, protective magic. If the stones fall to Semiazaz's coven, the stone table itself will be turned to the dark and used for sacrifices to the demons."

"How do you know all this?" Kailin asked, suspicion evident in her tone.

Impatience pinched along the spirit's features. "I have a bowl which I use to scry into the future. I see many outcomes. The clearer the vision in the bowl, the more likely that outcome will come to be."

"And the demons taking over the world..." Jackson started.

"Is the clearest of any," Drakkina said, her brows pinched. Kailin glimpsed sadness, regret, and anger in her changing face before the woman's gaze snapped back to her. "You have a destiny, Kailin, daughter of Gilla. One that will either save or destroy humankind. You must master your power, or it will be torn away and used to master you."

"Then teach me," Kailin said. Drakkina smiled, the darkness bleaching away to hope. Had the woman really thought she'd send her away? "Did your bowl show me...not cooperating, refusing to learn?"

Drakkina's gaze shifted slightly to Jackson. "It is one outcome that leads to her rapid death at the hands of the coven."

Kailin turned in her seat to follow Drakkina's gaze to Jackson. His handsome face had hardened beneath the brow of his hat. The set of his jaw reminded Kailin of the steely granite outcroppings in Scotland. "Teach her," he clipped, his gaze leveling away from Drakkina to meet Kailin's direct stare. "We cannot lose her."

"Agreed," Drakkina said.

"Are there weapons besides magic that can be used against them?" Jackson asked, his gaze shifting back to the floating apparition.

"You're the first warrior to ask." She paused as if considering his question. "There are objects, but they too involve magic. However, I do not scry a positive outcome at all without all of Gilla's daughters and their soul mates in the circle. If even one is missing, the outcome is horror." She shook her white hair. "So, you all have something to do with fighting the demons."

"Us, the soul mates," Jackson said. "You've seen me there?"

"Yes," Drakkina said with slow distinction so that the ending *s* carried.

Jackson didn't say anything, didn't smile. Kailin certainly didn't expect him to yell out a proposal to wed and become her soul mate. Yet it would have been nice if he'd teased a bit like before, as if he thought the idea of wedding her wasn't soul-shrinkingly terrible. Instead, the stone-cold set of his shoulders and the firm grip of his mouth made Kailin think of the wild horses in the States that would rather be whipped than take a bit in their mouths.

"You will be there or the world as we know it will perish." Drakkina's ominous voice resounded around them as if it came from the infinite number of sand particles in the surrounding dunes. It faded and so did the tingling in Kailin's birthmark.

The camels whined and twitched their ears. Qeb continued his prayers, his camel following Jackson's as they resumed their walk across the desert.

They traveled southwest for several more minutes while Kailin waited for someone other than herself to say something. Even an Arabic comment from Qeb could start a conversation. Kailin tightened her lips as she subdued the tight ball of power in her chest that begged to leach from her.

"Just because," she started, the pent-up pressure blasting the words from her mouth. She paused and dropped to a slow, distinct whisper. "Just because you might be at the stone circle for this hard-to-believe, end-of-world battle, even standing next to me, doesn't mean we have to be..."

"Soul mates? I think the fact that your magic doesn't work on me backs up her claim."

"I was going to say together, together forever, or in a relationship, or whatever."

"I think soul mate insinuates a relationship," he said with flat indifference.

Damn that tone. She'd rather hear a roguish joke from him than apathy. As if she was trying to tie him to her, trick him into wedding her.

Kailin threw her hands in the air and huffed. A small twist of sand blew off a dune to her right and she clamped down on the lightning surging below her skin. She gritted her teeth. "You can leave at any time, Mister Black."

"I wouldn't dare abandon the world, Doctor Whitaker. I happen to live in it."

"I'll send word for you when Judgment Day comes. I'm sure a powerful"—she indicated the warm air in front of them—"spirit, crone, witch, whatever she is, can get you to my stones posthaste to help us save the day. Until then, feel free to cut and run."

His eyes continued to survey the sand in front of them. "You still need me, unless you've suddenly purged your severe claustrophobia."

"I'll blow the whole mountain side away and lift up the Orb from the ruins."

He adjusted his hat to block the sun better. "Blowing apart a mountain is difficult to hide. What a powerful weapon to have under control." They rode silently for a minute before he called her.

"Kailin."

She turned in her saddle to see him. "What?"

Jackson rubbed his mouth, sliding his palm over his jaw as he met her gaze. "Every government in the world will target Anthony and you, either to force you to do their bidding by threatening your family or to kill you so that you can't be used against them. No, you won't expose yourself that way. You need me to crawl in the dirt."

She stared hard-lipped at him. Pressure behind her eyes made her blink. She looked back out over the dunes. "Fine. Bring me the Orb, take your treasure, and I'll see you when the spirit brings you to the stones. We need have nothing further to do with each other."

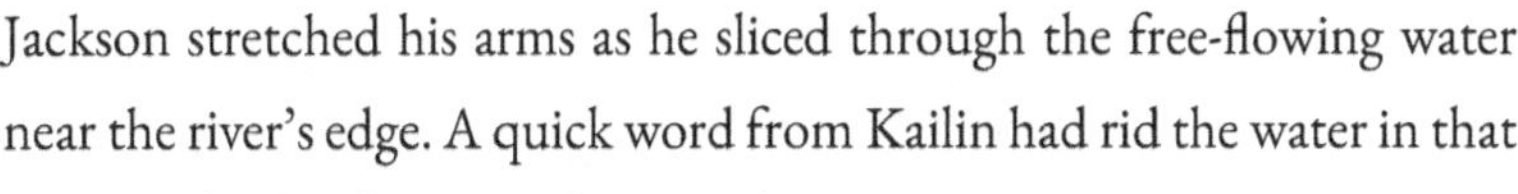

Jackson stretched his arms as he sliced through the free-flowing water near the river's edge. A quick word from Kailin had rid the water in that stretch of Nile of crocs and critters.

Kailin had gone farther upriver to bathe behind a bush that he'd first inspected for fiends and kidnappers, all while she'd rolled her eyes. She could certainly handle herself unless they surprised her. She'd changed into a fresh shirt and was letting her golden hair dry in the breeze as she walked back toward their resting caravan where Qeb took each camel to the river to drink.

Jackson watched a golden curl dance along Kailin's cheek as if it beckoned him. She had a graceful walk, even on the uneven ground. As if she'd adapted to the sands under her feet. Her gaze roamed the dunes off to the right where small twisters of sand danced. Was she practicing her control? Bloody hell, what amazing power she had inside. If anyone discovered it, they'd use her.

Tension weighed at his shoulders, and he rubbed the back of his neck. Wasn't that what he was doing? Using her? To get to the Orb. He sank back into the cool water to rinse the soap from his limbs, his gaze never leaving her. Damp patches from her hair made the fabric of her shirt cling to her body. The water turned the white shirt nearly transparent to show her thin corset beneath as it supported her full breasts. He adjusted his cock underwater as it came to life despite the cold.

Could they possibly be soul mates? Was that possible when one used the other, when one disliked the other without even knowing the whole horrible truth? Was there any way to fulfill his mission without making her hate him? Was his mission worth risking the whole world?

Jackson's toes sank into the mud and he stood, shaking his head so that his hair sent droplets in a shower around him. His eyes went directly back to her.

Kailin drank from a canteen, and he watched her slender neck work. She was breathtaking. He longed to kiss that smooth skin, taste the mix of water and slight salt. Smell her floral soap and wrap his hands in her soft tresses. If only she wouldn't set up barbed wire between them.

Jackson inhaled and waded toward shore. Kailin studied her fingernails as he emerged and grabbed a clean shirt from his pack. He let the breeze dry his skin.

She looked up at the sharp hill where rocks and sand had caved inward. From the outside the slope appeared as any eroded bank of sand along the Nile. "What we seek is there."

"The Orb?" He walked up to stand next to her, his shirt still in his hand.

She nodded. "There's a...hum of energy, familiar." She turned to meet his eyes. "I remember the feel. It's similar to the stones in Scotland. Like there's something near made of the same magic."

Her gaze dropped to his chest, and he watched her swallow. "Put your shirt on, Mister Black. We aren't heathens, even on expedition." She returned her gaze to the slope. "Anthony calls the hidden tomb the secret monument to his greatest treasure." She spoke quickly like she was nervous. "I am that treasure, his little Cleopatra, powerful enough to move mountains," she said.

"That you are," he answered and watched her take a breath as if she were trying to control herself. Her lips were parted and despite the dry heat, they looked soft.

"How should we enter?" she asked, her words louder than needed. She cleared her throat, lowering it. "I could dig with my power."

Jackson forced his gaze from her to the water that had been biting away at the bank. "The original entry is completely caved in and flooded," Jackson said.

"I'm sure that the bastards who took Anthony know that, which is why they've gone to the trouble to drag me here by kidnapping my father."

Kailin looked back to him, her gaze frozen on his chest. "Do you intend to continue half naked? Your skin will burn."

"Thank you for your concern. I was but drying off." He shifted his gaze to the white shirt molding to her breasts. Even in trousers, there was no missing the fact that she was a woman. "I prefer to dry before throwing a shirt on, so it won't stick to every nook and cranny."

Kailin gasped and turned, plucking at her thin cotton shirt while he threw his on over his still-damp head.

Qeb called behind them where he stood with the camels, their jaws drippy and continually chewing.

Jackson pointed and Qeb led one of the camels behind him away from the river. The others would follow. "We'll make a camp a ways back from the bank, in the shelter of the hill. Far enough to not be easy prey for the crocs."

Kailin scanned the free-flowing water. "If one comes up, I'll push him back."

"Better yet, roast croc is delicious." Jackson grabbed some of the bags that Qeb had lowered from the pack camel and tromped through the grass. His still-damp skin pulled against the thin cotton of his white shirt. He hoped the eyes he felt on his back were green-blue, framed with long lashes, and not narrowed in suspicion.

Delve into the carnal world of the flesh, Drakkina had recommended. It seemed unlikely Kailin would take the advice. If she did, it better be before they found the Orb. That didn't give him much time.

CHAPTER SEVENTEEN
DIGGING

Evening descended quickly in the shadow of the hill. Kailin straightened from her crouch near the saddlebag and stretched her back in a long arch. Her gaze drifted across the sand dunes. She would wait until darkness hid her abilities before digging in from the top. The attack last night proved they were being watched. She didn't quite know how she would locate the mysterious Orb of Life or why there was a dragonfly etched into it.

Dragonfly. Kailin froze. Did the Orb carry Drakkina's mark?

Jackson drew his gun, eyes trained on the dune line. "You saw something?"

"No."

Drakkina said the mark of the dragonfly on Kailin was hers. Did she know something of the Orb? "I thought of something I forgot to ask the apparition." She lowered back to the small fire.

"What was that?" He slowly re-holstered the gun, though kept his gaze far-reaching. The fire played off his features, cutting shadows across his strong jaw.

Kailin looked away. "She might know something about the Orb. Anthony mentioned that it has a dragonfly on it. Like my birthmark."

She flaked off a bite of the roasted fish Jackson had caught earlier. He'd insisted that he catch them without her magic. She'd schooled the fish underwater toward him. His eyes had narrowed when three fish jumped right into his hands but didn't say anything.

"Interesting," he murmured. "When do we take our walk?"

Kailin's eyes shifted to the dozing camel owner. She placed the rest of her fish in her mouth and licked her finger clean. "Now." Kailin stretched upward, lengthening the tight muscles of her shoulders and hamstrings after the full day of riding.

Jackson didn't follow but watched her stretch.

"What?" she asked impatiently.

"Still trying to remove the image of your lips sucking your fingers." He blinked and shook his head as if clearing his vision.

Kailin's chest squeezed simultaneously with her lips, yet relief gave her the room to inhale and release an exaggerated sigh as she rolled her eyes. The day of stilted apathy was over. Had he decided a course of action during his silence? Take his treasures and run or try to seduce her first?

"You're impossible," she muttered and grabbed a canteen of cooled, boiled water.

Jackson stood and rattled off instructions to Qeb, who nodded with his eyes closed.

Walking away from the small fire into the dark, cold air was like diving into a black lake. Kailin buttoned her leather duster and wrapped her scarf around her neck to keep the breeze from sparking more goose bumps down her chest. She refused to look behind her, but glanced overhead at the stars. Orion held ready. Cassiopeia sat upon her sideways throne. Cold and distant, her friends watched as she hiked up the dune. She listened to the deep tread and sliding sand of Jackson following her.

Coming to the top of their valley, she stood to catch her breath after the steep climb. Her gaze slid parallel to the Nile to the slightly sunken plateau under the star-sprinkled blackness. She breathed the refreshing air, teasing out the memories of that night near the beginning of her life when she stood here trembling despite Anthony's jacket. She'd been so young, Anthony guessed four years. Only glimpses of the memories remained, that and a tremor of the panic that nearly blew her and the hill completely apart. The river had raged that night, flooding the land up the base of the hill, sluicing away the erected braces for the dig.

Anthony had calmed her and helped her say the words to make the hole fill in with sand and dirt, burying the evidence of their unnatural escape. Then he'd scooped her up, held her close, and promised to care for her. That she remembered. She'd been lost, terrified, and totally vulnerable and she'd taken his instant love to heart.

Kailin's eyes welled with tears at the thought of her father's worry. He must know that his kidnappers would come for her. His concern for his little Cleo would pain him more than his discomfort. Whatever the Orb was, she'd find it and trade it. Anthony was worth much more than any treasure.

"Here?" Jackson asked near her.

She pointed to the low point. "The tomb sits under that dip."

"How far down?"

How far had she flown upward, propelling herself and Anthony out of the hole? "I'm not certain. I was only four years old when I last saw it."

Jackson walked forward, his shovel balanced on one shoulder.

"I can dig much faster." Kailin hurried after him. "Stand back. I wouldn't want to bury you."

Jackson stopped short of the dig site and leaned on the shovel. "Try not to throw the treasure out with the sand."

"I don't intend to dig like a dog after a bone," she said, stopping beside him. Extraction required finesse, not speed.

She held her arms straight out before her with the backs of her hands together, even with the sandy ground. Taking a deep breath, she concentrated on allowing a small amount of her magic out of her imagined pebble. She threaded the magic through the night to the dark, sandy ground about twenty feet before them, and opened her arms. "Part."

The sand moved, the sound grinding as the individual crystals of quartz slid against each other, pushing outward from the center, deepening the sunken spot. She moved sand until it mounded up on either side of the center. Was she digging deep enough? Where was the Orb? Where should she dig down?

Behind her eyes, Kailin imagined the dragonfly birthmark linked to the pebble of magic. The brown mark moved its wings, nearly shattering her concentration, but she caught it on an even breath. The small dragonfly lifted, flying outside her. She opened her eyes and followed the zipping spot of shadow over the pale sand. It hovered over the dip she'd parted. She moved closer. "Where?" Kailin murmured. "Seek your mate," she whispered so soft it was as if her lips fluttered over nothingness.

The shadow shot downward toward the far side of the plateau, diving into the sand. Kailin anchored her eyes to the spot and ran over to it. "Here," she said. "The Orb is somewhere below here."

Jackson stopped beside her. "You know that? How?"

She glanced at him. "Magic." Then looked back out to the spot that seemed to call to her. "Twist," she said and a mini tornado formed over the spot. It drilled into the dune, throwing a stream of sand and dirt up into the air.

Jackson cursed softly with a chuckle. She smiled at the precision. She'd been practicing all day as they rode. Small tornados at a distance so as not to be noticed. *Twist and out*, she thought as she drilled downward, breaking through layers of sand and rock. The tornado slammed into something hard about four feet down and dissolved.

Kailin held a stick she'd brought up with her from the camp. "Fire." The end blinked aflame. Jackson stood with her at the edge of the three-foot-diameter hole.

He tilted his head to look at her, his smile one of pride and amazement. "I'd say, Doctor Whitaker, that's the ceiling of a tomb." Sandy blocks fit together in tight lines.

Kailin smiled back at Jackson. "Thrilling, isn't it?"

He laughed lightly. "I'll make a treasure hunter out of you yet." Jackson took the torch and nodded toward the blocks. "Think you can do something about those?"

Kailin pulled on her magic, expanding it into a long knife-like force. "Cut," she punctuated the "t" at the end like a shot from her mouth. A fissure appeared where she stared, a long line that sliced down through the thick stone, mimicking a surgeon's blade. It followed her gaze as she imagined her pebble of magic cutting along the edges of the hole her tornado had dug. As the rubble gave way she lifted her hands and the rocks flew upward and out of the growing hole, where she held them suspended in silence above.

Jackson held the fire high to illuminate an open area below. The smell of dirt and ancient dust filled Kailin's nose, tickling, reminding her of the panic she'd felt here decades ago. She sucked in, trying to dispel the shadows of fear and...sneezed. The rocks she'd been holding shot outward into the air like a bomb had detonated.

Jackson flung the torch and grabbed her. He threw her to the sand and covered her and his own head as the fist-sized rocks thumped around them. Kailin's breath struggled to squeeze in past his weight. He cursed against her ear as a rock bounced off his back. Kailin had felt it through his chest. Debris continued to rain down on them for several long seconds. Then silence filled with the thump of Jackson's heart. He eased his weight onto his forearms braced on either side of her head and lifted.

"Are you hurt?" he asked but didn't roll away. Kailin blinked against the dust that still floated. His body lay intimately across her and without the cushion of petticoats she could feel all of him. And there was quite a lot of him to feel.

"I am well."

"Good," he said and stared down at her. "Oh, and God bless you."

Kailin couldn't help the grin that answered his smile. It was as natural as a laugh from one's heart. She shifted her gaze to his chin and moved under his weight, but he remained. "I'm sorry about that. I actually may have been able to throw them elsewhere before they hit you if you hadn't touched me."

"It happened rather fast," he said. "And bruises make one interesting."

Her gaze reconnected with his. The heat from his body infused her. The comfortable weight teased her. She was trapped, and her body was rapidly realizing that being Jackson's prisoner felt good. "Are you going to let me up?"

His lips quirked. "I haven't decided."

Kailin let out a small bark of laughter and pushed upward with her hands. Reluctantly, Jackson raised his body and rolled sideways to push up to stand. He reached down, and she grasped his warm, strong hand.

Jackson's eyes nearly sparked with excitement. "Shall we see what the great Doctor Kailin Whitaker has unearthed?"

She wiped her nose with a handkerchief from her duster jacket. "And no more sneezing," she murmured.

The torch had gone out but barely a thought made it relight when Jackson held it upright. He turned in a circle, looking out at the dark hills of sand. Nothing moved. Hopefully the night wind had covered the sound of rocks falling and sand moving.

Jackson maneuvered the flickering glow over the hole. "Perfectly convenient," Jackson complimented. "Without a sore back from hours of digging."

"Only a sore back from a falling rock." Kailin kneeled along the edge with Jackson.

He lowered the torch so that they could see the room below. Dirt and pebbles covered every surface, but she could make out a number of statues and jars lining the back wall, many having fallen over. "I see mosaics and glyphs under that dirt!" Kailin pointed down and to the back. "They could tell us about the Orb buried here, its purpose and how to use it."

"You sound like you want to go in."

She twisted her head to meet his grin. "Maybe. In the light."

His smile turned serious. "You have nothing to fear. Not when you can blast your way out. Come down with me. I want you there when we discover our treasure."

Kailin's stomach flipped about, either from the consideration of going below ground or from Jackson's desire for her to be by his side. The two of them working together to discover the past.

"I would also have you with me, so I know you're safe," he continued.

"I thought you were impressed enough to know that I can take care of myself," she said.

"Bullets can't be stopped if they aren't seen," he answered, his smile gone. He shoved the end of the torch into the sand and walked away from the light, scanning the dunes around them again. The three-quarters moon gave off silvery light.

Kailin knelt over the edge of the jagged hole where she could make out the hint of colors peeking through the dust layers on the walls. When she imagined running her palms over the glyphs, feeling where ancients had laid their own hands, her stomach curled into a ticklish twist. Kailin hung her head. "I can't believe I'm considering it."

All these years Anthony had begged and now, beside a man she knew had lied to her, someone who could mute her powers making her as vulnerable as an ordinary woman, she was preparing to face her insurmountable fear. Somehow though, Jackson made her feel safe.

He walked back over and knelt next to her, taking up the torch once more. "I don't see anyone."

She exhaled long. "I swore I'd never go below ground again."

"If it helps"—Jackson's words were very close to her ear, and her shoulder rose at the tickle—"I promise not to touch you down below."

He held himself away from her now even though he leaned so close it felt as if they touched. A sizzle of awareness slid along Kailin's skin down her neck where his breath feathered. Yet his body didn't touch hers. She could still sense her tight pebble of magic, roped and tied, wrestled into temporary submission.

Kailin couldn't say anything. She swallowed and slowly sat back on her heels. She nodded. "I'll go." By the flicker of torchlight she watched Jackson smile.

"But right now, we're still above ground," Jackson murmured as his gaze delved into her eyes, momentarily flicking to her lips when she wet them with a touch of her tongue slipping between.

Kailin kept her eyes open but didn't pull back. His empty hand brushed her cheek as his face neared. She held her breath, and he caught her chin in a gentle pinch. Kailin's eyes closed as his lips touched.

Crack! Lightning! Hot pain erupted through her skull, slamming her forward into Jackson's arms. "Kailin!" Jackson's voice faded as the night flooded her, swamping her with inky weight.

"Back," she whispered but it was no good. Jackson held her in his arms as she slipped into a pain-free layer between life and death.

CHAPTER EIGHTEEN
BURIED

Floating in a pool of black sludge, Kailin surrendered to the comfort of oblivion. In oblivion there was no time, only quiet comfort and sameness. If boredom surfaced, the mind would prepare to wake. Kailin heard the rush of her breath in and out for several unending cycles. She must be alive if she was breathing. Her head beat in time with her heart. Throbbing. More evidence of life. Oblivion was much more comfortable.

"Bloody fucking bastard!" Jackson's words shot through her sore head. *Wet.* Hot wet trickled down her neck. *Blood?* The thought nearly sent her diving back into the black. "That rock nearly split her head. She could be dying right now!"

A deep calm voice wavered before Kailin where she sat slumped against the warmth of Jackson. She knew it was him because he smelled good, but also because her pebble was nowhere. She rested against him, in his snug embrace, his arms wrapped around her body.

"The Orb of Life is sacred," the detached voice said. It was familiar. Kailin tried to force her eyelids open, but they were too heavy. She contented herself with listening. "It is not meant to be unearthed. We convinced her father of this, but now see that was foolishness. Doctor Anthony Whitaker was only the first to try and take the Orb. But others follow."

"So your plan is to kill off everyone coming to find it?" Jackson asked. "That's one hell of a long murder list."

"It is our sacred duty to protect what must be lost, that which should never have been forged in the first place."

The familiar voice broke through Kailin's groggy mind. *Moghadam!* The large man from Samantha's party. Kailin chiseled a crack in her lids. Like breaking the pressure of a sealed sarcophagus, her lids slid open easily. The light of several torches pierced her sight and she blinked.

"There, she stirs," Moghadam said. "Though it would have been far kinder for her to die instantly. I hear she is terrified of closed spaces."

Nausea gripped Kailin's stomach, either from the crack in her head or Moghadam's cryptic words. Jackson squeezed Kailin gently, cradling her against his chest. He seemed to pull the back of her head into him. Maybe to staunch the bleeding. His efforts hurt and she gasped on a stab of pain. It was then she realized his hands were tied around her front, binding them together. Her wrists were also tied together before her.

"You bloody dung worm, Moghadam!" Jackson swore in Arabic. "You dishonorable cur."

"My honor is sound, Mister Black. How is yours?"

Kailin tried to see past the sharp points of firelight to the faces beyond. There were at least ten men dressed in traditional Bedouin clothing. Keffiyehs encased their heads and long thobes flowed around their bodies where they stood by their horses. Kailin's gaze wove amongst them, but she didn't recognize anyone until she reached Qeb. He stood behind Moghadam in shadow, eyes darting between the large leader, Jackson, and her. He looked incredibly guilty.

"Qeb betrayed us," she mumbled.

"Seems it. I should have been more on guard." Jackson's voice was a rough growl near her ear, restrained fury infused with guilt. "How hurt are you?"

She wasn't sure. "The trickling on my neck seems to be stopping, but my head pounds."

"Bloody hell, Kailin."

"Quite literally," she whispered. "And I can't do anything to help our situation with you strapped to me. Do you think they know that?"

"Not certain," he answered, his lips so close they brushed the spine of her ear. "Qeb's told them that you have some sort of powers which is why they knocked you unconscious first when they attacked." The words rumbled in his chest. "We were bloody easy targets."

"I am as responsible," Kailin countered. She was used to feeling invincible with her magic. But threats stalked her now. Even some that her magic did nothing against, like the cobra if she'd been bitten and the bite of a rock cracking her head when she'd been wrapped up in the touch of Jackson's lips.

They sat in silence, Jackson pressed against her back, keeping the chill from penetrating while Moghadam investigated the hole.

"One shovel," Moghadam said and looked sideways at Jackson. His gaze slid to Kailin and he cocked his head. "One shovel and less than an hour if Qeb is to be believed. That is...unnaturally efficient."

"Let us go, and I won't hurt you," Kailin said and felt Jackson stiffen. "Keep me tied here and you won't make it out of this desert alive."

Moghadam laughed.

"Beware," Qeb said, his eyes open with wary waiting. He glanced around as if he expected to see a wall of sand swallow them in the dark.

"If you could hurt me, you'd have done so," Moghadam said.

"I threw you backwards last night. You and all your men." Kailin's gaze bit into the man's dark, flinty eyes.

Qeb retreated to stand amongst the horses. Moghadam continued to consider her, his features sharpening as he weighed the evidence of her threat. "Again, if you could do something *now*, you would have."

"I will," she bluffed. "Cut me loose and I will give you a chance to survive."

"What of your man?"

"He is not my man," Kailin said indignantly.

"That's not what it looked like when my rock hit your lovely head, lips parted and tipped up to receive his breath."

The villainous men around them kept silent. Kailin ignored the blush rushing across her face. Their torches would be soaring if she weren't tied to Jackson. Then they would know what her wrath meant. She stared directly at Moghadam with hatred in her gaze. Her words came softly, crisp and succinct. "Do not make me angry. You won't like me when I'm angry."

The threat, so pointed and honest, cut through Moghadam's hard smile. "I apologize, lovely lady, but I'm afraid I will test your temper tonight. Perhaps your hatred will lessen your terror. Hold onto that." He nodded to a bulky man nearby. "Lower them in."

"Untie us first," Jackson demanded.

"And have you climb and claw your way back out? No. You two can hold onto each other in the dark as we seal you in with your treasure. Death in each other's arms is rather romantic."

Lower? Down? Into the black hole? Kailin stomped down the terror that churned a swath of cold dread up her throat, but couldn't control the rapid exchange of breath, the hiss of barely subdued panic.

"Slow inhale," Jackson said against her ear. "Slow exhale." His arms tightened around her.

Slow in, slow out. Kailin concentrated on the words, but her breath still came in quick pants, drying her mouth. Stars flickered before her eyes. *Drakkina!* she screamed in her mind. *Drakkina, help us!* The blasted spirit was never around when needed.

"In," Moghadam ordered, and two men moved forward to grab them. Kailin used her leg strength to dig into the ground, but she was weak and so was the sand. It surrendered her easily as they dragged them.

Jackson held her close. "Lean into me when we fall."

Fall! In! Claw back out! Kailin's world shattered into shards of panic. She screamed and kicked backwards in the sand, but the men managed to lift them to the gaping hole in the hill. It was at least a ten-foot drop down, but the fall didn't knife white searing terror through her. It was the dark, engulfing walls. The smell of dirt filtering up. The thin, dusty, inadequate air. Rocks and earth above and around her, closing in on her body. A tomb!

"I've got you," Jackson's firm voice penetrated. "Kailin, I'll catch you. Relax or it will be worse."

For a brief moment she stopped screaming and breathed, processing his words. But then her boot caught the edge of the hole. Sand and pebbles rattled down on the stone floor below. Without the torch, the hole was a gaping mouth ready to swallow them, smothering them in all-consuming night and hopeless insanity. Hyperventilating, Kailin kicked with her boots against the edge until she felt nothing but air. Jackson held her before him on the edge.

"Tuck into me, Kailin!" he rasped. And then...

The hole consumed them with a flash of free-falling breeze. Somehow mid-fall, Jackson pushed forward so that their feet hit first, protecting their backs. Jarring pain crushed the air from her lungs as she slammed onto Jackson's chest, the two of them toppling backwards. He grunted, and she stared up at the torchlight illuminating the hole above like a fiery sun.

Sand rained down, stinging her eyes. She spat and sucked in breath, her vocal cords constricting on their own accord as the exhale narrowed into a scream. She was going to die! But worse than that, she was being buried alive.

Jackson spat out a mouthful of Kailin's hair he'd sucked in. She lay against his chest, staring up at the hole, screaming. This was no tantrum wail of a child or a woman feigning fright to lure the comfort of a man. Kailin's scream was shattering, heart-splitting terror, raw and uncensored. It was worse than the howl of the dying. It was the twisting, squeezing pain of torture.

All Jackson could do was hold her in her trapped position, his arms tied around her, hands bound before them both. He dug his heels against the stone and scooted them backwards so they wouldn't be hurt by the dirt and stones falling as Moghadam's men covered the hole with a slab.

"Throw down a torch!" Jackson yelled up. "It will eat up our oxygen quicker."

Moghadam's face appeared over the edge. "A mercy I think," he yelled over Kailin's screams. The bastard looked unnerved by her intense reaction. Hopefully the memory would haunt his nightmares for the rest of his life. Seconds later a torch dropped down, illuminating the small, half caved-in tomb around them. The slab slid into place, blocking out the stars above.

"Kailin. Love. Close your eyes." She paused for breath that turned to rattling sobs that were in complete contrast to the in-control woman he knew. It twisted his stomach as if a noose squeezed around his middle. "Imagine the bright blue sky above." Jackson used the same soothing tones he'd used with frightened horses back home, the same voice he'd managed during the worst of Cassy's illness. Even as dread crept through him, his voice rolled with a calming caress at Kailin's ear.

"Sparrows flit from an oak at the edge of a forest, but you're out in the open, on a huge prairie with waving grass as high as your knees." Kailin's sobs gentled to a light sniffing as she listened. Her breaths hitched but they held longer in and out. "The blades tickle under your skirts against your knees as you run free in the breeze that bends the grass. Above, white clouds float silently pushed by wind. Your owl circles, searching for a hare or mouse. It is open. You are free."

Jackson felt Kailin draw in a full breath, expanding her lungs. "You smell fresh grasses and the slight tang of coming rain." Jackson's gaze slipped along their tomb as he talked. Porcelain cats laid cracked on the far wall along with Canopic jars possibly holding the mummy's internal organs. Turquoise, red ochre, and gold shone through the dust on the walls, painted depictions of royal hunts, births, and the afterlife.

"You hear the squeak of the prairie dog diving into its burrow as your Tuto shoots down. The bird soars back up looking for easier prey."

He twisted to peer over his shoulder. The original entrance was behind them, caved in and set with years of mud and pressure from the flooding Nile. He glanced around. Surely there were more tunnels leading away from this small room.

"Horses, wild and free, run across the flat land, under the magnificent blue sky," he murmured near her ear and tracked her slower breathing. It was jagged with quick intakes, quivers from the sobs and strain of screaming. But it was slower. "That's it, Kailin. You are under the wide-open sky, safe and free."

The sarcophagus sat along one wall, dust covering the gold and embedded gems.

"Peaceful breezes pull at your hair, and you lay back into the grass to stare up at the passing clouds."

It looked as if the tomb hadn't been raided. Priceless pieces of golden treasure laid scattered with papyrus scrolls and statuary. As his gaze searched and his lips moved in slow, reassuring tones, Jackson's stomach clenched. The Orb must be here. Where was it?

"The breeze blows softly over your arms, and you inhale long, the cool fresh air." Kailin followed his words with a deep draw on the air around them. How many more of those inhales did they have between them? Orb or not, he had to get them out of here.

"Kailin, keep your eyes shut. I have to move us, find something sharp to cut these ropes. Once we're separated, you can easily get us out." The back of her hair brushed his chin as she nodded. "Good. Keep watching the white puffy clouds. Don't try to move. I've got you." She sucked in another slow, long breath. If she struggled it would take longer to get free. And she must be calm when he released them, or her magic would explode the whole tomb around them.

Spears leaned into the back corner. "Let's stand but keep your focus on the wide sky." She pulled her knees in and shifted her weight so they could roll forward into a crouch and then a stand. "Good, I'll guide you. Now shuffle your feet through the tall grasses around us."

"You're good at this," Kailin whispered.

Jackson stopped, a grin touching his dust-dry lips. "Getting in life-threatening positions or talking calmly?"

The smallest of chuckles twitched through her body. "Both, but I was referring to the beautiful description of the prairie."

"It was my home for decades."

"You miss it."

He continued to move them toward the corner with the spears. "Yes."

"Will you go home after this?" she asked.

Jackson opened his mouth, his chin brushing the top of her head, and then closed it again. Would he? It depended on whether his mission was successful or not. Could he ever return home if Cassy didn't survive?

"I don't know yet."

"I'd like to see it," she said.

"You are, right now. Keep focusing on it."

"I am," she said. "Intensely. Yet...I would like to touch the grass for real and breathe that beautiful azure, blue sky."

He inhaled and caught the slight floral scent that still hid in Kailin's hair. "Your smell reminds me of it." Two more steps and he stopped.

She laughed. "You mean the smell of terror and dirt."

Of sweet woman, my woman, rolled through his head. He frowned slightly at the possessive thought. "Of silent grandeur covered by a field of wildflowers."

She didn't answer. Jackson scanned the walls. Where was that damn Orb? It was supposed to give life. Could it give them air?

"There are spears in the corner," he said. "Sharp enough to saw through our ropes." She trembled but let him move them as one to the corner. He could tell the moment she opened her eyes. Her whole body stiffened and her breathing became shallow.

"Only a few moments longer, Atsila," he said.

Kailin kicked one of the spears over so that it hit the floor.

They knelt together. "We need to turn the blade up," she said breathlessly.

"Don't fall on it," Jackson warned. "You've bled enough today."

Kailin pulled her hands apart as far as she could, leaving an inch of rope between. "Relax," Jackson said. "I'll lower you over it." Her body sagged slightly, and he tipped them forward. His muscles contracted, keeping them in the awkward position over the deadly blade. It was his carnal dream to be pressing into her from behind, but it would be in much better circumstances.

He inhaled, pulling on the thinning oxygen to charge his muscles. Kailin knelt over the spearhead as he sawed the binding across the blade. Back and forth, back and forth, he rubbed against her as he rubbed the rope. Without the cushions of the usual skirts, he was sure she could feel him growing against her.

"Good God," Kailin huffed beneath her breath, confirming the thought.

He chuckled though his breath rasped out over the exertion. "I'm not apologizing either."

Back and forth they rocked while the individual lines of twine snapped one by one under the sharp assault against both their bindings. Jackson grunted softly as he strained forward while holding her body back from the blade.

The ancient blade severed the ropes, one right after the other, and Kailin's hands flew apart. Jackson lifted them back from the weapon but held onto her.

"Wait, Kailin. Don't blow us out yet."

"I am getting out now," she snapped, struggling in his grasp. The woman was amazingly strong. Near panic added to it. Her eyes shifted upward like she was already imagining the ceiling blowing heavenward.

"You could destroy this whole tomb if you blow up the hill again. We won't be able to find the Orb. Not to mention the fact that Moghadam and his men aren't far away yet. They'll see us escape and come after us tonight. And I want to have a chance to check your head before you start battling."

After a lengthy pause, Kailin said, "We need more air."

"Agreed," he said and realized that his respiration had increased as his body tried to find more oxygen in the stale air. "A few small holes up to the surface. Can you do that?"

"I think."

"Don't pull the whole thing down on us."

"If you keep making me mad, I might pull the whole thing down on *you*."

"Your dragonfly woman would be quite cross if you kill me before the end of the world."

"Let go of me before we both succumb to low oxygen and die in this bloody hole," she said.

Jackson exhaled long and loosened his grip. He groaned as his overextended arms pulled back. He shook them out as he let them drop from her sides. Loneliness instantly replaced Kailin in his embrace.

Kailin poked one slender finger up toward the dirt, away from the slab. "Hole, out," she demanded and the dirt sucked in on itself, upward, creating a long tubelike hole up through the ceiling. It was only about five inches wide, but it led upward foot after foot. "Out!" she insisted and with one little sound of raining dirt far above, she broke free. "Good

God how far are we buried down?" The pitch of her voice had risen to a shriek. Would Moghadam hear?

"Shhh...they could still be close." He reached for her hand but let her snatch it away. She was too panicked to risk losing her power. But power and panic were a dangerous combination.

"It doesn't matter how far we are down because you, Kailin Whitaker, can get yourself out of anything." He smiled at her and she met his gaze. Fear floated in her eyes. "You can." He nodded and waited until she nodded back with an inhale.

"I'll make a few more holes for air circulation, and we can look the site over before surfacing," she said with stilted calm, but he saw the tremor that passed over her shoulders.

"Good plan," he said although the only treasure he really cared about was the one fabled to bring life to the lifeless, bring health to the sickly, and body to the disembodied. He held the torch high to illuminate the small room as Kailin drilled two more holes.

"Did Anthony say where he thinks the Orb is in here?" he asked.

Kailin pivoted and held out her arms to stop him from traipsing to the back of the medium-sized tomb. "Wait."

Jackson halted, lifting his torch higher to push back the shadows. The room was about twenty feet square. "Anthony would have sprung any traps when he was here before."

She crouched and wiped away the dust that had settled in the cracks of the floor. "It's wise to be cautious around treasure that ancients didn't want robbed. And from what he's told me, he hadn't gotten far at all before the Nile crashed in and cut him off."

Jackson knew all of this, of course, but the Orb was so close. His need swelled up inside him, and he took a few breaths of the air that filtered down. "It's not a large room," he said.

Kailin had gone to the golden sarcophagus that sat near the wall. She ran her fingertips across the dust that had settled all over it. "He became mostly concerned with surviving, and then I dropped in."

"Dropped in?" he asked.

She shook her head without looking at him. "I was four, so I don't remember much of anything besides terror, but Tuto and I appeared here inside the tomb."

Jackson walked slowly to stand with her by the sarcophagus. His gaze followed her fingers as they explored the glyphs under the dust. Her nails were filed into soft curves and remarkably clean. Jackson could imagine her fingertips tracing the lines of his body. *Concentrate, you fool.* But he felt the tug between the Orb and Kailin like the rack, slowly pulling him apart at the bone.

Kailin wiped away the symbols across the top. "'Son of Pharaoh Ramses II and Queen Nefertari, Amun-her-khepeshef, lies here.'" The Egyptian glyphs wrapped around the magnificent sarcophagus, inlaid with semi-precious gems of turquoise and lapis.

"'Gone to Tuat, the underworld,'" Kailin continued, "'to be tested by Anubis and Thoth. If his heart proves worthy, he will pass to the Fields of Hotep.'" She glanced back at him. "Sometimes called the Fields of Offerings. Typical Egyptian mythology."

He held their torch closer. "There." He pointed. "It talks about the Orb."

Kailin's words came quicker with her excitement. "'The great Orb lies with Pharaoh's son, gifted to him by the ancient man from far across the world, protected by the gods. His army stands ready. Take the Orb only if you are prepared to die. You will be stripped of everything, first your clothes, then your skin, then your muscles and sinew down to your bones.'"

"Warnings are always ominous," Jackson said, his gaze scanning the broken pieces of marble beyond. He moved forward, the torchlight pressing into the dense black corner where the Orb may have rolled. Dust still settled from their disruption and the air moving down through Kailin's holes. He looked past life-sized statues of angular guards, a statue of an ox, and what could be a mummified cat.

"The Orb must be here somewhere."

"Wait," Kailin said, but he stepped quickly up to the guards, and a whistle shot in the stillness.

"Stop," Kailin yelled.

CHAPTER NINETEEN
GIFT FOR ONE

Jackson dropped to the floor, several pieces of broken pottery jabbing into his chest and stomach with cutting intensity, and he inhaled some of the dust. He twisted, his gaze flying to Kailin. He grabbed the guttering torch he'd dropped and pushed up, spinning in a crouch. Brandishing the light before him, he saw wide eyes in her moon-pale face. Her gaze was on a spear held unnaturally motionless in the air. Its deadly iron point was aimed right where he'd been standing. "Kailin?"

She dropped her extended arms, and the six foot long, lethal spear clattered to the rubble-strewn ground.

"You're not hurt?" he asked and stood, going to her. She shook her head, and his relief felt like a herd of wild mustangs set free. He wanted to pull her into his arms, to feel the warmth of her body and hear the thud of her heart, but he merely held her arm while propping the torch in the broken pottery around them.

"Bloody hell, Atsila." Jackson caught her face in his palms, brushing back the hair that had escaped her braid. "You could be impaled right now." His eyes searched her face, pale yet flushed with energy. "My foolishness—"

"Almost got *you* impaled, not me." She looked deep into his eyes. "I was careful and ready."

He huffed softly, releasing her face. "And I'm grateful for it." The thought that she could have been hit by some other trap made his stomach sick. She could be torn through, slumped on the ground right now before him. Her life blood flowing too fast to catch.

She studied his eyes, her brow furrowed. "Are you well?" Her hands rose to his shoulders, resting there.

No, he was not. Not with the thought that Kailin could be injured or killed. And it would be all his fault.

Silence hung between them as his confession swelled inside him until it sat on his tongue. His secrets. His quest.

She turned her face to the golden coffin. "Anthony said he thinks the Orb is inside the sarcophagus. But you are welcome to any of the other treasures in the room. Your fee." Her fingers flicked in the air behind her.

Treasures? A room full of treasures waited around him, full of mystery and ancient beauty. Yet he couldn't drag his gaze from the treasure before him. The woman who stood warm and alive. And then his gaze dropped to the lid of the sarcophagus as if tugged there by need, need for the Orb of Life, his one pursuit. Or what should be his only need. Kailin was confusing that within him.

Jackson breathed deeply and made himself release her. "Can you open it? Lift the lid?"

Her fingers brushed and teased the dirt away. "First," she said, a touch of awe in her voice. Curls from her braid coiled around her shoulders like golden little asps. He forced his eyes to the huge artifact.

"It's yellow quartzite," Kailin said and ran a hand over the dust-free hieroglyphs. "'Here lies our prince, Amun-her-khepeshef, son of the Great King Ramses II and Queen Nefertari.'"

Jackson bent over the etched death mask next to Kailin. She turned her head without straightening. He knew that look in her eyes, the thrill of discovery. Her lips curved upward. "That's...New Kingdom, nineteenth dynasty. I think he was the first son of Ramses II. The Pharaoh had forty or more sons and forty daughters. His first several sons died before they could inherit the throne. Anthony would know for certain if Amun-her-khepeshef was the first." She shook her head and stood, running her hand over the coffin. "It is utterly—" She stopped, her mouth open.

"Thrilling," he finished as he watched the color return to her cheeks. "Egyptian archeology." He smiled. "More fun than studying stones set in a circle in a farmer's field?"

She ignored his little jab and continued reading, her slim fingers moving over the glyphs like a blind man reading braille. "'I protect the Orb of Life by sealing it in here with me,'" she read. "'A gift from an ancient magic, an ancient man. I gift it to the one who carries its mark. Beware its power and never let it fall into the hands of thirteen demons.'"

"Thirteen?" he said. "Lends a bit of credence to the ghost's story," Jackson commented with a casual tone that belied the goose bumps crawling up his arms. "I'd say Anthony was bloody right about the Orb being here."

"A gift to the one who carries its mark," Kailin murmured. "Anthony must have found references to the Orb then. No one has been here since he and I, or the spears would have all been tripped."

"And there'd be more modern bodies on the floor," Jackson said, his gaze scanning the rubble. All he saw were relics wrought in gold, treasure that was all his. But he'd trade it all for the Orb of Life. Would he trade the Orb of Life for Kailin? He pushed the question down in his gut, smothering it.

"You found references to the Orb in other sources," she murmured, as if speaking to her father. "And you came back." She looked at Jackson. "Moghadam must have Anthony."

Jackson shook his head. "Moghadam and his radicals don't want anyone to have the Orb. He wouldn't take Anthony to make you retrieve it for him." He ran his fingers over the lid, following the trails of the design and glyphs, pushing against the gritty dirt and sand.

He felt Kailin's gaze and looked back over his shoulder.

"How did *you* know about the Orb, if you did not work with Anthony?" she asked. "Anthony told me in letters that he was keeping it a secret."

He didn't even pause but looked back at a cat motif in blue lapis on the lid. "It's referenced in several tombs. Moghadam apparently knows of it too. Your father isn't the only one interested in the Orb."

"Are you?"

Jackson turned slowly, meeting her steady gaze. "I promise you that we will free your father."

"And then?"

Lying was not something he wanted to start with Kailin. "Let's have this interrogation when we aren't buried beneath tons of rock and sand." He saw the hitch in her inhale, and his stomach clenched. Damn him for reminding her of her fear, but she wasn't letting the half answers he supplied satisfy. He needed to think about how to tell the truth and still not tell her that he very much intended to take the Orb. Once they found it and used it to get her father. "So let's find the Orb so we can get out of here." He rested his clenched fist on the stone.

Kailin swallowed hard, her face pale as she eyed the still-intact arched ceiling. She nodded but her lips parted on a series of little pants. He walked over to her and placed his hands on her upper arms. She tensed and pulled back.

"You take away my magic when you touch me," she whispered. "Right now, the knowledge that I can blast my way out of here with a single command is the only thing keeping me from screaming."

Jackson lowered his hands. He tipped his head and stepped aside. "You can retrieve the Orb quicker without me."

Kailin took a full breath and lifted her hands out before her. *She is glorious!* She stood straight, facing the rubble along the back of the tomb, legs and arms braced as if ready to block an army. The knot that had sat at her nape had unwound into a thick snaking braid down her back. Waves, teased loose, twisted in golden disarray around her head and shoulders. The sleeker boy's clothes showed her slender frame in such honest perfection that she looked even more womanly than if she'd been wearing a regal gown. Her face set in stony strength, the dried blood on her forehead adding to her fierce features. Purpose pulsed with each breath, purpose and the love for her father keeping her underground when she'd rather be anywhere else. Perhaps even in his bed.

The thought raced through Jackson's head, and he kicked it out. *Focus, fool!*

"Lift," she commanded. The lid of the sarcophagus vibrated, and bits of sand, stones, and dirt lifted from the etched glyphs and designs, up into the air like a fog or small sandstorm.

Kailin poked her straight finger upwards. "Hole, out," she yelled and a hole drilled upward through the ceiling for several long seconds until reaching open air. This hole was larger than the rest. With a little swirl of her fingers, she filtered a small tornado of rock and sand up and out into the night above them. Debris from around the tomb rose as well.

"Good thing you didn't drill into the Nile," Jackson said and stepped closer, his torchlight roaming the glyphs before him.

"We're headed away from the river," Kailin said as she stood directly under the hole, breathing.

Kailin's storm had cleaned away the dust and dirt around them. Artifacts lay scattered where they'd fallen when she'd originally blasted her way out of the tomb with Anthony years ago. Several Canopic jars lay on their sides, one broken with a stain beneath it, an organ that had dried away years ago. Golden creatures with delicately painted feathers and fur sat overturned, but his gaze slid over them to the treasure he sought.

She coughed, and he looked toward her. "Are you better now with the extra air?" he said.

"I am...handling it."

He gave her a lopsided grin. "Anthony will be exceedingly proud when he hears about this adventure."

A small smile softened her lips. She took a full breath and held her arms straight over the lid. "Lift." A gust of air whistled down the hole she'd bored, adding to the woeful atmosphere of death. And then the unmistakable sound of the airtight seal releasing around the edge resounded. The sound of scraping granite ceased as the side of the lid lifted. *Astounding.* It must weigh at least a ton. With slow precision, she tipped it so that it leaned upright against the side, as if it could be slid back over to seal it again.

Jackson held his breath as he watched, not the stone settle, but the slight woman who did it without much strain. *Amazing. Utterly powerful. Completely beautiful.* He shook his head. If any of his associates knew about Kailin's powers, she would be the most sought-after target in the world. *Dammit.* They mustn't ever know.

"The inner coffin seems to be...humming," Kailin said and Jackson turned his gaze to the golden inner coffin. Turquoise and amber stones sat amongst strokes of faded red ochre on the adorned lid.

"Do you feel it?" Kailin slid her finger along the edge. "It resonates."

"Not really, but there's a glow," Jackson murmured though the room felt altered somehow, like the air was full of something thick. "Ready to lift another ton or two?"

A rare smile transformed her face with the natural glow of self-confidence. "Anytime."

"Very well, Doctor Whitaker, let's take a look at the humming prince."

"Up." The lid opened with another rush of air, almost as if the mummy himself sucked in a deep breath. She set it propped half over the opening. A soft light radiated up from the open coffin.

They leaned over the open inner coffin. The wrapped mummy lay inside, undisturbed, guarded by his army and his scribe and father's general. Why must so many guard a non-ruling prince?

The answer nestled against the prince's side. They weren't guarding the prince, but what he held.

"That's it," she said.

There it was. The thing he sought with all his heart. The object of his greatest desire. The one thing that could save Cassy. "The Orb of Life."

"It...it has a dragonfly on it," she said. The shape of a dragonfly was etched into the surface of a large spherical rock. It looked exactly like the birthmark on her arm.

Kailin reached out with one steady finger to touch a thin wing. White fire seemed to ignite within, turning the rock into a small sun. "Good God!" She rested her palm against the rounded stone. "It's blinding."

"Stop touching it."

As soon as her skin broke contact, the light dimmed. She gasped as the blinding light disappeared.

"Damn, I can't see," Kailin said.

"Blink. Your eyes will adjust again."

Jackson's torchlight glowed and accented the stark shadows.

"The dragonfly matches the one on my arm." She glanced at her covered limb. "In fact, it's tingling now. Drakkina?" she called, but the ghost didn't appear. "Perhaps the Orb is making it tingle this time."

Jackson reached down into the sarcophagus and gingerly removed the Orb. He held it in his palms, but it didn't light up like when Kailin touched it. "It can't be a coincidence that there's a dragonfly on it. You must be connected to it somehow." Did that mean that only Kailin could make the Orb work?

She peered at the ball. "The dragonfly. Is it moving? Look! Its wings." She absently rubbed her own arm where he knew the matching birthmark sat along her silky white skin. He watched the amazement and curiosity light her features, making them even more stunning, more enthralling. She glanced up at him, and he froze in the direct line of her smile. "I've never seen anything like it," she whispered in awe and glanced back down, breaking the spell. "Something that could tie me to my family."

She touched it again with one finger. The light blossomed from within. "Good God," she repeated and yanked her finger back, blinking against the bright light.

"Did it do something to you?" Jackson grabbed her finger, inspecting the delicate pad. When he touched her, the light in the Orb went out completely.

"Some type of energy surge." She looked at him. "It gave me more magic I think, stronger power."

"Brilliant," he murmured. He released her finger, and the Orb resumed its muted glow.

"Frightening," she countered as if she'd missed the sarcasm in his voice. "For one person to contain so much power."

"It's a good thing you're on my side." He grinned, trying to lessen the tension. She nodded and his stomach twisted at her immediate agreement, but he pushed the guilt away behind the face of his sister. Kailin would still get her father back; he'd make sure of it. But then he'd have to get her to heal Cassy. That was if she didn't hate him and everything connected to him.

"You mute it when you touch me," she said. "You negate its powers when you extinguish mine. We must be connected."

A low rumble of thunder penetrated the thick ceiling. Odd. When was the last time he'd seen a lightning storm over the Egyptian desert? Never.

Kailin's gaze lifted to the ceiling. "I can't believe I'm standing in a tomb." She stared, lips parted around quick breaths.

"It's probably safer to be underground right now," Jackson said and pulled a silken cloth from the inner sarcophagus to wrap around the Orb.

"I would still like to be away from here as soon as possible." Kailin looked upward, and he glanced fear in her tight features. "I only want the Orb to trade for Anthony."

"You would..." he stopped, and her gaze swung to him, "give something so powerful to criminals?"

Her eyes searched his, and the space between her gently arched brows pinched. "Anthony is my only family. Plus, they may not be able to do anything with the Orb if it only responds to me."

She pulled her loosened hair out of her face but didn't tie it back. "You can come back with officials and workers once I've recovered my father. He will most likely want to help you excavate."

Jackson scanned the glyphs on the inside of the interior coffin. It showed how rattled Kailin was being in the tomb that she didn't translate more of the inscription. Amun-her-khepeshef's name reaffirmed the identity of the occupant, but the description about the Orb stopped him.

The Orb of Life gives power to the powerful, life to those still alive, resurrection to those half-dead, those possessing the other half of the whole. The Orb belongs to the one it is gifted to. I, Amun-her-khepeshef, loving prince, son of Ramses II, gift the Orb to the bearer of its mark, the mark of the ancient man who gave it to me to guard.

Kailin's mark. Had the prince, on his deathbed, gifted it to Kailin, the bearer of the mark? If the prince had, maybe the rock wouldn't work for anyone else, so they buried it with him. Jackson's forehead tightened.

Kailin stared up at the holes she'd drilled earlier. Thunder shook the ground overhead, sending down pebbles and sand. She shielded her eyes and coughed, shaking the dirt from her hair. She'd undone the rest of her braid, and the waves fell around her shoulders. She looked like an angel, radiant even surrounded by death and dirt.

"It's bad out there," she said as another ground-quaking explosion rained dirt. She looked at Jackson. "But I don't want to stay down here."

"Hmm," Jackson watched the flash of lightning pierce the little opening at the top of the hole. "Can you affect the weather?"

"Yes."

"Yes?" His eyes widened.

"Yes." She nodded to emphasize her proclamation.

"Is there anything you can't do?"

Her lips pinched together, stifling a grin. "Yes." She looked up. "I should be able to disrupt the weather pattern enough to send the lightning away."

"Can you do it from down here?" he asked. She bloody hell nodded. Jackson pointed at the hole. "I'd feel better about us standing out on the open desert once you've sent the lightning on its way."

"Back," Kailin murmured.

"You like to shove things around don't you," he said.

She didn't open her eyes. "Yet my magic can't even knock you off balance. Most annoying." She gritted her teeth. "Back." Thunder banged above them. "Move." She pressed her hands through the air together as if pushing a mass.

"Can you heal people with your magic?" Jackson asked. Surely Kailin would have said she could after meeting Cassy.

A scream echoed through the cavern, making Jackson spin. Kailin jumped.

"They're coming! Cac! You're calling them!" screeched the ghost as it spun like a mini sand tornado down the hole from the surface. Drakkina materialized in a cloud, her face pinched in frantic appeal. "Your magic! You are bringing them right to you!"

The ghost was looking at Kailin. "Who?" Jackson demanded. Drakkina turned to him, her wide eyes moving directly to the wrapped Orb and then to his eyes. If her face looked panicked before, it was nearly split with frantic fear now. "Who is coming?" Jackson repeated as thunder clanged through his head, cracking so loud his teeth hurt.

"The thirteen demons!"

CHAPTER TWENTY
HIDE WHERE?!

"The demons?" Kailin yelled above the storm. "Here? Is it time for the battle?" *Not now!* She wasn't ready!

Drakkina shook her head, her white-streaked hair flying wildly as if mimicking her franticness. "They are hunting you and your sisters, and"—she paused to look pointedly at Jackson's hands—"the Orb of Life. If I'd known it was here—"

"Why do demons want the Orb?" Jackson asked and Drakkina nearly sizzled with frustration.

"It has power!"

"That they can use even if they weren't gifted the Orb?" Jackson asked, his words brittle and coming fast.

"You must stop your magic now, Kailin," Drakkina said, "or they will kill you here and steal the Orb!"

"I've stopped."

"The Orb," Drakkina pointed. "It resonates with your magic."

Jackson opened the wrap around the Orb. Its center glowed as if it was an ember holding onto the energy of the fire that had charged it.

"But I'm not doing it!"

"Your magic calls it like my amulet would!" Drakkina shouted.

The wind wailed overhead, drafts fluting down the holes Kailin had dug. Booms of thunder shook the ground above. Jackson strode over to Kailin and grabbed her shoulder. The Orb went black. Only the glow of torchlight flickered in the room.

"Hold onto her!" Drakkina called. "Any use of magic calls them, pinpoints your location!"

"Your yelling does the same," Kailin murmured as she gazed up at the slab of heavy limestone that Moghadam's men moved over the ground after they'd thrown them down into the tomb.

Jackson's arm pulled her against his solid form. He anchored her in the darkness, the weight of the mountain on top of them. His powerful stance gave her strength. She breathed, utterly amazed at how calm she was.

A scraping noise above made them all look upward, and Kailin's heart shot into a race as if it had been the crack of a starter's pistol. A flicker of torchlight dropped down, followed by the snake of a rope to the floor as lightning split the sky open. A man dropped down the rope. At least he looked like a man, although Kailin had absolutely no idea what a demon looked like. Didn't they have wings and horns like the devil? Another followed the first.

"Moghadam!" Jackson growled. He stepped forward but the lightning reflected off metal in the zealot's hands, a gun, Jackson's gun. Jackson shoved Kailin behind him. "Bloody hell. Come to finish the job?"

A third man climbed down the rope, followed by three more who dropped more than climbed down, desperate to get out of the storm. "We're the only ones left," Moghadam yelled over the raging storm outside. "The sand and twisting sky have taken the rest."

"The demons," Drakkina said and Moghadam flashed the gun in her direction.

"Who are you?" he demanded.

Drakkina's image grew in the small space, her ethereal body charged with magical wind as her dragonflies zipped around. Good God, was her magic calling the demons too?

"I, little man, am more powerful than your puny weapon. Put it away."

The men behind Moghadam jumped back along the far wall, their clumsy retreat smashing a few more of the ceramic cats. "What are you?" Moghadam demanded.

"The only thing standing between you and those demons out there."

"Ghul!" one of the men behind him yelled and glanced wide-eyed toward the gap in the limestone slab marking the only entrance and exit.

"That's right," Drakkina hissed. "Demons, here to take your precious Orb."

"It is not theirs to take," Moghadam said, eyeing the hole illuminated against the bright discharges of lightning. "It belongs to the prince who lies here."

"Not anymore," Jackson challenged. Moghadam brought the point of Jackson's gun around to face him.

"Your prince gifted it away."

"To whom?"

"'I, Amun-her-khepeshef, gift the Orb to the bearer of its mark,'" Jackson quoted. "You must know the inscription, Moghadam, if you belong to some old brotherhood to protect the Orb."

Moghadam stared him down. "I see no mark on you."

"Not me," Jackson said and nodded to Kailin.

With Jackson's arm still around her, Kailin shoved her sleeve up to reveal her birthmark.

In a stride that made Jackson pull her further into his protective circle, Moghadam leaned over Kailin's arm, his thumb brushing her skin. Kailin fought the ridiculous urge to pull back. Certainly there were worse things to fear, like what was thundering outside.

"Hide!" Drakkina yelled. "Before they funnel down here and find you holding the blasted Orb!"

"She bears the mark," Moghadam said and the men behind him dropped to their knees. He looked into her eyes. "My queen." Moghadam bowed his head and stepped back. Wind circled through the tomb from the holes, whistling and rushing, as if it sought them. The pungent smell of rancid death came with it.

"Your queen you almost killed," Jackson retorted, his gaze searching as if to find a place for them to hide. But where could one hide from an otherworldly demon? The Orb still lay dormant, tucked under his arm. As long as he held onto Kailin, her magic didn't resonate with it and call the demons to her.

"They come for our queen?" Moghadam asked. Drakkina hovered nearby and Tuto swooped down through the opening. Dust floated down from the intricate mosaics lining the ceiling. Would the demons collapse the tomb, burying them here? Kailin's heart leapt, beating in time with a torrential surge of panic.

"Yes," Drakkina hissed and shot around the open sarcophagi.

"There is nowhere to hide," Kailin said. "Do we fight?"

"'Twould be like a child fighting a pack of hungry lions," Drakkina said. "Thirteen of them."

Jackson froze, his eyes scanning the interior. Moghadam yelled Arabic toward his men and they scrambled to find weapons. From what Drakkina had shown her, the weapons would be useless.

Jackson turned her to him. "You are going to have to trust me."

"Trust you?" she asked numbly. He nodded, the curls of his hair hitting across his forehead. "Trust you," she repeated. He gave one more brief nod, his lips tight, and turned with her hugged against his chest.

He set the Orb down against his leg and with one arm, tugged the pharaoh from his coffin. "Hide your prince," Jackson yelled to Moghadam, who took the mummy with much more reverence.

Jackson turned to Kailin. She stared into his gray eyes, darkened by the shadows and torchlight. His eyebrows rose slightly as he spoke and nodded at the same time, as if he were convincing a child or perhaps a lunatic. "We are going to hide inside."

"Inside? Inside *what*?" Her voice pinched high.

Jackson bent to stare directly in her eyes. Kailin couldn't even blink. She held her breath, knowing what he would say, what he was thinking, yet shoving the notion away because it was so horrific it would surely give her a brain attack and kill her on the spot.

"I'll keep you safe, Kailin, but we have to get in. It's full of magic, has hidden the Orb for thousands of years. They won't sense you or it once inside."

"Inside," she repeated around shallow breaths. Her head started to hurt. Here came the brain attack.

"Close your eyes. Hold onto me."

"Close my eyes." Kailin's eyes flickered shut and open as Jackson held her close.

"Moghadam, close the sarcophagus once we're inside," Jackson called. "When they're gone, let your queen out. Understand?"

"Aiwa! Aiwa!"

Kailin squeaked as Jackson lifted her. Without disconnecting, he settled her in the large sarcophagus. Kailin's stomach rolled and her lungs couldn't pull in air. Her head pounded. She was going to pass out or vomit or both. "Jackson!" she screamed.

"Shhh!" Drakkina hissed as she hovered. "They are coming down. I can smell them."

"You can smell them?" Kailin asked incredulously as Jackson's knee came down between her legs. The other leg followed as he climbed on top of her. His large body filled the space above Kailin as he descended, blocking out the torchlight and the mosaics pebbling the vaulted ceiling.

Moghadam leaned over. "We will protect you, my queen, you and the Orb of Life." Commitment and duty etched his hawk-like features. Kailin felt Moghadam nestle the rock down near her feet. Jackson slid to her side so that she didn't feel his weight as he pressed over her.

"Just stay alive, Moghadam," Jackson ordered. He looked at Kailin. "Close your eyes, Atsila."

Her eyes stung. She forced her lids to lower and rise and then to finally shut. She gritted her teeth together at the grating sound of the stone slab sliding along the edge of the coffin. Moghadam's men grunted as they threw their weight into shoving the lid, balancing it along the open top until...

The lid slid into place, locking out the wail and wind, locking out the stench of death blowing into the room, locking out their air.

"Out," she whispered. Nothing happened. Jackson's body laid snugly against her. Kailin was completely and terrifyingly trapped.

They lay in silence, their breath the only sound over the blood rushing through Kailin's ears. Her heart pounded to the point of pain against her ribs. Her tongue stuck to the parched roof of her mouth. Silent tears rolled down from the corners of her eyes to wet the hair at her temples. Jackson's breath was long, slow, as if he recovered thoughtfully after a long run. Hers was shallow, frantic, like the flutter of wings on a small bird dancing away from a snake. Her fingers sank into his arms, but he didn't flinch.

"They can't sense you in here. Drakkina will draw them away."

"Moghadam?"

"Will do whatever it takes to protect you now that he knows you are the Orb's rightful owner. His whole life revolves around that mission."

Kailin wiggled her foot and felt the hard Orb knock against her ankle bone. "Jackson, I...I can't get us out of here with you touching me."

"That's a good thing right now," he said. His breath touched her cheek. "Because you'd have us flying out of here if you could. And I think the demons would notice the hill being blown apart."

Kailin didn't respond. Her breath rasped through her constricted throat, past her lips. She felt Jackson shift slightly, but he couldn't seem to move his hands. His nose nuzzled against her temple. He must feel the wetness there, her unstoppable tears.

"You are safe here, Kailin. We're together and safe."

As if to mock him, the ground shook beneath them. Would the sarcophagus fall off its pedestal? Would the lid fly open, exposing them? Or slide off kilter, crushing them?

"Slow breaths, Kailin," he whispered in her ear and inhaled against her skin. "Lord, you smell like flowers." He ran his nose along her cheek until she felt him near her mouth.

Jackson's body draped along hers. The smell of leather, pine, and man surrounded her, blocking out the memory of the scent of death and decay that had wafted through the tomb right before they'd climbed inside this—no, no, she mustn't think it. Kailin's blood pumped and her energy soared. But there was nowhere to go, nowhere to funnel the excess.

"You are safe, Kailin," he whispered, his lips brushing past hers as he spoke. "You are outside, on the prairie. Tall grasses sway against your legs; the sweet dancing winds pull at your hair. The sky is so large that you lose yourself in it as you lay back staring at the endless blue. White clouds race past in all sorts of shapes. There is nothing but wide-open air and fresh life all around you."

Jackson's lips brushed against her mouth as if he spoke the calming words into her. Kailin tilted her head slightly to follow them, center them on her own. She moved her lips over his, waiting, her trapped energy begging for release.

Jackson's mouth pressed gingerly against her own. Kailin parted her lips.

As if a dam broke, he covered her mouth, slanting along her shape, tasting her. Without sight, her other senses took over, savoring his smell and taste, relishing the rock-hard feel of his body wrapped around her. She felt like she was melting into him, merging, protected instead of trapped. His fingers found her hand and intertwined with her fingers in the tight space next to their bodies. Bone and flesh against limestone. Kailin shoved the thought away and threw herself back into the kiss.

Their lips moved together. Their noses slid against each other as they slanted, giving and gaining better access. Her fingers tightened around his hand, rubbing along his fingers, another outlet for the growing sensation flooding through her. Sparked by the panic, Kailin's body burned. He grew against her leg, and she knew that if they were back in her room at the hotel, buttons would be flying.

Kailin breathed against his mouth. She couldn't think, couldn't concentrate on anything other than Jackson and the passion she was free to unleash. His heat and power wrapped totally around her, capturing her mind and body so that there was no room for panic. Terror was pushed out, obliterated by raw sensation. Never before had she relinquished control, but with Jackson touching her, she couldn't burn down the world.

Low thumps, deep vibrations, and high-pitched shrieking whispered through the sarcophagus walls. Kailin turned her face, listening. Her lips rested against the side of Jackson's cheek. She breathed. His thumb stroked her palm, and she kept her eyes clamped shut.

"You are *mine*," he whispered against her. "And I am yours. Bloody hell," he cursed low. She turned her face back to his, and he caught her lips once again in a crushing force, half passion, half uncontrollable lust.

She returned the kiss with as much as he gave, even more. No holding back. Her entire life was about constraint, but not now, not with him. She could release everything she felt against him and he would take it all. Wanted it all.

She had so much to give, so much she restrained on a daily basis, but with Jackson touching her, she would hold back nothing.

Drakkina forced her form to the ancient stone floor and changed the particles creating her body to look like Kailin.

The tall, dark Egyptian called Moghadam turned to her and gasped. "My queen! You must hide in the sarcophagus!" His wide eyes fell on the replicated sphere in her hands. "You must hide the Orb."

Excellent, he thought she was Kailin.

"I do not hide but will lead my hunters away. You must guard this room and bring the man out as soon as the demons are gone," she said in an imitation of Kailin's voice. It wasn't perfect but the man was too hyped up on warrior adrenaline to notice. He and his five followers couldn't know that Kailin still lay in the tomb. Otherwise, if the demons took them, they would give her location away. Hopefully the demons wouldn't care enough about her mate to want to waste time killing him.

A gust of wind whistled through the tomb. "It smells of retching and old flesh," Moghadam said.

Artifacts and bits of newly broken pottery flew with the force. Moghadam's men placed themselves between Drakkina and the hole above them in a ridiculous attempt to protect her.

"Hide," she demanded. "If you die, there will be no one to retrieve my mate from the sarcophagus."

Moghadam rattled off a command and the six of them fell back behind the sarcophagus with the first lid removed. She needed them alive to rescue Kailin and her mate as soon as possible. How much air would they have in that coffin? Humans—so damnably fragile!

A whirlwind spun down through the rectangular hole that led to the outside world. Drakkina expected Semiazaz, his white hair and black eyes that haunted her infrequent dreams. Instead, the mummy of the prince, which had been unceremoniously removed from his resting place when Jackson Black decided Kailin must hide with the Orb, stood.

Amun-her-khepeshef's wrapped arms rose woodenly, like a puppet on strings. The tips of skeletal fingers pressed out of the frayed ends like weathered gloves to unwind the stained wrapping from his head. As the wrapping loosened, a sunken skeletal face emerged, scraps of tanned skin stuck to the stained bones. Broken teeth moved and light peered from the black eye sockets. Drakkina stood mesmerized at the grotesque display of power.

"Child of Gilla," the mummy spoke. It was Semiazaz's smooth voice. "Give us the Orb and we will allow you to retain your life."

CHAPTER TWENTY-ONE
MASQUERADE

Semiazaz. He had taken leadership of the hapless coven, and Drakkina hated him with ice-sharp revulsion. She could not give up her existence until she saw every speck of his unclean soul destroyed in every thread of time. She would see it done to right her wrong.

"Yes, girl, give us the Orb, and you get to live," Semiazaz said.

Two other wrapped mummies, who had been propped in the corner behind the demon leader, tore at their face wrappings. Glittering fury sparked through their vacant eye sockets. "No!" one spat. "She dies!"

"I will tear her limbs apart," the other resurrected mummy threatened.

Drakkina searched the black eyes of Semiazaz but saw no sign of blue with gold rims. Was her lost Eógan somewhere in there? Could he be, like the scrying bowl had insinuated?

She held the imagined Orb in her hands. "You desire this?"

Semiazaz's face remained a blank mask of wrappings, but his black eyes sharpened into glinting shards of obsidian. He showed no sign of recognizing her in Kailin's form. "I will trade your life for it." More hissing and curses leaked from inside the dead prince's bones. The bound coven of thirteen demons must be held within the three mummies.

Drakkina set a rock, disguised as the Orb, on the cut stone floor next to her booted ankle. "You haven't the power to bring my death," she said, churning the small marble of magic inside that she held ready to unleash.

"Is it possible that Drakkina has left you so unprepared that you don't know that I can kill you with one thought?" he enunciated, his borrowed skull tipping slightly to view the plain rock on the floor that masqueraded as the great Orb of Life.

"Is it possible that you are so ignorant that you don't know the expanse of power gifted to me by Gilla, my mother?" she returned.

The prince's hollow, macabre gaze snapped level, his brown teeth moving without a bit of his lips remaining. "You will die soon enough, at the final battle as we have seen. I will take the Orb of Life now."

She kicked it gently with her foot. "The Orb is nothing more than a fabled rock."

"We felt its magic when you touched it," he replied evenly. His face turned toward the back where no doubt one of the men had given themselves away. Stupid human.

Drakkina shrugged and set her foot upon it. "I'm touching it now and it's doing nothing."

The mummy took a rigid step closer. "Did you gift it to Drakkina then? Does she hold power over both the Orb and the dragonfly amulet?"

Drakkina had made the image of her amulet look like Kailin's amber stone the girl wore around her neck. The real dragonfly amulet had been Drakkina's, the female half, and was hidden in the stone circle in Scotland. The Orb had belonged to Eógan, but he'd given it to Druce.

Druce had apparently added a layer of protection to the Orb by making it work only when near the amulet or the person to whom it was gifted. *Damn the man!*

Then Druce had gifted it to Prince Amun-her-khepeshef, when he realized that Eógan and Drakkina were swaying toward darkness, their power so great.

Drakkina felt the tension pull along the lines of her face and she forced a smooth visage of innocent youth. "Of course. You will never catch Drakkina, and she will never gift it to you."

One of the soldier mummies shrieked and stomped their rage. The other mummy roared and grabbed one of the mortal men in fury. The demons inhabiting the partially preserved mummy used their magic to yank him to the ceiling. They slammed his head into the limestone-dotted mosaic until bright red smeared along the carefully placed tiles. Dead. One less man able to push the slab back off the inner coffin.

"So," Drakkina said, trying to draw the attention from the rest. "There is nothing of use for you here."

"The Orb will work for us when we claim the amulet," Semiazaz said and rotated his half-wrapped mummy head along his stiff shoulders as if his white hair cascaded across them. His gaze moved like the sensing forked tongue of a cobra, judging, deciding when to strike. How long should she wait to draw them away? They had to follow her.

"Gilla and Druce created such beautiful children." He tilted the other way. "You say you are strong. How strong, exactly? There would be glory beyond your comprehension if you joined us."

"Join you?" It was ludicrous. She eyed their shapes. "You are so desperate to take a body again that you will inhabit a desiccated three-thousand-year-old corpse? Why would I join a desperate, pathetic, imprisoned coven?"

A hiss erupted from a mummy behind him. "Let me take her!" The voice was familiar.

"Ahh," Drakkina said. "Bast. In home territory again? It must rankle that the Orb was hidden here the whole time, in your own litter box, and you never knew."

Semiazaz's head swiveled to the thrashing feline demon. She shucked the mummified remains and floated in cat form in a black swirl of smoke. "Be still!" He turned back to Drakkina, his black eyes even more piercing. "You know Bast?"

"Drakkina has schooled me on all of you." She spoke without hesitation to mask her misstep.

"And yet you stand here acting like we are no threat," Semiazaz replied. "Even when you are trapped and know that we will kill you and strip away your magic."

"I am powerful," she articulated softly and images of twelve demons coalesced, leaving only Semiazaz in the mummy corpse. The other two abandoned mummies fell in heaps. The demons formed a circle, probably the maximum distance they could separate from one another, and began to move as one toward her.

Drakkina let out a trill of feminine laughter, taunting and luring to draw the stupid beasts after her. Her form remained that of Kailin's, and her essence shot up one of Kailin's holes, straight toward the sparking constellations. She didn't bother to count the bodies scattered below, blown against the dunes by the demons' tornado-fury. Her mind focused on the shift she must make at the right time. Too soon and her pursuers would lose her and return to the crypt. Too slow and they'd catch her and discover she wasn't Kailin, thus returning to the crypt after they killed her.

A shriek filled the sky below as the bound evil shot after her. *Yes!* Now where to shift? Drakkina's form slid between temporal lines, into the mist that made up fractions of time out of sync with the mortal world. Lines of time crisscrossed like a spider's lair, decades and centuries intersecting at distinct points where she could leap with ease. But she dove and wove through the mist, leaving a faint trail behind her. She wanted them confused and dizzy before they stopped following, so they'd be less likely to return to Kailin.

A crack of hot power shocked through her from behind. *Cac! Too close!*

Cease your flight, resonated through Drakkina's mind. Pure darkness, an oily sludge meant to suffocate her will and stop her.

Drakkina's mental blade of white magic slashed through Semiazaz's command. She dove through the mist between Merewin's era and the time Kat had inhabited for a few mortal days. Twisting and flexing, Drakkina dispersed her essence as close to the lines as possible. Where to land?

"Stop!" Semiazaz tried again. Drakkina sliced and dove into the years following Kat's exit. Her mist tingled with the thickness of mortal air and the sluggishness of time. It tugged on her form as she shot faster than a star, shooting toward a circle she couldn't see but knew was there. Kat's meadow, the one Gilla's daughter had protected with her magic and tied off into the very trees and stones that encircled it. Kat had hidden there, and a century later her sister Serena and her mate had hidden there, much to Drakkina's annoyance.

It was somewhere below. Blackberry brambles surrounded it. Pure of heart could find it. *Cac!* Pure of heart? What a foolish stipulation.

Demons shot through the treetops above her, scattering summer leaves like the shots from a more modern-day firearm. And witnesses below would swear of devils shooting through the branches. They wouldn't be too far off.

"Earth Mother, show me the way," Drakkina willed and dove, her eyes closed, her essence and trust in the Great Mother guiding her. She thought of Kailin's twin, Kat, and her specific twist of glamour magic that guarded the meadow. Like a glittery sliver of power, Kat's magic shimmered behind Drakkina's eyelids. She plummeted straight into the soft grass and yellow-buttoned daisies. Her form evaporated at impact with a mere dispersion of particles. She reformed as Drakkina on her back, staring up at the gray dawn lighting the circle made by the trees above her head.

She didn't need to breathe, yet she panted. A flare of heat smashed past the trees above her and circled. Could they see her, smell her, find her? Would Kat's magic hide her or bring the demons right to her? Drakkina watched. Pure of heart sounded much better now that she was in the meadow. Semiazaz's coven was as far from good as one could get.

Around the meadow, the leaves shook as the dark power searched and scattered more leaves. Shrieks and screeches chased birds and forest animals out of the woods and into the clearing where Drakkina lay along the earth, waiting, staring, praying.

"We've lost her!" the voice of Bast shot from the other side of a large blackberry bramble.

"Quiet," Semiazaz rebuked the furious group that literally shook the world around them. "She couldn't have just disappeared." His voice came without force. Semiazaz was close, very close. All became silent. Drakkina didn't try to cloak herself. That would require more magic and might be enough to make them sense her through Kat's glamour shields.

"I do not believe that the creature was Gilla's daughter," another voice, deep and restrained, offered.

"Neither do I," Semiazaz replied. A movement near a thinning of blackberry vines pulled Drakkina's gaze. Silently she sat up into a cross-legged position. If she was to be crushed out of all existence, it wouldn't be on her back.

"Drakkina," Bast hissed. But Drakkina's gaze centered on the man standing along the edge of the meadow. She had no physical heart, yet it stuttered painfully in her chest.

Eógan. He stood there, dark hair with specks of gray hitting below his shoulders. His blue tunic was the same that he'd worn to honor their union. Dragonflies were stitched along the edge that lay against his strong thighs. Broad shoulders stood proud yet relaxed. His sword remained, as always, strapped to his side.

Drakkina squeezed her eyes shut and opened them. He lingered, looking very much alive, although she knew he was not.

"'Kina," he called.

Drakkina felt the blade of sorrow twist in her. It was purely emotion since she had no body. She closed her eyes and prayed for numbness. *Please, Earth Mother.*

"Come to me. I am still here. Semiazaz may have taken my magic, but you can still save me. I am within him and can come back. He says that if you give him the Orb, he'll set me free."

"Lies," Drakkina whispered and ignored the tears leaking from her false eyes. She blinked, her gaze fastening on him, soaking in the sight of him even though she knew it was all Semiazaz's dark magic.

"'Kina, 'tis a good bargain. He has no use for you if you give him what he wants. We can be together again."

Drakkina walked up to the brambles, silently gazing at her lost love. The sun broke through amongst the old trees of the forest, beams of yellow and white like the thunderbolts of the ancient gods. They struck along Eógan's beautiful form, along his strong features and caught his eyes. Black. His eyes were obsidian orbs, not blue, not a hint of gold around the rims.

Drakkina turned away. *Lies.* If Eógan was inside Semiazaz, the demon had tainted him centuries ago. Even a man as strong as her love couldn't exist within such turmoil and darkness. Could he?

"I do not think she remains here," the deep-voiced demon said. Semiazaz continued to scan the area but didn't advance into the clearing. "I do not feel her essence or that of the Orb."

Bast hissed and several others shook within the trees. Semiazaz's black gaze drifted over the clearing and to the right as if he didn't trust his senses that nothing stood before him. With a sudden twist of power he transformed, the darker hair paling to slither like a silver snake down his back as he changed into his usual wise-man image. Drakkina released her breath. He was easier to view this way.

"Back to Egypt," Bast said.

"Nay," another called. "There was nothing of Drakkina or Gilla's daughter there when we left. The witch sent her and the true Orb elsewhere. We should return to the stones and start again."

"Egypt has too much magic," another boomed.

"Gives me pain to sort it through."

"Pain is dealing with all of you," Bast hissed.

"Enough," Semiazaz ordered with one last glimpse around. His eyes seemed to rest for a second on Drakkina but continued to scan the area.

"To the stones of the Scots. Perhaps Drakkina will become brave enough one day to face us there. Her cowardice is so like her mate's.

Perhaps if she knew how I still torture him, she'd meet me." He let the taunt and offer lay like a hovering ribbon of coal smoke. Enough to choke Drakkina if she breathed it in. Only years of honing the steel around her heart kept the pain minimal.

"Together then," he said and dissolved into power that warped the summer air, making it look as if a gray ripple of water fell where he'd appeared. The trees vibrated and then stilled.

CHAPTER TWENTY-TWO
BREATHLESS

Jackson had experienced long, deep kisses, but never like this. Soft, warm, and utterly feminine, Kailin tasted like heat and desperate passion. If they were safe in his home back on the prairie with the open sky above them, he would strip off her clothes and love every inch of her. But he couldn't love her here, trapped with fear driving her passion. He pulled back slightly and ran his barely moveable thumb against her hand and nuzzled her cheek with his nose.

"What?" she asked breathlessly and he hoped the panting was from the kiss and not the low oxygen level.

"I think they've gone."

Kailin's body tightened beneath him, straining to move. Her foot pushed against his boot. He gave her as much room as he could, but they were still clearly pinned together. With them touching, the orb didn't emit any light either. It was as if his eyes had been closed forever.

She huffed. "I can't put even a small distance between us to use my magic."

"It might be too soon to do that anyway. If Drakkina is leading them away, she surely doesn't need you to wave a flag back here." Jackson shifted. "Brace yourself, I'm going to try to push upward, and I don't want to hurt you."

Kailin lay flat and Jackson moved his hands around her until he found a place that was limestone and not soft female body. With most of the pressure on his knees instead of his feet, he didn't know what type of leverage he could get, but he'd try.

"One, two, threeeeee..." He rounded his back up. "Arrrrr!" He breathed and pushed. The lid seemed to shake a small bit but didn't slide. Muscle couldn't win against a ton of limestone, gold, and encrusted gems. He collapsed back on Kailin and tried not to suck in all their remaining air.

"I tried to use magic too, thinking maybe you weren't touching me," she whispered, "but I guess you still were." Several shallow inhales sounded like a sob. "We're really trapped in here."

"Only until Drakkina loses the demons and returns. Or Moghadam opens this up. He knows his queen is in here."

"What if the men are all dead?"

"Then Drakkina."

"What if Drakkina is dead? Or...more dead." Kailin's voice had become so tiny he could hardly hear it even though her lips brushed his ear.

"She's survived this long. She knows how to handle them." Jackson kissed Kailin's ear and then her cheek. "We're lying together on the wide-open prairie, blue skies, white puffy clouds, constant breeze. My mother had this huge patchwork quilt that we'd take out for picnics. We're lying on it." Jackson clutched Kailin's limp hand. "Full from sweet potato pie and rabbit stew with young garden carrots."

"I think you need to take me to this place, Jackson," Kailin whispered. "I promise."

"You promise?" she asked. "With a kiss?"

There was being a gentleman and then there was giving in because the lady certainly needed a kiss. "Of course." Jackson brushed back over to her parted lips. Gentle at first, he melted against her mouth. Warm, so warm. Kailin's lips were soft and generous, her body contoured and sloped like fertile hills. He tasted barely controlled passion, but the quiver running through her, against his length, was tainted by desperately tamped-down terror.

God, how was he going to get them out of there? Because he certainly wasn't surrendering Kailin to death now. He'd never known when his own life would be finished, but now he had something to live for. A promise. A promise to see home again and to take this amazing woman there where she would never be confined again. Not by cultural strictures or moral expectations and certainly not by feet of earth over her, imprisoned by gold and stone.

She slanted against him, her breath a rasp that roped in his mind away from the prairie and difficult promises. "Mine. My Atsila." He whispered the oath that continued to resonate within him. Heat slid down through his body. Smooth skin, the essence of flowers in her hair behind the ancient dust coating them. His hand was still up along her, and he touched the edge of her jaw, feeling a slip of hair there.

His short nails dug against the limestone, but the twenty-six-hundred-year-old chiseled sarcophagus certainly didn't give.

"I can't breathe," Kailin whispered. "There's no air."

"There is," he whispered against her mouth but didn't continue the kiss. "Blue sky full of air around us. Lean into me." She shivered, certainly not from cold. Terror, then. Jackson's stomach twisted tight as the warm trickle of her tears pressed between their cheeks. "Nothing but open air and prairie grass."

"Jackson." His name came tortured from her lips. "I...there's so much more I want to do."

He waited, but she didn't go on. "Small breaths. We'll be out of here soon. Then there will be more," he insinuated. "Much more." A breathless hitch that sounded like the start and stop of a chuckle came from her, easing the pain in his chest.

Damn. They had to get out of here. Jackson braced his back against the lid again and shoved. *Useless.* He shifted his feet around the Orb, but as long as he lay against Kailin, the Orb's power was muted. *Damn. Where is that witch?*

The air was thin around their smashed bodies, sparse. Jackson drew shallow inhales. He kissed Kailin's lips lightly. "Blue skies," he murmured. He held his breath and pushed upward, trying to separate his body from Kailin's. No use. Even with his eyes shut he sensed the dizziness that comes with the lack of oxygen. Maybe if he died first, his body wouldn't mute her magic and she could escape. His fingers moved along his pant line, but then he remembered Moghadam had taken his gun.

There were other ways to die. "Kailin, I need your scarf."

"What?"

Her voice sounded as thin as the air. "Your scarf." Jackson used his teeth to tug at the fabric around her neck. If he could ball it into his mouth, stopping the oxygen completely, he could be the first to die, the only one to die.

"Listen Kailin. When I...pass out, I think your magic will work again. You need to get yourself out then."

"My magic," she repeated.

"Breathe, Kailin. You need to think. When I stop moving," he said, purposely not inhaling against the burn in his chest. Stars sparked in his periphery. "You need to blast your way out of here. I know you can. Do you understand?"

"Blast us out," she whispered.

"Good. I'm going to stop talking now. Kailin, I...I'm sorry." He kissed her. There was so much more he wanted to do, so much more he wanted to say, explain, in case she found out his true mission. She would think the worst. Maybe that's what he deserved. "I never meant to hurt you," he whispered and began to eat the dusty cloth. His chest burned, and his lungs tried to pull against the blockage in his mouth. He fought the instinct to spit it out and gulp whatever air was left. He needed to die before Kailin passed out.

Hiss! The seal of the limestone lid broke, releasing the vacuum. Jackson's heart slammed hard in his chest, and he spit and coughed against the dense folds until the scarf was out of his mouth. The heavy lid scraped along the edge of the narrow coffin. He sucked in air, his lungs demanding while stars sparked across his field of vision.

He looked down at Kailin's closed eyes, her lips parted but unmoving. "Breathe, Kailin," he ordered. The lid ground across the top of their prison slowly, too slowly. "Kailin!". Jackson moved his mouth across Kailin's and blew into her lips. Was she unconscious? Was she...dead? "Kailin!"

Deep voices babbled in Arabic outside the sarcophagus. The lid scraped the rest of the way across the top and crashed down one side to the floor. Jackson pushed up on his knees, pulling Kailin's limp body with him. "Kailin, we're out. Breathe," he ordered, using one hand to hold her chin, but she was limp.

Panic ricochetted inside him like gravel in a tornado. He leaped down onto the stone floor and lifted her, laying her out there. His chest clamped tight. He tried to inhale deeply himself but could only concentrate on trying to detect movement in Kailin. He ran his hands over her face, splaying back her hair.

"We saw her leave," Moghadam insisted.

Jackson ignored him, watching Kailin for signs of life. He rested his hand on her chest and felt the thud of her heart. He sucked in an inhale so fast that he coughed over the sob as his head fell forward, his eyes closed. *Thank you, God.*

Her lips moved and Jackson's chest opened enough for him to fill his lungs. He'd been given a second chance. The cramp in his chest uncoiled. Kailin was alive.

"Our queen," one man murmured.

"Give her some room," Moghadam commanded. Jackson leaned back and released her to stand.

Boom! The tomb's ceiling blasted upward. A fountain of dirt and artifacts shot like an explosion into the inky night sky. Around them, men screamed in surprise, two of them flying out with the artifacts. Kailin lifted her arms at the same time her eyes flicked open.

"Out," she whispered and rose within the storm like Athena rising to the heavens. She glanced down at Jackson as she disappeared into the dark. "Jackson." She moved her hands, but nothing tugged at him. Her telekinesis still had no effect on him. Even the Orb had risen out of its silken wrap, a firefly glow lighting it from within, while he watched from below.

Moghadam was praying, and his two remaining men crouched by the sarcophagus.

Jackson glanced around for a rope or something climbable. But the sarcophagus was the only thing remaining in the tomb. Once Kailin's panic ebbed, she'd be furious at herself for the destruction, her shattering of the etchings and mosaics on the ceiling.

Jackson cupped his hands around his mouth. "Kailin throw the Orb back down to me. It magnifies your magic and could call the demons back." Kailin dropped the Orb over the hole, letting gravity carry it. Jackson caught the slightly glowing ball.

With the Orb under his arm, Jackson looked at the stunned men. "She can lift you out." He rubbed a grimy hand over his dust-covered face. "I'm going to hitch a ride." He pointed at the long sash around Moghadam's waist.

"Jackson?" Kailin stood on the edge of the chasm she'd erupted in her panic. Sand sifted down from her feet. The stars wreathed her head in the blackness of the once again clear sky. The constellations, his longtime friends, watched in awe with him. "Drakkina and the demons seem to be gone."

"Let's keep it that way," he said.

Moghadam yelled up, and the two men that had been unnaturally lifted yelled back.

"I didn't kill them," Kailin said, frowning down at the leader.

"It would be your right, my queen."

Kailin huffed, a hand going to her riotous hair hanging around her shoulders. "Ridiculous." In the firelight from a torch somewhere behind her she looked like a dark angel shot down to earth, tumbled in the sand and dirt of cruel humanity.

The separation between them physically hurt inside Jackson.

"Moghadam," Jackson said and took the proffered sash. The tall leader spoke in Arabic to his two men, and they too gave him their sashes, which he wrapped together to make a long, sturdy rope. He tied them quickly around his legs like a harness, all the while keeping the muted Orb under his arm.

Moghadam tried to take it from him. "I will protect it for the queen."

"No," Jackson said, "I mute its magic more, so the demons won't return." He spoke as if he were an expert on the bizarreness of the situation. Really he only muted it completely when he touched Kailin.

Jackson gave the end of the wrapped sashes to Moghadam, which he fastened around himself, his two men taking part of the length to help pull Jackson's weight.

Jackson looked up at Kailin. "They'll pull me up with them."

She nodded and stood so that he only saw her hands out flat over the hole. The men gasped and prayed as their feet left the carved floor, all three of them clasping the rope looped around their arms so that they were pulled upside down. The sash dug into Jackson's groin as he rose into the air, holding tightly to the Orb with one hand and the rope with the other. The cold desert night greeted him like a literal breath of fresh air, and Kailin lowered them gently to the puckered sand.

Jackson yanked the sash from his legs and strode over to Kailin, pulling her into his arms. Stiff and cold, she felt like a neglected mummy. "I've got you," he whispered. Kailin softened, pressing back into him, and he wrapped his whole body around her as she allowed the scope of what they'd survived bubble up to her consciousness.

"We almost died," she whispered. "In a...coffin."

The Orb was a hard annoyance, and Jackson let it drop to his boots on the sand, clasping her completely to his chest. "But we didn't."

The seven of them stood among the broken artifacts on the newly sculpted mounds of debris, rock, and sand. The one man who had been killed below by the demons was found and prayed over by Moghadam and his men.

"We will search for the others in the daylight," Moghadam said, eyeing the cold blackness of the desert. "The cyclone scattered them. Perhaps some will be alive."

"I panicked," Kailin said, pulling back to look into his face.

"Seems like a reasonable reaction considering you were half unconscious and stuck in a tomb."

"I could have killed the rest of us. I was out of control."

"Moghadam's men don't even seem dented. You must have set them down softly."

"I blew the room to bits." Her profile turned to him, her eyes glittering slightly from the torchlight. "All the artifacts. The prince."

"We'll find things in the daylight. Not now." He had to get her somewhere safe. Jackson scanned the night but only stars seemed to watch. He fought the chill down his spine that had nothing to do with the plummeting temperature and everything to do with the thought of the demons coming back. He had no idea how to protect Kailin if that happened.

She shook her head. "I'm the dangerous one. One person shouldn't have such power," she whispered, trying to pull away from him.

"If you think that," Jackson said, trying to put some lightness in his tone, "then we should definitely stay connected."

A shadow dove from the clouds, a silent and graceful form, making Moghadam's men gasp, one falling to the sand to prostrate. Kailin's owl landed with two wing flaps near her legs. His white face twisted back and forth as if taking count of those who had survived.

He made a raspy cry.

"Tuto." Kailin relaxed and crouched down to touch his head.

Her absence in Jackson's arms felt cold, and a press of loneliness made him frown. He looked at Moghadam. "Do you have a way for us to get off this desert tonight? Your queen could use a bath and a good night's sleep where demons can't suck her away."

Moghadam ran a hand over his face while nodding. He too glanced at the open space around them. "We did."

Kailin straightened. "Did I blow them up too?"

Moghadam stared at her, frozen for a second. "I...I don't think so, my queen. The demons' cyclone took much, but we will keep you safe." His eyes flitted to his companions who nodded quickly as if they too felt the ridiculousness of Moghadam's boast after their army had been slaughtered and their "queen" held more power than any of them.

"We had a camp nearby," Jackson said.

"Aiwa, yes," Moghadam nodded and swept his arm out and bowed to indicate Kailin to go first. His men were intent on finding anything of use in the carnage littering the sand.

Tuto leapt into the darkness of night, soaring in silent circles. Jackson secured the Orb in a leather satchel he found on the sand as they began to walk toward their camp. He wouldn't let anyone else possess it.

The sand sifted under his boots as he kept hold of Kailin's arm. Her long strides wobbled, and Jackson steadied her. Far below was a small spark of what remained of their fire. Qeb must have taken the camels, and who knew if they were even alive after the demon's storm. The need to tuck Kailin away somewhere safe made his blood thrum and his gaze scan the dark landscape. Where? He wasn't sure. Where did one hide from demons? A church? A tomb could mask her magic. Which tombs could he access, and how would he get her inside one again?

The chilled desert breeze sliced against Jackson's neck, making him glance behind him. Something wasn't right. "Wait." He paused, his hand halting Kailin's descent. The stars, the constellations, something seemed warped. "Damn," he muttered and Moghadam turned to study the night sky. The darkness, dotted with familiar points of light, wavered like water. It was as if he stared at a reflection of the night sky in a pond.

"The stars," Moghadam began.

"Let's move," Jackson cut him off and propelled Kailin ahead of him down the hill while simultaneously holding her up. The Orb thumped against his hip within the leather pouch.

"What is it?" Kailin tried to stretch her neck around.

The wind picked up sand along the dune, flinging the grains against them. It stung the back of Jackson's neck. He kept Kailin in front of him, blocking her body. A whooshing sound flooded the silence before disappearing. Jackson and Kailin ran down the slope, still connected, Kailin still muted.

Stop! a voice filtered across the sand, straight into Jackson's mind. *Give me the Orb!* It was a voice Jackson knew.

CHAPTER TWENTY-THREE
LION'S DEN

Drakkina pulsed energy into her form so they could see her as she hovered over the dunes. "Give me the Orb." She was so close to it, yet without permission, she couldn't claim it. "It belongs to me."

"It belongs to the one it was gifted to," the Egyptian leader yelled. "Kailin Whitaker."

Drakkina floated down to earth but didn't bother to funnel enough magic into her feet to make them appear. "It belonged to my husband and matches the other half of my amulet." She indicated the ethereal rendition of her dragonfly medallion that hung on a mirage of a chain around her neck. She'd returned the real amulet to its protective hole in the circle of stones in Scotland. She couldn't risk the demons finding it. "The two must be reunited."

"Why?" Jackson Black demanded. "What power will you have when the two are brought together again?"

Damn intelligent man. Drakkina narrowed her eyes. She did not have to answer his questions. She turned her gaze to Gilla's daughter who stood straight and silent, judging her.

"I lured the demons away," Drakkina said and floated closer.

Kailin met her gaze with steel. "And we nearly suffocated to death in a sarcophagus."

Drakkina cursed. "It was the only way to hide your power from them."

"I would rather fight," she said. Jackson nodded in agreement.

"You aren't ready. You'd destroy the world before you could outmaneuver Semiazaz and his coven."

"Which is not her fault," Jackson said.

Drakkina nodded. "I couldn't find you to teach you, child," she said, floating closer to Kailin. "Gilla sent you somewhere where your magic would be difficult to trace. The ancient magic here shields you. It's so potent, its power mixes with yours to confuse your magic signature, confuse the demons."

"I need you to teach me to control it," Kailin said.

"Gift me the Orb," Drakkina answered.

"That's too steep a price," Jackson answered. "We don't know what we're bargaining with yet."

Drakkina's eyes shifted to Jackson. "What are you going to do with it?"

"It has the power to bring life," Jackson threw back. "What are *you* going to do with it? Come back to life?"

Damn perceptive man! "I will have the power to trap the demons once more so they can't wreak havoc on the worlds."

"Worlds?" Moghadam asked. He remained apart but had taken a defensive step closer to Kailin.

"The temporal worlds," Drakkina answered automatically. She was tired of explaining, but humans seemed to require mounds of information. "The demons plan to collapse the web of temporal lines holding apart every line of time, bringing all times and people into existence together. It will be stacks of humanity piled together, ripe for their picking." She paused for dramatic effect, though the truth hardly needed embellishment. "Most will die again immediately, suffocated, crushed, but others will remain to be fed upon, played with, and enslaved on a new world created as a playground for ultimate evil."

Drakkina didn't need to inhale or exhale but she held her breath anyway while the small, dusty group considered her nightmarish prediction. There on the white moon-splashed hills of sand she smoothed her visage into a practiced mask of bland indifference.

"Why help us?" the leader of the raiders asked.

"Because of my oath to Kailin's mother." They didn't need to know more than that. Drakkina's essence was locked in limbo until she could fix the mess she had made in her greed millennia ago. Anguish still twisted her heart.

It was her own disregard of the Earth Mother's warning that had doomed the worlds when she bound the demons together. Stripped of their independence and most of their power, Drakkina had sought to tie them so close they would destroy each other in their frustration and hatred. She'd been wrong, as the Earth Mother had predicted. They'd grown strong, a miscalculation, and now they could touch the mortal world. They had calmed into a deadly force that could work together instead of against one another.

"Kailin." Drakkina hovered close to the slender blond woman who looked so much like her twin, Kat, and just as defiant. "You hold the strongest, most commanding of Gilla's powers."

Kailin stared into her eyes. "I don't want it," she whispered, her smooth lips moving in the moonlight.

"'Tis your responsibility to hold onto the gift. To use it for good, use it to battle the demons who slaughtered your father, stole his gifts, and killed your mother. She sent you away with her most powerful gift so you could use it to save yourself, your sisters, and the world."

"I would give it to you."

"No," Jackson said. "Don't give her anything." The cowherd's eyes narrowed as if he saw through to her unspoken reasons.

Drakkina wasn't surprised. A liar could sniff untruths and half truths easier than those who blindly trusted the good in people.

Drakkina ignored him. "The magic from Gilla is a gift to be kept, not given away. Give me the Orb and I'll teach you to control it, use it."

Kailin turned away, her booted feet sinking into the sand, and trudged down the dune toward the Nile that now reflected the moon's glow along its snaking current. Jackson never let go of her and she seemed to allow his harness. Moghadam and his men trudged after them.

Drakkina swallowed her curse. The girl was as stubborn as Druce. Trust was too hard to earn. It took time, energy, and being cordial. It took honesty, which Drakkina wasn't ready to offer.

"Very well," Drakkina said across the sand. "I will teach you to control your powers without you giving me Eógan's Orb. But don't give it to anyone else either." Drakkina looked at Jackson. "Let the cowherd hold it so it doesn't emit magic."

"I will use it to get my father back," Kailin said though she continued to trudge precariously forward.

"Druce is not coming back," Drakkina spat and then cleared her throat. "No one comes back when demons steal their souls."

"Anthony Whitaker is the father I know," Kailin stated. "He is missing and I will use everything I can to bring him safely home."

Drakkina's make-believe heart thumped hard, and she let it dissolve so she could concentrate on keeping the panic out of her voice. If Kailin gave the Orb away, how could she ever retrieve it from someone who was criminal enough to kidnap an innocent?

"The Orb of Life must be at the final battle, and it must be ours," Drakkina said. "Don't give it away. Semiazaz could trick them into giving it to him and then we will be lost. I am talking about the fate of the whole world, Kailin."

The girl's steps slowed, and she turned back to Drakkina. Drakkina tried to look trustworthy, strong, and rational. Her image shifted about her with her unpracticed efforts while her iridescent swarm of dragonflies danced in agitation around her. "I will teach you to harness the Orb's power, tie it to your own, but don't gift it to anyone, especially someone you can't trust."

"I won't bargain with the devil," Kailin said.

"By the Earth Mother, child!" Drakkina said with honest frustration. "I want the world to go on. I need to fix my wrongs, and I can't do that without Gilla's daughters, their mates, my amulet and that blasted Orb!" She sputtered. "I am at fault." She threw her arms in the air. "I am bringing doom to this world." She jabbed a finger in the air at Kailin. "And I am going to fix it."

Everyone stared at her. If blood still streamed through Drakkina, she would have felt a blush of embarrassment, but she held her head high. "We must work together to save...everything."

Kailin tipped her head slightly, studying her. "I will not gift the Orb to another, but I will get my father back."

It would have to do. For now.

While Jackson held her arm, Kailin let emotions gush within her, a luxurious torrent she'd never allowed before. They sat, arms looped casually together, beside a small fire Jackson had started at their meager camp.

Jackson's hand moved and Kailin yanked in her control, but his grasp slid down her arm to her fingers. Strong and warm, his hand intertwined with her cold digits. He squeezed gently, his fingers sliding all the way to the juncture of her own, an intimate grasp.

She thought to pull away, disentangle, but the strength and warmth of his skin made her own fingers curl into his. It wasn't a weak need for comfort, Kailin justified. With her emotions so raw and her control taxed, it was safer to be connected firmly to the one man who could save her from herself. And save the world from what Drakkina called her gift.

"Do you believe her? Drakkina?" Kailin looked up at Jackson's strong profile.

His jaw clenched and his lips slid back, showing white teeth. "I'm sure the Orb would benefit her personally. She doesn't seem the altruistic type."

"She can't take it. It must be given."

He released a sigh that sounded...frustrated. "A built-in safeguard. Items that don't have power don't need that level of protection. I'd say your rock is pretty damn powerful."

Kailin let Jackson cup her hand, blowing warm air on her cold fingers. "But if I don't know what to do with the Orb," she said, "I could really do some damage."

"Whether Drakkina's motives are purely personal or because she really wants to help this world or because she has some loyalty to your mother…" Jackson shrugged. "Don't know, but I think she'll teach you to control your power and maybe the Orb."

"She knows about my family."

"And you don't?"

Kailin shook her head with only the briefest movement. "I don't remember them." She heard the sorrow in her voice.

Jackson drew Kailin closer. She stared at the exposed skin of his neck where he'd tied a blue square of linen like a loose cravat. She could make out the simple weave of the knot in the moonlight.

Jackson's warm thumb slid across her cheek. "Before this is over, we'll find out what you want to know. Everyone should know from where they hail." He sat back.

"Don't let go," Kailin said. Her emotions were too exposed to trust her control.

Jackson threaded his fingers back through hers, a smile tugging at the corner of his mouth. His lips came close to her ear. "I don't intend to let you go, Kailin." His American twang rolled her name like the rub of his thumb across her palm. It tickled and made heat spread through her at the same time. Kailin scrunched her shoulder toward her ear in defense.

"Baths and using the water closet will be embarrassing to say the least," she teased softly.

Jackson huffed a small laugh and pulled back, giving her room while staying connected. Relief and disappointment collided inside Kailin in a mini geyser. She should want distance. After all, Jackson Black was the most dangerous man she'd ever met, because her powers were useless against him. *Ugh!* Danger was seductive. Like taming a lion. Kailin had never met someone who was truly dangerous before, since she could control the world around her with a thought. Jackson Black was not only handsome, virile, and seductive, he was also definitely lion material.

Moghadam walked over. "My queen, I would see you off this cold desert tonight. My men and I can run to the closest town and return with lights, horses, and ammunition." Even though the man talked to her, his gaze moved to Jackson.

"You found no live horses?" she asked, looking out into the darkness.

"Most ran off with the storm and chaos," Moghadam said. He looked out at the black desert. "But I would not leave you."

"I will keep her safe here until you return," Jackson said.

"And I will keep Mister Black safe until you return," Kailin said without missing a beat.

"No magic," Jackson reminded her.

She nodded. "Of course." This impotence was maddening.

"I can take the Orb, hide it." Moghadam bowed as he spoke. "I will keep it safe for you."

"I will keep it safe for myself," Kailin answered and smiled to hide her irritation. She'd always protected herself and her belongings before. Demons could swoop in and destroy her, but the Orb stood a better chance with her over the militant man with mere pride for protection.

He bowed again. "As you wish, my queen."

That irritated her too. "My queen" was meant for Queen Victoria, not her because she had a strange birthmark that resembled a dragonfly. The title made her even more abnormal, something she'd been hiding her whole life. "And my name is Kailin or Miss Whitaker or Doctor Whitaker."

"Yes," Moghadam nodded and headed out. He spouted off some directions to his small group of men. Two headed in one direction, and Moghadam and the other two ran back the way they'd come.

Jackson's hold pulled her in toward his chest, but he didn't try to kiss her. A confusing twist of disappointment made her feel hollow.

"I doubt they will return before dawn," Jackson said, "so we better make up some shelter if we want any sleep."

"I agree," she said.

"Can I let go?" he asked.

She tipped her nose up slightly, grounding herself in the familiar gesture. "I thought you said you never would."

"Water closets and bathtubs, remember."

"Are you planning to take a swim in the Nile?"

Jackson laughed softly and unclasped her hand slowly. Kailin tensed as her power flooded back into her. She immediately encircled it within an imagined ball, squeezing it smaller until it resembled a pebble in her mind. It was easier this time. Maybe with practice it would become as easy as breathing. Practice and Drakkina's guidance.

Kailin rose and joined Jackson where he slid the strap of a satchel over his head and one arm and placed the Orb in it. "It's less of a demon-beacon away from you."

I trust him with it. He knew he couldn't use it since it was gifted to her.

She shook out several folded blankets while Jackson snapped a canvas tarp that had been buried in the sand. At least on excavations in Scotland she didn't feel the grit of sand in her clothes and hair.

She took a few of the metal stakes Jackson held. "I've put up my fair share of tents," she said. "Or did you forget that I'm not the feather-wearing, needlepointing type of woman?"

He grinned. "I'm not likely to forget that." His roguish look made her want to grin back.

She looked around at the dark emptiness. "In Scotland I tack or tie canvas between trees," she said and watched Jackson erect a folded pole, hooking it into the grommet in the center of the canvas tarp.

"No trees out here. Luckily, the storm didn't carry off everything," he said and grunted while manually drilling the pole into the dense ground. In the cast of firelight, Kailin admired the bulges of muscle under Jackson's sleeves. He glanced at her as if feeling her gaze, and she looked down, busying herself with threading a metal stake into a grommet. Crouching, she twisted and pushed the stake into the cold grains of sand, but it was ridiculously hard without the use of magic.

"Here," Jackson said, walking around the large square of coarse fabric to her. He placed his hand over her own. It was warm and strong. She swallowed hard.

Jackson squeezed, then took the stake. "The sand is hard, and I'm better at ramming through things." His smile was obvious in his tone, but there was a softer undercurrent that hinted at want, need, desire.

They worked together in the darkness, which to Kailin seemed to push them tighter into a ring that was only the two of them. There were small words between them, but mostly only the wind over the dunes, keeping its own conversation.

"That should hold," Jackson said and tossed the remaining blankets into the tent.

Kailin gathered up the three waterskins and small sack of figs, nuts, and Aish Baladi flatbread that they'd found dotting the rising slope of the dune.

Jackson ducked through the slit of the tent, but Kailin stopped before it, arms full, and wet her dry lips. Her heart pounded, and she concentrated on keeping control of the pebble of magic she imagined sat below her breastbone.

Ridiculous. Why was she so nervous to share a tent with the man? *Because he's a lion, that's why.* And Drakkina had said they were soul mates. Yet it was beyond ridiculous to continue to stand outside the shelter. She drew in a fortifying breath and stepped into the lion's den.

CHAPTER TWENTY-FOUR
LA PETITE MORT TO DESTROY THE WORLD

Jackson kept his eyes on his task of flattening the wrinkles out of the blankets. Good, she'd decided to come inside instead of standing out there all night.

She took a deep breath and then spoke casually. "I brought in the food and water."

"Good. Time to eat and rest." He took the satchel off and set it near the found provisions.

"Rest?"

"Sleep."

"Yes, of course," Kailin said, sounding the smallest amount flustered. Any crack in her even resolve was huge. The woman had been through enough to make anyone quake, yet she held herself in check.

She shouldn't have to always be in control, but with her power she had no choice. Kailin must be exhausted. The room was shielded from moonlight, but he'd found a broken lantern that still worked without the glass globe. It cast a warm light, and he watched her settle on a blanket.

Jackson took several gulps from a canteen while Kailin unpacked the fare she'd found. "Not what you usually eat on expedition in Scotland?" Jackson asked.

Kailin smiled. "I lived on oat cakes, fish, edible mushrooms, and flowers for three months."

He gave her a look of sympathy. "No mushrooms and flowers here at present."

Kailin smiled. "No, but I'd be happy to get the grit out of what we have."

He opened his mouth, but she held up a hand. "I won't use magic to clean it."

His gaze connected with Kailin's. She was beautiful with her hair free of her braid in wild disarray from the wind. Her heart-shaped face was smooth and smattered with freckles that she probably despised, but they came from working outdoors, and he loved them. They were like the constellations that he'd called friends. Her lips curved in a soft smile, so unlike her rigidness when they were back in the city. Jackson found it hard to inhale.

They ate in near silence, and he turned the lantern wick down to conserve the oil. Soft inhales and exhales from Kailin whispered between them, like someone trying not to be noticed. She failed completely. Jackson was very aware of her.

"Tasty," he said, and she startled. He swallowed the flatbread. "Anxious?"

She let out a smooth sigh. He wondered what it would feel like across his skin.

"I only truly relax outside. Under the stars."

Jackson stood slowly, as if confronting a horse that could bolt. "Come on." He reached out, and after a moment, she laid her hand in his. He stooped without releasing her and grabbed the blankets he'd smoothed. The constant currents of breeze rushed around them in the crisp night as they emerged under a black blanket of sky bedecked with diamond-like stars.

Jackson released her hand and a sudden breeze of hot air brushed him. He glanced at Kailin.

"Sorry," she murmured. "My concentration is a bit shaken tonight."

"No wonder you're a beacon for the demons. I'll have to stay attached to you." He quickly snapped the blanket up and then down on the sand next to the tent.

Jackson took her hand, and with his other, executed an exaggerated flourish toward the spread. "Your bed beneath the stars, milady."

Kailin lowered smoothly to sit on her heels. Jackson managed to pull another blanket around them while keeping ahold of her hand. "Lean back," he said, tugging her slightly as he reclined. He'd left the lantern in the tent, so the scant light of a quarter moon reflected silver along her hair.

"Why?"

Did the woman think he'd pounce on her if she were horizontal? "To look at the stars. They are glorious out here when there isn't a demon storm obscuring them."

"Hopefully that doesn't happen often," she said, leaning back next to him, their shoulders pressed together as they stared overhead.

"Only once, I've heard, and that may be only a myth," he said.

She sniffed a little laugh. Their hands remained joined between them. Without a campfire, the stars glittered like polished diamonds. Familiar figures stood out, watching.

"Poor Andromeda," Kailin said and pointed upward. "Chained, waiting for the sea monster to rip her apart because of her proud mother's boasts." She stared upward while he turned his face to trace the gentle slope of her nose in profile.

"Forever trapped." She shivered.

"Up there is wide open space though. No monsters, only eternal freedom."

Kailin continued to stargaze. "I have no idea what freedom feels like." She shook her head, the back of it brushing the blanket.

Jackson rolled the tiniest amount closer to her so that his leg pressed against her own. The blanket held their body heat around them, and with their hands clasped it felt...*companionable*. No, that wasn't the word. It felt...right.

"Freedom comes in all shapes and forms," he said. "I suppose Andromeda isn't completely free, since she must rise and move across the sky each night. But we all have boundaries, restrictions."

"Some have more than others."

Jackson remained still as if a little movement would destroy the moment. The slight smell of jasmine still infused the air around Kailin. Damn, but the woman sweated out the sweet smell.

He kept his eyes on the heavens, but he barely saw the stars. His complete focus anchored on the complicated woman next to him. Silence and space surrounded them, their fingers intertwined and tucked between the press of their bodies. As if they were shipwrecked, alone, surrounded by desert and enclosed under heaven's starry canvas. The only thing missing was the song of the crickets back home.

He squeezed her hand. "You know you can surrender when I touch you." She stiffened next to him. "That tight rein you always keep on your power must be a constant battle."

Her body relaxed even though her hold tightened on his hand. "It is," she whispered.

"You've had to struggle to keep it subdued your whole life."

She didn't say anything. She didn't have to. It was clear there in the dark without the distractions and chaos of life.

"I don't want pity," she whispered.

"Good 'cause I'm not dealing out any." Silence.

"You grew up in the States, west of the Mississippi," she said, the soft notes of her voice like a song. Did she sing? He'd love to hear her sing.

"Yes," he answered.

"Was it dangerous living in Indian Territory?"

"It's dangerous anywhere in the world. You have to be mindful, respectful, and think two steps ahead of danger."

"That's where you learned Cherokee."

"Yes, Atsila."

"Fire," she whispered.

The silence began to grow awkward. He could feel the walls erecting between them, her hold on him lessening as she pulled away mentally.

Hell, he didn't talk about himself or about the past. The past was gone and there was nothing to be done about it. But he wanted her to trust him. "My parents were adventurous," he said, his voice too loud. Softening it, he said "They moved right next to the 'savages,' as people called them. I was born on the small farm my parents had started."

"Only you and Cassy?" she asked.

"I had an older brother. Kyle."

"Had?"

"He died of influenza."

"I'm sorry."

Jackson paused for a long moment. "The savages," he exaggerated, "who knew more about living than any white man, tried to save them."

"Is that when you lost your parents?"

"Yes." Jackson felt her fingers readjust in his, sliding tighter into a solid grasp. "Cassy worked alongside the medicine man and survived the exposure."

"Your sister is brave."

"She's the strongest of us all." He swallowed past the familiar lump in his throat. Talking about the bloody past was foolish. It only brought pain. But Kailin squeezed his hand, and he continued. "She was living out there alone and got sick. The poliomyelitis. She'll die if I don't find something to save her."

"Which is why you brought her to Egypt," Kailin said as if she suddenly saw everything as clearly as the stars. But she didn't. She didn't know his secret. How he would do anything to save his sister, to make it up to her for not being there when the rest of his family wasted away beneath her once-strong hands. For leaving them all and heading out on his own in search of treasure. She didn't know how he would make it up to her, to them.

⚬

Kailin waited but no further information came as they laid under the stars, the wind cooling her face as she stared upward. Her mind worked through the picture Jackson's words had created. A boy raised with an older brother and a younger sister, on a farm in Indian Territory. His playmates were the natives people feared and despised. Being the middle child, the younger boy, he'd probably wanted to find his fortune elsewhere and left when he could. And when he returned, most of his family lay buried. Only his sister remained.

She refused the burn of pity tears at the back of her eyes. Jackson Black didn't want pity any more than she did. How about comfort? Everyone could use some comfort.

Jackson turned more toward her. "You should probably get some sleep."

Did she really want to sleep?

The heat from his body filled the small space under the blanket. Warm and all man, Jackson exuded power and strength without a bit of magic to back him up. That was true courage. Unlike she, who spent most of her days afraid of making a mistake like she had tonight. A mistake that blew the side of a hill apart, risking irreplaceable lives and artifacts. Panic, anger, loss of control. She'd battled them her whole life. Never letting herself let go or else—*boom!*

Kailin exhaled deeply. *Am I going to be a virgin all my life?* Because she certainly couldn't let herself be out of control with someone else. At one time, she'd considered marrying, but it would have to be someone boring, a man who couldn't make her feel...well, anything close to passion. The thought left her empty.

No, she wanted to feel something more than worry and regret and constant restraint. She wanted to surrender, lower her defenses, let herself feel life.

Kailin caught a glimmer in her periphery.

"A shooting star," Jackson said. Kailin followed the faint fire trail in the sky. "The Micmac Indians," Jackson continued, "say that's one of two sisters trying to get home. The elder made it and the shooting star is the younger one who messed up and was turned to flame. Yet she still tries to return to her people."

Kailin held her breath as the diamond faded into the black tapestry. She drew in air to fill her lungs with courage and rolled toward Jackson so that one elbow propped her over his chest.

His gaze turned to her. Intense. Questioning. Waiting. He stared.

"A lost sister trying to find her way to a home that no longer exists," she said. She shook her head and wet her bottom lip. His gaze shifted there. Was he breathing? Kailin inhaled and lowered her face to his.

She touched his lips gently, but Jackson's heat plunged into her on contact, melting her hasty plan to keep control into a puddle. His strong hands cradled her face, tilting her over him to deepen the kiss. His taste, the feel of his hands over her cheeks, down the skin of her neck, sent heat throughout Kailin's body. What was this magic that he wielded? Panic bristled inside.

"Whoa there," he whispered and brushed his lips against hers, rolling her to the side. He wasn't over her but next to her. She could still see the sky. He lowered his lips slowly, watching her face. Kailin inhaled his familiar scent and felt his warmth, snapping tingles through her.

Kailin reached behind his head, and Jackson groaned against her lips. His strong fingers parted through her hair, fanning it wide across the coarse blanket. "God, little fire, you are so beautiful," he murmured against her mouth. His hands returned to her face as he poured more and more molten heat into her body. It melted Kailin's insides, all except for her heart which beat like a wild horse thudding across a moor.

"Let go, Kailin," Jackson said against her ear, sending a cascade of shivers down her neck and across her chest, making her nipples pearl. He followed the shivers with his kiss to the hollow of her neck. "I'll catch you." He trailed lower, his fingers freeing the buttons of the shirt tailored to fit her.

Her breath flew from her lips as his kisses moved lower still to the top of her full breast, pushed upward by the corset she wore underneath. Her control shattered and she released a blast of power. She gasped. "No."

Jackson pulled back, concern across his shadowed features. "I'll stop."

"No," she shook her head and huffed. "I let go of my control, and we are all still here." She smiled. There was no pebble inside her throbbing to explode. Oh, there was throbbing, but not from her source of magic. That had dissolved like chalk in water. "Wait one moment."

She exhaled and imagined fire streaking over the dunes, earthquakes, a flood surge from the Nile, and wind contracting into a tight, destructive tornado. Opening her eyes, she clasped Jackson close, her hand bolted to his muscular shoulder. "Don't let go of me," she whispered.

"And if I do?" he asked, studying her face.

A small grin pushed through her concern. "Possibly the end of the world."

Jackson met her smile with his own. "Then I'll hold on to you forever." He stroked his hand through her hair as he kissed her. Hot and full of ripe promises, his kiss washed away any further thought of control.

Suddenly her own clothes felt confining, and she broke the kiss to slide the brushed cotton off one shoulder and then the other. She was giddily aware that Jackson watched with a look of anticipation mixed with worship on his handsome face.

Kailin pushed Jackson down and leaned over him. She threw a leg over his hips and straddled him like a horse, the blanket still draped around her shoulders. With a small shift, the juncture of her legs pressed against his rising member.

"Holy Lord," he murmured on a groan. He sounded tortured as everything about him hardened. Even with Jackson muting her magic, she still had power over him. The idea thrilled her.

She worked open the laces on the front of her corset. His fingers joined hers in their attack on all that was holding her clothes in place. Their eyes met, and in his she saw barely controlled passion. Kailin wanted him to lose control like she had.

The last of Kailin's hooks parted and she threw the bodice off. Letting the blanket fall from her naked shoulders. She sat upright, letting him see her, and felt his gaze rake down from her face to her breasts.

"Oh, Little Fire," he drawled.

Slowly she lifted her breasts, plump and peaked in her hands. She ignored the chill of the breeze as the moonlight shone down on her pale skin, casting her in silver.

Jackson groaned, and sat up, quickly yanking off his shirt. He pulled her to his warm chest. With her legs still straddled over him, her clitoris rubbed against his hard cock, pulsing in answer to a rhythm they began to set.

Their lips moved together, tasting, testing, and she ran her fingers through his thick hair. The hair on his chest teased her nipples, and his fingers stroked down her naked spine as her long tresses tickled her skin. "Little fire," he said against her lips. "I think we'll have to change your name to Wildfire."

Kailin smiled into his face and tossed her hair, almost drunk on her freedom. She'd dropped all control and the world continued to lie still around them, unharmed, unmoved.

He ran his hand down her madly thumping chest. He was gorgeous, rugged, mountainous. She'd never let herself notice for too long before, but now... Now she could touch and look at him, all of him. Three days of beard roughened his square jaw. Brown hair she knew had sprays of sun-kissed gold lay in sexy disarray almost to his chin. Jackson was a delicious cross between Perseus and a wild man from the plains that grew him. Bronze and muscled, not afraid to dirty his hands, yet clever and cultured without having to prove it to others.

His hand looked dark against the paleness of her breast. Kailin shivered as his thumb drew circles around her nipple.

"Atsila," Jackson murmured. "It's cold. Come back down here." He pulled the blanket back over her shoulders and guided them both to the ground.

"Mmmm...warm." She draped herself over him like another blanket.

He rubbed warm hands down the skin of her bare back. "You're as cold as a sheared sheep in winter." Strong arms came around her, holding her close, but she didn't feel trapped at all.

"Have you cradled a sheared sheep in winter?" Kailin asked against the hollow of his throat. She let her tongue slip out to wantonly touch his skin, tasting the salt there.

Jackson groaned and she shifted slightly, rubbing against his bulge below. "Yes, I have."

"Have what?" She'd lost track as she tried to let her fear of the unknown evaporate like her controls. Copulating was nothing new to humankind. It was a simple response to life's pressure to procreate. Why should she worry about it? Well, there was the procreation part.

"Held a freezing lamb against my chest in winter."

"Oh. Was it lost?"

He paused for a long moment. "I found her in a white-out and carried her home under my coat."

Kailin's mind dismissed his words and followed his hands. They ran down her hips to loosen the rope she'd been using as a belt to hold up the men's trousers. She snuggled into his chest and raised her hips to give him room. He chuckled and worked her pants down, running his hands over her hips and buttocks. It occurred to her that no one but she had ever touched that part of her body before. No one she remembered.

When his fingers trailed down her bloomers to the material slit between each legging, she stiffened. Apparently, she wasn't as wanton as she'd hoped.

He stroked her thigh on the outside of the thin white linen. Jackson lowered his face to brush against her lips. "This is where I stop." The words sounded like he was informing himself as much as her.

"What?" she raised her head, looking down at him, her body still thrumming with need.

"I've been waiting until you signaled. I'm glad it wasn't much further." He kissed her parted lips while stroking down her spine and over her buttocks. "You're a virgin, Kailin."

"What does that matter?" she asked. Did he not want her because she was inexperienced? Didn't men like innocence in a woman?

"I'm not going to take you outside wedlock. I may come across like an ill-mannered rogue, but I'm not." His arms tightened, drawing her down to lay across his naked chest. "Although you are damn tempting," he murmured against her hair. He inhaled long and a small growl issued. "Damn tempting."

She worked her hands between them and propped her forearms on his chest to frown at him. "You aren't taking me. I'm...taking you. I *am* the one on top." She quirked an eyebrow at him and hoped he could see her expression in the moonlight.

With a tensing of muscle, he rolled her off him to her side so they faced each other. "Not anymore." His teasing smile faded. "Kailin," he said, brushing the side of her face. "I am not the marrying type, and I won't ruin you—"

"Ruin? How archaic," she said, her temper piqued. "And I'm not the marrying type either, so you can ruin me, that is, if I say yes. And I'm saying yes."

His brows pinched, and she wanted to reach over and smooth the anxiousness away. "Not the marrying type?"

"How could I marry?" She flopped onto her back to stare up at the diamonds above. But the constellations didn't bring peace. Staring up into the vastness of space, she felt lonely. "Do you think I could marry someone I couldn't lose control with? How could I copulate with all my shields up, protecting the world from my devastating power?" She left the obvious lying between them. She wasn't about to ask Jackson to marry her. "Plus, Drakkina said we were soul mates." Her words sped up. "She'd be quite happy if you...ruined me."

"I..." he started and then stopped. "You don't know me, Kailin."

"I know you held a baby sheep under your coat to save it. I know you feel guilty for not being home when your parents and brother died. I know you love your sister. I know you lied about working closely with Anthony, and that you wish to see the wide-open prairie again." He opened his mouth, so she put a finger over his lips.

"I know you are honorable and therefore have a good reason for lying to me, which we'll talk about when I'm not half naked." She removed her finger. "And I heard... In the sarcophagus, you whispered...that I was yours, your woman. I think that's as good as I'll get to being married."

He shook his head, reaching over to capture her chin, stroking his thumb slowly along her lip. "You think too little of yourself."

"It's true though; you have to see. I can't be with another man. What if he brought me to la petite mort?" Kailin had read the verses by Chaucer and Shakespeare about the womanly orgasm that brought on a trance-like swoon akin to a mini-death. She knew that by touching herself, she could bring herself pleasure without a man being involved. But she hadn't dared to do so when it could cause chaos and damage. But with Jackson muting her powers, she might be able to experience what poets glorified and maids whispered over.

"If I... well major earthquakes could rock the world, floods, brush fires." She raised her arm, moving her hand for emphasis as she spoke, which brought the smile back to his face. Kailin dropped her arm and slid closer to him, resting her hand on his sculpted chest, in an effort not to look as desperate as she felt. "Don't make me beg, Jackson. We're two adults."

"What if you get pregnant?"

"I've never lived up to cultural acceptance, and I've always wanted a baby. One with gray-blue eyes and golden-brown hair suits me just fine."

He stared at her, not a single blink.

"Jackson?"

In one fast exhale, Jackson grabbed her, rolling so that she lay beneath him.

CHAPTER TWENTY-FIVE
TOTAL SURRENDER

He held himself on his elbows propped on either side of her face. His lips crushed down onto hers, full of wild heat as if she'd released him off a chain. Had he been holding himself back? And now he'd let go, like she had. They kissed for long moments, each one growing in intensity. Kailin moaned against his mouth as she threw a leg over his hips so that her pelvis pressed against the large bulge in his trousers.

Jackson stroked her shoulder, and then slid his palm along her full breast, teasing the nipple. It felt good, so very good. He continued to kiss her while his hand trailed over her skin, as if mapping an unexplored landscape. Sensation tingled along every inch, and she didn't have to stop it for fear of what her powers might do.

Kailin rubbed bare legs against his and reached down to unclasp his trousers. He growled low and shucked the trousers and his underclothes in seconds. Her hand came in contact with him and she tensed. It was large. She'd never even seen a real man naked, and all the sculptures and

Classical art she'd studied had the member small, nothing like Jackson's erect penis.

His hand stopped over her abdomen, his breath ragged. "We can stop," he said.

All Kailin could do was shake her head.

"I want to hear you say it."

"Say what?" she whispered, still holding him, her fingers taking in the length and breadth. Was Jackson large by manly standards? Who the hell could she ask that of? Bruce? She nearly laughed.

"Say what you want."

"You, Jackson Black, I want you." She stroked him. "Even if you are gargantuan in comparison to other men."

A deep chuckle exploded from his chest. "Gargantuan?

"I did not mean to offend," she said, sliding her hand up to his chest. "I am sure it works fine even large."

She felt the suppressed mirth in his chest as a rumble. "It works just fine, brilliantly in fact," he said and caught her hand, kissing it. He pulled her into him, and the last coherent thought Kailin had was that they were indeed alone under the bright stars. Not even Tuto circled. No demons swirled death nearby. No Drakkina interfered or watched. Not even magic threatened their inner circle under the cocooning blanket. Only Jackson. Only Kailin. Together.

Moans hummed up her throat as Jackson kissed his way down the column. His tongue tasted her skin, probably as salty has his. "I wish I could bathe first," she said.

"I prefer you dirty to croc-bitten," he murmured and kissed and licked his way to her nipple. Her breath hitched as he encircled it with his lips, his teeth tickling the tip. "You taste delicious exactly the way you are."

Jackson sent ripples of sensation through her chest as his hand wove a trail down her stomach to her bloomers. Kailin lost herself in Jackson's mouth on her skin. She ran frantic fingers through his soft, thick hair. The sensation of the cotton of her bloomers sliding down her legs added to the excitement. Jackson kissed her lips and then blazed a trail up to her ear.

"You are everything amazing, Kailin Whitaker," he said before moving back to her mouth. He slanted her face to deepen the kiss, and she devoured him right back. He groaned and his hand coursed down the side of her breast to her hip, stroking, his rough palm tickling her smooth skin. Their kisses were hot, all-consuming kisses, and Kailin couldn't tell where she stopped and Jackson began. They were becoming one.

She turned further into him so that they lay facing each other. She ran fingers down his broad back, marveling at the rippled strength there, the heat he gave off. She reached his buttocks and squeezed. He groaned and rolled her back down, stroking down her stomach. Could he feel the butterflies flitting there? Where molten heat singed their wings until they flew, leaving only lava pooling in her pelvis?

He stroked her legs and hips, her inner thighs, but not her core. Lord, she craved his touch. Kailin grasped the back of his hand and guided it to her. "Touch me," she breathed into him. "Touch me here."

Jackson pushed the heel of his hand down, grinding against a deliciously sweet spot that begged for more. Kailin surged upward into his palm. Over and over she pressed in a primal rhythm that felt as natural as the cadence of her heart. He continued to grind into her as his finger slipped below.

He groaned, breathing heavy against her cheek. "Atsila, my wildfire, you are so hot and ready."

"Please," she whispered, widening her knees, the very center of her on fire with pulsing want. Wild horses hammered through her. Rushing heat built higher and higher until she felt consumed. "I want all of it, all of you."

Jackson shifted, rising above her, centering. She wrapped her legs around his back, resting her heels on his naked buttocks.

"Open your eyes, Kailin."

She hadn't realized that she'd squeezed them shut and blinked open. His face was dark with shadows, but the moon gave enough light for her to see the fierce set of his features as he held himself over her aching body. The tip of his cock found her, and she used her legs to pull him into her.

"Mine," he groaned and thrust, filling her completely.

She barely felt the sting she'd read about in a medical book and was slightly stunned that her body could take all of him.

He stilled, buried completely inside her. Did he not feel the urge to move? Kailin lifted her hips and moaned softly as she rocked. "It's not over, is it?"

He choked a bit. "No."

"Then move," she said, pressing against him. Her fingers curved into his shoulders.

Jackson's lips met hers and her hips rose against his loins. He groaned. "I don't want to hurt you."

"I'm not some fragile papyrus," she said. "And I'm on fire."

He frowned, still not moving, so she added, "In a good way. Now move."

Jackson leaned in, kissing her, pouring more heat into her. Kailin's hips rose again and this time he answered. He slid so deep that she felt his cock reach toward her very center, binding them together as one. A primitive rhythm claimed Kailin's entire focus. There was no magic to control, no boundaries to keep up. She was open and consumed, outside and now inside. She gave herself over to all the sensations, reveling in them, swimming deeply in them, in the essence of Jackson.

"Mine," she said as they moved together. "My man."

"Mine," he answered and kissed her. "My woman." He dove once more for a soul-consuming kiss, and they writhed as one, giving and taking, rising and falling. He rose higher on her pelvis so that with each thrust he rubbed against her sensitive clitoris.

"Oh yes," she said, feeling a rise like a crescendo in a symphony. Their movements became more frantic, and she heard Jackson's heavy breaths. "I think..." She didn't know what she thought, but she felt need, intense need.

"Don't think, just feel," he instructed, his jaw tight as the intensity rose higher and higher.

Kailin strained, reaching for the promise of some primitive ecstasy that she could barely believe. Yet it was there, within sight. She could almost find it. "Jackson," she moaned as he rubbed faster, his body moving in an erotic ride over hers, fully surrounding her soft body in muscle and man. The wave built with each thrust. Kailin pounded upward against him. "Oh God, Jackson!" She found the crest and dove blindly over.

"Kailin! Atsila!" Jackson roared. Wave after wave jolted through her body, like lightning radiating out from her pelvis, reaching every muscle, every single nerve ending. The rush of blood pounded with her moan and Jackson's back muscles contracted over her, his arms flexed on either side of her face.

For long moments, their bodies continued the ride. Slowing slightly with each exhale, squeezing out every last drop of exquisite sensation.

Jackson leaned over her, kissing Kailin gently on love-swollen lips. They stared at each other as their breaths climbed back down. His muscular, large body was heavy even though mere moments ago she'd urged him to pound into her even harder. He must have felt her wiggle and shift, and he tried to roll to the side.

"Stay," she whispered.

"I don't want to crush you."

She smiled. "You seemed to a moment ago."

"You weren't complaining." He tried to move again, but she held tight. He held himself on his forearms to give her space to breathe.

"Wait. For a moment." Jackson studied her face, and Kailin wet her lips. "It's the first time I've been totally surrounded by something and not panicked."

"Surrounded." He glanced at his biceps on either side of her head. "You're definitely one trapped woman."

"Trapped?" She laughed, happiness bubbling out of her. "I've never felt so free. Imagine that." She shook her head. "And yet I can't even see the sky."

He held over her for another moment. She shrieked slightly when he rolled them and covered their heads with the blanket. In complete darkness Jackson enveloped her again within his arms. Against his chest, their heat still lingered.

"Wildfire, you are amazing," Jackson murmured into her hair. "And I'm not letting you go."

For the first time ever, Kailin fell asleep peacefully, without being able to see the sky.

Dark, peaceful warmth surrounded Kailin on all sides like a perfectly heated bath. Comfort melted along her bones as she luxuriated in the subtle fragrance of man and their combined scent. She sighed inside the confines of her dream. Sunset colors blended with storm clouds and collapsed into perfect gray-blue eyes.

"Shhh," his whisper penetrated her sleep. "Don't move. Someone's out there."

Kailin's awareness flooded back into her body with a jolt of magic. Luckily, Jackson's body still lay against her, dampening her power, once again saving whoever or whatever moved about their small camp in the valley.

She and Jackson lay beneath the blanket twenty feet from the tent. Kailin kept her body perfectly still, but her eyes opened to a dazzling show of stars and a lightening toward the east. Dawn was approaching fast. Could Moghadam have returned?

The stark click of a gun cocking startled Kailin. A quick squeeze from Jackson told her it was his. She gritted her teeth. If she used her magic, would it call the demons? Would people try to manipulate her if they knew about her abilities? She had power but couldn't use it without extreme consequences. *Damn useless.* Very well, she'd let Jackson take the lead.

Silence was followed by a slight rustling of the canvas. *Damnation!* The intruders were in the tent with the Orb while she was naked beneath the blanket.

"Jackson, the Orb," she whispered where her lips brushed against his jaw.

"When I roll away, get dressed fast," he instructed on a slow exhale. "Then run."

Yes, to getting dressed. Hell no, to running away. He had to know that.

Jackson lifted the side of the blanket and rolled away from Kailin. The cold off the desert sands washed under and across her bare skin. Kailin fought the shiver as she silently grabbed her trousers. No time for drawers. She shoved her hand about under the blanket as quietly as possible until she found her shirt and shrugged into it. Hell, the bloody buttons were on the inside. She buttoned them anyway.

Jackson had dressed in his trousers with suspenders over his shirt before she'd woken. He walked bent over, a keffiyeh wrapped around his head as if to hide his identity. He pushed into the tent.

"Looking for me?" Jackson's voice cut through the dark. "Back out of there. Leave the Orb."

A man spoke softly in Arabic. Kailin heard her name.

"She's returned to Luxor," Jackson said. "There's no one here to stop me from shooting a thief so don't tempt me."

"Ahh, Mister Black." The cool, articulate voice stopped Kailin in mid-crouch. "Do you really think I'd send one hired local to retrieve the Orb of Life?" She knew that voice.

"Where's Anthony Whitaker?" Jackson asked and Kailin heard the shuffling of feet. She crouched back down, her toes turning in the cold sand. At least six bodies stood outlined by the slow lightening of the sky behind them.

Jackson's form was the tallest. A second man held a gun to his head. *No!* Kailin's magic welled up in her, but she held tight to it. Uncontrolled, her magic was no help at all.

"Doctor Whitaker is waiting for his daughter to return to her hotel room."

"You've released him?" Jackson asked.

"Of course. It was tiring holding him and his servant blindly captive. And one of my sources made it back last night after the strange storm."

"One of Moghadam's men?"

"So Moghadam thought. Of course he's no one's man now. Blathering idiot ranting about cyclones and evil wind. I had to put him out of his misery."

Kailin watched the outlines, unable to move or look away. Though logic dictated that if it became light enough for her to identify the leader, it would be light enough for his men to spot her. But she couldn't leave. Not when a gun sat at Jackson's temple, not when she was almost certain of the identity of the man with the familiar voice. Kailin lay flat against the cold sand, wishing she could turn tan and blend in like a viper.

"As soon as I heard you had the Orb, I released the good doctor and came to find it before you disappeared with it. A treasure hunter like you could never release the ultimate prize."

Kailin shifted to ease the tension in her muscles. The tent blocked the speaker but the hair on the back of her neck prickled. The voice was practiced, British, and smooth. Yet she'd never heard it so calculated, so cold. As she edged the final inch, her neck straining to see around the canvas, the man's words stopped her.

"I'm so glad Kailin left. I plan to marry her eventually, so I didn't want to kill her."

"She's mine, Dallinton," Jackson said, jarring Kailin out of her initial shock. Her eyes froze on Jackson. She was his? Her face flushed as she remembered their declarations last night.

Yes, she pinched her lips together. She was his, and he was hers. And she wasn't about to let anyone shoot the man she loved. Her heart pounded in her ears. The realization spread through her chest as if the warmth of the sun was exploding inside. Her stomach flipped and she concentrated on silent breath.

She blinked. Dallinton? Henry Dallinton, the milksop hanging on Samantha's skirts?

Henry Dallinton laughed. The cold, empty sound squelched the sun inside Kailin, making her shiver.

"She's yours?" Dallinton snorted. "Kailin Whitaker can't belong to a dead man."

"You need me," Jackson said. "You don't know how the Orb works."

Kailin lay on her stomach, scooting slowly in the predawn shadows until she could see the front half of Henry Dallinton. He stood in a long pale duster and a felt hat and sported a rifle. One of his men still held a gun to Jackson's head, the keffiyeh draped around his broad shoulders. If the villain fired, there'd be no way she could stop the bullet from penetrating Jackson's brain. Her heart pounded through her chest against the sand. She'd found love and now it could fall through her fingers. Kailin's chin rested in an indent of sand.

"Kailin will help me unravel its mysteries, and I will be the most powerful man alive," Henry said.

"I doubt your bosses will let that happen."

Henry laughed. "The British government is utterly foolish. Like your bloody government. Both of them hired you, a known treasure hunter, to steal the Orb for them, when I have little doubt that you planned to take it for your own."

Kailin's attention was drawn from the gun. Take it for his own? *Deny it.* She waited.

"Kailin will never help you," Jackson said.

Henry huffed dramatically. "Really, Black, do you actually think the woman will mourn your death when she finds out your role in her father's abduction?"

Kailin's lungs emptied numbly, injected with the poisonous words. Jackson didn't say anything. She blankly noticed the other men tightening the circle around Jackson.

"The only man her dear father saw during the whole ordeal was you when you lured him away from his apartments. When she identifies your body and her father realizes who you are, she'll be thankful she didn't fall prey to your duplicity." Henry stared into Jackson's unwavering face and tilted his head. "Or has she already?"

Say something! Say he's lying, that you had nothing to do with Anthony! Kailin's silent scream thudded behind her temples while she stared without seeing. Memories flooded her mind. Jackson jumping over her railing, delivering the ransom note, insisting he help her find the Orb. The lie about her name and working with Anthony twisted in Kailin's stomach until she felt like she could throw up.

"Kailin knows nothing," Jackson said between his teeth. "Leave it that way."

"Certainly not," Henry growled. "If the twit has somehow lost her heart or worse to a scoundrel like you, I have every intention of punishing her for it."

"You want the Orb. Leave her alone," Jackson said, ice in his voice.

"I only wanted the Orb until I saw her. She's a beauty despite her regal snobbery." Henry squinted. "Oh, don't condemn me, Black. You want the same things: the Orb and the girl. You took my money quick enough to help abduct her father and bring her to Egypt. I knew all along that you wouldn't be able to give up the treasure. What were you planning to do? Steal the girl's heart and then her treasure?" Henry shook his head and *tsk*ed. "She'll be glad I killed you. Maybe she'll thank me properly"—he laughed then—"or rather improperly."

"Do not touch her," Jackson threatened, his voice so cold that Henry's cocky smile faltered, but then righted itself.

"Oh, I certainly will," Henry said, his eyes shifting to the hired man holding the gun. Henry's nod to the man shot through Kailin, melting the ice that held her paralyzed. Instinct took over, the building blocks of basic, uncluttered truth. *Jackson cannot die!* No matter what was real and terribly true.

Jackson dove at the same time Henry's eyes shifted. Jackson's back leg kicked out, catching the armed man's kneecap. The gun exploded with a crack that splintered through the dawn stillness.

"No!" Kailin leapt upright out of the sand. Her power pulsed out of her toward the bullet, toward Jackson. The man who'd lied to her, kidnapped Anthony, and wanted the Orb for himself. "No!" she screamed, her arms rising. Everyone turned toward her, everyone except Jackson.

The bullet struck his back, its power slamming him face first to the sand. Blood wet his shirt from the inside, spreading outward in a ragged circle from the impact point. The bright, primal color sucked the breath from Kailin. "No." The word came out with a sob.

CHAPTER TWENTY-SIX
SHATTERED HEART

"Kailin, thank goodness you're well," Henry called. "This scoundrel has duped you. Anthony is safe at your hotel."

Jackson lay still, unmoving. "Jackson?"

Power frothed into billows inside Kailin, filling her focus, pushing the pain to the breaking point. Heat, angry and vengeful, wafted out of her, magic exciting the metal structure of the weapons in the disjointed circle of villains. The men grunted and gasped, dropping their guns to watch dumbfounded as the metal warped and sizzled in the sand, fusing with the grains.

"You shot him," Kailin called, her hands raised, magic at her fingertips.

"Kailin," Henry said, his hand out as if she were a stalking puma. "He's nothing but a liar, a paid mercenary bent on tricking you, laughing at you."

Kailin unleashed a blast of magic, her hand pointed to the sand under Henry Dallinton's feet. "Down," she mouthed with such ice that the word nearly froze her lips. *Wham!*

Henry screamed as the sand beneath him flew upward a hundred feet into the air as he sank down into the dune. "Down," she snarled until all that remained was Henry's head, his lifted chin resting on the sand.

"Help!" he yelled, his eyes wildly searching the group of thugs around them. "Pull me out of here!" Two large men ran toward Kailin while two others began to dig with their hands around Henry's head.

A twitch of her fingers tossed the men running toward her into the air. Loud curses and screams ensued as she moved her hands, directing the thugs to weave amongst each other at her whim. "Far," she whispered and watched the men fly through the dawn back across the dunes a mile or two. She almost dropped her arms, but at the last minute lowered them slowly before turning back to Henry.

She flicked her finger and the tent exploded. The Orb lay exposed, throbbing with her power.

"Kailin! Listen to me!" Henry yelled and spit at the sand pecking his face in the wind. His wide eyes blinked furiously at the sand. "Calm down. Let's talk about this." Henry screamed as geysers of fire shot up from the sand, encircling him in a cell of flames. Fury like she'd never let herself feel raced freely through her limbs.

"Freak!" he screamed, but Kailin barely heard him.

She stared paralyzed as the blood oozed through Jackson's shirt. Red spread across his back in the seconds since she'd reacted. His head lay toward her, eyes open, his white scarf thrown outward across the sand. He didn't say anything. He didn't have to. Regret, anger, pain twisted in his gray eyes until they blinked long and closed.

"No!" Kailin screamed and dropped to the hard ground next to him. A geyser of sand rose around them to slice the clouds above. "Jackson! Don't die!" she yelled.

"Kailin—" Henry started. Kailin flipped her hand and Henry's body flew up out of the dune to follow his men, his yell fading in the distance.

With barely a thought, Kailin summoned the Orb. It rolled across the shifting landscape to her side. Her fingers dug into the sand next to Jackson. She didn't touch him. That wouldn't help.

The Orb glowed, drenched in the waves of her uncontrolled magic. She picked it up. Its mass filled her cupped hands. It felt warm, almost hot. There was nothing to guide her, just instinct or perhaps the Orb itself. Sand and heat swirled around Kailin. She straightened to stand tall, holding the glowing sphere, centering it above Jackson's blood-drenched back.

"Kailin!" a frantic whisper penetrated the wind, but she ignored it, her entire being focused on Jackson spread out below her.

"Heal him," she spoke aloud and funneled her magic and vision of his healed body into the Orb. "Heal him."

Kailin's magic focused into a sharp stream down into the Orb in her hands, and the whirlwind of sand cut off, dropping around them. "Kailin! The demons! Stop!" the whisper grew to a shout as the world around her grew quiet once more.

"Heal him," she whispered, the words thrumming through her body, pounding with her heart. The Orb glowed brighter, expanding its light to encompass Kailin and Jackson.

"They are coming now," Drakkina's voice became a whisper from outside the Orb's glow.

Kailin knelt over Jackson's prone body, hovering without touching. The Orb spread heat within its surrounding area. The heat penetrated her body, warming her muscles, her very bones, seeking and mending sore spots. Kailin dared not open Jackson's shirt. If she touched him and muted the magic, could she make the Orb work again?

"Heal him," she whispered and watched his back rise with an inhale and fall. The light hummed, heated, and penetrated, resonating under them until they sat on a thin surface of warped glass made from sand.

Jackson rolled over, his hand rising to her hair that dangled over one shoulder to the desert floor. One touch, one glance of his finger across a single strand of hair and the Orb sucked the magic back into itself.

"I have to get you out of here!" Drakkina screeched. "By the Holy Earth Mother, control your magic. Cap it, tie it within yourself, but stop flapping it around like a white flag!" She waved her arms over her head, scattering her dragonflies. "Look here, demons! Come and get me!"

"Atsila." Jackson sat up, his blood soaking the front of his shirt like the back. A dark pool of it stained the sand where he'd fallen, and in the center of it, a bullet.

She looked away. "Don't call me that," she said. "Don't call me anything." Kailin stood up and set the Orb back on the sand so as not to touch it. It remained nearly dormant without her magic engulfing it.

"Kailin," Jackson said. "I…"

"Who do you think you are?" Kailin felt tears scorch the back of her eyes.

"Someone who doesn't deserve you."

Wind whipped across the dunes as dark clouds gathered on the horizon. Their shirts and Jackson's keffiyeh snapped around them. Tuto screeched as he circled them turkey-vulture-style, gliding on the shifting currents of air.

"Quick, Kailin, you and the Orb must hide," Drakkina said. She ran her hand over her face and up into her wild hair. "Where, where? Where do I send her?"

Kailin stared in horror at Jackson. He didn't say anything but looked at her, his gaze roaming her face, her form, as if memorizing her.

"You lied," she said. "You...used me."

Jackson didn't refute anything, didn't try to explain. His eyes appeared...sad.

How could she have been so blind? She was intelligent, yet Jackson's large, handsome form and sly tongue had duped her, shown her to be the idiot in this farce. She turned away and looked at Drakkina.

"Send me somewhere then, far away."

"Yes, yes, but where? Somewhere you can be hidden, you and that blasted Orb." Drakkina looked at her. "I could stuff you in a tomb."

"Not if you want to keep what's left of your essence together," Kailin threatened, readying her magic to strike, like a cloud gathering lightning to sear the earth.

"Cac! Put that magic away, girl." Drakkina flapped her hands. "It pinpoints your position."

Kailin studied the racing clouds. Electrical discharges cracked through the thunderheads. "Actually, I think I'll stay. Today is a good day for that final battle." Pain and fury mixed inside Kailin. Hurling her destructive magic at the demons that murdered her parents and threatened all humankind seemed appropriate.

Thunder shattered the wail of the wind. Kailin's hair flew up on the gusty currents, tendrils twisting and snagging together. She stared up at the building chaos of evil and hardened her heart. She held the magic coiled and ready like a curse sitting on her tongue.

"Gift me the Orb!" Drakkina shouted.

"No!" Kailin and Jackson yelled at the same time. Kailin glared at him.

"Get Kailin out of here—and the Orb," Jackson yelled. He stood, his shirt stained as if painted with a bullseye.

"I'm not going anywhere!" she yelled back. "I'm ready for this fight." The hairs along her body stood on end as the magic flowed under her skin. "Let them come." She stared up at the mass of black as it formed a funnel.

"Don't be stupid, girl!" Drakkina screamed. "They'll rip you apart like your father, like Gilla!"

"You don't know that," Kailin said, her voice above the roar. "I'm more powerful than you can imagine." With that, Kailin released her pent-up energy, her anger, her shame and embarrassment into a mighty blast that sent the top of a dune shooting up into the tornado. Sand, earth, rock, and buried relics shot out from the funnel cloud to be strewn for miles around. The debris fell around them, bouncing like hail. Jackson dodged a falling jar that shattered on the dune.

"Better slither underground, Mister Black," Kailin warned, her armor of ice in its familiar place. "This is likely to become ugly." She turned her gaze back to the demons and raised her arms. White lightning shot from her hands, splintering over miles up into the air. Kailin cupped her hands, the palms forming a ball, and the energy wrapped around the tornado, encapsulating it. The dark clouds condensed.

"Just like Druce!" Drakkina yelled, but Kailin ignored her rant.

She hurled a blast of power toward the demons. Her bullet of magic smacked against a barrier and dissipated as if it were mere wind against a wall. She gathered more energy, pulling from the glowing Orb she balanced on the tops of her bare feet. The Orb throbbed in time with her heartbeat, linked to her, centering her magic into a dagger.

"What can I do?" Jackson yelled and Kailin realized he was talking to Drakkina, not her.

She ignored them and concentrated on funneling a lifetime of muted magic into a weapon of demonic destruction. *Whoosh*! She sent a stream of disruptive force toward the demon storm.

Her magic pooled into the center of the funnel. She could see its white light. What would happen? Could it blow them apart? Could she single-handedly destroy the greatest threat to humanity the world had ever seen? It would make a lifetime of controlling this cursed gift worthwhile. It would maybe even ease the pain of her own stupidity, her gullible foolishness to believe a liar with the most mesmerizing gray-blue eyes. He'd helped abduct Anthony. *I'm such a fool.*

Whoosh! She snapped another blast. It added to the pool in the center. She frowned. It was as if she had fed it.

"Stop throwing your tantrum," Drakkina yelled.

The white light intensified. It was hard to look at. *Boom!* The white magic slammed back down to the earth, hitting a dune to the south, shattering it. Kailin found herself on the ground, the wind knocked out of her.

The world shook as if in fear. Ripples of earthquakes shuddered under her back. Wind threw rocks the size of billiard balls across her line of sight overhead. Tuto swooped down to land next to her on the sand, the safest place to be. Bloody hell, what had she done?

"Get her out of here!" Jackson roared as he yanked her to her feet. A rock hit her toe with enough force to break it, and the pain shot through her. She grabbed it, wincing, and wrestled her arm free of Jackson's grasp.

She hobbled to the side and grabbed the Orb, tucking it under her arm. She wasn't losing the prize everyone wanted. As she touched the sphere, her toe instantly stopped aching.

"On the currents of my blood," Drakkina intoned, her face raised to the black sky. "On the currents of my need to save this world and for redemption, send them, Earth Mother, within my thread of power!"

"No, wait!" Kailin yelled as the desert warped before her eyes. She focused on the tent as it flapped free of all but one of its stakes.

"Hold onto her," Drakkina called over the wind. Jackson grabbed Kailin against him. "And don't lose the bloody Orb!"

"Let go of me," Kailin ordered, impotent without her magic.

"Stop being a bullseye for them," he said against her ear.

Kailin would have responded but she was too busy trying to hold her body together. Her fingers dug into Jackson. "I'm unraveling."

"Hold on," he said as if he knew what the hell was going on. Which he couldn't. Once again Jackson Black was acting.

The world began to flash past Kailin's eyes. Up in the sky, the sun flew through its daily arc, then the moon, chasing one another in a stellar game of tag. Then again, faster and faster, until it was a blur of light. Kailin tried to speak, but no noise came. She tried to blink but only the flashing light remained in sight. She tried to breathe but couldn't feel the breeze of breath slide through her mouth. Did she even have a mouth?

Pay attention and learn, child. Drakkina's voice floated through Kailin's mind instead of her ears. The flashing slowed. *Hold onto her so they don't realize she's there.*

Was Drakkina speaking to Jackson? Was Jackson still with her? She couldn't feel anything. Was this what it felt like to be paralyzed? To die?

I will lead the demons of your time away, so they don't destroy Egypt of 1871. Then I will retrieve you. By the blessed Earth Mother, stay quiet and hidden!

The moon overhead slowed to a standstill. Kailin looked down and realized they were falling. She instantly threw out a net of magic to catch herself and realized that Jackson held tight. Her magic didn't work!

"Ahh!" she began to scream but Jackson's hand covered her mouth. His hold tightened on her as they fell through branches toward the earth.

She closed her eyes, and he released her mouth, wrapping arms around her. She buried her face in his chest.

She hated him, despised that he'd tricked her into falling in love with him. Yet if she was about to die upon impact, she was glad it would be in his arms.

Instead of jarring pain and oblivion, Kailin's toes and then heels touched a cushiony, damp ground. She opened her eyes, pulling away. Jackson let her move but held onto her arm. She was too stunned to yank away.

They stood in a dark forest of old, soaring trees. The silvery moon threw splashes of light down through the shadowed canopy to fall upon gnarled roots and moss-covered boulders. This place was familiar. Kailin peered through the night and glimpsed a far-off standing stone. Even without the tug on her birthmark, Kailin knew that the stone was one of ten standing around a stone slab table.

They were in the thick forest near the stone circle that she had studied since she was old enough to demand her own expedition. She'd studied every inch of the circle, digging at the ancient hearth, holding the shards of pottery, lying upon the stone slab to stare up at the stars, wondering why the only time she wasn't pulled in a direction was when her being resided within the stones.

A branch snapped in the woods. "Shhh," Jackson breathed against her ear, sending a shiver through her that she ignored. He pivoted her with him behind a thick oak as a movement flitted around several trees. It stopped. A cloak, silvery blond hair, piercing eyes that moved directly to their hiding place. The man was tall and broad, and contained magic. Even with Jackson holding her, Kailin could feel it.

"I will kill you Semiazaz, you and your horde," the man spoke with calm arrogance. "Show yourself."

"No," Jackson whispered before Kailin could even lean that way.

Tuto landed silently onto a branch above. The man had to have seen the bird, though he kept his eyes level with Kailin's gaze. As if he saw her clearly.

"Spooked by an owl, Druce?"

Druce? This was her father.

Another man approached. As his ethereal form slid against the tree branches, they shriveled, bending limply toward the ground. He moved closer, and his body solidified. She tried to gather her magic, but it lay limp in her body like the tree limbs. Jackson's arms had moved around her, and he held her back up against his chest.

"Eógan?"

"Yes, Druce, it is I."

"Drakkina said that Semiazaz had absorbed your spirit, killed you completely."

"Semiazaz can't contain me, or you. His hands are tied to those other twelve demons. Their powers are tangled up in the chaos of confinement. My mate made certain of that long before you existed. But they are growing stronger."

"I will hunt them. Kill them before they can harm any more of the world, before they can grow more powerful."

Druce practically crackled in the darkness, his energy was so strong. Kailin could feel its resonance like a deep chime within her. His power was magnificent, beautiful in its complexity and mass.

"Strong and eager," the one called Eógan said and smiled. "But you do not have Gilla by your side."

"And you do not have Drakkina," Druce threw back.

Eógan laughed. "Let us hunt as brothers then."

"I would keep them safe, keep Gilla from it all."

"Aye, wizard, leave Gilla to tend your daughters and the bairn."

"The bairn?" Druce said and paused, his head cocked as if he listened to some warning. "You know about the bairn?"

"News travels fast," Eógan said. "The babe is special."

"You have been away. How...?"

Eógan's smile cracked, lips pulling back suddenly in agony. In the darkness the shadows along his face changed places as if the skin stretched over moving bones. Kailin's throat tightened, preventing breath or warning. Druce backed up, magic in the palms of his hands.

"Run, Druce," Eógan's voice was the same yet strained through a wall of suffering. "It is a tr...a...p." Eógan spit out the final "p" and doubled over.

Druce glanced back toward the trees where Kailin stood. *Run home, child. Kailin, run to Mama*, settled firmly into her mind. Kailin sucked in a breath, fear spreading through her like a fast-acting poison.

Eógan lifted his head as a long white beard grew rapidly from his chin. His shoulders broadened and he grew upward, his bulk carrying him high into the silvery, moon-painted trees.

Druce released a bolt of magic straight into the growing, twisting mass of demonic souls. The giant staggered under the impact. "Strong, but alone," the voice came twisted and tangled as if many pitches spoke as one, creating a haphazard echo. "Foolish."

"Be gone, Semiazaz!" Druce ordered and bombarded the demons with a volley of mystical energy, spears of white light at various parts. Strikes hit at different angles, searching for weaknesses. "Take your evil brethren from these lands or stay and die."

The voices laughed, the pitches sliding along Kailin's spine. She felt Jackson pull her tighter against him behind the tree. She surrendered into the cloak of his arms, hiding her magic from the demons. Yet her father had felt her presence. Would Semiazaz and his forced companions also sense her magic?

"When else would we meet you alone without your mate?"

"Come then," Druce said with calm determination. "Truth and love make my magic stronger than yours. Let this be the final battle then."

"Without your family as witness? What a shame none will watch you destroy the plague of humankind. Perhaps we should summon them. Eehh...your girls." A grin spread upon the bearded face.

"You will die now," Druce roared and cupped his hands like Kailin had done on the desert. His magic surrounded the twisting group coalesced into the image of Semiazaz.

"It doesn't work," Kailin whispered.

"Shhh," Jackson said in her ear.

Druce shot white magic into the center of the mass but instead of shattering the evil, the mass absorbed it, the same as Kailin's magic. He would fail. Drakkina had told her so. The demons would kill him and strip his magic. The pearl of a tear slipped over her bottom lid. Maybe she could change the past. Maybe—

"No!" Druce roared and threw his magic with a push of his clenched hands. Kailin yanked away from Jackson, summoning her powers to add to her father's. *No!* Drakkina's voice penetrated in her mind as Jackson's arms hugged her back into him. The witch's voice pierced, nearly immobilizing her.

"Let go!" Kailin yelled but her words were caught in the inky roar of pure evil as it crushed like a black wave down upon her father. She watched in desperate shock as her father crumpled under the weight of what looked like a ten-foot wave of dark water that then morphed into a circle of beasts.

They all stood within feet of one another, though they looked like they strained to be apart. Kailin recognized Semiazaz with his long, white beard, but there were others. Their faces were distorted grimaces, some with gnashing teeth. One catlike woman hissed and scratched the air as if she wished to tear Druce's withered body apart.

"Take it!" a demon with black wings roared. "Then we can take Gilla."

"Yes, Semiazaz, take his magic before he's totally dead," the feline hissed.

Kailin tried to pull away, although she wasn't sure what her magic could do against so much power, not when her father's immense magic had failed. But she didn't get the chance.

Kailin felt her body melt, unravel as Drakkina's words whispered in the background. *On the currents of my power gifted by the Earth Mother, send them now.*

CHAPTER TWENTY-SEVEN
REVELATIONS

Kailin tried to close her eyes, but it already seemed as if her lids were gone. She watched the arc of moon chasing the sun five times before dark clouds obliterated both spheres. Her body grew heavy as once again she and Jackson and the Orb landed.

This time they were within the ten stones. There was a house surrounding the stone slab with tall stalks of corn thrashing from the wind in a side garden. Herbs lay against the ground as if trampled. The two of them stood near a back window. One of the wooden shutters hung crooked due to a missing peg. Outside the stone circle on the far side stood a line of wolves.

"Damn…" Jackson swore softly. "Are those diced snakes?"

Kailin glanced toward the front door where she could see what looked like sliced snakes writhing in the cornflowers growing along a pebbled path. Their blood splattered against the lavender heads and yellow buttercups.

"Scottish adders," she said.

"Are we in Scotland?"

She nodded, the back of her head brushing his chest as they stared out together. "These are the stones I've studied my whole life. This is where I'm from."

"Guessing that this isn't here now. I mean we're here now but now isn't our now, is it?"

She shook her head. "It's a long time ago."

Kailin stepped out of his arms, but he clasped her wrist like a manacle. Her curiosity was too intense to care.

She bent to peek through the swaying shutter into the large cottage. It seemed to be a bright day, but the clouds covered most of the sun. She could make out thatch raining down inside from the roof. There, near the slab, stood a woman and a child. Kailin strained to hear them, but she couldn't.

"Mama?" she whispered and watched as the woman hugged the child tightly and kissed her. She tucked a large white feather into her dress. *My dress!* It looked like the same dress she'd been wearing when Anthony found her in the pharaoh's tomb.

Jackson pulled Kailin from the window to stand flat beside him against the house. He unwound the long keffiyeh from his neck and tied it into a makeshift satchel. "Demons are coming."

Kailin nodded silently and crouched low as Jackson took the Orb and slid it into the bag. Kailin lifted slightly to peer through the window again and felt him place the satchel's strap over her head to fall across her chest, the weight of the Orb secure against her.

The woman who must be her mother held her arms wide. Her long braid swung down her back to her calves as she stared up at the ceiling. "I freely gift ye with my most dangerous power, to move things, elements, solids, people. On the currents of my blood, on the currents of my love, on the currents of my power given by the Earth Mother, send her now within my last remaining thread."

Kailin couldn't breathe. The child reached for her mother, one small hand tightly fisted as if she held something. *An amber stone.* But the child couldn't reach her mother, because she was already thinning into a long thread of yellow. Magic pulsed in the thread that shot upward through a tiny crack in the thatch. Straight to nineteenth-century Egypt.

Above the wind and branches hitting the house, a resonating chanting had begun. The demons stood as they had in the clearing, but instead of Semiazaz at the front it looked to be her father, Druce.

"Come out, Gilla. 'Tis I, your husband. I have control of these demons now. Come out, love!"

"You are no longer Druce," Gilla screamed from within. Anger pinched her face. "You killed Druce and now you've come for me and my children."

Gilla ran to the hearth and began to pry at one of the stones. She worked quickly, her slender fingers bleeding at the effort of scratching at the mortar. The rock fell out onto the floor, and she shoved her hand into the hole. "Nay! Where did you take the Orb, Druce?"

Kailin glanced at the Orb in the satchel against her hip. The Orb had been given to the pharaoh by a magical man who made him promise to gift it to someone with the same dragonfly birthmark. Had Druce taken the Orb and hidden it in ancient Egypt before the demons had killed him? Could the Orb help Gilla now?

No, came Drakkina's voice in Kailin's head. *If you give Gilla the Orb, the demons will only take it from her. Watch and learn or hide.*

Kailin sniffed at the tears coursing down her cheeks as she watched her mother run across the room and scoop up a baby out of a wooden cradle. The bairn Semiazaz, as Eógan, had mentioned. The one that was somehow special.

The baby looked so small. Another sister? It must be only a week or so old. Yet its eyes were open wide. They stared...straight at Kailin. She gasped and for a brief moment crouched below the window frame.

Trees thrashed wildly around the standing stones. Wildflowers and homegrown vegetables lay flat where rocks and magic had trampled them. The demons couldn't stretch all the way around the perimeter, so she and Jackson were safe from their sight, but not their animals.

"Wolves." Jackson crouched next to her. "Where the hell is Drakkina?"

Kailin shook her head and peeked again into the room. Gilla held the baby on her lap while sitting on top of the stone slab. She kissed its head and smiled calmly at it. She spoke quietly against its miniature ear.

She looked upward. "Drakkina! Where are you? I beg you! Save my bairn. I have no magic left!" She placed the little baby over her shoulder and gently patted its back while she cupped its thin baby hair. "Please, Drakkina. I had to use the power to send the girls. There's nothing left."

The baby fastened its large eyes directly on the window where Kailin hid. Could it sense her behind the swaying shutter? Where was the baby now? Dead? The thought twisted Kailin's gut. She'd been saved, but now there was nothing left to save her last sister or her mother.

"Drakkina!" screeched Gilla as the ceiling began to cave in, thatch raining down. Gilla covered the baby with the wide sleeve of her dusty white robe. Drakkina appeared in the room and relief swelled tears out of Kailin's eyes.

"I can't help," Drakkina said sadly.

"Aye, ye can send the bairn like I sent the girls."

Drakkina shook her ethereal head, dragonflies flitting around her sparkling hair.

Fury clenched inside Kailin.

"There she is." Jackson nodded at the figure in the room.

That's Drakkina of the past. Kailin turned her head. Another Drakkina looked at her, lips and eyes tight with regret. *If I influence this timeline...* The apparition looked sad. She shook her head. *My scrying bowl shows only failure if I interfere with this timeline.*

"So you left them to die, and you're going to let it happen again?" Judgment tightened the lines of Kailin's face.

Jackson's arms came around her, but she shook them off. He let her go but continued to hold one of her wrists.

The wolves stood at the perimeter of the circle. One would snap and the others would follow. Tails bristled and saliva dripped like they were starving and incensed by the smell of fresh, taunting prey.

"If they cross that line, I'm letting go of Kailin," Jackson warned. "Get us out of here."

"No," Kailin said. "We have to help them."

Drakkina floated closer. *Your mother knew that she couldn't let her magic fall into the demons' hands. That's why she sent each of you with one of her powers. It was necessary to protect the world and you. Don't let her efforts and death be in vain, Kailin.*

"But the baby?"

Has his own powers. Drakkina's mouth tightened as if she held information back. *You must go.*

"Holy Lord," Kailin breathed when she turned back to the window. A black oily cloud roiled down the chimney.

"They're crossing the line," Jackson said and released Kailin's arm.

Magic shot up inside Kailin, throbbing on the waves of her terror and fury. She didn't even glance behind her but sent a pulse of magic there. Several cries and whimpers came from the advancing beasts, and they scattered into the forest.

Kailin, no! Drakkina yelled inside her head.

The Drakkina of the past lifted the baby from Gilla. "The babe must die." This Drakkina was stone, her face firm, convicted.

"No!" Gilla and Kailin yelled at the same time.

Drakkina laid the baby on the stone table. He was wearing a long, linen gown, his arms free, but he didn't struggle.

"Send him away," Gilla said, desperate.

"'Tis too late." The stony Drakkina inside the collapsing cottage raised her arms in the air. Her ethereal body seemed to solidify as her power built. Gilla came up behind and grabbed her around the waist.

With a small gurgle, the baby lifted a dimpled fist toward Drakkina. With a little punch in the air, Drakkina flew backwards, knocking Gilla over too.

Kailin's mouth dropped open. Had the newborn thrown the most powerful being she'd ever encountered across the room? Drakkina rose, flying back across the room to hover above the baby. Another punch of its dimpled fist broke holes in her vaporous form.

The Drakkina outside with them was speaking while the one inside fought against a newborn. *On the currents of my wish for redemption, on the currents of my love for this family and humanity, on the currents of my power given by the Earth Mother, send them now within my thread.*

"Not yet!" Kailin ran around the side of the house, the Orb banging against her hip.

"Kailin!" Jackson yelled, but it was too late. Kailin glanced back and saw his body warp, twisting into a single yellow thread. It shot off into the thunderclouds. Kailin turned back to the cottage and ran inside.

Gilla pushed off the ground, her eyes wide with shock.

"I'm Kailin." The words came fast in gusts.

"Kailin?" Gilla said. "I sent you somewhere safe. Why are you here, grown to womanhood?"

Black smoke twisted and billowed around the ceiling.

"Don't let them touch the babe!" Drakkina of old yelled and shook her head. "They'll taint it, use it against the world."

"It's a baby, not an it," Kailin shot back. Using her magic, combined with the energy pulsing into her from the Orb pressed against her through the thin scarf, she lifted the baby through the air and settled him into Gilla's outstretched arms. The baby smiled. Could babies that young really smile? Wasn't that gas? As if on cue, the baby burped and smiled some more. Was it reading her mind?

"It seems so," the hardened Drakkina said sarcastically. Her dragonflies buzzed around her.

Then one by one around the room, each demon descended from the black cloud into a solid form, feet, paws and talons on the earthen floor.

"The boy child is ours," Semiazaz commanded from his stand in the middle. He turned his obsidian eyes on Kailin and tipped his head. "A sister? All grown up."

Kailin released her magic in a blast straight at the leader. Semiazaz staggered backwards, a look of utter bewilderment on his face. "Grown up and fierce." His eyes shifted to her satchel. "And with Eógan's Orb."

"Leave here!" Kailin yelled. "Before you feel the full force of my power."

Drakkina looked pointedly at Kailin. "You don't belong here. There will be repercussions." She began to chant the now familiar spell for transforming people into threads and sending them flying into another time period when Semiazaz suddenly changed back into the one named Eógan. It was enough to make Drakkina stutter, and two demons lunged at the baby, grabbing it from Gilla.

"Earth Mother protect my bairn," Gilla said raising her arms as if to unleash her own magic. Was she bluffing? The two demons actually cringed, and Kailin felt a jolt of pride. Her mother had been extremely powerful, and they didn't know that all her magic was gone.

The demons melted into a thin black layer, covering the baby with shadow. Kailin's baby brother hovered in the chilled room wrapped in malodorous taint.

Drakkina sent a thin edge of ethereal power along the baby's skin. Was she trying to kill him or merely slice off the demonic layer? Did she still consider the baby too dangerous like she'd said to Gilla?

"Stop!" Kailin whipped her magic toward the baby.

Protection, purity, light. She envisioned clean love, a blast of sisterly devotion and desperation. The baby whimpered, eyes wide as the oil melted away from its pale skin. It hovered, under whose power, Kailin wasn't certain.

"On the currents of my desperation to save this world, Earth Mother, send the babe now!" Drakkina's words blew out with a faint wind. The infant moved its small, clenched fists and wailed, but he still elongated into a thread and shot off through the torn and blasted thatched roof.

"Leave him alone!" Gilla shrieked and raised her hands again.

"Die," Eógan said and Semiazaz's white beard snaked downward, transforming him. He shot a blast of black, sparking magic, right into Gilla. She didn't even cry out, her body withering in half a second.

"Gilla! Mama!" Kailin screamed and ran for the ashes that sifted down through the air to land on the piled fabric that had been her mother's robes. Dust, warm from her body, ran through her fingers. "Mama," she whispered, taking the shawl that still held her scent of baked bread and dried flowers. The scent caught so fiercely at Kailin's memory that her stomach clenched and she choked. She'd lost her all over again.

Kailin threw the shawl around her shoulders, buckling the small silver clasp to keep it in place. Her fingers slid back to her mother's clothes, now speckled with tears. Feeling something hard, she pulled a tooth belonging to a large animal from the ash. She tucked it into the pocket of her hastily pulled-on pants. Tears stung again and she glanced toward the window where Jackson had disappeared. Where was he? Kailin closed her eyes. She felt hopelessly and completely alone.

CHAPTER TWENTY-EIGHT
TIME TO BATTLE?

From somewhere behind her Kailin heard the demon, Semiazaz, speak. "We'll take Gilla's daughter then and the Orb. The boy will be easy to follow. You really should have killed the lad, Drakkina. He's more powerful than both his parents. He'll be a worthy leader of our coven."

"Kill the girl now," hissed one of the demons. "She dissolved the souls of Elathan and Erubus!"

Kailin looked to see Semiazaz's small black eyes boring into her. "No, Gilla's daughter but gave us room to"—he rolled his shoulders—"stretch, shall we say." The other materialized demons took several steps away from each other. A large, winged demon pushed through the remaining stones of a wall and growled with laughter.

"Elathan and Erubus merely slid along with the boy to wherever Drakkina sent him," Semiazaz said and smiled. "We'll find them easily." Several of the demons flew or ran out beyond the stones. Semiazaz rolled his eyes. "Once these children have had a small chance to play first."

Kailin straightened and spun around, her mother's shawl flaring outward. "Let's finish this here." Magic crackled down her arms and needled her fingertips. "While some of you are out exploring your quasi-freedom."

"Gilla's daughter, no," the old Drakkina intoned as if trying to bend her to her will, but Kailin's power was too strong. "They can still kill you," the witch said, "and we will lose the final battle."

"I have the Orb." Kailin pulled the sides of the satchel down to reveal the large, brilliantly glowing stone nestled in its folds. The remaining demons turned toward her, arms wide in a similar fashion. Their dark magic arced between their separated fingers to join with each other.

You don't have the dragonfly pendant, my dragonfly. Drakkina's voice urged inside Kailin's mind, though the witch in the room didn't give any indication that she was communicating. *They work together like soul mates.* Kailin glanced at the window where the other Drakkina, the one from her time, floated on the edge, watching with horror on her face.

The Drakkina in the room shook her head, scattering wispy dragonflies. "The Orb may not be enough. Don't fight them here. It's not time."

"This seems like a perfectly good time," Semiazaz said casually.

The Earth Mother predicts ultimate doom if the final battle happens without all the sisters and their soul mates in this circle. Kailin didn't know which Drakkina spoke in her mind.

"What choice do I have here?" Kailin whispered. Her power sizzled under her skin, but her confidence waned as the cat-like demon hissed.

"Consider this, child," Semiazaz said, his voice booming through the crumbling room. "It would be easier to join us. You won't be harnessed like we are, and you can care for your brother. The two of you could

easily rule the world. With power like yours only death will stop you."
He touched his long beard. "Do you really want to die today?"

The spell. You know it. Use it. The words held an added cadence,
making it from the Drakkina outside. *Kailin, run! Please, child, leave
this place. We need you.*

"Leave Gilla's girl alone, Semiazaz," the cold Drakkina ordered.

Kailin began to chant in her head. *On the currents of my blood, on
the currents of my love for...for my family, for this world*, which included
Jackson Black, *for the love of Gilla and her Earth Mother, send me home!*

As she said the words, tamping down the fear of getting lost among a
temporal web she knew nothing about, Kailin funneled the magic she
held churning inside into the words, the prayer, the spell. Could she
actually thread her way somewhere without getting lost amongst the
millions of years of earthly existence?

The only place she could think to go was home. But where was home?
Wasn't she technically standing in her home? Or was it Anthony's manor
in England? Or was it the tomb where she appeared to him decades ago?
Home was more than a mere place. It was a feeling, safety and familiarity.

She concentrated for a moment on Anthony but wasn't sure he was
still there waiting for her in Egypt. She thought of Bruce and the manor
house in England with its fragrant arching gardens. But she'd always felt
restless there, which was part of why she'd gone on expedition as soon as
Anthony would let her.

She thought of the stone circle where she currently stood, but without
a house and a coven of eager demons crowding it. She'd studied the layers
of earth, each stone and tree, the central slab, the cut of each monolith.
But it wasn't home either.

Where was it? She had to find it and feel it so well its mere existence
would draw her to it. Images of smiling over burnt feathers shot into

Kailin's mind. Of staring up at familiar constellations with the warmth of a strong arm snug against hers, fingers glancing off her own. The sound of a firm, calm voice guiding her through the desert of panic inside a sarcophagus. The feel of breath along her skin. His smell, his taste, his touch. *Jackson.*

"Come to us, daughter of Druce and Gilla," Semiazaz intoned as if it were the opening to a dark ritual.

Ruse or not, Jackson was the one she could pick out of a million strands of time. Jackson, yes; he could lead her home. She knew him on every sensory level.

On the currents of my…love, send me home, send me to Jackson Black.

The room wavered and for a split second the old nightmare of Kailin's childhood flooded her. She scooped up the Orb in its satchel and threw the strap over her head as her chant beat with her heart.

"She's escaping!" hissed the catlike demon.

She heard the Drakkina in the room curse, but the other Drakkina spoke into her mind. *Yes, child, follow your string home. I'll lead them another way.*

Tall, broad, smooth shoulders. Wavy brown hair, sun-touched around his tan face, and a jaw bristled with three days' growth. A cowboy's hat tipped at the right angle to shield smiling gray-blue eyes. A natural sway in the saddle, a rhythm that carried his body with masculine, lion-like grace.

Kailin felt hot and melting as she shot through the sky before the flashing sun and moon chasing each other across a blue, then gray, then black sky. She thought of the way his muscles rippled under the tips of her fingers as she licked them along his skin, her nails grazing the taut sinew, biceps bunching, straining. The sounds he'd made while loving her, groaning on the tip of carnal torture and pleasure, rumbled through her ears.

Home. Fly home. Kailin tried to keep her magic centered on the word although her mind kept a constant tether on the one man she knew as well as any home. She barely noticed as she shot between, over, and under translucent lines of time, strung together in an intricate design much like a thousand spiders' webs coming together in a complex tunnel.

A white, nearly full moon and the spire of trees greeted Kailin. Pine trees? Not dunes? A chilled wind rustled the branches. A short screech sounded from a birch tree as Kailin descended into the same circle of stones she'd just left. She plopped hard onto the silvery ground covered with moss and cornflowers.

She rolled up into a crouch, which was rather hard with the weight of the Orb over her shoulder, her mother's shawl hiding it. She whipped around trying to see everywhere at once. Tuto swooped down through the black sky and landed on top of one of the standing stones she'd studied her whole life.

A hulking shadow stretched out on top of the central slab table, her family cottage completely gone. Kailin readied her magic. Thick, long legs swept off the table to the ground.

Her heart thumped hard. "Jackson?"

In two long strides, Jackson was upon her. His hands gripped her shoulders in an unbreakable hold. "Dammit, Kailin Whitaker, where have you been?" He didn't let her respond. He didn't even let her inhale.

His lips descended onto hers. She pushed the satchel with the Orb in it behind her to rest on her back, as Jackson's hands wrapped around her shoulders.

His strong hands cupped her cheeks, cradling her head between them. He pulled back, bending to search her face, his thumbs stroking her cheeks.

Jackson shook his head. "I was yanked away from you. You were left with those demons. I couldn't get back to you. I couldn't find you. Not even here, in this circle." He swallowed hard, his eyes momentarily searching the star-speckled sky. He opened his mouth and then closed it again. "I couldn't believe that I'd lost you." He looked back at her. "You and the Orb."

The breeze shook through Kailin, but she resisted when he tried to pull her into his arms again. "Jackson." She wet her lips and tried to ignore how numb they felt. "You did lose me. When you helped them take Anthony. You didn't even know me, but you lost me."

Something changed along the shadows of his face. A hardness slipped over the relief that had pulled Kailin into the last amazing kiss. The farewell kiss. She waited, hoping he would say something, anything that would make the past irrelevant, make all that happened before dissipate with a simple explanation. He'd been working with Anthony. It was a trick to fool the real villains. He and Anthony had planned it all out over ales and darts. Anything.

Jackson nodded, though it looked like it took its toll. "You're right, Kailin. I'm sorry. I didn't know you. Choices had to be made, hard choices. Do you...?" He ran his hand through his hair. "Do you still have the Orb? Can it heal?"

Tuto screeched from his perch on the stone, lifting off and circling Kailin. Pressure against her leg was punctuated by a low growl. She jumped forward on a gasp.

"A wolf!" Jackson yelled and shoved Kailin behind him. In quick succession he pulled his pistol and cocked it.

"Wait!" Kailin said, grabbing his arm.

They stared at the large beast. Its black fur appeared almost gray in the moonlight. Yellow eyes reflected back at them. It seemed to watch Jackson's gun while trying to sidestep its way around him to Kailin. Its black lips peeled back, showing long white canines.

"Where the hell did he come from? I've been out here for months. I would have noticed a monster that large," Jackson said evenly.

Months?

There was no time for questions. Kailin slapped her pants pocket, searching. "The tooth." It was gone. "My mother had a fang in her pocket when she was killed. I took it and threaded here."

Tuto screeched again in his tight circle. His talons reached down to pluck at the beast's head. The wolf ignored the bird and kept its eyes locked on the weapon.

"Put the gun down," she whispered.

"Down?"

"I think he's supposed to protect whoever brings him through."

"What?" But Jackson lowered his gun and the large wolf's back end sat.

"I watched my mother slide an owl feather in my dress as a child, before she sent me. Anthony said Tuto appeared in the tomb when I did. I think I brought the wolf through with me because of the tooth."

"By God." Jackson ran a hand through his hair. "What are you going to do with a pet wolf?"

"I don't know." Kailin moved forward, her hand outstretched. With a small forward thrust, the beast rubbed its head in her palm. "Hi there."

What a bizarre...day, month, who knew. Exhaustion suddenly weighed along the taut muscles in Kailin's body. Emotions were tiring and she'd been bombarded with fear, fury, loss, sadness, disbelief, regret, bitterness, and probably a few more. It was all too much.

An animal scampered off in the woods beyond the stone circle, and the wolf's ears perked up. It tipped its nose to the breeze.

"Go ahead," she said and flapped her hand. "You'll be less scary when full. I hope." The wolf turned and trotted off into the forest as if he understood her words. Kailin shook her head and slumped down in front of the dying fire.

Jackson grabbed a blanket from on top of the stone slab and shook it, placing it around her shoulders. He threw some twigs and dry heather onto the chars. His movements were strong, quiet, and undemanding. Kailin let out a long exhale and watched Jackson blow life back into the last shreds of fire. He added strips of wood and finally larger branches. He moved about the campfire as if he'd been making them his whole life.

"You still want the Orb?" she asked as the wood spit and cracked.

"It healed me." He touched his chest where a bullet had gone through. "It holds power over life and death, Kailin."

Kailin heart took on the weight of stone. He wanted the Orb, not her. That's why he'd been trying to find her. "Drakkina has it," she lied. "I gifted it to her so she can bring it to the final battle."

He exhaled, looking away toward the forest. "Well then."

After a moment, he sat across from her while she stood, her feet damp from the cold grass.

"You give me no explanations, Jackson, only lies or silence."

His eyes met hers over the flames. "Would any explanation suffice, fix the fact that I helped kidnap your father?"

"No, but you knew that, knew that the night we were together." She played with the cuff of her shirt, realizing it was still turned inside out from that night. All that had happened, and she had done so without bloomers on under her trousers.

His teeth came down on his bottom lip, the one Kailin knew tasted like security and heat and delicious frenzy. She shook her head and dropped her gaze to the orange-yellow flames.

"You planned to take the Orb all along," she said.

He tossed another thin log onto the fire, making the carefully erected triangle collapse. The flames hissed around the assault before turning to lap at the new fuel.

"Yes."

Kailin's laugh came out like a choke. "Bloody awful, huh, to find out that the only person who can make the Orb work is the one it's gifted to. Even though you did seduce me, if you'd stolen it away during the night, you wouldn't have been able to do anything with it."

Jackson straightened so fast it was as if he jumped, though Kailin was fairly certain his boots didn't leave the ground. His long stride crossed the fire in the space of her gasp. He grabbed her upper arms, his breathing ragged. He opened his mouth to say something.

Say something! Say anything!

Instead, Jackson raised his hand to her face. With one curved finger he caught a tear as it welled out of her lower lid. The second tear really wet his finger. They came then, tears, more tears than Kailin could remember releasing ever before. The sound of the fire and night breeze in the trees played in the background as she wet the front of Jackson's linen shirt, a shirt without a bloodstain and hole. He'd pulled her into him, letting her rest her face against his heart.

"I am sorry, Kailin."

Kailin didn't shake, she didn't wail or snort. She just...surrendered, released everything as if she had liquefied and he was a cup to catch her.

Fight, fear, and ice bled out with her tears, leaving hollow, weak Kailin. More alone than ever.

"Go home, Mister Black. Leave me alone." Kailin pulled away from his arms.

CHAPTER TWENTY-NINE
OLD FRIENDS

Kailin breathed in the dewy air of the forest and no longer smelled the tang of char from the campfire where she'd left Jackson sleeping. Feeling the weight of the Orb in its satchel hit against her bum, she trudged forward in the woolen socks Jackson had given her.

She held aside a limb and paused to take in the rugged castle in the distance. Dawn was beginning to throw rays of sun over the mountain that stood at its back. Everything was clear and fresh. The vista always took her breath away. Dawn reflected against the castle's surrounding walls beyond the small village that sat before it.

The wolf following her growled low a split second before a voice broke the silence. "Foolish."

Having felt the tingle of her birthmark, Kailin didn't jump but let the branch slap backwards into Drakkina's pinched face. The pine needles slipped through the witch's ethereal form as she walked more than floated behind Kailin out onto the soggy moor. Drakkina shook her head. "Kailin, you could have been taken, used by the dark. Or worse," she said, "you could have been killed."

"But I wasn't." Kailin trudged forward. Tuto made advancing circles overhead to keep watch while the new addition loped behind.

"He's still following you," Drakkina said.

"Tell Jackson to go home."

"I mean the wolf."

Kailin glanced at the large black beast. "The wolf showed up when I..." she gestured above her head, "landed. He must have threaded with me because I took a fang from my mother's robes."

"Actually, the tooth was given to your baby brother. The wolf is his guardian," Drakkina said.

Kailin paused in her stride. The wolf belonged to the baby like Tuto belonged to her. Regret flattened her stomach, but she started walking again. She'd have to care for the wolf herself since her brother was gone.

Drakkina pointed at the distant castle. "They are kin to you, through Serena and Keenan Maclean and their son William."

Kailin tripped on a clump of heather, the satchel swinging at the end of its looped strap. The witch shrugged. "Your eldest sister made her home close to the original."

Kailin pulled her mother's shawl closed before her. "What year is this?"

"In which calendar?"

Kailin frowned. The witch was playing with her. "The one created by Pope Gregory XIII in the sixteenth century."

Drakkina slipped an ancient-looking pocket watch from her waistband. "Eighteen-seventy-two."

Kailin tripped again.

"You really need to find some boots," Drakkina chided.

"How long have I been gone?"

Drakkina ticked off time on her fingers. Kailin examined the melted patches of snow. It was spring in the Highlands. "It's April or May, isn't it?" She spun to look at Drakkina. "I've been gone for months!" She'd been so encompassed by her misery over Jackson's treachery that she hadn't even thought about time.

"You're lucky you made it back to your own century. It was your first time using a travel spell. You could have landed in a very inhospitable locale or time. Volcanos poured lava around here in the past."

Kailin exhaled loudly. "Anthony must be so worried."

"Aye, he's looking for you. He'll love your new pet."

Kailin closed her eyes. "Can you get word to him that I'll come home soon? That I'm well?"

"Do I look like a messenger?" Drakkina asked and pointed toward the sky. "Send your bird."

Kailin could hear the roll in Drakkina's eyes. She'd already turned back toward the soaring mountain behind Kilchurn Castle, home to the Macleans. Kailin made her legs plod onward, her wet feet growing colder.

"I'll send Tuto to Anthony, but tell Jackson to go home, not to follow me," she said.

"He's already headed south."

Kailin's inhale stuttered. *Jackson's leaving.* She blinked back tears. *He won't even try to fight for me. No explanations.*

"He's merely following your command, Kailin."

Kailin glared at her. "Stop reading my mind."

"He's your soulmate, woman."

Kailin turned on the spirit. "How could he be if he doesn't love me enough to tell me the truth?"

Drakkina snorted. "Love. None of you know what you're doing, and yet I'm expected to sit back and let it all unfold." She held out her arms, swathed in blue flowing fabric. "As if the temporal world doesn't depend upon you. Love takes time and communication."

"He's the one not communicating!"

"Stubborn, stubborn," Drakkina said and huffed. "I'm going to find Merewin to talk some sense into you. No one's more stubborn than she."

The tingle in Kailin's birthmark melted away as the witch faded. Kailin closed her eyes and leaned forward, resting her hands on her knees. Tears ran silently for several minutes, and a light rain began to fall from the gathered clouds. She breathed deeply and straightened. *Control. I must have control.* She wiped the tears from her eyes and cheeks.

Several horses left the village of thatched houses before the castle. Apparently, she'd been spotted.

"Perhaps you should stay in the forest nearby," she said to the wolf. With a little flick of his full tail, the wolf loped off into the trees that were green-tipped with buds.

The Macleans were kin? Kailin would have to look further into that. Drakkina may be unpredictable, but so far she hadn't lied. After what Kailin had witnessed in the stone circle of the past, it was very likely that her siblings had been sent to different time periods. But where had the baby boy gone? What was his name? The demons had held him, covered him. Hopefully her brother had lived. Drakkina should know.

"Hail!" one of the riders called.

Kailin switched the satchel with the Orb onto the other shoulder and held up an arm. "Hail, Macleans of Kilchurn. Doctor Kailin Whitaker. I am in need of a pair of proper boots and a horse." She recognized the chief at the lead, William, named after his great-grandfather. "And a hot cup of tea."

"Ah, Kailin lass, ye know that we only serve tea with a splash of good Highland whisky in it. Perhaps then ye will explain the beastie watching ye from the thicket."

She laughed and would have blown off his tam o'shanter with her magic, but she didn't want to draw any demonic attention to these good people.

"Plus, after what Judith read in your mind," William said and shook his head, "I'd say ye have a mighty need for that whisky."

Kailin's smile faded, and she huffed. "Very true."

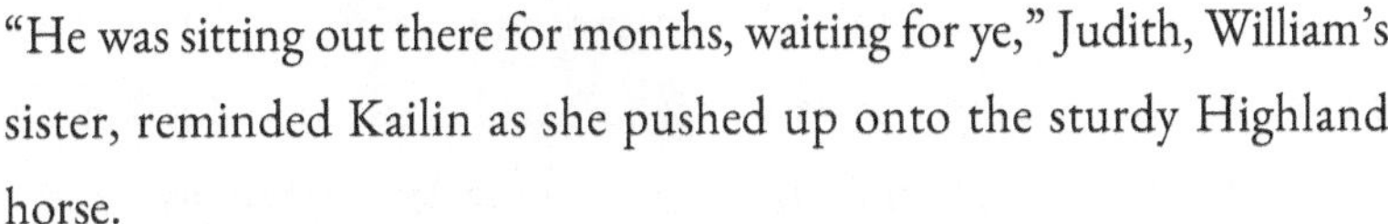

"He was sitting out there for months, waiting for ye," Judith, William's sister, reminded Kailin as she pushed up onto the sturdy Highland horse.

"Waiting for me," Kailin asked, "or for the Orb?" She glanced at the lump in the leather bag hanging near her leg.

Judith frowned and huffed. "I don't doubt *your* magic, but you doubt mine."

Kailin touched her friend's hand. "You can see me move things with your own eyes, your own interpretations. I cannot see in your head. I don't mean—"

"I know." Judith smiled. "Ye want to believe me but your own"—she flapped her hands—"your own worries about being accepted make it difficult."

A blush heated her cheeks. "There are no secrets from you, are there?" The woman came from a long maternal line of telepaths, able to read minds and emotions and sometimes the future.

"Nay." Judith laughed but then grew serious. "I'm telling ye, Kailin. He loves ye. Aye, he thought about the powerfully healing stone, but he thought of ye too. If ye'd let him explain instead of leaving—"

"He had all night to say something, to explain."

Judith nodded, her eyes straying to her husband, who spoke with William. "Men have to work past their own foolishness too." She turned her gaze back to Kailin. "Jackson Black has reasons—"

"Reasons for lying to me, kidnapping my father, seducing me, plotting to steal the Orb from me."

Judith closed her eyes as if she were holding onto her wild, Highland temper. She opened those bright brown eyes while tugging on her long braid. "Aye, he has a sick sister."

Cassy. Kailin inhaled the still-frosty morning air quickly. Was all his subterfuge because he was desperate to heal his sister? Kailin's heart thudded hard, and she concentrated on keeping her magic in its place.

She turned to William, and Judith's husband, Sean. "Thank you for your grand hospitality and your mare. I will return her."

"Sean will make certain of that," William said and Sean pulled another horse around. "He'll escort ye home, Kailin."

Kailin sighed. "Really William, do I have to show you that I will be totally fine on my own?"

William walked over and patted the neck of her mare. He lowered his voice. "We've all noticed ye haven't used your magic since you came two days ago. Even when keeping control of your temper, lass, you dump at least one bowl of soup in someone's lap."

She would have snapped back but there was real concern in William's eyes. He would make some lass a very good husband someday. Kailin pursed her lips in an *O* and blew gently. Loud guffaws grew behind William. "Feeling a draft?" Kailin smirked.

"Holy! William, drop yer kilt," Judith called.

William didn't move but allowed the whole bailey to get a good view of his bare arse, compliments of Kailin's magic.

William chuckled and shook his head. "Sean, ye can stay home with my sister," William called out and Kailin let the kilt drop back into place.

He winked at Kailin. "Aye, ye need a man that your magic doesn't work on. Go find this Jackson Black." A small shadow fell across his face. "But if he lies to ye again, send word. The Macleans will become *involved*," he stressed with much male bravado.

Kailin smiled. "You'd brave getting English soil on your boots for me?"

She teased but William remained serious. "Aye lass, we would, I would. Ye're kin."

"Drakkina told you?"

"Judith knew, and aye, the meddlesome spirit confirmed it." He nodded. "Ye'll always have a home at Kilchurn. And ye can keep the mare."

Pools of tears stung her eyes. "Thank you." She blinked them back. The emotion in her voice showed that her gratitude encompassed much more than the horse.

William nodded and patted the back of the mare, and Kailin trotted through the bailey toward the gates.

—◆◇◆—

The tingling on Kailin's arm put her on alert. "Drakkina," she said and watched her breath puff out into the early morning air.

You need to get rid of that Orb. The witch's voice echoed in Kailin's mind. Drakkina's ethereal form materialized off to her right. The mare shied to the other side of the pebbled path. She was sure-footed, used to Highland paths, but too far over and they'd tumble down a ridiculously perilous mountain slope.

Kailin ran her palm over the mare's shaggy neck, guiding her back to the center.

"I thought you were visiting my most stubborn sister."

"I did," Drakkina said, frowning, "but she doesn't want to interfere unless it's life and death."

Drakkina flapped her arms around. "Which all this is. To start with, you need to gift the Orb to me. Its magic will call the demons back to you."

Kailin wished she had Judith's ability to read minds. Her eyes narrowed. "So, if I give the Orb away—"

"Gift it away," Drakkina corrected.

"Gift the Orb away, then it won't enhance my magic so much that it would call to them."

Drakkina nodded as dragonflies zipped around her veiled hair.

"Don't they know where I live now, so to speak?"

"You didn't come back exactly at the time you left. They've already searched that time. You came back months later. You're on a completely different thread of time. Even a day can throw them off."

"They aren't here now."

"You haven't been using much magic. I only felt it a little over an hour ago."

The kilt lift. She doubted she could go through life without using her magic. It was a reflex.

"So, you must gift the Orb to me so I can safeguard it for the final battle."

"How do I do that?"

Drakkina smiled triumphantly. "You state your name while holding it and state clearly that you are gifting it to me, Drakkina of the ancient Callum clan. And then it will no longer enhance your magic or call the demons any more than before in your life."

"Will the Orb call the demons to you?"

"I know where to hide it."

"Hmm... But if you were, say a normal mortal. Would...if it were gifted to you, if you had no power, would it call the demons?"

Drakkina frowned. Kailin wasn't very good at lying and the spirit wasn't stupid. "I don't recall if the last mortal, that pharaoh prince in the tomb, was killed by the demons or not."

Kailin nodded as if she was contemplating, but she knew. It was her life's work to decipher hieroglyphs and the age of mummies or remains that people brought out of tombs for her to inspect. The prince had died as an adult from an assassin's strike to his head. Could that have been Semiazaz? There were no glyphs in the tomb that mentioned supernatural tornados or demonic beings. In addition, the Orb wouldn't have been entombed with him.

Kailin pulled the bag with the Orb into her lap. The mare walked calmly around the mountain edge, following a path leading into a meadow. Kailin swayed naturally with her gait and rolled the sides of the bag down so that the Orb of Life sat like an egg in its leather nest in her lap. Best not to touch it.

"Fine then," Kailin nodded. "Let's get this thing turned off to me."

Drakkina smiled again. "Cup it, you must touch it. I'll keep watch and try to block your magic beacon for the time you need. Be quick."

Kailin picked the Orb out of the leather nest. It tingled up her arms and glowed even without her magic. It pulled at her powers, filling her with unnatural strength. She would be invincible with this in her hands.

"Are you sure it wouldn't be better for me to finish them off before the final battle?"

"Don't be a fool, Kailin," Drakkina said softly. "Druce—"

"But I have the Orb; he didn't. I feel so powerful."

"We need all the sisters and their mates in the circle for the final battle to end in our favor. I've seen this in the scrying bowl. Wisdom from the Earth Mother, wisdom you must heed."

Kailin stared at the brilliant, bluish white, glowing Orb. "I, Kailin Whitaker, daughter of Gilla and Druce..." She spoke slowly, enunciating each word with her oath. "I gift the Orb of Life to...Jackson Black." Kailin shot a mental picture of Jackson with a bolt of her own magic into the Orb.

"No!" Drakkina yelled and dropped her arms, but it was too late. The magic sizzle from the Orb faded, leaving only a round, rather ordinary-looking large rock with a dragonfly painted on it.

Kailin shoved it back into the leather bag and tied it tight. She took up the reins. "I'm sorry, Drakkina, but I don't know you, at least not very well. Hell, I don't even know if you're one of them"—she pointed to the sky and swirled her finger like a tornado—"disguised as Drakkina."

"But you'd be gifting it to Drakkina. It would only work for me," she said in a voice both breathless and high-pitched, like the whine of a child who knew she'd lost an argument.

"We will bring it to the final battle." Meanwhile, if Jackson could use it for Cassy, he'd have what he'd been after all along.

"So you are going to him? To give him the Orb. Have you accepted him as your mate?" There was hope in her voice. It irritated Kailin.

Kailin kept her words icy. "I don't know, but if you say he needs to be there, he'll be there. I will tell him to bring the Orb."

Drakkina started to fade.

"Wait," Kailin called out. "What happened to the baby? The boy, my brother? You only mention my sisters. Can we give him back his guardian wolf?"

"He was touched by darkness."

Kailin didn't know what that meant, but Drakkina said it as if she was proclaiming his death, such sadness in her tone. It leaked out with regret. Her face pinched tight as if holding in a sob.

"Where did he go?"

Drakkina shook her head. "He's lost to us." And then she disappeared.

CHAPTER THIRTY
A GIFT

"Do I look like a twig! Too tight," Kailin complained to the maid who yanked on the ties of her corset. It had been weeks since she'd been forced to shove her body back into current style with a too-tight cinching and bustle. The maid murmured an apology in Arabic, translated by the amber stone Kailin still wore.

Kailin closed her eyes and breathed. "I'm sorry," she said and the maid paused, eyes wide. She was young and probably used to being bullied. Kailin forced a smile and made a mental note to pay her extra for her impatience today. It wasn't the girl's fault that Kailin was as nervous as a girl going to her first ball.

Rap! Rap! "Are you ready, Cleo?" Anthony called from the adjoining room.

"Not quite. These bloody costumes are what hold women back from ruling the world, you know."

Her father's muffled laughter through the door brought out her first real smile of the evening. He'd insisted on returning to Egypt with her when she showed up at Whitaker House on a Highland mare. It was all she could do to convince Bruce to stay behind, but Anthony wouldn't be swayed despite being kidnapped the last time he was there.

The maid continued to tie and fasten the hooks and tapes that held Kailin's crinoline over her hips. She stepped high upon a chair to lower the raspberry-colored organdy material over Kailin's head without brushing the intricate curls and matching ribbon in her blond hair.

"I could hide a sarcophagus under these skirts," she mumbled as she waited for the maid to close her gown and tie the loose organdy ribbons at her back.

"See." The maid pointed at the reflecting glass and beckoned her to look into it.

Kailin blinked at the elegant woman standing tall before her. *Who are you?* Dusted, bathed, brushed, nails filed and clean. Her hair curled and twirled up high on her head with raspberry-hued ribbons. The square neckline was quite modern and low to show a hint of her cinched bosom. Pale gold braid that matched her hair edged the dress as if keeping the fabric fenced away from her exposed skin. White pearls and raspberry-colored glass beads dotted the gold braid, adding to the interest. The braid ran along the edge of the gathered upper skirt, accenting the break in the layers of flowing fabric.

"Beau...ti...ful," the maid said in stilted English.

Kailin smiled and nodded, though she wasn't feeling beautiful. Inside her stomach twisted around the small fare of beef and vegetables she'd eaten. *Ridiculous!* It was merely a ball. She would bring the Orb, pass it to Jackson, and leave.

It was risky, this gifting. What if Jackson planned to sell the Orb? No one else could make it work. She'd remind him to keep it at least until the final battle, whenever that was to happen. Then he could do what he wanted with it. She wouldn't tell him how she'd gifted it to him either, although it wasn't complicated.

If Drakkina hadn't been pressuring her, perhaps it would still be her Orb, but then her magic would be a beacon to the demons, bringing them down on hapless Luxor. No, it was better to gift the Orb away, but not to Drakkina. She was still an unknown. Her cold judgment about killing her infant brother, even though she seemed different now, still sat in the front of Kailin's mind.

Perhaps once she spoke with her sisters about the priestess, Kailin would trust her more. Perhaps she should have gifted the Orb to Anthony. But it was Jackson who was supposed to be at the final battle, not Anthony. And maybe it could help sweet Cassy.

"Ready?" Anthony called once more.

"Yes." Kailin flipped open a broad, white-plumed fan with a gold braid dangling in a loop while sliding her feet into golden slippers. She coiled the fan's braid around her wrist and fluttered its soft span back and forth in little coy movements before her face. Only her eyes peeked over the edge as Anthony walked in. Even in his late fifties, the man was still handsome with sharp blue eyes, a full head of silvery hair, and a strong body from climbing through tombs.

"My dearest Cleo," Anthony said. "You are a vision."

Musa, his manservant, nodded sedately behind him in agreement. He had also been released unharmed with her father.

Kailin fanned herself playfully. "A fluffy vision of raspberry cream."

Anthony took her gloved fingers and kissed the top of her hand. "With your coloring and golden hair, the raspberry hue is gorgeous. No fluff, just sleek, sophisticated beauty."

Kailin half smiled. "So says my papa."

"And I heartily agree, Miss Doctor Whitaker," Musa said from the doorway. He used both her titles since he refused to call them by their given names and two doctor Whitakers was confusing.

"Along with everyone else who will set eyes on you," her father said. "Well, perhaps not Samantha."

"Good God. Will she be there?"

He shrugged. "I'm assuming Miss Cassandra Black invited all the prominent Brits in the area."

"It certainly would make a statement if she *didn't* invite her."

"Sorry, love," Anthony said and looped his arm through hers. "I think she'll be there with her father. We don't need to attend, although you seem intent on finding this Black fellow." Anthony frowned. "Although slippery, he should be at his own home."

Kailin pressed several coins into the maid's hand as she left the room on Anthony's arm. The Orb felt heavy in Kailin's satchel to match the weight in her stomach.

The air was cool and dry as they stepped onto Hotel Moudira's terrace. Kailin's gaze fell across the small round table where she and Jackson had laughed over Samantha's smoldering feathers. Kailin frowned, remembering the seemingly gentlemanly Henry Dallinton, who had not been seen after that night on the desert.

Moghadam stepped from the shadows with the wolf beside him. The two had become uneasy comrades in their quest to protect Kailin.

"Bloody hell," Anthony cursed in a hushed tone, his hand against his heart. The pair, large man and hulking beast, walked behind them as they had been doing since they arrived in Luxor. Kailin had started calling the wolf Tenebris, meaning *dark* in Latin, since his fur blended in with the night. She had needed a name instead of "wolf" to help pass him off as a large dog to board the boats to Luxor. Luckily, they'd boarded at night, and she'd let Tenebris have her cabin. She'd paid extra for the cleaning upon disembarking.

Moghadam had called himself her guard, or actually "his queen's guard" to be exact, despite Kailin telling him that she had gifted the Orb to Jackson. Maybe Moghadam would guard him instead. A small smile touched Kailin's lips as she thought of that scuffle.

"Do you think he'll jump in with us?" Anthony asked as he lifted Kailin into the open carriage he'd hired for the night. The driver eyed the large Egyptian with a mix of fear and annoyance and then cursed when he saw Tenebris. When Moghadam climbed upon a horse to follow, the driver tapped the old gelding to move on.

Anthony settled back opposite Kailin. He exhaled long. Kailin knew that look and the knot in her stomach twisted again.

"So," he began, his graying eyebrows raised. "Still not talking about..." He pointed to her bag and then Moghadam. "And Black, his whole role in this and why I shouldn't have the guard lock him up when I see him tonight?"

What could she tell Anthony? He was the closest family she'd ever had. The man whose life was put in danger on account of the Orb and the mess that followed. A man who loved her and wanted to understand what was causing the new nightmares plaguing his dear Cleo.

Kailin sighed. "Papa," she started and paused, then opened her mouth, then shut it. The horse clopped down the street. "I found out where I came from."

Shock and concern lost to fascination in the lines of his face. "Where? When, I guess I should say."

Kailin smiled. It wouldn't be too difficult to convince her father that time travel was possible.

"I saw my mother." Her smiled faded as she remembered Gilla's desperate work to save her children. "I saw my father killed." Her eyes shifted to Anthony. "My father by blood."

Anthony leaned forward and squeezed her hand. "Terrible," he murmured. There was sorrow in his eyes.

She lowered her voice, so the driver wouldn't hear her words, translated by the amber stone she always wore. "I lived in that stone circle on the coast of Scotland at the very turn of the millennium."

"One thousand AD?"

She nodded. "Approximately."

"Fascinating," he whispered. "Your clothes pointed to that time period." He eyed her bag. "Did the Orb take you there?"

She shook her head. "There's this…" How to explain Drakkina? "This spirit woman, a witch of some kind who seems to be trying to save the world from a group of thirteen demons. I saw them. They are more powerful than me."

"Impossible," Anthony swore, but worry deepened the lines of his face. Kailin didn't know if it was concern for the demons or concern for her sanity. "You are the most powerful being I've ever encountered who could be verified," he whispered, eyeing the driver who seemed more distracted by the wolf and rider flanking him.

"Unfortunately possible," Kailin said. "The demons are drawn to my magic; they want it, and killing me," she whispered, "seems to be how they can get it."

"And the Orb?"

"The Orb enhances my magic, calls them like a beacon. They want it too."

"You need to get rid of it then. I knew I should have destroyed all reference to the Orb."

"The Orb only belongs to one person at a time," she continued. "I've...I've gifted it to Jackson. I need to hand it to him."

Anthony slammed back in his seat, dumbfounded. "But that's what he's been after all this time. Why, he helped Dallinton and whoever he was working for in the US government to kidnap me. He lied to you."

Kailin's stomach tightened so much she thought she might double over.

"And you're giving it to him?" Anthony asked. Kailin recognized tightly held anger in her father. By nature he wasn't violent, but this was stretching his limits.

"The witch said that Jackson Black needs to be at the final battle with me against the demons. My sisters will be there too...with their soul mates."

"Soul mates?"

"My sisters are apparently spread across time. Hidden. Drakkina says I can meet them someday soon. Won't that be amazing? Maybe you can talk to them about their worlds."

"Black is your soul mate?" Anthony almost squeaked. Unfortunately, the huge hook she had tried to snag him with hadn't been enough distraction. If that didn't work, nothing would.

"Drakkina, that's the witch's name. She says he is."

Anthony studied her. "And what do you believe?"

The carriage rumbled and jerked to a stop before the large, lit house the Blacks had been leasing while in Egypt. Violin music poured out into the night from the open front doors. Tuto flew in a silent arc around the house and landed on one of the chimneys. The stars were out, her silent friends. Unfortunately, they were also Jackson's friends. Could she ever confide in them again?

"Cleo? You believe her, this Drakkina?"

Kailin looked down at her gloved hands folded in her lap. "I don't know."

"Why does he want the Orb?"

"He said he's a treasure hunter." She looked up into Anthony's concerned eyes.

"But you think there's more," Anthony finished for her.

Tears burned the back of her eyes. "I really hope so."

Anthony rubbed her clasped hands between his big paws. "A true scientist doesn't stop at what seems to be the obvious. It's in your nature to ferret out the whole truth, Cleo." He touched her chin, making her look up. "Kailin, daughter. Find out the truth, and if it's not to our liking"—he tipped his head to Moghadam and Tenebris—"we'll set your watchdogs on him."

Kailin grinned a little as the weight of not telling Anthony anything lifted. Questions would follow for certain, but the beginning had gone well. After a lifetime of seeing her own magic, Anthony was able to handle the bizarre information she'd dumped in his lap. Her adopted father had always been on a constant quest for the sensational. Even if he didn't personally possess magic, it was in his nature to accept it. Had it been an accident that Gilla and her sacred Earth Mother had sent her to Anthony? Kailin's grin spread. She'd been an orphan, but she'd had the best father.

"I love you," she said, her throat dry.

Anthony looked startled but a soft smile filled his face with vivid happiness. "And I love you, my Cleo. Now let's go find that soul mate of yours."

"Papa!" she gasped in rebuke as he chuckled and helped her up. Her father saluted Moghadam after lifting Kailin to the ground. Tenebris loped off into the bushes on the side of the house. Moghadam followed behind, his gaze most likely scanning the dark bushes for demons. They ascended the steps to the open doors where a servant allowed them entrance.

The foyer was bright with candlelight set in shining chandeliers. The polished floors had thick rugs from the Orient, and vases of flowers adorned side tables. It was tastefully beautiful.

Kailin's smile faltered when she heard Samantha's high-pitched laughter from the punch table in the ballroom. Memories of Champagne geysers at the last ball made Kailin cringe. She tucked her hand securely into Anthony's elbow.

"We'll fade into one of the salons," Anthony said, reading her stiff spine.

"It may make the night a more pleasant one," Kailin said from behind her fan.

Anthony laughed. "Heaven help this soul mate of yours."

"Seems my magic doesn't work on my soul mate," Kailin grumbled low.

Anthony tripped on an imaginary step and a chuckle punctuated the shake of his head. "This gets better all the time."

"Hmm, not from my point of view."

Anthony led Kailin around the dancers to the far side of the room. Her heart felt higher up in her chest as it pounded. He should be here. It was his house. Jackson's sister seemed anxious to wring everything she could out of life despite her illness. Having a ball made sense with that in mind. The invitation had come from Cassy, but Kailin assumed Jackson would help her.

"We should find Cassandra Black," Kailin told Anthony and he nodded.

Kailin felt the prickle of eyes along her form. Whispers and behind-fan discussions about her were probably ensuing with vigor. She shouldn't have come. Her name had been linked to the explosion at the site as well as the disappearance of Henry Dallinton and his men. Even though nothing could be proven, she was still a suspect. There was also her disappearance for months to cause conjecture. Some had thought that she'd run off to the States with Jackson Black or Henry Dallinton.

Why am I here? Because she needed to pass the blasted Orb to Jackson, that's why. She wasn't about to visit his home on an ordinary day when she'd be cornered alone with the man. She didn't want to endure his nonanswers, their crushing weight again like that night in the stone circle.

"I don't see the scoundrel," Anthony said, picking up on Kailin's tension. He seemed ready to whisk her back to the carriage. "Wait here. I will check the outer rooms for his sister. Watchdog there will keep an eye on you," Anthony added, nodding to Moghadam who circulated the room, nodding to peers.

Kailin gave a small snort of indignation that went along well with her easily donned ice queen persona.

"Kailin Whitacker! You look well."

Kailin turned to see Ian McGivens striding through the dancers to her side.

Samantha's father squeezed her shoulders as an embrace. "Anthony was so worried when you disappeared. He thought you had traded yourself for him."

Kailin allowed a more sincere smile for her father's friend and co-investigator. "I was in the Highlands visiting some friends near my dig site. I had some delays finding my way home."

"I suppose we will never know how you got out of Egypt without any of us knowing."

"I'm afraid it's a rather drab story." Kailin patted his arm. "Have you seen our hostess tonight, Cassandra Black? I wish to pay my respects."

Ian continued his stare for a long moment before seeming to break out of his engrossing thoughts about Kailin's missing time. "Ah...yes. She was in the main hall looking rather pale. I think she may have retired to rest for a while."

"Is her brother here?" Kailin held her breath. Was Cassy getting worse? Where was Jackson then? He wouldn't abandon his sister, although he had left her to try to find Kailin in Scotland. Had he been trying to find the Orb in order to heal Cassy? Could it heal her now that she'd gifted it to him?

Ian shrugged. "I haven't seen him at all. But tell me, Kailin, have you seen Henry Dallinton? He disappeared the same night you did. We thought he might be with you."

Kailin mimicked his shrug and capped the fire burning her cheeks. "I haven't seen him either, but I've only recently returned to Egypt. Excuse me." Kailin swept her skirt around as she turned to exit the room. Moghadam followed. Anthony met her at the arched opening into the front hall.

He shook his head. "Can't find either of them. Cassandra asked Samantha to hostess while she rested. Samantha's lording it over the room in there."

Kailin turned in a tight circle, surveying the rooms. "I have to get to Cassy. Jackson might be with her if she's not feeling well." They both looked at the long, exposed flight of stairs leading to the bedchambers above.

"You'll need a distraction to keep Samantha from pointing you out," Anthony said.

Tuto, Kailin called in her mind and envisioned a distraction. Less than a minute later, a loud screech came from outside the front doors. Kailin waited, a smile on her face. *Clever owl.*

In a flash of white feathers, Tuto's large wingspan swooped through the front doors to soar up into the vaulted ceiling among the chandeliers. Kailin covered her mouth, as hanging from her pet's beak was a two-foot-long sand boa. The snake was not venomous, but most of the room either didn't know that or didn't care. Tuto flew overhead, letting the serpent dangle from his talons over the crowd. He seemed rather intent on following Samantha with it as she screamed.

Kailin hurried up the stairs; the heavy Orb banged against her leg in its bag. As she clipped along the hallway, she opened and closed doors to empty rooms. The second to the last room on the right was cracked open, and a flowery smell wafted out of it. "Cassandra?" she called softly and pushed the door open.

Cassy lay on her side across her bed. Ruffles of pink wrapped around her legs as if they'd tripped her, tying her there. "Cassy!" Kailin grabbed her own skirts to get to her new friend. *Please be alive. Oh God, please!*

CHAPTER THIRTY-ONE
BATTLEFIELD BELOW

"Kailin?" Cassy murmured.

Thank God or the Earth Mother or whatever deity might be watching out for the girl.

Kailin gingerly lifted the slight frame of Cassandra Black into a sitting position. She looked worse than the last time she'd seen her. Much worse, close-to-death worse. Her skin was pale, not the pale of someone avoiding the sun but of someone who'd lost all vitality. Dark circles marred the paper-thin skin under her eyes. She could only lift her lids halfway, making her look almost asleep. She tried to wet her lips, but her tongue seemed to stick in her mouth and she gave up. She might not be dead, but she was close.

"Where is Jackson?"

A small smile cracked her dry lips. "He thinks my party is foolish." She pulled in a slow, labored breath.

With the way Cassy looked, Kailin had to agree. "He should be here."

"He's in his study underground, with the sulfur pool. He's always there, trying to find a cure."

"Under this house?"

Cassy nodded but it looked like it took a lot for her to do so. "He's always trying to save me." She finally produced enough moisture to wet her lips. She smiled. "When I was five, I wandered off into a blizzard on the prairie. I was lost for sure. Jackson and my older brother were out looking for me. Kyle gave up, but Jackson refused. He found me, said he heard me whimpering somehow in that wind and snow. I was so cold.

"He took my soggy, frozen coat off and stuck me under his own coat against his warm chest. He rode us home through that storm like that, guiding the horse even when it wanted to give up. He wouldn't let it. Jackson saved me, saved us. He always has."

She wheezed, pulling in air. "That's why he's down there even as a party dances over his head. He won't give up trying."

Kailin had frozen to the bed. The lamb story Jackson had told her. The lamb hadn't been a lamb. It had been Cassy, his sister. He would do anything for her. She was all he had left of his family.

Kailin closed her eyes. Jackson was saving his sister again, no matter what. The Orb had been his chance. He'd lied, he'd helped kidnap her father, he may have even tried to steal the Orb from her. But it had all been to save his sister. Perhaps he had hoped to save Cassy and still win Kailin's heart, so he'd hidden his plans.

"Damn," Kailin whispered.

The frail girl had closed her eyes again, her lips parted. "Cassy! Don't fall asleep. We have to get to Jackson. Cassy?" She didn't respond but sounded like she battled to pull in air. Was there time? There had to be time.

The door squeaked open and Kailin snapped around. "Jackson?"

"I heard you yell," Moghadam said in the doorway, his eyes widening at the sight of Cassy across the bed.

"We need to take her to Jackson. He's on a lower level of this house where some healing waters are supposed to be. We need to get her to him."

Moghadam lifted the fluff-enshrouded girl off the pastel coverlet. Chaos echoed from the main hall, but most people sounded as if they were leaving. Luckily Cassy wasn't witnessing the frantic stampede to abandon her party. Tuto still tormented Samantha in the corner while they plunged through the room, Cassy in Moghadam's arms, and Kailin jogging to keep up with his strides.

"Heavens!" Mrs. Pierce yelled from an alcove and took off after them. "Cassy, Cassy!"

"We need to get her to Jackson, below ground," Kailin ordered. "How do we get there?"

Mrs. Pierce waved frantically and yanked her skirts high to her knees to run through to the back of the manor. Kailin cursed under her breath at the hindering skirts. Her leather sack, carrying the Orb, thumped along one thigh through the many petticoats.

"Blimey!" Anthony yelled and ran after them.

Mrs. Pierce rammed through a wooden door and grabbed a lit sconce on the wall as she barreled down the narrow stairs. Kailin glanced back at Moghadam, who cradled Cassy against his chest so her head wouldn't hit the stone sides.

"Cleo," Anthony yelled, but Kailin leapt down the steps into the darkness. The dry smell of sand and earth accented the sound of grit on the wooden steps under her slippers. Jackson was somewhere up ahead, and she had to reach him.

"Come," Mrs. Pierce called. The woman was spry in an emergency. Kailin followed with Moghadam, Cassy, and Anthony behind.

"Jackson!" Kailin shouted into the darkness, her eyes focused on the circle of light blocked mostly by Mrs. Pierce's bulk. A bit of magic made the light grow. Mrs. Pierce gasped quietly, looking up at the flame, and held it higher, lighting the way.

"Jackson!" Kailin called ahead and saw a door at the bottom of the stairwell swing inward.

"Kailin?"

Mrs. Pierce nearly barreled right through Jackson like a charging rhino. He steadied the woman before she could do herself harm, but his eyes focused on Kailin.

"What are you—?"

"Cassy," Kailin sucked in air and glanced over her shoulder. "She's..."

"Good God," Jackson cursed and gingerly took his sister from Moghadam's arms. "What happened?"

"She was tired," Mrs. Pierce cried. Anthony handed the grief-stricken woman his handkerchief. "I took her upstairs to lie down and went to fetch her some broth."

"I found her," Kailin said. "She was talking and then couldn't breathe. She lost consciousness."

Jackson set his sister beside an open bath cut into the ground. Steam and sulfur rose from the surface, causing water to drip from the low ceiling. The house must have been built around the hot spring. Was that why Jackson had rented the large manor for his sister?

A hand rested on Kailin's shoulder. Anthony stared at her, his graying eyebrows raised in utter shock. "Are you well? Here?" His gaze took in the surrounding stone and darkness. "It's rather tomb-like."

Kailin blinked. She'd climbed down into this dark, closed pit without a moment of hesitation. Her stomach clenched with the sudden reminder, but she shut it out. "I'll have to tell you about a time I was locked in a sarcophagus."

"Holy Ra," he muttered.

Jackson hovered over Cassy, listening to her labored breathing, brushing back the hair from her face.

"Jackson, you need to heal her," Kailin said and wrestled the bag off her shoulder to pull out the Orb.

"Your enhanced magic with it will call the dem—" he started.

"I've gifted it to you," Kailin said, her eyes connecting with him. "Days ago. It's yours. Use it to heal her." She shoved the Orb into his hands, and the slight glow within intensified, making them blink and shield their eyes.

Moghadam stepped back while Anthony surged forward. "Good Heavens," her father whispered. Even Mrs. Pierce froze in awe. Magic swirled in oily colors along its surface, illuminating the dragonfly.

"What's going on down here?" another voice called.

"Stand back, Ian," Anthony said somewhere behind Kailin. "They're trying to save the girl."

"Hold it over Cassy's chest." The rasping draws of her breathing had ceased. "Imagine her lungs working," she whispered. Jackson stared into Kailin's eyes and nodded. "Imagine them pink and healthy, moving in and out."

She wasn't a healer. She couldn't detect precisely what was hurting Cassy, but Kailin knew enough about human anatomy to know what should look healthy. "Think of Cassy's heart pumping blood everywhere, her muscles thick and fed by the blood, her nerves running minutely through her limbs, sending signals to her brain."

Systematically, Kailin told Jackson what his sister's body should look like if she were healthy. It was all a whisper, a breath of words over the pulsing Orb as Jackson held it over his sister.

She watched him, his gaze holding onto her as if she were the only thing keeping him from slipping away in the raging pulse of power. She nodded encouragement and watched him swallow hard. Small beads of perspiration appeared on his forehead, but he didn't show any other sign of the great weight of wielding power over life and death.

Strong, honorable, determined to risk everything for the people he loved. Jackson Black fought now for treasure, the treasure in the delicate life of his sister.

"What are they doing?" Ian asked.

"Don't meddle," Anthony chided. Kailin could hear their shoes scuff on sand across the rock floor.

"Dear God in heaven," Mrs. Pierce prayed.

"Imagine her smiling, Jackson," Kailin instructed. "Happy and awake, breathing and laughing, running."

The glow from the Orb flowed down onto Cassy's chest, covering it, absorbing into her through the bodice of her dress.

"Oh!" Mrs. Pierce cried. "Her chest is rising."

Kailen bent over Jackson's sister. "Cassy?"

Moghadam murmured a prayer in Arabic. Cassy's head rolled to the side and then back again. Her eyes flickered open. "Am... Am I in a cave?"

Kailin glanced at Jackson, who didn't even seem to be breathing as he stared at Cassy. The glow from the Orb ebbed, the bright blue-white rays sucking back into it.

"You're in Jackson's underground...workshop, apothecary," Kailin said with a wave of her arm toward the ceiling. "How do you feel?"

Jackson's gaze ran up and down his sister. Cassy bent her knees and gasped as she sat upright. "I...I feel...good." Her tone reflected awe and the fervent prayers of thanksgiving flowing from Mrs. Pierce.

Jackson pushed the Orb into Kailin's hands and grabbed his sister into a fierce hug. "Oh Cassy," he breathed into her hair. "You're alive." He cradled Cassy, but his gaze moved to Kailin. "Thank you."

"You did it," Kailin said softly. "You saved her."

For a second he looked like he would argue, but he closed his eyes and hugged his little sister into his chest.

"You're smashing my dress, Jackson," Cassy said, a smile in her voice.

He pulled away. "Can you stand?"

"Perhaps," Cassy said.

Jackson lifted her easily and slowly let her legs slide to the cavern floor. Cautiously, he released her.

Mrs. Pierce covered her mouth and sobbed happily against her palm.

Anthony laughed. "I'd say you are standing, Miss Black."

Kailin laughed too. It was cut off abruptly when Jackson scooped Kailin into his arms and spun them in a circle with a "Whoop!"

Dizziness collided with giddiness and joy inside her. They'd done it, Jackson and the Orb.

Jackson's face was filled with bewilderment and open happiness. He set her down, a hand going to his forehead where he brushed back his hair. "I only..." He stared into Kailin's eyes. "I needed to try everything to save her," he said. "If there was a chance to save her, I had to try."

"I would have helped you, helped her, had I known what you were about," she said.

His brows pinched. "I was trying to find a way to tell you when everything came crashing down. You have every reason to hate me." His words were stilted, twisted, a glimpse of the unfounded hate he had for himself over leaving his family.

"How could I hate a man who saved his little sister in a blizzard?"

He rubbed both hands through his hair. "I... Thank you, Kailin."

"I forgive you, but you need to work on your communication skills," she said and exhaled. "And so do I. I was so wrapped up in my quest to save Anthony that I didn't think about your reasons."

Jackson reeled her back into his arms, and his lips met hers, warm and firm, full of passion and promise. The kiss funneled down into Kailin, heating her from the inside out until her skin flushed. Her entire being fell into Jackson and she pushed even closer within the circle of his arms as she slanted against his lips. Safety, acceptance, understanding surrounded her. She felt free and caught at the same time. Her heart thumped with a need that went beyond the physical.

She pulled back gently, her eyes opening. "I love you, Jackson Black."

Surprise and then something more, much more, intensified the spark of life in his eyes. "I love you, Kailin Whitaker, and I will never let you walk away from me again." With that he yanked her closer against his body. "I will love you forever." The words sounded like an oath.

"And I will love you forever," she said. They both stiffened as a sizzle ran through Kailin at their words.

"What...was that?" he whispered.

Kailin smiled. "Perhaps Drakkina was right about the soul mates."

"What the bloody hell do you think you're doing?" Anthony said, making Jackson twist, pulling Kailin to the side.

Ian McGivens stood holding the Orb of Life. But the object that pulled everyone's attention wasn't the Orb, it was the pistol he leveled at Kailin.

CHAPTER THIRTY-TWO
LOSING CONTROL

"I'm taking what should have been mine to begin with, Anthony. I funded your expedition. I insisted you find this amazing power. Yet right when you were about to find it, you stopped looking, gave up, and wouldn't tell anyone where you thought it lay buried."

Mrs. Pierce had flattened Cassy against the wall and stood in front of her charge. Nothing would likely get around her frame. Anthony stood in front of Mrs. Pierce. But Ian seemed intent on keeping his weapon turned toward Kailin and Jackson. Moghadam tried to move in front of her, but Ian waved the gun at him to stall his intent.

"No, Moghadam," Kailin said. The radical was going to get himself killed trying to protect her when she didn't need protecting. Kailin centered her magic, readying it, controlling it.

Kailin stared at the aging archeologist-gone-renegade. Was he the real power behind this scheme to find the Orb? He'd been his father's colleague forever.

"It is too powerful," Anthony said. "It makes good men do foolish things. Put down the gun, Ian."

Ian ignored him. "Dallinton got too greedy. Wanted you"—he nodded to Kailin—"and the power behind the Orb."

Stupid man. Was Ian so uninformed that he thought a simple gun could hurt her? She held her magic in check, waiting to hear all the man said first. If she yanked his gun away, he'd stop talking.

"What powers do you think it has?" Anthony asked.

Ian smiled. "Not completely sure yet, but it looks like it can save a life. Which makes it more valuable than anything I've ever witnessed."

"You have no idea of its greatness," Moghadam swore.

"I'll learn."

"Father?" Samantha's voice came from the dark stairwell. "Are you down there? People are looking for the Blacks."

"Stay up there, sweetheart," Ian called. "Tell them...there's been an accident down here. Send for a surgeon."

A surgeon? Good Lord! He was going to shoot them.

"The Orb is useless to you," Kailin said. "It can only be wielded by the one it's gifted to," Kailin said. "Otherwise, it's merely a rock."

He frowned momentarily, his eyes shifting between Jackson and her. Jackson pulled her behind his back.

"Let go," she whispered. With him touching her, they were all in danger. He dropped her arm, and she moved back to his side.

"Take it," Jackson said. "It's yours. Leave with your treasure then."

Ian ignored Jackson. "I'm guessing that you, my dear, are the owner of this magic. I've heard the whispers about you and your...gifts. With you gone, the power will fall on whoever is holding it."

It happened too fast. Ian fired the gun as Kailin threw up her magic and Jackson lunged in front of her. She unleashed her energy to stop the bullet, and her power evaporated as Jackson's back slid along her arm. The bang echoed around the cavern. Cassy screamed, and Jackson fell to the floor, his head hitting the rocks with a *thunk*.

Moghadam tackled Ian as the deranged man took aim again at Kailin. She growled, and with a toss of her arm, Ian and his gun flew in different directions. Moghadam hit the floor as Ian slid out of his grasp, slamming up against one wall while the gun skittered across the rocks on another wall. Ian tried to stand but with a flash of her fingers, he found himself stuck to the floor.

"Stay still, Ian, if you know what's good for you," Anthony yelled and jumped to seize the archeologist's firearm while Moghadam grabbed rope.

Kailin dropped to the ground next to Jackson. Blood spread out under his chest. "Oh God," she whispered and pushed him over, yanking his shirt open. A coin-sized hole gaped near his heart next to a scar from the first pistol shot that had gone through him. His eyes remained shut. "Jackson!"

"Here, Cleo." Anthony handed her the Orb that had rolled from Ian's grasp. Kailin held it over Jackson's chest where blood poured out of the hole. She funneled her magic into it, but it fell flat around the heavy rock in her hands. *Bloody hell!* She'd gifted it to Jackson. He was the only one to make it work, and he was unconscious, bleeding to death beneath her helpless hands.

"No," she seethed and closed her eyes, forcing her magic into the rock, boring into it with her mind until she felt it vibrate.

"Kailin," Anthony said. "Cleo." He grabbed her hands gently. "You'll crush it."

"I don't care. It's useless."

He pried gently as her claws dug into the rock until its weight was no longer hers to hold. Her hands pressed down upon the warm, sticky wetness that continued to spread out from the hole. Cassy knelt beside her.

"We must stop the blood." She balled up a frilly length of torn petticoat and pressed it against the gaping hole.

"Jackson," Kailin called. "You have to wake up. You have to make the Orb work. Or say you gift it to me." Then she could heal him. Why had she ever gifted the Orb away? "Please, Jackson. Don't leave me." Her vision blurred as tears turned her eyes to oceans. She was drowning. She'd found someone who wasn't afraid of her powers, wasn't worried she'd accidentally snap their neck or throw them through the air. She'd found the one who was her equal. "No, don't leave me. I need you. The world needs you."

Kailin's hands shook as she moved them across Jackson. Her magic couldn't even button his shirt, let alone push together his flesh. He was her soul mate. Her magic didn't work on him. What fool created that rule?

"Drakkina!" Kailin yelled, her gaze searching the empty air above them.

Anthony was asking her things, his face a mask of worry. Probably for her sanity and then the safety of the world. She almost laughed. What would happen if she went insane? If Jackson...if he...she couldn't think it, wouldn't think it.

"Drakkina, where are you? I need you now! One of your soldiers in the final battle is dying!"

Her birthmark tingled, and Kailin grabbed her arm, smearing blood on her raspberry-hued sleeve. "Drakkina get in here now!"

Child, I'm here. Drakkina's voice echoed inside Kailin's head. The ageless woman materialized next to her, causing several gasps.

"He's been shot."

"Again? A bad habit he's developed," she said.

"He's dying."

"And you gifted the Orb to him."

Kailin's focus remained on the dark red wetting the delicate lace of the petticoat. "Can I get it back?"

"No."

"What will happen to it if…?" Anthony left the words hang.

"It will revert back to its creator, Eógin. He's dead," Drakkina said, "so it will go to me."

Kailin's eyes snapped to Drakkina. Would the crone let Jackson die so she could have the Orb again?

Drakkina stared back as if reading her fiery gaze. Her lips quirked with a mix of wryness and sorrow. "I'll forgive you that, as you don't know me very well. Merewin will heal him." She vanished like a flame snuffed.

"Drakkina!" she yelled but the witch was gone.

Kailin turned back to Jackson, his head heavy in her lap. She leaned close to his face and fanned her hand over his broad chest. A shade of pale worked its way across his tanned skin. Was his heart slowing? It seemed like it wasn't trying as hard. "Dammit, Black, stay with me," she whispered. "You promised to take me to your prairie, wide-open sky, remember?"

She pressed her lips in a one-sided kiss. "Please, Jackson. I love you. We love each other. You said it and can't take it back." He didn't move, and a sob rolled out of Kailin. "Don't leave me, Jackson. The world may not survive me if you leave me."

Kailin bowed over his face and rested her forehead against his. She inhaled his familiar scent that was tainted by the iron smell of blood. She ran her hand down his scratchy cheek, her fingers spreading through his hair. Soaking him in. Her fingers curled into his shirt. *Not letting go, never letting go*. She'd surrender everything else, but not him.

Behind her Cassy gasped, but Kailin continued to fill her senses with Jackson. Something slammed against the wall. The sound of papers flapping against the ceiling made Kailin glance up. The room swirled with a low level of magic.

"Cleo," Anthony said, close to her. "Try to control it."

"It's not me. I can do nothing when holding onto Jackson."

Anthony's lips pursed into a sad line. "He's fading, and so is his ability to mute your power." The realization that Jackson was really dying struck Kailin like a physical blow. *Crack, crash!* A line of glass beakers along a table exploded. Jars on a long shelf against a wall shattered as a wind swirled up, scattering more papers like dove's wings. Mrs. Pierce and Cassy gasped, holding onto each other. Moghadam left the bound Ian on the floor and fought his way through the roiling turmoil whipping through the air to shield them.

"No!" Kailin screamed and lines in the granite around them cracked down the walls. She sobbed and the floor shook, knocking books off the shelves.

"You're too powerful, Cleo," Anthony pleaded. "Mrs. Pierce, take Cassandra above. The house might come down on us."

No! He can't die. Not now. Not when I've just found him, just forgiven him. Pain gripped Kailin's body, prying open the gates she held around her magic. Surrendering.

Through the pain flooding Kailin's head, a small but tenacious voice shot deep like a needle. *Calm yourself, Kailin. Your sister is here.*

"Sister," a different voice said, making Kailin glance up. A woman floated nearby. Her brown-gold hair swirled about her shoulders, her curvaceous body swathed in ancient robes. She held an infant to her breast and looked at Drakkina. "Don't drop her. Hauk's probably already planning to slice you through for borrowing us without warning."

"You had to bring the babe?" Drakkina complained and took the swaddled infant.

"Ariana was attached at the time you decided to whisk me away," the younger apparition snapped. "Another moment and Hauk would be here too. He was lunging for us."

"Cac," Drakkina cursed. "No place for a bairn." She pulled the baby closer into the shelter of her arms.

"She may be the bairn you said will be at the final battle," Kailin's sister said.

"Only one babe at the final battle, a newborn," Drakkina said as if it was a consecrated rule. "Unless the final battle starts today, your child will be too old."

The mother nodded to Kailin. "I am Merewin, your older sister."

"Can you save him?" Kailin asked.

"I will try," she said, giving a worried smile. She closed her eyes and laid her ethereal hands along Jackson's chest over his gaping hole.

Kailin could feel the pulse of her magic, and the blood slowed.

Merewin's beautiful face relaxed, and she opened her eyes. "His life force might be fading but it's stronger than any I've felt. He beats back death with a battle-axe."

Kailin sucked in air on a sob, and the hovering papers around them floated to the floor. The woman, her sister, inhaled long and closed her eyes again. "By the Earth Mother, heal this man. He has much yet to do with my sister."

The baby burped.

Drakkina gasped. "She spit up!"

"All the time," Merewin murmured.

Kailin watched Jackson. Was his face regaining some color? His eyelashes! They...moved. Eyes, gray as a coming storm in the dim room, sparked with life. "Kailin?"

Merewin's shoulders slumped as she sat back on her heels. "Very full of life force."

"Jackson?" Kailin said and ran her hands along his face.

Jackson looked down at his bloody chest, running a finger over the healed gunshot under the hole in the fabric. He gave her a lop-sided grin. "Another shirt ruined."

Kailin laughed, though it sounded a lot like a sob, her head falling forward between her shoulders. "I thought you were going to die."

"I promised to take you to open, blue skies," he said.

"We will talk another time, sister," Merewin called as she pulled the infant girl from a grinning Drakkina. She tucked her tightly against her shoulder.

Drakkina fussed at a stain on her robe but smiled at the baby as the infant reached for one of her circling dragonflies.

"Thank you," Kailin called to her as the hazy image of her holding her baby began to fade.

She and Jackson rose slowly from the ground. "Yes, thank you," Jackson said.

Merewin cocked her head. "You do look like Kat. Drakkina, you need to bring us together."

"The final battle is coming soon enough," Drakkina said, her smile vanishing.

"Perhaps a festival first, at Ribe. My people know how to celebrate," she said with a wink. Her body faded more as she nuzzled the baby. "May the Earth Mother and Freya be with you." Mother and child disappeared.

Jackson swung Kailin toward him, his hand going to her face. The emotion in his eyes said more than a book of words. There was nothing he could utter that could top the love she saw there.

Kailin leaned her forehead into his. "I love you too," she whispered. He hauled her up against him in a crush of love. She yielded into his kiss, surrendering to the onslaught of power surging through her. It wasn't the power of her magic, though. It was the power of love. Uncontrollable, immense, overwhelming love.

Behind her Samantha screeched, Moghadam growled, Ian cursed, and Anthony's calm voice answered questions posed by several of the local authorities who had run down the steps. Cassy asked questions and Mrs. Pierce hushed. Jackson pulled slightly back to smile down into Kailin's gaze. A bubble of laughter broke from her.

He chuckled. "It's a hell of a lot quieter on the prairie."

Kailin's smile grew. "Time for a new adventure."

"Together," he qualified.

"Together," she agreed and tugged at the back of his head to pull his lips closer. The chaos in the small underground room dissolved as Kailin lost herself in Jackson's all-consuming kiss.

EPILOGUE

Six Years Later

"That one is definitely a rabbit," Kailin said and pointed directly above from where she lay flat on the quilted blanket.

"I'd say more like a two-headed snake," Jackson said next to her and squeezed her hand.

"There are no two-headed snakes." She turned and stared at his profile. Her stomach flipped gently as she studied his handsome features. Tanned and healthy, strong and virile, he was the most exquisite example of a cowboy here in the States, living and thriving west of the Mississippi. He turned his face to her as if he knew she was admiring him.

"I've seen one."

"One what?" She couldn't help but grin at his teasing boast.

Jackson pushed up on his elbows and leaned over her. "A two-headed snake."

She exhaled on a tiny laugh. "One that's mistaken for a rabbit?"

He leaned in and kissed her lightly. "The cloud was obviously a snake."

She laughed at his stubbornness and rolled away across the quilt. She sent a small burst of magic toward the sky. "Oh really." She pointed up.

His laugh jumped through her like lightning, warming her giddiness into a deep comfortable heat down in her stomach.

"Only you could change a vicious, legendary snake into a fluffy bunny."

Kailin smiled up at her creation in the clouds. The too-perfect-to-be-natural cloud rabbit floated along on the continual breeze across the wide-open prairie sky.

Kailin met Jackson's gray-blue eyes. Even after years now of staring into his gaze, the love and respect that shone there still comforted and thrilled her at the same time.

He rolled over to her, losing his cowboy hat in the process. But he didn't seem to care as he leaned on his elbow over her. His lips moved with purpose and Kailin's heart started its wild thumping. Mmmm...this picnic had been a grand idea.

"I told you the wide-open prairie was amazing," he mumbled by her ear.

"Mama! Papa!"

Jackson's exhale turned into a groan. "She got away from Cassy and Tenebris."

"Cassy has her hands full with little Leo," Kailin said. "Maybe she's coming to get me to nurse him."

Jackson rolled off Kailin, and she refastened her buttons with one thought. Her fingers tucked at the curls that had sprung from her upswept hair. She glanced at their beautiful daughter skipping through the scattered clumps of bending wildflowers.

"Someone's with her," Jackson said, planting his hat back on his head. He helped her stand.

"Maybe Anthony's early."

Jackson unhooked his holster, so his pistol was accessible. "It's not him."

Kailin squinted. "Who is he?"

"Come here, little treasure," Jackson called and their daughter, Emma, leapt through the grasses toward them. She laughed as he caught her in his arms. "Who's with you?"

"Drustan," she twirped in her five-year-old voice. "He's nice."

As the man moved through the grasses, they seemed to bend away from him. Kailin frowned. "Something's odd."

Emma giggled. "He said that you'd think he was strange. He said everyone does, but I don't. I think he's funny."

The click of Jackson's gun showed he agreed with Kailin's assessment.

"Don't shoot him, Papa!"

"Hush, Emma," Kailin said as the man, or rather the boy, approached. He was too young to be called a man, yet he was tall. His hair hung across his eyes, and he walked with a grace like a young cougar stalking unconcerned in his own territory.

"Who are you looking for?" Jackson called out and the boy stopped, several long strides away. Emma wiggled down from Jackson and took off back toward the stranger.

"Emma, no," Kailin called but didn't reveal her magic to the stranger. He was only a boy, an odd boy, but just a boy. Why then were the hairs on her nape standing as straight as a pharaoh's staff?

"Come meet them," Emma called as she ran forward.

Stop!

"Stop!" the boy yelled in perfect sync with Kailin's mental scream. But Emma barreled ahead and grabbed the boy's hand to pull him. "No," he yelled and yanked it back.

Kailin was already running. Something was terribly wrong. The look on her young daughter's face was a mix of shock and pain. She dropped to her knees in the tall grass, her pink flowered dress flounced out into a circle around her. Jackson somehow beat her to Emma and scooped her up.

"Papa?" she rasped.

"What did you do to her?" Kailin yelled at the stranger.

The boy's lips thinned. "I told her not to touch me."

"What are you?" Kailin asked, but the boy merely stared at Emma, a look of horror on his angular face.

"Kailin!" Jackson set Emma down on the ground. "Bring it to me."

"I am sorry, Kailin," the strange boy whispered, but Kailin couldn't think of anything but the wooden box where Jackson kept the Orb of Life nestled in soft lamb's wool. She funneled her magic to flip open the lid and pluck the large stone from its spot. It raced toward them through the air, across the open prairie, under the azure sky toward the only one who could wield its power.

"Give her to me," Kailin said but Jackson set her on the quilt that Kailin whipped toward them through the grass. She knelt next to her first born, touching her face, listening to her frantically racing heart. "What's wrong with her?" she demanded.

"I told her not to touch me," the boy repeated. Without looking away, he took a step to the side as the Orb flew past him, missing him by inches.

"What's wrong with her?" Kailin insisted, shouting each word.

"I'm like poison to children," he said. His eyes shifted to the Orb as Jackson held it above Emma's small chest. "Adults...are affected differently."

Jackson's eyes closed. Kailin could feel the magic energy flowing out of the Orb as he used it to seek out injury in their small daughter. "Treat it like rattlesnake poison," Kailin said. "Can the Orb suck it out of her?"

"Damn, it's thick, like tar," Jackson mumbled.

The boy cringed, his dark blue eyes hard and staring.

Kailin's magic surged in her. Fury, as vast as the sea of prairie around them, filled her, boiling to the surface. The boy would pay! Her gaze moved back to him as her magic sharpened into a dagger. He looked...tortured, pained, his face contorted into an agony that resembled guilt.

"Go ahead," he said, his eyes locked with hers. "Do it."

"Mama?"

Kailin turned to see Emma sitting up. Kailin dropped to her knees before her, grabbing Emma to her chest.

"What happened?" Emma asked.

Kailin's eyes met Jackson's. Sweat glistened on his forehead.

"It's all out of her?" she asked over Emma's sweet-smelling head.

He nodded and the weight of relief pressed along Kailin's body.

"Mama, you're squeezing too hard."

Kailin pulled back, kissing Emma's forehead.

"Who the bloody hell are you?" Jackson asked. "Why did you come here?"

"I..." The boy paused as Tenebris loped over the prairie, Tuto swooping overhead as if pinpointing their small group in the tall grasses. The large wolf ran to the boy, his sensitive nose in the air. He stopped and stared directly into the boy's face.

"Tenebris," Kailin called, but the boy didn't back away. He was brave before the huge wolf. Would he hurt the wolf like Emma?

"Tenebris," she called again. "Come."

Tenebris dropped his rump to the ground and pointed his nose high. With a huge gulp of air, he let loose a howl, building, building until it was so loud that Emma plugged her ears with her little fingers.

The boy didn't flinch. His gaze moved to Kailin's. Tenebris lowered his belly to the ground as his howl ran out. "He knows me," the boy said as if the wolf had introduced himself. "But I don't know him." He tilted his head as if examining the animal. "It seems I should."

"Tenebris," Emma called and patted her leg, but the wolf remained before the boy.

"Who are you?" Kailin asked, hugging her daughter closer, but a part of her already knew. The breeze across the prairie grass started the ripple of goose bumps along her arms. The chill ran to her chest and up her back to her nape. "Are you...?"

"I too am a child of Druce and Gilla." His too-long hair flopped over one eye as he glanced back down at Tenebris. "I wanted to see you, daughter of Druce and Gilla."

Kailin's breath hitched, and she readied her magic again. "Emma, run home now. Directly to Aunt Cassy. Do you understand?"

"Yes, Mama." With one last wary glance at the boy, she sprinted through the cornflowers, as healthy as she was before meeting him.

Kailin stood beside, but not touching, Jackson.

"You're my brother," she said. "I thought the demons... I thought they killed you."

A small smile played along the boy's lips. "I remember you," the boy said. "You tried to save me."

She shook her head. "You were an infant."

His smile broadened. "I remember. You're very powerful, powerful enough to push Semiazaz."

"Where have you been? That was over six years ago." Jackson asked, and the boy's eyes shifted to him, his smile faltering.

"It was over nine hundred years ago," he said. "You have strong emotions for my sister."

"Yes, I do," Jackson replied without skipping a beat. "Let's start with your name then," Jackson said.

The wind that flowed constantly across the plains stepped up a notch. The boy's head whipped around to stare off to the west. Dark clouds gathered there, pinching downward into a tornado. Tenebris sat up, his hackles bunching. A low growl came from his rolled-back lips.

"Cac," Kailin said Drakkina's favorite curse. "Demons."

"The Orb drew them," the boy said. "But they'll follow me."

"Wait. Where are you going?" Kailin asked.

The boy bowed slightly. "I am Drustan."

"Son of Druce, son of wisdom, son of magic," Kailin translated.

Her brother looked at Tenebris. "Come."

"Tenebris?" Kailin said, her stomach clenching.

"He was meant for me," Drustan said.

"But he's been with us—"

"I am alone in this world," her brother said, "except for them." He indicated the dark billowing clouds. "I can touch no one." His eyes strayed in the direction Emma had run.

The wind gusted, yanking Kailin's hair. She dragged it out of her eyes and bent to the ground as the large wolf ran over and licked her cheek. She hugged him tight and Jackson ran his hand down their pet's back.

"Kailin, we need to go," Jackson said tightly.

"Take care of her," the boy said to Jackson. "Come, Tenebris." The wolf leaped up at the summons.

"Will you be safe? Will I see you again?" Kailin asked.

The boy turned and laid his hand on the wolf's head. Their bodies blurred as they raced toward the unnatural storm. His voice echoed in Kailin's mind. *Yes, you will see me at the end of the world. Goodbye, sister.*

Finish the epic journey to save the temporal web in the fifth and final book of the Dragonfly Chronicles. Drustan, the infant brother to the four sisters, inherited vast power from his parents. Whisked away and raised by the coven of thirteen bound demons, he is groomed to be the ruler of the new world under their control. But then he meets Anna, the woman from his dreams, the only person he can touch without causing her illness and death. Will she be able to convince him to go against his upbringing at the final battle?

If you haven't read each sister's story, do so before Drustan's book, SACRIFICE, releases. They all come together with their soul mates and Drakkina to fight the ultimate evil.

The Dragonfly Chronicles are published wide and in e-book and print formats.

Book #1: PROPHECY – 18th century Romany tribe & Scottish Highlands

Book #2: MAGICK – 10th century Vikings

Book #3: MASQUERADE – Current day & 16th century Elizabethan England

Book #4: SURRENDER – 19th century Egypt

Book #5: SACRIFICE – Late 19th century Scotland

If you loved this book, please leave a review where you purchased it or on Goodreads. By letting your friends and book groups know that you loved SURRENDER (in person or on social media), you're helping me be seen in this wide ocean of publishing. Recommendations and reviews are the number one way to thank an author. Thank you! *Heather/Eleri*

ABOUT THE AUTHOR

Eleri Drake is the penname of Heather McCollum, a *USA Today* and *Publishers Weekly* bestselling author of Scottish historical romance. Books written under the pseudonym Eleri Drake contain fantasy elements to make the adventure and passion even more fun.

Growing up, Eleri/Heather dreamed of fairies and magic. She would swim in her family swimming pool with her legs together, hoping they'd fuse, and she'd turn into a mermaid. Her favorite television show was *Bewitched* where she wished to be Tabitha, the playful, trouble-making little witch child. Now she can funnel all her whimsy into these romantasies set back in time.

Social Media Links for Eleri Drake

Let's stay in touch!

Join my Heather/Eleri newsletter at:

https://www.heathermccollum.com/about/newsletter/

Newsletter

Acknowledgments

Thank you, awesome readers, for continuing your reading journey with me! I love knowing that I've given someone a happily-ever-after. It makes the months of writing, editing, formatting, and marketing so worth it.

With the current state of world chaos, taking a break to dive into an alternate world where you know good always wins is healthy and empowering. Thank you for taking care of yourself.

Also, thank you to my wonderful editor, Melinda DeJongh! Here's to many more projects together. And to my family and friends who never cease cheering me on. Love you all so much!

At the end of each of my books, I ask that you, my awesome readers, please remind yourselves of the whispered symptoms of ovarian cancer. I am now a thirteen-year survivor, one of the lucky ones. Please don't rely on luck. If you experience any of these symptoms consistently for three weeks or more, go see your GYN.

- Bloating

- Eating less and feeling full faster

- Abdominal pain

- Trouble with your bladder

Other symptoms may include indigestion, back pain, pain with intercourse, constipation, fatigue, and menstrual irregularities.

OTHER SERIES BY HEATHER MCCOLLUM

HIGHLAND HEARTS

First Book – Captured Heart
Enemies to Lovers

Set in the early 16th century Highlands. A Scottish Historical Romance series, spanning generations, with a touch of magic. The women in the Macbain Clan have the power to heal, a "gift" that gets passed down through family lines. Those with the gift must evade witch hunters and deal with suspicion. They harness herbal lore and learn to use their magic to help those they love.

HIGHLAND ISLES

First Book – The Beast of Aros Castle
Marriage of Convenience

Set in the mid-16th century on the western isles off Scotland. Fun banter and laugh-out-loud adventures with the broody chiefs of the clans and the feisty women who find their way into their lives. Mysteries and secrets abound!

THE CAMPBELLS

First Book – The Scottish Rogue
Enemies to Lovers

Set in the 17th century in Scotland. Two English sisters journey to Scotland to start a school for the local people in a castle that their brother bought (or so he thought). They quickly realize that on top of learning to read, cipher numbers, and serve tea, the girls need to learn how to defend themselves against both Scottish and English villains. The school becomes a self-defense school, and the pupils are called the Roses (beautiful but with dangerous thorns).

SONS OF SINCLAIR

First Book – Highland Conquest
Enemies to Lovers

Set in the late 16th century northern Scotland. Four brothers were raised by a mad, war-loving father to be the biblical four horsemen of the apocalypse. They are mere flesh and bone, but they were raised to be Conquest, War, Judgement, and Death. Learning to love, the most powerful prize of all, challenges all their beliefs.

BROTHERS OF WOLF ISLE

First Book – The Highlander's Unexpected Proposal
Marriage of Convenience

Set in the 16th century off the west coast of Scotland. Five brothers are trying to rebuild their clan on their ancestral isle, but the isle is said to be cursed. To break the curse, they must learn truths about love. The original idea for this series was loosely based on the musical *Seven Brides for Seven Brothers*.

THE QUEEN'S HIGHLANDERS

First Book – The Highlander & the Queen's Sacrifice
Secrets, Body Guard, Tudor

Set in 16th century London at Queen Elizabeth's court. Three of the queen's ladies get mixed up with visiting Highlanders to expose assassination plots. Poisoned gowns, a chastity belt, a 16th c woman chemist, and masquerade fun!

BROTHERHOOD OF SOLWAY MOSS

First Book – The Highlander's Wild Flame
Enemies to Lovers

Set in the mid 16th century Highlands. Four Highlanders, who were raised as enemies, escape an English dungeon by working together. When they return to the Isle of Skye, they pledge to convince their feuding families to unite to strengthen Scotland. Alliances are only as strong as the emotions behind them, love being the most powerful. Strong women and a witch work to bring elements of fire, air, water, and earth together to strengthen their isle.

Rohaise the Red (novella ghost story)

Based on a true haunting in Scotland.

The troubled spirit's name is Rohaise, and her yearning to live once again is fierce, fierce enough to kill for love and freedom.

Heather McCollum's Library of
Scottish Historical Romances